THE WORTHY AND THE WILLFUL

T. MARIE ALEXANDER

The Worthy and the Willful
Copyright © 2023 by T. Marie Alexander

All rights reserved.

Copy Editing and proofreading by Tanya Keetch

Paperback 2nd Edition

No part of this book may be reproduced in any form or by any electronic or mechanical means including information storage and retrieval systems, without permission in writing from the author. The only exception is by a reviewer, who may quote short passages in a review.

This book is a work of fiction. Names, characters, places, and incidents are products of the author's imagination or are used fictitiously. Any resemblance to actual persons, dead or alive, events, or locales is entirely coincidental.

Please visit my website at www.tmariealexander.com

ISBN: 978-1-7352320-8-9

WARNING

Although this novel features a young adult main character in high school, it is a dark contemporary romance and is not suitable for younger teens due to mature content and language. This book is much more graphic and triggering than the previous two books in the series. The recommended age is eighteen+.

PROLOGUE

WRAN

2 days ago

I should have killed him in Aspen as well.

Snarling, my fingers flex repeatedly against the tree bark as I kneel down and attempt to shroud myself in darkness. Rox stands in the window of Cade's house, head tilted upwards towards the starry night sky. She sighs and her shoulders drop as she stares blankly at the stars we both have cherished over the years. How I wish I could wash that look from her face. The stars are meant to be our happy place. Her eyes drop from the sky and scan the barren street as if searching for someone. As if she can feel my eyes on her. When she doesn't find anything, she takes one more longing look up at the stars before turning from the window.

Once the room is cloaked in shadow, I make my way across the street to the massive southern style home and look to where Rox just stood. She's on the second floor.

When I decided to come back here, I didn't think about how I was going to get in without alerting that fucker Cade. All I knew is that I needed to see Rox without *him* around. She wasn't herself when she shooed me away earlier today. The life had drained from her eyes, and she seemed almost regretful. For what, I don't know, but I do know he did something to her. I can't let that stand. I can't let my girl stay here another minute.

Searching the area, I look for anything to help me get inside this house. When my only options come down to scaling a tree and the rocks at my feet, I choose the rocks. It's not like this would be my first time breaking and entering. Picking up the biggest one I can find, I glance back towards the window. It's not the subtle entrance I want, but it'll get her attention. I'll just have to stay unseen until he disappears.

I wish I could make him disappear.

Just as I'm about to pitch the rock through her window, my phone goes off and I drop the rock in a haste to get to the device. I hiss at it when I see Josh's name flashing across the screen. Why is he calling me this late at night?

Swiping the answer key, I hiss into the phone. "What?"

"You're making a mistake," Josh says into the phone like I'm supposed to know what he means.

"What?"

"Back away from the window, Wran."

"How do you . . .?" My head snaps back, and I search the street. I narrow my eyes when I see my brother's police cruiser a little way down the road.

I should have known he would follow me when I left the house. He doesn't know how to stay out of anything.

"Go home, Josh. I told you to let us handle this."

"Wran, just think," he huffs on the other end of the phone. "Be smart about this."

"I don't want to think! I want my girl back, and I want that fucker out of her life. He did something to her. There's no way she would stay with him otherwise. I know it."

"It's called guilt, and it's a real thing, little brother," Josh throws back at me. "You barging in there isn't going to make it go away."

"What does Rox have to be guilty about?" I bend down and retrieve the rock I dropped. Taking a step back from the house, I look up at the window again. My thumb strokes the jagged texture as I contemplate breaking the window. It might not do much damage, but it would do enough to cause him the amount of annoyance he causes me.

"Wran, you know Rox. You know her better than any-one, and you know how she reacts when she thinks some-thing is her fault."

"Yeah, like a fucking masochist."

"She thinks what happened to Cade is her fault and she's going to try to make up for it, he states. "You didn't see the ways she looked at the hospital when he walked away from her. She was crushed. She lost another friend. She's going to try to make up for that and you are not going to be able to stop her by putting a rock through his window."

I turn around and glare at the cruiser. "What am I supposed to do then? Let her stay here. Let him manipulate this whole situation. He blew a fucking whistle at her, Josh! Like she was some dog. You're asking me to let that stand."

"No. I know you would never do that. What I am asking is that you find a better way that doesn't consist of you breaking and entering and causing her to run straight into his arms."

I glance behind at the window again and let out a sigh. I hate when my brother's right. "What am I supposed to do?"

"You fight for her in a way that she will respond positively to. You let her learn because sometimes loving someone means letting them make mistakes and growing from those mistakes. She will come back. It's Rox. She's never that far from us."

I let the rock slip from my hold at Josh's words. "You sound like a fucking counseling pamphlet. You expect me to just watch her with him?"

"No, you give her something to want to come back to."

"Fine, I'll relent for now, but if that fucker so much as lays a hand on my girl, I will bury him alive."

"And I'll help you."

I end the call with a huff and force one foot in front of the other until I'm away from Rox and down the street to my brother's cruiser. He lowers the window and arches a brow at me. I scowl at him. If something happens to Rox,

I'm blaming him. This could've all been over with tonight if he hadn't shown up. I'd be able to talk some sense into her and she'd be away from that rich prick.

"Need a ride home?" Josh asks.

"Fuck you," I seethe and get inside the car.

CHAPTER 1

ROX

Present

A chime sounds throughout the house, and I quickly remove the pancakes from the griddle. Spinning around, I race out of the kitchen to the door. I open it to see Claire standing there in a flirty dress and her signature heels. Her hair is pulled up into a ponytail today. I frown at her presence. I thought by staying here, Cade would come around and let me help. Let me prove just how sorry I truly am. She's here, though, which can only mean he called her. I gulp and step aside, allowing Claire into the foyer. She looks me up and down, her lips slanted down.

"Why are you here?" she asks as I shut the door.

I turn to my former friend and shrug. "He's my friend. I want to help."

Claire rolls her eyes at my statement. "You're being ridiculous and stupid. He doesn't want you here."

"You don't know that. Maybe he'll come around."

Claire scoffs and then sniffs the air. "Are you cooking?"

"Yeah. What's it to you?"

She shakes her at head at me. "I'm going to give it to you straight so you don't make an utter fool of yourself. You broke someone's heart. Back the fuck off and give him space. That's the only way he's going to come around. You are being clingy. And guys don't like clingy."

"He told me I could stay here. He wants me here, Claire."

"He was being nice."

I stare at Claire for what seems like forever. I know she's telling the truth. If anyone knows how Cade is feeling, it's her. The weekend has passed since Cade's accident, and he hasn't so much as looked at me since he told me to choose him over Wran when Wran showed up here on Friday. I did. I chose to stay with my best friend; he needed me more than Wran. But Cade hasn't so much as spoken to me since he made me do that. It's been a lonely weekend.

A noise behind me has me turning around and away from the truth Claire speaks. Cade wheels himself over to us, but he doesn't even acknowledge my presence. His attention is solely on Claire.

"Did you take your meds? I left them in that container beside your bed," Claire tells him.

Cade nods. "You ready?"

"Are you in any pain?"

Cade finally looks at me, but his eyes are angry and hard. The darkest, steeliest blue I have ever seen them. "Not the kind of pain pills will fix. Because they don't really fix anything, do they, Rox?"

I bite down on my bottom lip, my eyes dropping from his. "I'm sorry."

He scoffs, and I can already feel the tears welling up.

"Are you ready to go?" he asks Claire again.

I peek up at her from under my lashes to see her watching me. There's pity in her eyes and it's the first time I've seen pity on Claire's face since we were in middle school.

Sighing, she nods and steps aside Cade. She grabs the back of his wheelchair and begins rolling him out the door. Just as the door closes, I remember the breakfast I made and the fact that Cade is usually my way to school.

"Wait!" I shout after them. I rush out the door and Claire turns to me. Cade glares over his shoulder. "How am I supposed to get to school?"

I eye the white convertible. I can't get in that with the wheelchair.

"Try calling Belmont." Cade sneers. "He's boyfriend material. Maybe he's not too busy screwing someone else to pick you up."

I don't say anything to the jab. For all I know that is exactly what Wran is doing. He hasn't tried to call or text or anything since Friday when I told him I chose Cade. I expected him to come back. To fight harder. To show Cade that

I didn't make the wrong choice, but it's been radio silence where Wran is concerned.

"But I made you breakfast," I tell him, trying to get the conversation away from Wran. I pull my phone out and look at the time. "We have time to eat breakfast. There's even enough for Claire."

"You were raised by that Neanderthal. I want nothing your hands have touched. It might be poisoned." He looks to Claire. "Let's go already."

Claire doesn't say a word as she carefully wheels Cade down the steps of his house. I watch as she moves him over to the car and he struggles to get up and climb inside. This is all my fault. I've lost my best friend, and I don't think he wants me back.

They leave without a glance back at me and something breaks even more inside me. The tears I've been holding back finally fall and I wipe them away. I deserve this. I deserve to hurt just as much as he. Glancing down at my phone, I pull up my contacts. My eyes immediately zero in on Wran's number, but I bypass it. Cade expects me to go running to Wran. That's what I always do. I can't this time. I scroll through the numbers until I find the one I want. The name Psycho Pixie has me shifting on the soles of my feet. The last time I talked to Raven, things didn't end so well. I basically blew her off after she showed some concern about me and my wellbeing. I have no one else besides her and Josh, and I can't turn to him. Letting out a breath, I press the call key and wait for it to ring.

The phone rings a few times before it cuts off. There's shuffling in the background, but no one says a word.

Taking the plunge, I speak first. "Raven? It's Rox."

"I'm sorry. You must have the wrong number. I don't know anybody by that name," she says into the phone.

"Wait, please don't hang up!" I practically yell into the phone. "I'm sorry. About the way I treated you and for basically ditching you at that party. I'm really, really sorry."

She lets out a huff. "I couldn't give two shits about you ditching some lame party. I was only there because my friends were playing a set. We were worried about you and then you didn't even give us the time of day. That was really shitty, Roxy."

"I know. I could give you a million reasons as to why that happened, but at the end of the day, it happened. And I'm sorry. I didn't mean to act like . . . like—"

"Claire, Cade, and all the other jerks with an inheritance up their ass."

"Yeah."

There's more shuffling on her end of the phone, and I watch as a car bypasses the house. I turn around and head inside, heading straight up the stairs to the room I've inhabited.

"So, what is this call really about?" Raven finally asks. "I can't imagine you decided to call after a couple of weeks out of the blue just to apologize. What do you want?"

I run my hand through my hair. I hate that she's right about me wanting something. It shouldn't have taken needing a ride to school just to finally call and properly apologize to her. I should have made time to do that. Although, I have no clue where the time would have come from. It's literally only been a few days since my whacko bio mom was carted off to the loony bin.

"I, uh, need a ride to school if you don't mind." My voice comes out low and embarrassed.

"Huh, I knew it was something. It's always something with people like you," she huffs out. "What happened to Cade?"

I stiffen at his name and the way she's clumping me in with people like Claire. I don't have a nice inheritance. I don't have the big house or the big dreams. I'm just a waitress, and for some reason, her putting me in that category feels like nails in a coffin.

"What do you mean people like me?"

"Selfish. Self-entitled. Arrogant. I could go on and on."

"Please don't," I tell her and go over to where my backpack lies. "Look, I really am sorry. I don't know what else to say. If that was a no to the ride, then I should probably start walking. Thanks for answering."

"I didn't say no."

"So you will?" I verify.

"I'm not the selfish one and it's supposed to rain today. What type of person would I be if I made you walk?"

"Thank you."

"Whatever. Where are you?"

"Do you know where Cade lives?"

"Yeah. Be there in five. And Rox?"

"Yes?" I hesitate.

"You're forgiven. Just don't be such a bitch again."

I let out a choked laugh. "You got it. Thanks again."

It's pouring outside when Raven pulls into Cade's driveway. She's driving an old beat up Toyota that looks to have seen better days, but I'm not complaining. She's taking me to school and I'm grateful.

Locking the door behind me, I rush down the steps and to the waiting car. Raven pops it open and I jump inside, shivering. Raven arches a brow at me and I frown. I haven't been home since coming back here. And I don't have the appropriate clothes. All my rain jackets were left behind when I decided I needed space from Wran. Suppose I should get those back. Or not. I suppose I should be trying to figure out what I'm doing. I can't possibly stay here forever. And I can't leave Wran thinking my feelings for him have changed. Out of everything that's happened, my feelings for Wran Belmont are the one thing I am positive of.

"You look like a drowned rat," Raven observes and reverses the car. "I told you it was going to rain."

"I know, but I kind of don't have a rain jacket or shoes here." I wiggle my toes in my sandals and grimace. "It's all at Wran's place."

"I could run you home if you want."

I ponder her question for a moment. As much as I want to see Wran, I know if Cade found out, our friendship would be even more in the toilet. I need to let him calm down and come to terms with everything before seeing Wran again. No matter how badly I want to. I just really hope he's okay. Cade didn't give me any time Friday to explain to Wran why I wasn't choosing him. And if I know Wran, he's probably out somewhere angry and drunk, maybe even punching things. I hope neither.

"No, that's alright. I just want to get to school. I have an exam in calculus, and I need to ask my teacher a few questions before it begins."

She nods, and I sit in silence as we drive through downtown to get to our little school. When we make it there, Raven parks on side of the building, right next to Claire's white convertible. I stare at the car in regret. I can't believe he called her. Sure, I don't have a license or anything, but I could have driven his car to get to school. He didn't have to call Claire. I was right there.

I sigh and grab my backpack.

"You gonna tell me what's going on with you and lover boy?" Raven asks as she gets out of her car. "You two seemed awfully close a few weeks ago."

"Cade's just mad right now. I'm sure he'll come around."

Raven scratches at her forehead and kicks her door closed. "He's mad, but you are still living with him. Strange."

I bite down on my bottom lip, not sure what to say to that. Cade wants me at his house. That much I know. He wouldn't have had me choose him over Wran if he didn't. I just don't know the reason why since he refuses to talk to me. With another sigh, I follow Raven up the stairs to the school and go inside. She walks ahead of me without saying another word. Movement up ahead snags my attention and I see Cade glaring down the hall at me. I make my way down to him, but he slams his locker shut and wheels himself away from me. I brush my hair behind my ear and quickly glance around the hall to see if anyone noticed his dismissal of me. The only people watching me are Raven and her friends.

I bite down on my lip and hesitate to go over to them. But they're all together and now is probably the best time to apologize to them all. It wasn't just Raven who spent time looking for me the night of the party; they all did, and they all deserve an apology.

Going over to them, my head hung a little low from embarrassment, I give them a shy smile. Lex crosses her arms and glares at me, but I can't blame her. Charlie doesn't look the least bit concerned or bothered by my presence. I don't know if that's a good thing or a bad thing.

"So um . . ." I start, but am quickly cut off.

"You went to him," Raven says. "He seemed pissed."

"Yeah." I glance at the small crew before continuing, "A lot happened this past weekend, and he's mad that I don't feel the way he does."

"Aww. Sucks for him," Lex says, sarcastically. "So, why are you here?"

I shift on my feet as I glance from her to Raven and back to her. "I want to apologize to you all for ditching you at the party. I heard you sounded great."

I cringe at the lie. Why did I just say that? No one mentioned how they sounded. And it's not like I needed to say that. Inhaling, I lift my head and stare at them straight on. Now is no time for me to cower.

"Actually, no I didn't hear that. Sorry. I'm just nervous. I'm really sorry for ditching you all. A lot has been going on in my life recently, and I wasn't thinking about anything besides the people that are closest to me. I made a mistake, and I really would like a second chance to prove that I can be a good friend." I look to Raven. "I'm not selfish or self-entitled or anything. I really am sorry. If it makes you all feel better, I do have a legitimate excuse for leaving the party and forgetting about you."

And what is that?

"I almost got ran over by a truck and Cade took me to the hospital."

Lex's eyes widen, and she steps forward. "Are you serious? Do you know who did it? Are you okay? Oh my god, we've been jerks to you and you almost got ran over!"

Raven elbows her in the side and she immediately calms down.

"Sorry," she mumbles and shifts her backpack to her other shoulder.

"So, will you all please forgive me? And can we try this friend thing again?"

Charlie shrugs and picks up his guitar. "We're cool."

That's all he says before he walks away from the group. My eyes flicker between Raven and Lex in a questioning manner. If they aren't okay with this, then I'm pretty sure Charlie isn't going to tolerate it. He seems like the type that would follow whatever his friend chooses.

Raven nods and Lex follows suit.

"I have one condition though," Raven tells me.

"Okay."

"You have to sit with us at lunch."

My brows crinkle together in confusion. "That's all? I sit with you at lunch and all is forgiven?"

"Yup."

"Plus," Lex adds, "You have to wear pink on Wednesday."

"Pink on Wednesdays? Why?"

She laughs. "It's a joke, silly. I saw it in a movie. You're forgiven. Just don't do it again. If you almost die again, just don't forget about the small people. We might not have trust funds, but we do have feelings."

"You have my word," I tell them both.

"Awesome!" Lex claps and bounces on her heels. "We're going to be BFFs!"

CHAPTER 2

ROX

I head over to where Raven and Lex wait in line for lunch and stand next to them. Scanning the selection, my stomach lurches at the brown, gloopy mess and withered lettuce. I'll wait until my shift at Aunt May's to eat. My friends both ignore the week old lettuce and grab a salad and apple. I follow them over to the table they sat at a couple of weeks prior. Guess this is their normal table. Charlie is already seated and strumming his guitar. I take the seat next to him and glance over the music sheets on the table. I can't read music, but what he's playing sounds great.

"That's amazing." I smile at him, not really knowing how to start a conversation here.

"Yeah, it is," Lex says. "He's been working on this piece for weeks for some scholarship competition. He never be-lieves us when we tell him it's good."

Charlie's fingers fall still, and he glares across the table at Lex. "It can't just be good. It needs to be the best. I need that scholarship, or I won't be able to go to music school."

"I get it," I tell him. "I used to be the same way about my art."

"Right. You paint." He shoots the girls a glare. "At least someone understands the mind of an artist."

"It really does sound great."

"You should hear it on the piano. It sounds like some legit Mozart," Raven says.

"You play the piano too?"

He nods and picks up the sheet laying in front of him. He scratches out some notes just as Claire and Cade come through the cafeteria door. My eyes immediately zone in on Cade. He doesn't even look my way. There's a group of people behind them. Girls in cheer uniforms and guys in what looks like track pants. He's with his people. I watch as they all make their way across to the table that the athletes normally sit at. The girl with the red hair from before takes a seat in Cade's lap, and I frown at that. Surely, having some girl sitting in his lap isn't good for his knee. It probably hurts.

"Rox?" Raven queries.

I pull my eyes away from the jocks and turn to her. "Yeah?"

"We asked if you wanted to come over after school. Charlie will be practicing the piece on the piano if you want to hear."

"I wish I could, but I have to work at Aunt May's." It's not a lie. Aunt May didn't really want me to come back to work so soon after everything happened, but I need some piece of normal. She's the only person outside of Cade and the Belmonts that know about my bio mom and what happened. I'm surprised the school didn't ask questions, but then again, this school never does.

"Oh, alright," she says and I hear the dejection in her voice. I don't want them to think I'm doing this on purpose.

"How about you guys come by for dessert later tonight? Aunt May always has lava cake on Monday nights, and I swear it's like cutting into a cloud."

"You had me at lava cake!" Lex says and shoves a forkful of lettuce in her mouth.

"You sure?" Raven asks. "You don't want to ask someone else?" Her eyes cut to the table a few rows down from us. I shake my head. "Alright then. We'll see you tonight."

We spend the rest of lunch talking about Charlie's piece. I don't glance at Cade's table at all after that. When the bell dismissing lunch chimes, I head to my locker and grab a sketchbook before heading to my study hall. Once there, I head to the back of the room to the desk by the window. Before the second bell even rings, I have an outline of a woman drawn. She's standing on the side of the road, her long hair blowing in the wind. As I go to darken the lines, the intercom comes on.

"Roxanna Belmont, please report to the counselor's office. Again, Roxanna Belmont, report to the counselor's office."

I roll my eyes and stuff my sketchbook in my backpack. Hopefully, Josh didn't say anything to Ms. Flannigan about what happened last week. I really don't want to talk to her about finding out my mom isn't really my mom, but my aunt. I still haven't quite wrapped my head around that whole circumstance. Or the fact that everyone that raised me are certifiable. How can that much crazy be in one family? I shudder at the thought. At least I'm not them.

Getting up, I head out of the room. I make it a few paces down the hall when I notice Cade at his locker. He has a top locker and is struggling to reach it. I watch as he tries to rise from his wheelchair. He winces and in return, I do the same. I knew he was in pain. I glance down the hall, but there's not really anyone else out here. I take in a deep breath before heading his way. I mean, it's not like I could head to Ms. Flannigan without walking past him. Cade would have noticed me anyway.

"I can help with that," I announce as I come to a stop next to him.

He freezes and stops trying to reach the locker. His jaw flexes and it takes him a good minute before he unclenches, and he turns to me. I expect a glare, but all I get is a renounced, uninterested expression.

"You're not good with social cues, are you, Roxanna?" Cade speaks, but it doesn't sound like the Cade I've gotten to know over the last couple of months.

"I just thought . . . you looked like you could use the help, and I was here." I sigh and my head drops. "Cade, please—"

"Are you still in love with him?" Cade cuts me off.

My head rises and my eyes meet his cold, hard ones. I could lie. I could tell him that Wran doesn't mean that much to me. I could tell him that in the heat of everything that was happening last week, I reverted to what was comfortable. But that would all be lies. And he would know it.

"I've always told you how I felt about both you and Wran. I never led you on, so please don't do this."

Cade's eyes narrow at my statement, and before I have a chance to stop him, he's forcing himself up from his wheelchair. He grimaces and hisses, the pain written all over his face, but he doesn't make a move to sit. Cade slowly comes to me. He leans in close, resting both his arms on the lockers beside my head and shifts his weight off his bad knee.

His eyes roam my face for a second, and then he leans into me. I can feel his hot breath against my ear.

"You never led me on?" I shake my head and he chuckles. His hand to the left of my head drops and lands on my hip. His thumb caresses the sliver of skin where my shirt and skirt meet. "Really? So you writhing underneath me in the library, begging for more, was not you leading me on?"

"Cade—" My voice cracks on his name when his fingers skirt underneath my top. "Stop."

I push back into the lockers, to escape his wandering hand. For the life of me, I want to push his hand away, but I don't want to hurt him any more than I already have.

"Do you really want to make up for ruining my life?" he whispers in my ear. "I know one way you can do that."

My eyes widen when he grasps my boob and squeezes. I shake my head at him and scan the hall. We're alone. Completely alone. I shake my head at him again. Cade can't really be suggesting what I think he is right now. This isn't Cade. This isn't my Cade. Sure, I know I hurt him. I can admit to my fault. Maybe I led him on that day in the library. Maybe I've been leading him on this entire time; I don't know. This though . . . this is unreasonable. This is just . . . just . . . nauseating. The guy I've grown to know wouldn't proposition me like this. He wouldn't be grabbing me like this in a freaking school hallway.

I grab Cade's hand and pull it away from my chest. "I'm not going to have sex with you."

Cade's eyes tighten and his fist comes down next to my head, hitting the locker with a clang. I flinch away from his clenching and unclenching hand. "If you can spread these pretty little legs for that piece of trash Belmont, then sex with me shouldn't be that bad. Besides, you owe me. I'm only choosing that payment."

"H–he's not trash," my voice comes out shaky.

Cade's face reddens and his nostrils flare. He jerks his hand from where it lays beside my head, and it instantly goes around my throat. He doesn't squeeze or anything, but that doesn't stop my hands from going up to his.

"No, he's not trash," Cade hisses, pushing in closer to me. "He's just a child molester. You were fifteen when you had Harley. He was twenty, twenty-one. What kind of sick, perverted man looks at a fifteen-year-old like that. But if you like manipulative and abusive men, I can be that man. I should have known that would be your type considering who your father was."

His hand on my throat tightens and I shove him hard. He cries out as he shifts his weight on to his hurt leg. He collapses to the tile floor, and I gasp. I drop down next to him.

"I'm so sorry," I apologize and go to help him up.

He wrenches away from me. "The only thing I want from you now is that sweet pussy. Until then, stay the fuck away from me, Roxanna!"

My body stills at his words. He's in pain. I shouldn't take anything he's saying right now to heart.

I lick my lips and straighten my shoulders. "I'm sorry. Please just let me help you."

"No!" he barks. "I don't need your help with anything! I don't want anything from you. Get that through your head. You mean nothing to me now. You can't fix this, so stop trying."

"You don't mean that."

His face scrunches up at me. "Yes, I do. You're toxic, just like Belmonts. Everyone around you gets hurt. I'm done hurting, Rox. I've given you my future. There's no more I can give. So stop trying to force things that aren't going to happen."

"Cade—"

"Didn't you get called to the counselor's office? Wouldn't want to keep Ms. Flannigan waiting," he cuts me off and shuffles on the tile floor to get to his wheelchair.

I watch as he winces but gets up. If he would only let me help him, he wouldn't be in so much pain. "Cade—"

"Go!" he shouts.

I flinch at his abrasive tone and look around the hall. We're still alone. Dropping my head, I retrieve my backpack from the floor and give Cade a nod. He needs space; I can try that. I move around him and rush to the end of the hall where Ms. Flannigan's office is located. I stop right outside the door and turn to look at Cade. His eyes are trained my way, but I can't really make out the expression painting his face.

Time, I tell myself. *I just need to give him time.*

Surely, he will get over this.

Right?

With a sigh, I knock on Ms. Flannigan's door. The door opens seconds later, and she stands with a smile on her face. I step inside the office, and she goes over to her desk. I search the small room. For what, I don't know, but a part of me expects to find some cop cuffs laying around.

"How are you?" Her soft voice pulls my attention to her. I shrug. I highly doubt she called me in here to see how I am. "Roxanna, Josh has—"

"I'm going to stop you there, Ms. Flannigan," I interrupt her before she can even begin. "I don't know what Josh has said to you about me, but I can guess. And I don't want to talk about it."

She nods and sits up straight. She clasps her hands on top of the desk. "To be perfectly clear, Ms. Raine, Josh hasn't mentioned your situation at all to me. He only said he was worried."

I frown at her use of my real surname. She knows I hate it.

"And since Josh and I are doing what we are doing, I do care about him and the things that stress him out. But I also care about you. I have a television. I watch the news. And the fact that Cade came in early this morning to tell me to find someone else to give your introductory speech, leads me to think there's a lot more going on in your life. Maybe a little too much for someone of your age."

I cross my arms over my chest and sit back in the chair. "So what? Everyone deals with stuff."

"Not everyone has a father that was released from prison, kidnapped them, was drugged, school, a job, and a toddler that's in social services custody. Not to mention, you're living with Cade, and he seems extremely upset right now."

"How do you know I'm staying with Cade?" I thought I was being careful about the people I let in on that. If it got back to Lynn, my social worker, that I haven't even been staying at my apartment, that's just going to make her ask more questions. I don't need her asking more questions. She's already trying to get custody of my daughter.

"My parents live in the area. I've seen you come and go on multiple occasions."

Great. Just freaking great.

Who else know about my living arrangements?

"Roxanna," Ms. Flannigan starts again. "You have a little over a month until you graduate. I know your life right now isn't a musical, but life after high school is much tougher. I like to think I can help my students. I think talking to someone can help you, which is why I've been given the green light to pull you from your free period the remainder of the year and for you to talk."

My eyes narrow at Ms. Flannigan. "What do you mean?"

"You'll be having daily meetings with me from this point forward. And talking will be worth a participation score that can affect your overall standing. All your teachers agree that this is for the best. Your grades have been dropping, you've missed plenty of school over the last couple of months, and now your best friend is injured and upset."

"You can't do that!" I shout at her. "Josh won't agree to this. He'll never make me talk if I don't want to."

Ms. Flannigan sighs. "Josh doesn't have a say in this. As much as I care about him, this is about you. This is about Roxanna Raine, not Roxanna Belmont."

"They are the same person," I tell her. No matter if I go by Raine or Belmont, I'm still me. My problems aren't going to go away.

"I believe you're wrong. I have gotten to know two different version of Roxanna, but we can discuss that when you are ready to hear about it. That is not today. As for right now," Ms. Flannigan opens her desk drawer and pulls out a small black, white, and gold notebook, "I want you to take this and begin journaling. One entry a day. I won't read it or anything, but I will be checking it for participation."

She slides the notebook over to me and I stare at it. She wants me to keep a diary. I haven't had a diary since before I met the Belmonts, and those memories are still a little bit fuzzy. Writing isn't really my go to media for expressing myself, not that I really want to. There's nothing I can write in this book that is going to help me with my problems.

Nothing.

Nada.

Zilch.

I don't understand why it matters suddenly. The teachers at this school have never cared about any of the students. In the past, they have all looked the other way, and let us handle things the way we see fit. I mean, these are the same teachers that let Josh enroll me under a fake name and didn't even report me to social services. As much as I hated it, everyone knew I was Roxanna Raine. Everyone knew I shouldn't have been with the Belmonts. Yet, not one person cared. And I'm grateful for that. Ms. Flannigan needs to go back to being one of those teachers.

I don't want to talk about any of this. I just want it to go away. Dwelling on negativity is only going to breed more negativity. I need all the positive energy I can get and talking about what has been happening isn't going to achieve that.

Ms. Flannigan shifts in her chair. "Look, Roxanna, I know this is the last thing you want. No one wants to talk about the messed up crap in their lives. Not even me, and that's my specialty. But I also know that we can get stuck if we don't learn to deal with those things. The last thing anyone wants to be is trapped inside a nightmare they don't wake up from."

I look up at her. I understand that.

"Is this the life you want?" she asks me. "Do you want to be a waitress forever? Do you want to constantly look over your shoulder forever? Do you want to constantly deny yourself things you want just because you believe you can't have them? Like art school?"

I shake my head at her. No, I don't want that. I've never wanted that, but this is reality. I'm glad I learned sooner rather than later.

"This is life, Ms. Flannigan." I look her in the eyes as I say this. "I had hope once before. I believed in Neverland and finding my Peter Pan and wishing on stars and all the stupid things girls believe in. It got me here, and now I'm learning to live with it. The only thing I genuinely want now is my daughter, and I will have her."

She sits back in her chair, head tilted to the side and sighs. "If that's true, then that's sad."

She gestures to the notebook again. Reluctantly, I take the book and stuff it inside my backpack. If I must do this, then I guess I'll do it. It's no different than anything else in my life. Not like I have a choice.

"May I please go?" I ask.

Ms. Flannigan nods. "Yeah, we'll pick this up tomorrow. Just remember to do the journal entry."

I give her a tight smile and get up. "Of course."

CHAPTER 3

WRAN

"You're still here?"

I peek over my shoulder and grunt at the sight of Josh hovering above me. Closing my eyes again, I do my best to ignore him. He's been acting this way the entire weekend. Controlling. Annoying. Trying anything to get me out of the house. I have every right to be here though. Just because he lives in our mother's house, doesn't mean he owns it. At least not solely. From the way he's been acting, you'd think I was a tyrant on a rampage. All I've been doing is laying here.

"I thought we discussed this, Wran. You need to get off the couch and do something. Anything. Moping around isn't going to make her come back."

I open my eyes again and raise a brow at him. I have not been moping. Guys don't mope. Besides, the only time we've discussed her is the night he stopped me from breaking into that rich prick's house. Other than that, I haven't heard a word out of his pie hole. Then again, I haven't really been paying him any attention. Josh has the tendency to give his opinion even when it isn't asked for.

I throw an arm across my eyes. "Go fuck yourself."

"Wran," he chastises.

"What?"

Josh's hand flies out and a hot sting lands across my head. I jerk towards him and narrow my eyes. Really? The fucker's hitting me now. I rise on the couch and scowl at him. My hands fist the sofa's material, but I do my best not to overreact. I breathe in once and then out. Rising, I come face to face with my brother.

"What, Josh?" I ask him again.

"You have an apartment. Why aren't you there?" He moves over to the recliner and sits.

"You have a job. Why aren't you there?" I retort. "I'm not a child, you know. I don't need my big brother coming to check up on me."

"You've been moping all weekend over a girl like some prepubescent boy. You and I both know Rox will be back. So why are you letting this get to you?"

I flop back down on the couch. Yeah, I know my girl loves me. That didn't make her come home with me on Friday. That wasn't enough for her to choose me. Not to mention, I haven't heard from her since our little talk outside *his* house. If Josh saw her face, heard her words, he would understand. There's also the fact that I don't want to be at the apartment without Rox. It doesn't feel right.

And being around all her things will only make me put a fist through the wall right now. Thomas, my therapist at Pleasure House Rehabilitation Center, would recommend I remove myself from the toxic environment. Staying at this house and away from Rox's things is me trying to do what he would suggest.

Josh sighs. "Wran, I'm not going to tell you what to do. You are right. Your ass is grown, and my days of babying you are over. Like I told you the other night, give Rox a reason to come back. Hell, get a job or something. Something to keep you from focusing solely on her."

A job?

I do need one of those.

"Police station hiring?" I ask him sarcastically.

"No."

Leaning forward, I rest my elbows on my knees. "I don't want to be a cop anyway. You guys are crooked as fuck."

Josh doesn't respond to my dig at his career choice. In actuality, I commend him. I could never be a cop. Then again, I said the army wasn't for me and ended up being a part of that for three years. Hell, I'm probably still in the army. I only got discharged for the fractured shoulder.

"So what are you going to do?" Josh inquires.

"Whatever it takes to get Rox back."

"I meant about a job. She's going to college soon and I can't pay for that by myself."

"You don't have to worry about that. Her college is taken care of. We just have to convince her to go." Getting up from the couch, I stretch. There's some popping and it feels good. "But you are right about the job. I do need one. I was considering going back to the garage."

Josh nods. "Thought you hated that place."

I shake my head. "No. I just hate how they did me. I really wanted to be partner, and I think I deserved to. But we don't always get what we want."

Josh chortles. "Wow, Wran Belmont actually sounded like an adult for once."

I cut my eyes to him in a warning manner. There's nothing funny about that situation. The night I found out the garage was looking for a co-owner, I went straight to my buddy for a recommendation. His gramps own the garage and I had been working there since I was sixteen. I thought if anyone were going to get the position, it would be me. But since I didn't have a degree, any formal training as a mechanic, and was from the wrong side of town, I wasn't even considered. Jesse told me to my face that I would never be good enough for such a thing. Okay, so he didn't say that exactly, but he made it sure I knew I wasn't qualified for the job. Even though I had been there longer than anybody else and could do practically every job there. Not even Jesse could say that.

That also happen to be the night that I broke and took Rox's virginity. I was drunk and angry, and she kept touching me with those soft hands. Hands that shouldn't have been anywhere near me when I was that upset. I don't know what got into her that day, but she knew what she wanted.

Sure, we had been messing around, but I made it clear that it would never go farther than that. After Jesse told me I wasn't good enough to be co-owner and then Rox throwing herself at me the way she did, I broke.

I crumbled and finally got something that I wanted but didn't deserve.

"I think the garage could use you. It hasn't been the same since Gramps died," Josh voices.

Jerking my head towards him, I arch a brow. I knew Gramps was sick before I quit. That was the main reason they were searching for a partner, but I hadn't heard from anyone that he had passed. Jesse was probably a wreck. He was closer with the ol' man than he was his own father.

"I hadn't heard that Gramps died."

Josh nods. "Yeah, about two years ago. Jesse owns it now."

"Jesse and who?"

"Just Jesse. You should go see him. He asked about you a while back."

Ha! I highly doubt that. We didn't leave things on good terms. "What happened to you not babying me?"

"Habits die hard. Besides, I don't think it's babying to tell your ass to get a job."

I laugh to myself. The day Josh stops meddling in people's lives will be the day I decide I'm actually worthy of Rox. It's never going to fully happen.

"Anyway, I'm on lunch. Just thought I'd check in on you," my brother says and rubs the back of his head, a sheepish look appearing on his face. "Do you think you're going to be here tonight?

I cross my arms and smirk at him. "You have a hot date or something."

Josh meets my mocking eyes. "Yeah, I do. And I would prefer if you weren't here."

"Alright. I won't be here. Hearing you pounding some chick is not something I want to ever experience."

"Never said it was going there."

I shrug, not believing him for a second. If a man wants the house to himself for a date, he's most definitely got fucking on the mind. Anyhow, I'll be making myself scarce.

Josh goes to turn, but I stop him. "Wait. You said Jesse asked about me?"

My brother nods. "Just about whenever I see him. I don't know what happened with you two, but he sounds regretful when we cross paths. You should really head to the garage."

I grunt but nod. Jesse was my best bud a while back. When everyone decided Josh and I were no longer worthy of them, Jesse stuck around. All the trouble I got into, he was right by my side. We understood each other. We understood how backwards this small town of Kingston can be. He didn't fit the mold due to his tan skin. No one wanted to see a mixed-race boy come from the outside and infiltrate the carefully constructed structure of Kingston. Just like none of them want to see two young men fending for themselves because their pops is an alcoholic.

As terrible as it is, that's what Kingston really is. It might seem like a picturesque little town on the outside, but it is toxic. The main reason I want Rox out of it and away from toxic thinking guys like Cade.

The door slams and I'm pulled out of my nostalgic thoughts. Jesse turned out to be just like *them*, but if he's feeling regretful, I might as well use that to my advantage. Patting myself down, I find my phone. I immediately pull up the garage's number. I stare at it for a while. I haven't thought about calling the garage since the day I quit. Never thought I'd be calling it up again. I press the button and the phone rings. It cuts off mid-second ring.

"Thanks for calling Gramps' Garage. This is Jesse speaking."

I yank the phone from my ear and take a deep breath. Fuck, I wasn't expecting him to answer. When I worked there, a receptionist took all the calls. I thought I at least had three minutes before confronting him.

"Hello?" I hear come through the phone.

Relaxing a bit, I bring the phone back to my ear. "Jesse?"

There's silence.

I don't speak either.

"Who's this?" Jesse asks.

"Ah, man, it hasn't been that long," I say into the phone. Fuck, I sound like a teenage girl.

"Belmont?"

"Yup." I move the phone to my other ear.

"Wran Belmont?" he clarifies.

"Bro, c'mon, seriously? Yeah, it's me."

"Damn, man. I wasn't expecting to hear from a ghost today. Where you at?" There's some shuffling on his end of the phone and then a loud clank as if something fell or was dropped.

"Pops' old place with Josh. He told me you been asking about me." I sit back down on the couch and let out a long breath. Can't believe I'm talking to Jesse again. "You busy?"

"Nah. It's snails around here right now. You should come down."

"For sure. Give me ten." I leap from the couch and go in search of my keys.

"Alright. See ya then."

The phone cuts off and I come to a stop next to the console table in the entryway. I slump against the wall and let out a long breath. Okay, this is happening. I'm going back to the garage. I'm seeing Jesse again after he basically told me I was a low life that wouldn't amount to anything. At the time, I was so used to hearing that. I heard it from Pops and Josh on an almost daily basis. Right, so Josh didn't say that exactly. He just kept shoving college pamphlets in my face and telling me to think about my future. It was basically the same thing as telling me I would amount to nothing.

Maybe asking for a job won't be that bad. Maybe I won't lose too much pride by going back there.

Yeah, right…

The last thing I told Jesse was that I didn't need him or that fucking garage, and now I need a job. Sure, I could probably get a job in Arlington, but that's an hour drive one way. I don't want to spend two hours of my day on the road. That's two hours I could be spending trying to get my girl away from Cade. A low growl slip from my lips at the thought of him. I knew that fucker would turn out just like the rest of *them*. Him and that wannabe pick-up truck had arrogant, pretentious, and entitled written all over it. Even if I were willing to let Rox go, which I'm not, I wouldn't want her to be with someone like him. He's not good enough for her. Hell, I'm not even good enough for her.

Stuffing my phone in my pocket, I straighten my posture and grab the keys to Josh's bike. As much as I love my car, today feels like a bike type of day. Not to mention, it's almost time for Rox to get out of school. A motorcycle is cozier than a car. And she needs to remember why she loves me in the first place. I also just want her wrapped around me again. I miss that feeling more than I want to admit.

I stare at the light blue bricks of the garage that blends with the sky. It's old with peeling painted doors. Most car garages nowadays have automatic doors, but not this one. It still has the old barn style doors that must be pushed open by hand. I expected Jesse to upgrade this place once he took over. He used to talk all the time about how the garage would get more business if it were updated. Gramps wouldn't let him though. Said somethings need to remain the same for the charm to be seen. I understand those words now. This garage is the only thing that has remained the same since I left three years ago.

Hopping off the bike, I remove the helmet and balance it on the handles before turning to go to the garage. There's no receptionist when I walk inside. I frown and glance around. There's no one here. Aside from the junk cars littering the outside, this place looks abandoned.

"Jesse!" I call out and his name echoes off the walls.

There's no way he is going to be hiring. Not if the appearance of this place is any clue. It was never this barren before. Rustling from behind has me turning around to the sound. The door that leads to the actual garage part of the building opens and my old friend walks through in blue jean coveralls and oil stains. I raise a brow at him. Why the fucker's dressed like that, I have no clue. Jesse couldn't fix a car to save his life.

"Hey, man!" Jesse trots over to me and pulls me into a hug. "It's good to see you."

I jerk out of his hold and run a hand over my head, hoping he doesn't notice my quick reaction. He's always been the affectionate type, and it's still weird.

"Yeah, yeah. You too," I say, running my hand up the outside of my jeans and glancing around. "Josh told me about Gramps. Sorry to hear that."

And I was. As much as the people on this side of town, the side that is full of pompous rich assholes, irks me out,

Gramps was cool. Well, for an old geezer that is. He reminded me much of Aunt May. Caring and too damn nosy for their own good, but he was good people.

"It's been hard without him. Gramps was the glue that kept things together, and now everything's gone to shit. The fam's making it though," he tells me and leans against the receptionist's desk. He crosses his arms. "So why'd the infamous Wran Belmont call me up?"

I shrug, not about to ask for a job after seeing this place. "Ah, well, you know. Just checkin' in on an old friend."

He nods. "Uh-huh, and I believe that. Not."

"Why can't I check in?"

He lifts one finger and grins. "One, you shorten your words when you're lying or drunk. Two, I'm sure you told me you would never step foot inside this building again. And three, there is no three."

"Whatever," I mutter. Forgot this fucker know me just as well as I know him.

Jesse straightens. "So, what can I do for you? Need the car worked on?

I choke out a laugh. "If I needed that, I would do it myself. She still runs like she's new."

"So what?"

I let out a long breath and glance around one more time. This is Jesse I'm talking to. As much as what happened between us is still a sour point, he does indeed know me. That takes lying out of the question. Guess, I might as well give him the truth.

Looking at him straight on, I tell him, "I need a job, but from the looks of this place, I don't think—"

"Done," he interrupts me with a grin on his face.

I take a step back, all too aware of how he said that. "Why?"

He gestures to himself. "I'm not a mechanic. For Gramps' sake, I thought I could do this, but I can't. People would rather drive to Arlington than use Gramps' now. If they knew you were back in town, maybe business would pick up. You used to get a ton of business."

"So what you are saying is that you need me."

"We need each other," he clarifies.

"Sorta like partners?"

Jesse lets out a long sigh and pulls his eyes from me. He scratches at the back of his neck. "You know, with what happened back then, I never meant it the way you took it. No, I didn't want to give you that position. I didn't want you to be tied to this place. You had everything I wanted, and I didn't want to burden a friend with this future. If I had known, you genuinely wanted partner, it would have been yours. You had never mentioned anything before then about even wanting your own business."

"I never thought I could have it," I tell him honestly. Having my own business or even being a partner with someone never crossed my mind until he mentioned it that day. Up until then, I was solely focused on Rox. What she needed and wanted. I was just her provider, and I was happy with that. Partner made me think and believe, even if it was just for a few hours, that Rox and I could have more. We could live in a nice house with a dog. We could have dishes that weren't bought from the dollar store. I could be enough for her.

And I want that more than anything.

To be enough for Roxanna Raine.

To be worth her.

I thought getting partner would do that for me. Although I still want partner, I now know that it's not going to change how she sees me or how I see myself. It'll just be another way to provide more for her. And I want that too. I want to be the person she needs. I want to be her Peter Pan again.

"Well," Jesse drags out. "I'm sorry I didn't see it sooner. I'm sorry I hurt my best mate. But if Gramps is going to have a new partner, we should probably get that in writing. And you should probably tell me what I need to do to get this business back up and running."

My head jerks to him. Did he just . . . "You serious, man?"

He nods. "Like I said, I'm not a mechanic. And you, Wran Belmont, are magic at restoring cars and fixing them. This place needs you. It hasn't been the same since you quit. Think of this as us getting back on good footing."

Before I know what I'm doing, I'm grabbing Jesse and pulling him into a hug. "Thanks, fucker. I won't let you down."

Jesse chuckles and pulls back. "I know."

CHAPTER 4

WRAN

The deafening chime of the school's bell has me jumping off the bike and heading up the steps. I've been sitting out here for about ten minutes waiting on that bell. I would have gone inside, but I didn't want to seem like some creep waiting at her locker. Again. Not to mention, I don't want to run in to fucking Claire. Everything that happened last month could have been prevented if that girl could take a hint. I'm not trying to have her cause more trouble.

Opening the door and making my way down the hall, my girl makes it to her locker. She has her books in her arms, and she's struggling to hold them all. I glance around the hall for the douche, but Cade's nowhere to be found. I figured he'd be trying to weasel his way in now that she's chosen him. I know I would. Especially if she meant as much to me as he claims she does to him. A book slips from Rox's hold, and I rush down the hall, dodging questionable glances, and grab the book before she even realizes it's on the floor.

"Think you dropped something." I rise and her eyes snap to me. She takes the book and then searches the halls with a nervous gleam in her eyes.

"What are you doing here?" Rox whispers and shifts on her feet. "You shouldn't be here."

I lean my head down and whisper right along with her. "Well, I am. Why are we whispering?"

She gulps and maneuvers the books in her arms. She glances over her shoulder once before turning around to me. "I'm not whispering."

"Sure, you weren't." I step in closer to her and nudge her out the way. I put in the combination and open the locker.

Rox gapes at me. "How'd you know my combo?"

"This school has been using our birthdays as combos since I went here. Pretty simple to figure it out." I take her books and shove them inside the locker. "Now, let's go."

"Go?" she screeches. "Go where?"

"Well, that wasn't a no, so I'll take that as a good sign." I grin down at her. "Maybe he hasn't won after all."

My girl's brows crease and then she frowns when she realizes what I said. She shakes her head. "Wran, you shouldn't have come here. You know I can't go with you."

I grab her hand and begin pulling her towards the door. Despite her words, she doesn't put up a fight. We make it all the way to the door when a locker door slams. Rox's body goes tense, and I try hauling her out despite knowing what she's going to say. She doesn't move though. Instead, she stands in the door, face hard and unmoving. I don't look over her shoulder. I know if I do that fucker Cade is going to be there.

Rox pulls her wrist from my hold, and my hands instantly ball into fist. This fucker is really starting to get on my nerves. It was one thing when he claimed to be her friend and he was doing nothing wrong. This passive aggressive bullshit he's pulling now is going too far. Using my index finger, I tilt Rox's chin up to me. Her eyes don't meet mine though and she steps away from my touch. She takes a step back and then another and another. My jaw clenches as my eyes survey the thinning crowd for that bastard. When our eyes meet, his has a gleam in them. A low growl leave my lips and I take a step in his direction. Rox's small hands swing out and take ahold of my arms. With wide eyes, she shakes her head. She glances from me to him and then back to me. She does that a couple time before she yanks my hand and pulls me out of the school building. Smart. If we would have stayed in there any longer, Dr. Thomas would be having me as a patient again. And this time it would have been court mandated.

Guess she's more scared of what I might do to that fucker.

"Let's go," she speaks.

"Aww, I mean more than that fucker, huh?" I tease and follow her down the school's steps.

"Shut up, Wran." She examines the front of the school. "Where did you park?"

I point to the bike and her eyes follow my finger. She glances from the bike to me and then back to the bike. She shakes her head.

"No," she states plainly. "I'm not getting on that."

"Oh c'mon. It's just a motorcycle." I urge her forward. Again, she doesn't put up much of a fight, and I'm grateful. I can't really haul her on a motorcycle. That's a death sentence for us both.

"It's not that bad," I try to reassure her. "Who knows? You might even like it. You know, your legs wrapped around me. You're front against my back. Although, I wouldn't be opposed to your back against my front if only you could drive."

She scoffs and elbow me in the stomach. I just grin. "Don't be disgusting. And that sounds like something you would like."

I look her over and smirk. "I most definitely wouldn't mind having you wound around me. Besides, we have a kid. She needs a sibling and there are a ton of different positions to make that happen."

Rox roll her eyes, and gesture to the bike. "How do I get on this thing?"

I hop on the bike and hand her the helmet. She puts it on and lifts the visor. "Throw a leg over and wrap your arms around my waist."

"You did this on purpose," she grumbles as she follows my instructions.

"Yup." It's my only response.

If forcing her onto a motorcycle is the only way to get close to her, I'm doing it.

"So where are we going? I have work," she states.

I shake my head and speed off without answering her question. A yelp leaves her lips, and she tightens her arms even more around my waist. Her bodily heat has me clenching the handles tighter and I groan to myself. Fuck, this was supposed to get her hot and bothered. Not me. Maybe taking the bike was a mistake.

When we make it to the outer part of town where the drive-in is located, I come to a stop. Rox's arms don't relax. She even gives a little wiggle and scoots in closer to me. My eyes drop to her hands. They're clenching and unclenching like she doesn't know what to do with them. I could give her a few ideas, but I don't think she would approve of them.

Rox legs clenches around mine, and my eyes drift from her hands to her legs. Her bare legs.

Fuuuuck.

Maybe Josh is on to something with this bike. I can literally feel Rox pressing into me through my shirt. And the only thing separating her core from me is whatever thin material she's wearing underneath that skirt. I feel myself harden at the mere idea of her grinding against me.

Fucking, fuck.

Really, dumbass idea.

"We're here," I croak out, but don't move. I could stay here all day just like this if it meant having my girl this bothered and wrapped around me.

"Are we going on a date?" she asks in a breathy voice. I gulp at the sound. I'm getting a bike.

"Do you want this to be a date?"

That's not exactly what I had in mind when I came to get her. I honestly just wanted to see her. To talk to her. We haven't really talked in a month. And before that, I was just trying to piss her off like I used to before everything happened.

"I have work."

"That's not a no," I state.

A gust of air replaces her warmth and I instantly regret saying that. "We can't go out."

I get off the bike and come face to face with her. "Give me one good reason, Roxanna. Because I'm pretty damn sure your body thinks otherwise."

"One good reason and you'll take me to Aunt May's for my shift?" she asks me. I nod. "Besides the fact that my relationship hurts the one friend I've had in years—"

"Fuck Cade," I interrupt. "That prick is not a damn good reason."

"Fine. How about the fact that Lynn is going to do everything in her power to take Harley from me? How about the fact that you being Harley's father puts a target on your back? We can't be together, Wran. No matter what we want, we can't rewrite the stars. They obviously don't want us together."

"So you do want me?" I ask, taking a step towards her.

She puts up a hand. "That's not what I said."

"I believe you said and I quote, 'No matter what we want.' Sounds like you want me. And if you do, why the hell did you choose that prick?"

Rox looks away from me. I tilt her chin back up towards me. I need her to look at me. I need there to be no misunderstanding between us. I need to know that I have a chance. I need her to know that I don't accept what she said on Friday. We are meant for each other. We have overcome so much more than Cade.

"Rox, you know I love you," I tell her, being more vulnerable than I ever have before. "If you don't love me anymore, if everything we've been through and overcome means nothing, then tell me that. I'll stop trying. I can't say I'll stop loving you because I won't. But if Cade is really what you desire, I'll step aside. You'll only see me when I visit Harley."

Her eyes widen as she smooths the front of her skirt. Crossing her arms, she breaks eye contact with me and begins chewing on her bottom lip. I lift her face upward. I don't need the shy, timid, and unsure Rox right now. I need the girl that wasn't afraid to claim me three years ago even though I was an ass to her. I need that girl to speak up now and tell me what I should do.

"I–I," she hesitates and shakes her head, slowly retreating away from me. "Wran, love isn't always enough, but what choices do I have? If I choose you, I lose Cade. If I choose Cade, I'm . . . he'll never be happy if I'm with you."

I close the distance she put between us and take ahold of her face in my hand. My thumb caresses her cheek. "Don't think about what he wants. Don't think about what I want. What do you want?"

She looks up at me, eyes glued to mine. Her breathing picks up and she nuzzles her face even more in my hand. She pushes up on her toes, her eyes hooded. For a second, it seems like she's going to give us what we both want, but she pulls back. She doesn't go far, but she also doesn't continue. She doesn't kiss me.

"I don't know what I want," she tells me. "For so long, I wanted you. That's all I wanted. Then you left, and I didn't know who or what I was without you. Then I had Harley, and my life became being good enough to even see her. I don't know who I am. I don't know what I want anymore."

I let out a sigh. This isn't the first time she's said something like that. "Okay. I get that. Just tell me if you love me or not."

Her eyes soften and she lifts on her toes. All I have to do is lean down and our lips would touch. I'm tempted. I'm so fucking tempted, but I know she would run if I did. Instead, I just stay where I am. I'm not doing anything anymore until she initiates it. I want to know for sure that she wants what's being offered.

"That has never been a concern. I love you so much, Wran Belmont." She rises more and place a gentle peck on the corner of my mouth.

The hairs on the back of my neck rise at the softness of her mouth. My dick hardens and I step away from her. Fuck, if a simple little kiss has me wanting more, then we probably shouldn't be this close if that's all I can hope for from her. I let out a deep breath and turn slightly away from her, masking the hard-on I am sporting. Fuck, I have to get back on a motorcycle with her.

Clearing my throat, I respond to her, "Good. That's, um, really good. What better way to help you rediscover you than taking you out. We can start over with no expectations."

Rox brows draw closer, and she shuffles on her feet, peeking up at me through thick lashes. "Haven't you suggested that before?"

"Yes, but I was lying before. I'm not now. I will be the guy you fell for in the beginning. No sex. No talking of sex. It'll be like we're friends."

"We've never been friends."

I run a hand over my head. "Yeah, I know. I'm trying though. I can't eradicate you from my life, so I will take what I can get."

"And what if I want sex?" She takes a step towards me, her eyes trained on my stiffened crotch.

My eyebrows go up. "Is that what you want?"

She bites down on her lip, but then shake her head. I let out a breath. Thank fuck she doesn't want that. As much as I want her right now, I don't know if I could be the guy to offer that and ask for nothing more. I've done that in the past with a ton of girls. Sometimes just to piss Rox off or to get her jealous, but I can't do that now. Not with her. Rox is my lost girl. The mother of my child. I can't fuck her and pretend like it means nothing.

"Good," I tell her. "For a minute there, I thought I was going to have to give you one of Josh's lectures. We raised you better than that."

"You did," she says and walks past me and over to the bike. She runs a hand on the leather seat and then turn around to me. "To be honest with you, I kinda do want that. I've only done it that one time, and that night was such a rush. For once, I want to be a reckless teenager. I want to experience what everyone else does."

"Being a teenager is overrated. I hear they get into a lot of shit they regret later." I go over to her and lean against the bike. "I think you are perfect just the way you are."

She looks up at me with a frown. "You can't say that."

"Which part?"

"Both."

"Rox?"

She turns into me. "Yeah?"

I mimic her movements, bringing us closer. "Come back home. I miss you."

Rox shift on her feet and searches my face. "Wran . . . You know I can't. Not right now. Let me be there for Cade. Let me take care of him. When I see that his physical therapy is working, I'll come home. But I really need him to forgive me. I need my friend back."

"Why is he so important to you?" I ask her. I really don't understand this. For fuck sake, he blew a whistle at her. From what I can see, he's been a fucking douche since Friday. He doesn't deserve Rox. She could do a hell of a lot better than him for a friend.

Maybe this is mine and Josh's fault. Maybe if we weren't so strict and protective of her when she was a kid, she wouldn't feel the need to seek approval from the likes of someone like him.

"Okay. Stay there with him. But I want you to call me every night," I tell her. She goes to object, but I place a finger against her lips. "Don't. It's nothing we haven't done before. It's just talking."

She crosses her arms. "What's your game?"

I raise my hand. "No game, babe. I just want each party involved in this on equal footing. If Cade gets you at his house, I want to hear your voice until you fall asleep."

Rox stares at me for a minute before nodding in agreement.

Fuck yeah!

Before I know what I'm doing, I'm grabbing Rox and pulling her to me. She gasps and her body tenses against me. I start to drop my arms, but then her body relaxes and she snuggles into my arms, running her cheek against my chest like a cute little cat. Lowering my head, I place a peck on the top of her head and smile into her hair.

Cade might have her now, but there's no way she's staying. This proves it. We're meant to be together. One way or another, I'm going to have my girl back. Both of them.

A loud squawking goes off and Rox springs away from me. She pats down her mini skirt and pull out her phone. She immediately silences the device. Looking from her phone to me, she sighs.

"You think you can give me a ride to Aunt May's? My shift starts in thirty."

"You never have to ask."

With a shy smile playing at her lips, she turns away from me and grabs the helmet. Rox gestures towards the bike. I hop on and she immediately gets on behind me with no objections this time around. Her arms go around my middle with ease. My eyes drop to where her fingers play with the edge of my shirt. I smirk at that.

Cranking the bike, I swerve around, kicking up gravel, and head back towards town. At least now I know how to get my girl back. She wants a little freedom. She wants to experience what it truly means to be a teenager. Then I'll show her.

CHAPTER 5

ROX

Wran comes to a stop across the street of our one and only small-town diner. I look at the people going inside Aunt May's with a sigh. It's busy. Especially for a Monday. Taking the helmet off, I pull my leg from across the bike and get off. There's a slight twinge in my chest as I do and a part of me want to get back on the bike. To ride off with him for just the day. I can't though. It would be reckless and thoughtless.

I hand the helmet over and Wran takes it. I don't let it go though. It's the only thing connecting us in this moment. A part of me feels like letting this helmet go is letting him go. It's not, but I still don't want to let Wran leave. All weekend I waited for him to come back to Cade's place. I waited for him to put up a fight and to drag me back to our small apartment. He never showed up, and now I don't want him to go even though I know I should let him.

With a deep breath, my fingers fall from the helmet one at a time. I take a step away from the bike. Wran's eyes travel over me. There's so much I want to say to him right now. I wish I could explain this whole situation better, but I can't. My words haven't been coming out right lately. I know for a fact they didn't come out right back at the drive-in.

I don't love Cade the way I love Wran. I don't want Cade like I want Wran. It's so easy for me to tell myself, but it's not quite that easy to tell Wran. The words get jumbled up and I end up spewing out crap that doesn't make sense. Sure, I have no clue who I am without him. I've changed so much, but that hasn't really affected my feelings towards him. At least I don't think so.

Ugh! Why is it so freaking hard to just tell him how I feel? What I want.

I shake my head. I know why, and it's not something I want to admit to myself. I take another step away from him. There's not even a point to me thinking this. Until Cade is well enough, until he forgives me, there can be no Wran and me. I'm really hoping Wran has enough faith in me to know that he's all I want.

"Rox?" Wran eases up on the bike.

"Yes?" My voice comes out pathetic and weak, like I'm begging for his words. Like I need them like I need the very oxygen to breathe.

"There's one more thing I wanted to ask you about."

"What is it?" I drop my eyes and play at the loose thread of my denim skirt.

"Saturday you go to see Harley. Josh mentioned that you get to see her until there's an official trial. I'm coming with you."

I stare at him dumbfounded. I didn't really want him to come with me. Him being there is just going to give Lynn more ammo to use against me. I had thought after Wran risked everything to save Harley when my psycho father kidnapped her, he would have earned points in Lynn's books. He didn't. If anything, it will just escalate things. It gave Lynn the answer she needed to who fathered Harley, which is something social services have been trying to get me to admit for the last almost three years. If Wran comes to this visitation on Saturday, Lynn is going to want to make him take a paternity test. I figured the longer we keep Wran away from Harley and Lynn, the longer I might have with my daughter. They can't just straight up accuse him of fathering my child without undeniable proof. And no test means no proof.

At least, I'm hoping that's how it works.

"Um," my stomach drops, and my hands gets twitchy. I cross my legs and then uncross them as I try to explain that coming is a terrible idea. Not only for my situation, but for him too. Lynn is going to interrogate him. Just like she did Josh when she thought it was him who fathered Harley. I don't want Wran going through that. "Can I think about it?"

Wran runs a hand over his hair. It's longer now than when he first came back from the military, but still shorter than what it used to be. "That wasn't me asking permission,

Rox. I'm going. She's my daughter. I have every right to see her. Especially if there's a chance that I won't get to know her at all."

My eyes widen at his tone, and I bite down on my lip to keep it from trembling. Frantic, I shake my head at him. While I understand where he is coming from, I don't want him there. It's not a good idea. "Wran, you can't."

"Yes, I can. This isn't something up for debate. I want to see my daughter. You and Josh left me in the dark for nearly three years. You knew I would have been back in a heartbeat if I had known. So don't you dare try to take this from me now."

My shoulders slump in defeat and I nod. He does have the right to see her. I can't even imagine what went through his mind when he found out about Harley. The fact that it didn't come from me probably made it worse.

"Okay." I cross my arms and kick at the pebbles at my feet. "Just please be on your best behavior."

"I will." He mimics my posture and smirks. "I'll even wear a tie if that makes you feel better."

"Yes," I tell him with all seriousness. "That would make me feel a hundred percent better."

"Alright." His hands twitch on the bike's handles. "I guess I'm picking you up when your shift is over?"

I bite the inside of my jaw and kick at another rock. I don't meet his gaze as I shake my head. "Could you actually send Josh? I don't think it would be a good idea for you to take me to Cade's place."

Wran's jaw go tense, but he nods. "I'll send him your way. Just don't forget to call me tonight."

He cranks the bike and speeds off before I can go back on my word. A plume of dust rises causing me to go into a coughing fit. I back away, heading towards the diner. The door opens just as I make it there and a bunch of people I've never seen before, which is odd in Kingston, stream out.

Inside, Aunt May is standing at the register. There's people standing in a line and some leaning against the window. Confused, I go over to her. She gives me a smile and continues with the customer.

"What's going on?" I ask her. There are never this many people here. Not on a Monday.

Aunt May shrugs, and I leave it at that. I head to the back of the house to clock in. Hopefully, all these people will clear out fast. I don't really feel like dealing with a bunch of out-of-towners. Not after the weekend I've had. And now after the talk with Wran. With a heaviness in my stomach, I grab one of the extra aprons hanging on the hook beside the door. Aunt May doesn't really have a dress code, but with so many new people here, I don't want to walk out in my cut off tee.

I head back out, prancing up to May's side. She gives me a once over and grins. "How you doing, darlin'?"

"I'm okay. Ready to work," I tell her.

"Was that Wran droppin' you off?" I nod. "You tell that boy he coulda came in. Ain't seen him in a while."

"I don't think you would want him in here right now."

"And why's that?"

I gesture to all the people. "There's a ton of out-of-towners here."

"Point taken, darlin. I don't need that boy startin' anything this week."

The last time so many people stopped in Kingston, Wran got into a fight here at the diner. I was eleven and Claire thought one of the older men was hot. I acted as her wing woman, girl, whatever, but instead of him going for her, the bastard tried to pick us both up. Offered us a threesome. We fled. Wran did not. Aunt May lost a lot of customers that day.

I lean forward on the counter. "So what's with all the people? Your famous lava cake on sale or something?"

"Nothin' like that. They're all headed to that big festival up north. We get swamped every year 'round this time."

Right. I completely forgot about the festival. I haven't been to it since I was like thirteen. Wran and Josh would take me every year, but once I got older, it just stopped. Now that I think about it, a lot of things stopped that didn't make sense to me back then. At least now I know that all those unrequited feelings I had towards Wran as a preteen weren't quite unrequited.

I sigh, causing Aunt May to glance in my direction. "Something on your mind?"

I stare at her for a long minute. Aunt May is always the person I come to talk to when I need some advice, but she must be getting tired of hearing about me and Wran and

Cade. Surely, she has more on her plate than stupid teenage drama. All these people are evident enough of that.

My head drops and I neglect to answer the question. "So what section do you need me to do today?"

"First of all young lady, I need you to answer my question." Dropping the money in the register, Aunt May arches a brow at me and places her hands on her hips, foot tapping. "Go on and tell me."

"Aunt May . . ."

"Don'tcha Aunt May me. I been takin' care of your behind since I came to this town. You're like a daughter to me. Now, talk."

I look out at all the customers. This really isn't the place to be talking about anything. Anyone could overhear. And I kind of don't want random people knowing my problems. "How about we take care of all these people first and then I'll talk to you. Although, I'm pretty sure you can already guess as to what has me down."

"What the boy done this time?" I shake my head at her. "Well, then, alright. Hop on in, but once these people clear out, I want some answers. It's a shame I have to hear stuff from other people. Just a darn ol' shame."

I grin at her. "Yes, ma'am."

Taking a note pad, I go to the first table in the section I usually work. There's a man in a leather jacket sitting there with a half-eaten burger and an empty cup. With a smile, I come to a stop beside his table and point to his glass.

"I been waiting forever for that girl to get me another drink." He points behind me to where Mercedes stands grinning and twirling her hair as she chats up some man in a polo and khakis. Someone should probably tell her that he's probably married. Whenever I went to those festivals, it was full of people with kids. Hence, families. I highly doubt the man she's talking to is single.

I turn back to the customer with a wide smile. "Well, I'm here now. What are you having?"

"Coke."

I smile at him and take the cup. "Alright, I'll be right back."

It doesn't take long to refill the cup and return it to the man. He thanks me, and I move on to the next customer. I keep the pace for a good four hours, ignoring Aunt May every time she beckons me over.

By the time the out-of-towners leave, I'm spent. I didn't even get a chance to talk to Raven when she came in for her lava cake. I go to head back to the lockers when the door chimes. We were so busy that I didn't even get to take a break. I was hoping for at least five minutes before hopping into the closing routine. Pulling a smile together, I turn around to greet the new arrivals. The smile falls as soon as I see who it is. Claire stands with Cade in his chair, along with half the school. Okay, so maybe not half, but a good chunk of the people Cade was hanging out with earlier.

I don't make a move. Maybe if I just stay here, they will all leave.

Cade wheels himself forward as if challenging me. His eyes never waiver from mine as he reaches into his pocket and pulls out a shiny, red whistle. It dangles in his hand for a second, swinging back and forth, until he raises it to his mouth and blows.

I search the diner for some help, but no one's here. Aunt May went home an hour ago and left her manager to close for the night. He's been out back smoking for the last thirty minutes, and Mercedes is no help whatsoever.

Releasing a deep breath, words finally fine me. "Cade," I choke out. "Don't do this here."

The corner of his mouth twerks up. "Aren't you going to seat us?"

"I . . . um," I bite down on my lip and look at the others behind him. My eyes drift back to Cade and the red whistle he's rolling in his palm. Heat rushes to my cheeks as I fiddle with the edge of the apron. I can't believe he would do this. And here of all places. He knows how much this job means to me. Swallowing back a lump, I tell him, "We're closing in like twenty minutes—"

"Which means there's still time. So, seat us. Unless we need to report a difficult waitress. Pretty sure Lynn would love knowing that bit of information."

My back goes rigid at his threat. I search the small crowd for any reaction but get none. I'm not surprised. The only other person that could know what Cade is referring to is Claire. I search her for any reaction to his threat and get none. My full attention goes back to my friend. Cade can make my life a living hell for all I care, but I draw the line at him messing with my child.

I step closer to his wheelchair and peer down at him. "Don't you dare."

"Then seat us, Roxanna." The coldness in his tone and the steel in his eyes gives me shivers and not the good kind either.

Reluctantly, I do as he says. There are a few laughs as I do so, but they mean nothing to me. I've gone through worse, and if Cade thinks this is going to break me, then we must not have been as close as I thought. I can handle this. And in the end, I will have my friend back. I will fix what I broke.

I keep telling myself that as I seat them all. Cade just needs to get the pain out of his system and then we will be fine.

He will be fine.

At least I hope so.

Breathing in, I take the notepad from my apron pocket and begin taking orders. By the time I make it to the table with Claire and Cade and the red-haired chick, it's already closing time. I can't believe it took the entire twenty minutes just to take ten people's orders.

I look at Claire, waiting for her to tell me what she wants, but she merely shakes her head and points to Cade. I turn to Cade and the girl and wait for their order. Cade smirks at me before he begins listing off half the menu. I don't say a word as I write everything down. When he's done, I simply walk away.

Timothy's the cook that's on schedule for tonight. It's actually his first day back since the oil accident. I know for a fact that he's not going to cook all this food, but hopefully if Cade sees that I'm at least playing along with his little game, tonight will end without any more problems. Pushing through the door, I stop when I notice Timothy cleaning everything up. He glances over his shoulder at me, and I wave the notepad around. He frowns and begins shaking his head.

"That better not be no order. Fryer's off for tonight."

"Well, um, it's actually multiple orders," I tell him.

He looks past me and out the prep station window. He's shaking his head before he even looks at me again. "Nope. Get your friends out of here."

I don't correct him on the assumption that they're my friends. "I tried."

"Nine. We close at nine." He tilts his head up to the clock above the door. "It's officially nine-oh-one."

"I know, but-"

"Nine, Roxanna. I gotta get home. I can't have my wife calling up my phone. I don't know if you know this, but married women are crazy. If I get off at nine, I better be home at nine-oh-five, or I'm sleeping on the couch." He points to the front of the house. "Get them out of here. I ain't doing no more cooking."

I give him a short nod and head back out the door. I grab a tray with all the drinks ordered. Maybe this will appease him. I doubt it, but it's something. I give everyone their sodas, leaving Cade's for last.

"How long on the food?" Cade asks before I even have time to set his Coke down.

"As long as it takes you to get home," I mutter just loud enough for him to hear me.

I hastily turn around, hoping I can get away from his table before he understands the meaning behind my words. I'm not so lucky.

"What do you mean?"

I don't turn around to face him. He knows exactly what I mean. He and his friends won't be getting food here.

"Roxanna," he says my name with a warning. "I'm hungry. I want food."

My feet stay rooted where they are, and I make no move to address him. He knows what time Aunt May's closes. He knows what time the cooks stop cooking. The only reason he is here is to torture me.

"Come here." When I still don't move, he shouts, "Now! You really don't want to know the *or else*."

Exhaling, I do as he says and move back over to him. He shoves the red-haired girl off his lap. For a second, I'm relieved. He really doesn't need her sitting on his injured knee. That will only make recovery longer. My relief is short lived though when he pats his thigh for me to replace the girl.

"Babe!" the girl screeches.

I wince at the shrill in her voice. Cade doesn't regard her though. His eyes are solely focused on me. He arches a brow at me when I make no effort to obey him. The girl lets out a huff and cross her arms, but she doesn't leave. I probably would have run out of this diner if I was her. It's humiliating. This whole thing is humiliating. Maybe I should be the one running.

Cade grabs my hand and pull me down on him. He winces. None of his friends even attempt to see if he's okay. And these are the people he would rather hang out with. Cade's hand comes down on my thigh. His finger moves in agonizing circles. My eyes look around at the others watching our interaction before my eyes go towards the kitchen. I can't see through the prep window, but something tells me Timothy is not coming to my rescue. He's probably taking the trash out by now.

"I came here to eat," Cade whispers in my ear. "Yet, you're telling me that's not going to happen."

His fingers inch up my thigh as his free arm winds around my waist. My breath stills in my throat. "Just go home, please. I have to close up."

"I'll go home once I've eaten." Cade's hand lurch underneath my skirt and grips the edge of my underwear.

"Cade!" I scream and jerk up, but his arm around my waist has me restrained. "Stop. Please, stop. I will make you food myself."

"Too late. I'm hungry now."

My thighs tighten as his finger invades me, and I cry out. Tears instantly stream down my cheeks as I shake my head at this. This can't be happening. This can't be happening. My eyes flick from person to person in the group, hoping someone will help. They all just watch. Trembling, another cry slip from my lips as I see a guy with his phone out.

My whole body freeze as I watch him aim the phone at me. "Please no. Please."

Cade's finger come to a halt inside me and his body tenses against my own. "Come here."

Cade finally pulls his finger from me as the guy prances over as if he wasn't just recording this. I jerk back, and this time Cade lets me go. I land on the floor, tears still streaming down my face. I can't believe this just happened. I can't believe Cade just . . . just . . . I shake my head to myself, and wipe at the tears.

I look up just in time to see Cade snatching the phone from the boy.

"What the hell do you think you're doing?" Cade demands of him. He smashes the guy's phone on the tile floor and I flinch.

"What the fuck?" the jock yells, his face going red and blotchy. "That's my phone!"

The vein in Cade's neck pops as he snarls up at his friend. "And you were using it for something I strictly said not to."

"If you're going to have an audience, what difference does it make?"

I shrink into myself. Cade planned this. My humiliation is why he's really here. I get to my feet, ready to bolt, but Cade's head snap to me. "Don't you dare move, Roxanna." My body freezes. I can't take the risk of him doing something worse than this.

Cade looks around at all the students in his entourage. "Leave."

He doesn't have to repeat himself. They all scatter, including the guy that was recording this. Claire is the only one that stays behind. Cade looks up at me for a second before crossing his arms.

I mimic his gesture with a snarl. "Anything else?"

He smirks and pulls his finger up to his mouth. I'm pretty sure it's the finger he used to invade me with and my stomach churns at the sight. "You're not as sweet as I imagined."

"Fuck. You."

He wipes his hands down his jeans. "I'm going to be out late. Make sure you're in your bed at my house by the time I get home."

I shake my head at him. "Why? You obviously don't want me there. So why torture us both? Wasn't this enough?"

"It'll be enough when I feel like you've hurt as much as I have. Until then, you're going to be a really good friend and take what I offer."

"No." I don't have to take anything of this. Tonight was too far.

"Yes. And to answer your other question, I would rather us both be in torment than for you to go back to Belmont. That's the only reason you're at my house. He will not win."

I have nothing else to say as I watch Cade and Claire leave the diner. As soon as I can no longer make them out, my butt finds a seat and the tears begin again.

CHAPTER 6

CLAIRE

I come to a stop in front of Cade's house. Tonight was a lot. After the diner, all he wanted was to drive around. Seeing as we live in Kingston, there wasn't much to see. I didn't say a word to him after the diner. As cruel as I've been to Rox over the years, that was even too far for me. I would have warned her if I'd known that was his plan.

Turning my ignition off, I get out the car and go around to get his wheelchair from the trunk. Once I've gotten it situated, I go to the passenger side and help him out. I glance up at the house but it's completely dark. I don't know if Rox came back here or not. I hope not. Cade's been crazy since last Friday, and the part of me that forgave Rox for what happened with my folks doesn't want to see her go through what Cade put her through at that diner again.

It was disgusting.

It was vile and mean and so many things I didn't think Cade was capable of.

Obviously, my judgement was shit wrong.

He practically raped her.

And the look on her face . . . I don't think I'll ever be able to unsee the betrayal, hurt, and fear he put there. I don't think I've ever truly seen Rox weak. Shy and uncomfortable in her own skin, yeah, but not weak. She practically crumbled when Cade did what he did. And in front of an audience no less. God, I can't believe I just stood there and watched. Hell, I'm mean. I'm a bully, but I would never do something like that.

I don't make a move to wheel Cade up to his house. There are some things I need to tell him and if I don't right now, I'm going to chicken out. Brooding boys have always been my weakness. It's a weakness I plan to cut off though. Starting now. With Cade. If he can do that to the girl he's in love with, then he's not the guy I thought. I have no intention of falling prey to someone like him. And if I stay, I know I will. Just like Rox.

"Cade," I wrap my arms around my middle and look down at him.

He meets my eyes and frown. "Don't."

"That was beyond wrong," I tell him and shift on my heels. "Hell, that was just messed up."

Cade grins up at me. "This coming from the girl that poured a milkshake over her head."

"A milkshake is something completely different than what you did." I can't even bring myself to say what he did out loud. Not when I just stood by and allowed it to happen. "You should find someone else to take you to school tomorrow. I want nothing to do with shit like that."

"Okay."

"Okay?" I ask him. That can't be all.

"Yeah. You want no part in this. I'm okay with that. I have no beef with you. The only person I want to hurt is her."

My arms drop to my side, and I let out a sigh. I move so that my side is against the car. "I know you're hurt right now, Cade, but do you really think this is the way to get back at her? So what if she's not in love with you? Let Wran have her. You know just as well as everyone else in this town that they were going to end up together. He's the father of her kid."

Cade snarls up at me from his chair. "No. Belmont is not winning. He doesn't get to just show up and lay claim to something that's mine."

"But she's not property, Cade. She didn't deserve to be treated like it in front of all those people."

He snarls at me from thin lips. "She's whatever I want her to be right now. Besides, she's the one so bent on making it up to me. She could walk out that door if I was truly hurting her. Rox probably likes this. Probably feels like foreplay after all the crap she went through with Belmont."

I shake my head at him without correcting his assumption about Wran. I was around for most of his and Rox's early relationship. If it can even be called that. Sure, he pulled some pranks on her. Sure, he was mean to her sometimes, but Wran never did anything to truly hurt her. Not like what Cade did tonight.

"You're not the guy I thought you were," I finally tell him. "Hopefully, you can get over this, but until you do, count me out."

Cade shrugs. "Fine. See you around, I guess."

Giving him a short nod, I wheel him up to his house and leave.

CHAPTER 7

ROX

I yawn as I sit up on the old lumpy couch. It's been a while since I've slept in the Josh's cellar, but this was the only place I could think to come after that run in with Cade. I couldn't go back to his house and I didn't want to explain to Wran or Josh why I needed to stay with them. Both brothers would have gone ballistic, and I didn't want to deal with the fallout. Since Josh doesn't come around back anymore, the cellar was the perfect place to wither away.

That was five days ago. You would think I would be the most fearless person alive after dealing with my parents over the last couple of months, but I'm not. I turned my phone off and haven't spoken to anyone since Monday night. I didn't want to know what they were saying. I didn't want to know if it had gotten back to Lynn and if I'd lost complete custody of Harley. I didn't want to hear Josh saying that I should have handled things better.

I let myself have those days, but now I have to face the music. The world isn't going to stop just because Cade sealed our fate. And neither is the custody battle for Harley. I have to be okay. I have to make everyone believe I am okay. That's the only way I'm going to eventually be okay.

Grabbing my phone from where it lay on top of a box, I power it on. A few notifications pop up, and I click to see what they are. They're all calls from Wran and a few frantic messages. No one else. I at least thought there would be calls from the school and Josh. Especially considering that I haven't been in classes all week. No one seeing me for five days is sort of a big deal. I guess. Or not. Most definitely not seeing as only Wran bothered to check in on me. Then again, me disappearing seems to be a habit lately. Everyone's probably used to it.

With another yawn, I rise from the couch, and glance around the depressing cellar. God, I have so many memories here. So many with Wran. I wish I could talk to him about all this. I wish I could talk to anyone. Peeking at my phone, the thought of calling him crosses my mind. He doesn't need to know what happened. I could just call to hear his voice.

I scowl at the thought. There's no way I'm going to be that girl. I've lived three years without Wran. I managed things on my own without him for far too long to turn into this desperate, starstruck damsel again. This will all blow over. It has to blow over. Because I need it to blow over.

I reach for my shoes and steel myself for the day ahead. There's no way I'm letting what he did ruin my day. It's the only day I get with Harley a week and we're having some fun.

My phone starts ringing as I make my way up the stairs leading to the exit of the cellar. I glance back at all the boxes, dust, and dingy sheets before answering the phone.

I bring the phone to my ear. "Hello?"

"Where are you?" I cringe at the harshness in Josh's voice. "We're going to be late."

I check the time on the phone and wince at how late it is. Without my alarm, I slept later than I normally do on a Saturday. "Geez, no 'morning, Rox. How are you?'"

"I know how you are. Practically everyone does. Just get here before we miss our appointment."

I freeze on the stairs and inhale. He can't mean . . . surely if Cade . . . I shake my head. No, Cade wouldn't go that far. Last night was one thing, but he wouldn't let the entire town in on our problem. He knows what that would do to me.

I run my hand over my face and take in another deep breath. "Josh, what do you mean?"

"I mean get here or we're leaving without you!" I can practically feel the spittle and I draw the phone away.

Ending the call, I push through the cellar doors and head around the house to find Josh pacing and Wran leaning against the car. Both brothers' heads snap in my direction as I come to a stop. My head instantly drops, and I do my best to avoid eye contact with them. I may not know what Josh meant by his statement, but I know it has to do with

Cade. And there's no way I can explain what happened. I let Cade do that to me. I practically sat there while everyone watched me. I feel my eyes getting wet, and I swivel around so the guys can't see me. I wipe at my eyes. This is not happening today. My daughter needs me. Josh and Wran need me if there's any hope getting her back.

I am fine.

I am fine.

I am fine.

I say that over and over in my head until I'm sure the tears aren't going to fall. Turning back towards the guys, I can clearly see the concern on their faces. I smile and walk past Josh to the car. Giving Wran a little shove, I slide inside.

"I thought you said we're going to be late. Chop-chop guys."

"Rox-"

"Get in the car, Wran," I cut him off before he even begins.

He doesn't hesitate to get in. And without saying a word, Josh follows suit. I know they want answers. I know it's not like me to be late on a day when we see Harley. And I know eventually I'm going to have to talk to them, but for today I just want to forget.

Josh backs out of the driveway and for the first fif-teen minutes, no one makes a noise. It's just us and the sound of wind whooshing by. It's not until we see the leaving Kingston sign that Wran straps on his seatbelt and drop an arm around my shoulder. I roll my eyes and shrug his arm away. I know his tactics, and I'm not falling for them. I don't want to talk. They will just have to accept that fact.

"So bro, what's the plan for today? How do these meetings usually go?" Wran questions when I don't make a move to acknowledge his hand resting on my thigh.

"Well, usually we go, and we have a few hours with her. Sometimes we take her to the mall, the zoo, or for ice cream. Today is going to be a little different. We'll be meeting with our lawyer. You need to meet him, and I packed a picnic."

A picnic?

"Picnic?" Wran asks. "Josh, you do realize we're not the picnicking type of group?"

"I figured while I talk with Bennett, it would be nice for you all to have some family time."

Is he serious right now? "Family time?" I ask the same time Wran says, "Thought you would butt the fuck out."

Josh shrugs. "This is the first time you're actually spending time with Harley, Wran. Didn't think you would want to spend it sitting around the whole time talking to Bennett. Besides, you've been working hard this week. It's been a while since you've had a serious nine-to-five job."

I glance up at Wran. He has a job. When did he get a job? "You're working now?"

"I would have told you. It's new. Kinda." He runs a hand over his head. "You remember the night we first had—"

I slap a hand over his mouth and look over my shoulder at Josh. His eyes are on the road. With my face hot, I turn back to Wran. "How could I forget?"

His gaze shifts past me and at the driver for a second before coming back to me. "Yeah, well, that night I found out that the garage was looking to make someone partner. I thought I had the job, hands down. There was a communication issue, and I didn't get the job. Not until a week ago. I now own a percentage of Gramps' Garage."

"What?" I shriek. "Really? Oh my god, Wran!"

I practically throw myself across the small space separating us and wrap my arms around his neck. This is unbelievable. Wran used to spend all his spare time at that place. It was literally his home away from home. He loved that place. He also loved coming home covered in oil and then rubbing up against me. I always hated when he did that. Oil isn't the best smelling and neither is a sweaty mechanic.

Wran's arms tighten around me. And for a second, I let myself have this moment with him. I let myself feel safe in his embrace. His fingers move in circles across my lower back, and it feels good, like being home. I glance up into his eyes only to find his on me. He smiles, and my stomach flutters. It's like a swarm of butterflies going off within me, and I can't help the smile that cracks along my face. I love when Wran smiles. They're too rare, and as much as I wish it wasn't so, fifteen-year-old me lived for those rare smiles. Eighteen-year-old me lives for them too.

Josh clears his throat, and the spell is broken. Wran halts his fingers on my back, and I shift back to the middle of the car. The smile falls from my lips. As great as the news is, it doesn't change anything. Lynn will never allow this.

Josh will never allow this. And I could never allow this. My social worker made it perfectly clear that there would be no tolerance for misbehavior from me. She made it clear three years ago that no Belmont would be Harley's father. I suppose part of me always knew it would come down to me choosing Harley or Wran. And that's not a choice for me. I will never choose anyone over her.

I will never choose Wran if it means giving up the love of my life.

Slumping down, I lean my head against Wran's shoulder and close my eyes. Warmth encompasses me, and I crack one eye open to see his arm around me. He tilts his head down and places a gentle peck on my forehead.

"Sleep," he whispers, and I close my eyes again.

3 years ago

"*Rox!*" *Josh's booming voice jolts me awake.* "*Rox, where are you?*"

"*Here,*" *I attempt, but the word barely comes out.*

It takes all my strength just to sit up against the tub, but I manage it. I let my head fall against the cool tile and close my eyes.

"*Rox!*" *Josh calls my name again before I hear the telltale creaking of the bathroom door opening.*

I open my eyes to stare up at him.

Josh comes over and sits on the toilet. He places the back of his hand against my forehead, and swiftly pull it away. "Jesus, you're burning up."

"I–I'm fine," I croak out.

"I got a call from the school telling me you ran out of first period. Have you been in this bathroom since this morning?"

I don't answer him.

He runs his hand through his hair, and it reminds me of how Wran used to do that. Tears prink my eyes at the thought of Wran. Being with me was so bad that he ran away to the military. No goodbye. No nothing. Just a stupid letter.

"Hey, hey, why are you crying?" Josh slides from the toilet and pulls me into his embrace. "You're not in trouble. Just wish you would have called if you weren't feeling good."

"I'm fine," I say again.

Josh runs his hand up and down my back. "We'll get you to the doctor and you will be."

"No!" I jerk back and nausea floods me. Bile floods my mouth and I double over.

Josh grabs for the tissue and immediately starts dab-bing at the dribble on my pants leg. I shove his hand away from me. I don't need him. I don't need anyone. I can do this on my own.

"Rox, you're burning up, throwing up. Your skin is clammy and pale. You are sick. We are going."

He reaches for me, and I react without thinking. I grab the bar of soap sitting on the tub and throw it at him. It's more like a toss, weak and clumsily done. Josh dodges it easily.

"What's your problem? Why don't you want to go to the doctor? You're sick!" he shouts at me.

I shake my head. "Please. I'm not sick."

"You are!" He glares down at me, and a part of me hates making him worry like this.

"No. I'm not. I'm—"

My voice cracks. If I speak those words, there's no going back. The pretending will have to stop, and everything will change. Josh will hate me. I'll have no one. Wran's already left me. I can't lose Josh too. And he will leave. He will kick me out. The tears flow more freely, and I can't draw them back. If I say the words I've been neglecting for weeks, I'll lose everything. No school, no friends, no life. Everything. I choke on a cry and lower my head back to the tile tub.

"You're what, Roxanna?" Josh voice comes out strained.

I wipe at the tears and suck in a deep breath before giving Josh my full attention. I can't keep this secret any longer. It's literally tearing me apart. Besides, what's the worst thing that can happen?

"I'm pregnant." My voice comes out steady and calm. Like a clear sky after a raging storm.

Josh's eyes widen before he shakes his head at me. Rubbing at his temple, he backs away from me and my truth.

He shakes his head again and slumps against the bathroom sink. "I must have misheard you. What did you just say?"

I don't repeat myself. He heard me loud and clear.

"What did you say?" Josh shouts at me and I flinch at the sudden anger. "Say it again."

I bite down on my lip and shake my head. "Please don't make me."

"Say it," he demands. "I want to hear you say it again, Roxanna Raine."

He says my real name like it's a curse. Like I'm some demented villain like my father. Dropping my eyes from him, I repeat the words that sealed my fate a month ago. "I–I'm pregnant."

"Who's the father?"

My eyes squeeze shut. "You already know."

"Fuck!" Josh shouts. "How could you two be so stupid?"

The tears begin again and I pull my knees up to my chest. "I'm sorry."

"Sorry?" Josh laughs. "Sorry can't fix this, Roxanna. I knew you two living together was a bad idea. You're barely fifteen fucking years old!"

I bury my face in my knees. He acts as if I don't know this. I know very well what being pregnant means. It's not like I planned this. I've only ever done it once. Once for crying out loud.

"Get up." He straightens and squares his shoulders. "We can fix this before it's too late."

My head snaps up to him. I've done enough internet searches to know he can only mean one thing. "What do you mean?"

Josh stares down at me through cold eyes. "The only way we can, Rox."

I shake my head at him and square my shoulders back in defiance. I might be only fifteen, but he's not taking my baby. Wran left. This baby may be the only thing I ever have of him again. "No."

"Yes!" He leans down and grab ahold of me, pulling me from the floor. "I'm trying to protect you and my brother. Don't be stupid, Roxanna. You're not ready to be a mom, and I'm not letting him go to prison over something like this."

"You are not killing my baby!" I shout at him. Pulling out of his hold, I glare at him. "You will have to kill me to get to my baby."

Josh turns away from me and in the next instant, his hand goes through the wall. Nausea rolls through me again, and I buckle down to the toilet. Nothing comes up and I try to breathe through the dry heaves. Josh comes to my side and slumps down beside me. He pats my back but keeps quiet. When my breathing's back to normal and I'm no longer on the verge of puking out my intestines, Josh scoots over and allows me to sit beside him.

He sighs. "I don't know what to do about this, Roxanna. I can't fix this. I won't be able to protect Wran or you when people start asking questions. The best thing to do in this situation is to get rid of it, but I'm not going to force you."

I lean my head against his shoulder. "I'll lie. I won't say anything."

"And school? What happens when you start showing?"

"I won't go back. I'll homeschool. I'll go away somewhere, but I will not give him up. Wran already left. I can't lose anything else."

Josh wraps his arms around me and runs his hands up the outside of my arm. "I'll figure this out. I promise. We still need to get you to a doctor though. We can go to one in Arlington."

I nod into his chest. "Okay."

"Rox?"

"Yeah?"

"I need you to promise me you won't tell anyone this baby belongs to Wran. He'll go to prison, and I don't believe that will do anyone any good."

I nod into his chest. "I promise, but what about him?"

"I'll handle my brother. Now, go put on some fresh clothes so we can get you checked out."

My eyes flutter open at the soft touch against my shoulder. I lift my head to see Wran gazing down at me, the sun haloing his head like a crown. I smile at him.

"You okay?" He bends down, so we're eye level. "You were crying in your sleep."

My gaze shift from him to the empty parking lot and glass building beyond it. I gulp and nod. Of course, I'm okay. I have to be okay. That's the only way I'll eventually be okay.

CHAPTER 8

WRAN

Rox wipes her eyes and I see the moment she puts back up her walls. Her face hardens and pales. Those gorgeous amethyst eyes I love so much dull. She's terrified about something, and I hate there's nothing I can do about it. Josh told me before we left that Lynn is going to want to do a DNA test today to confirm I'm Harley's father. That confirmation will solidify my involvement with a minor and there's no way Rox or I will see our daughter again. However, if this is the last time I get to see Harley, I'm taking it. And I don't care what Rox or Lynn thinks about it.

Hell, it still baffles me that Rox lost custody to begin with. I might not know how DHS fully operates, but I do know they shouldn't have taken Harley for this long. Rox should have been given a period to work through whatever happened. Being here today is evidence enough that things somewhere, somehow didn't go the way they should have.

I offer a hand to Rox, and she takes it. Her hand's clammy and I can visibly see her gulp.

"Wran?" she utters my name, her eyes still trained straight ahead though. "Promise me you'll be on your best behavior."

I nod to her. It doesn't really matter how well behaved I am, today is only going one way. Everyone in Kingston has seen what that fucker did to Rox. Lucky for me, Claire of all people thought I should know before everyone else. She came to me Tuesday evening to explain that Cade had lost his mind. Said he was pissed that Rox wasn't at his place where she belonged. My hands clench just remembering the way she made Rox sound like that fucker's property. I would have killed him if it wasn't for her talking me down. The next day, I received a message with the video.

You might have been the one to fuck her first, but I will be her last. And I will make it hurt.

I thought it would be good to give her space this past week. I thought she would eventually confide in me about Cade, but that didn't happen. She stayed hidden away like she always does when things go wrong. For the life of me, I shouldn't have let her. She doesn't know about the video leaking. She doesn't know that Lynn knows. This meeting could be the one thing that breaks my little, lost girl, and I don't know if I can handle seeing her break.

Rox place her small hand in mine, and I tug her out of the car. Her chest slams against mine and her breathing hitches for a second before she rights herself. I really wish she would stop doing that. It doesn't change that I know she's affected by me or that she knows I know. I'm not going to push it though. She needs to come to me on her own terms. She glances down at her outfit and frowns. I tilt her head up and smile at her.

"You look beautiful," I tell her.

Her frown deepens. "I had this on Monday. I've had this on all week. I feel disgusting."

I don't tell her that I know or that Lynn will probably know. "It doesn't matter. You could be wearing a t-shirt covered in horse shit and you would look amazing. Just calm down."

"Yes, please," Josh says. "Calm down and let's walk. You two can walk and talk at the same time."

That brings a smile to Rox's face, and she finally moves. We enter the building, and she immediately sets her belongings in a plastic gray basket. I take in the stark white walls and the metal detector before following Rox's example. These people really know how to make this place feel welcoming. We clear the check point and I follow my brother down a long hall. We come to a door and push through. My feet come to a halt as the atmosphere suddenly changes from bleak to depressing. There are motifs on the wall of sea animals. Colors that would bring a smile to any child's face and a sitting room. We bypass that and head down another hall full of doors. Josh pushes through one and I can immediately hear laughter coming from inside.

I smile at the sound of my daughter's laugh. She sounds happy. So happy, and I missed all of this. I missed all of Harley's firsts. I let those thoughts leave my mind. I have now. Now is what matters. I walk inside the room and come to a stop when I see my brother holding Harley like she's his own. She has her hands on his face, covering his eyes. Her black curls bounce when she glances my way, and it's like I can't breathe. I knew I had a daughter. I even met her a few times, but things were so hectic, and my family was in danger so I didn't really take it in. I just knew I had to save her. I had to save them.

My feet lead me over to her and her eyes don't leave me. I take her from Josh without thinking and hug her tightly. Probably a little too tight. She wiggles in my hold, and I let her pull back. She smiles, and that one little act shatters me. I thought Rox had a hold on me, but how I feel isn't even comparable to the ways this child just captured my heart.

"I love you," I whisper to her.

"Wran?"

I jerk my eyes away from the child when my name is called. Rox, Lynn, a woman I haven't met, and some man stand across the room. I hadn't even registered them when I walked through those doors. I peek at Rox to see if I just made a huge mistake, but she just has a goofy grin on her face. Passing Harley back over to Josh, I head over to the desk where Rox stands.

"Sorry about that," I tell them. I'm in no way sorry at all.

"It's perfectly fine, Mr. Belmont. And understandable," the man beside Lynn says. We have some pressing things to discuss before you head on your way."

He gestures to the chairs placed on our side of the wooden desk. There are two of them and three of us. Rox takes the one directly in front of Lynn and Josh motions for me to take the other. I do and he hands me Harley. She starts bouncing on my knee and I'm not sure if I should stop her or what. Hell, I don't even know how to act in this moment. All I know is that my daughter is here. My . . . well, Rox is here. This may very well be the last time I see Harley and Rox in the same room.

Lynn takes her chair and jumps right in. "So, we know Wran is the father of Harley. It's strikingly obvious. However, we have informed Josh that a DNA test will be required today for medical purposes and proof."

"My colleague is sugar-coating things," the man states. "We've asked Roxanna on many occasions about you, but she has neglected to inform us. We can only imagine why that must be since neither Belmont would have been legally able to father that child."

His eyes drop to my daughter, and I scowl at the fucker. Who the fuck does he think he is? Rox had every right not to tell them who she's been with. Sure, she was young, but hell, I didn't rape her. I didn't harm her. I would never. Standing from the chair, I hand Harley over to Josh. She goes willingly, the grin and smile on her face moments ago gone.

I turn to the man. "Maybe we should discuss this without the child in the room."

He glances at Harley and I want to so desperately to put a fist in his face. I inhale and exhale, keeping my cool. I promised I would be on my best behavior.

"Of course," Lynn cuts in. "Josh, why don't you take her to the play center while we discuss this situation."

My eyes trail after my brother until the door shuts and I turn back to the group of people threatening to take away my child. Rox takes ahold of my hand and pulls me down. I take the seat, remaining calm.

"Wran, this is my colleague, Mr. Hanover. Roxanna met him a while ago when this all started. This isn't meant to be an interrogation. It's that we have been trying to get Roxanna to admit you are the father for quite some time."

"Why?" I ask. "What difference does it make? You people act like we did something unthinkable."

"It was," the man says. "You were what, twenty, twenty-one years old? She was fifteen. You see how that sounds, Mr. Belmont?"

I don't correct him on my age. Everyone assumes I was already twenty when it happened. I was still a fucking teenager myself. Sure, I should have been smarter, but I wasn't. I didn't turn twenty until the day I actually left Kingston and Rox behind.

"Yes. I very well know what it looks like. You think that didn't bother me. You think I go around screwing little girls for fun? I don't. I've never looked at a child that way."

"But you did. And she got pregnant and started doing drugs."

"I didn't," Rox voice comes out low and unsure. "I didn't do drugs. I've told you that. I was drugged."

"Hear say," the man says and he disregards her. He trains his glare back on me. "Why would any judge let you people have custody of a child?"

"Us people? You both seem to forget Rox and I have known each other for most of our lives. We grew up together. Yes, I'm a little bit older. Five years is nothing. Would I have liked things to be different? Yes, but they weren't. I didn't know about Harley. No one even thought to notify me. And if you think I'm not going to fight for my child, my right, then you are crazy. I've done nothing wrong."

"You raped a fifteen year old girl!" the man shouts and stares me down with a scowl.

"Charlie!" Lynn cuts in. "Now is not the time for accusations."

"He didn't rape me," Rox tells them. I glance over at her. "I wanted it. I'd been in love with him for years, and that night I wanted it. It wasn't planned."

The younger woman behind Lynn nods. Up until now, I'd completely forgotten she was in the room. "I understand."

Lynn lets out a sigh and hands me a cup. "Wran, can you please provide us with a urine sample? Afterwards, you can go have your fun with Harley. Today will be the last day until after the trial you'll get to see her."

"What?" Rox shrieks. "No! You can't do that. There hasn't even been a date set. There's no telling when that will be. You can't take my daughter for that long."

"Actually," the girl behind Lynn speaks, "a date has been set. Your lawyer should have received the letter."

"This isn't fair!" Rox shouts. "This isn't fair."

"We believe it's in the best interest of Harley that visitation is limited until a decision has been made. Especially after what occurred this past week?"

Fuck!

"Huh? What do you mean?" The confusion is clear on Rox's face. She has no clue what Cade has done. She must not have seen the video and talking about this in front of them is not the right way for her to find out. That prick has screwed her over one too many times for my liking.

Lynn looks over at the man, but there's no sympathy on his face. Rox is finding out about the video now.

"Your little sex tape."

I scoff at the accusation. That wasn't a fucking sex tape. Anyone in their right mind can tell she's being fucking assaulted. Rox is clearly uncomfortable in that video.

The girl behind him grimace. At least someone in this room has some tack.

"I don't have a . . . I don't understand." Rox turns to me. "What is he talking about?"

I run my hand over my head. How the fuck do I tell her that her so called best friend released a video of him finger fucking her in a diner full of football players? One where she visibly looks betrayed and haunted. One that the whole fucking town of Kingston has seen at this point.

"Wran?" she begs. "Please tell me."

"Um."

"Can I tell her alone?" the girl behind Lynn asks. "Mom, let me."

So, she's Lynn's daughter.

With reluctance, Lynn and I both nod. It's cowardly, but I just can't bring myself to shatter Rox. Not when I know she cares deeply for that bastard. And this will do exactly that. I yank the cup off the desk and head out of the office. I will deal with the fall out later. Lynn follows me out and stops me before I get too far down the hall.

"Please excuse Charlie. He was never meant to attack you like that. I can understand a young girl falling in love. I can understand you two growing up together and getting close, but this is our job. We must follow the law."

I nod at her. She's not telling me something I don't know. "Yeah, but that doesn't change that you are trying to take my daughter."

"You're right," she agrees. "It doesn't. But I think it's best for Harley. She'll be in a stable environment. She'll be loved and taken care of. Isn't that what truly matters, Wran?"

I glare at the lady. She knows I can't answer that. Either answer would be like renouncing my rights to Harley, and I will never do that. Instead, I hold up the little plastic cup and walk down the hall, searching for a restroom.

By the time I make it back to the office, Josh is there with a pink backpack swung over his shoulder. Rox has ahold of Harley's hand, but her face is completely void of emotions. Her purple eyes are shiny as if she's holding back tears. I want to say something to soothe her, but I know if I do, the dam will fall and I don't want that.

Harley pulls her hand from Rox's and walks over to where I stand. I set the cup down on a shelf against the wall and bend down to my daughter.

"Daddy. Poshy said you're my daddy. You said so too."

"Yes," I tell her.

"I want to go to the zoo." She pouts and it's the cutest thing I have ever seen. However, I don't think the zoo is on the agenda for the day. Josh being Josh already has a picnic planned out.

"I have something even more fun we can do. You like ice cream?"

She nods.

"Let's go get ice cream."

"Yay, yay, yay!" She bounces in place before leaping at me. Taken off guard, I stumble back but manage to catch her. Damn, this child has a lot of energy. I don't remember Rox or I having nearly this much.

Picking her up, I head out the door. I hear Lynn telling Rox to have her back on time. I shake my head at the absurdity of it all. I don't know how Rox and Josh delt with these people. Not for this long. Maybe it was for the best that my brother kept this little secret from me. I don't know if I would have had the strength then needed to keep my cool.

Once we have Harley buckled in, she falls asleep instantly. Rox assures me that this is normal. It doesn't take too long to get to Bennett's house and we're out of the car before I know it. Apparently, he's the lawyer my brother got Rox when I was at Pleasure House. Rox takes Harley, and I smile at them. Someway, somehow, I will have them both. I will have my family permanently.

Bennett greets us as we walk up the steps of his house. Correction, this isn't a house. It's a fucking mansion which can only mean he's one of *them*. I know I shouldn't judge, but I already don't like him. His kind are always the same. Smile in your face. Stab you in the back. Look how things turned out with Cade.

"Wran," Bennett holds out his hand. "It's been a while."

"We know each other?" I ask him. There's no way I know him.

He grins. "Not per se. But I've heard a lot about you. I went to Kingston High a few years ahead of you."

I grunt at him the same time Harley starts to stir in Rox's hold. Rox sets her down and she rubs at her eyes. The kid glances around, taking in her surroundings. I'm really hoping she doesn't remember the ice cream. When her eyes land on Bennett though, she races over to him. Harley's small arms go around his leg and he bends down to haul her up. I narrow my eyes on the man. What the hell? I look from Rox to Josh, but they are acting like this shit is fucking normal. There should be no reason my daughter is clinging to this man. I grab ahold of Harley from Tanner, but she doesn't relent. I give her a little tug. Nothing. She's not releasing her hold on him.

"It's okay," Bennett assures me. "She kinda likes me."

What the fuck? This is not okay.

"Rox?" I question and take a step back from Bennett.

"He's really good with kids," she explains. I scoff. Maybe a little too good if my daughter is clinging to him like that. She didn't even come to me and I'm her dad.

Something's not right with this picture.

"How about we discuss the court trial letter you received?" Josh changes the subject. "That way we can get to the park for that picnic."

"Right, right," Tanner says and steps inside the house. We all follow and I come to a stop at the pristineness of the house. Everything is white and made of marble. I knew this guy was one of them. He screams rich prick. "I would have called earlier this week when I got the letter, but I knew you would be here this weekend."

Tanner gestures for us all to take a seat. I glance down at my dark slacks and frown. Yup, no. Not sitting on his stuff. I don't want to owe him anything. Pretty sure I can't afford to have this stuff cleaned, even with my new position. Not until we start getting Gramps' back up and running to full compacity.

"I think I'll stand." I point to my daughter. "I can take her."

She shakes her head. "Staying with yellow man."

"Yellow man?" I ask her.

"Like the sun."

Okay then. I suppose that's one way to look at it. Strange but okay.

"So about this court date?" I ask as Rox and Josh take seats on the white sectional. I'm surprised Rox would sit on it. She's usually the prissy one about things like this. Guess she's growing out of that. That fucker Cade's house is probably just like this. She would have to get use to the luxury if she's staying with him. God, I really hope she isn't still planning to stay with him after what he did.

"Yes, so the trial has been set for a month from now." Bennett turns to Rox. "So around the time you graduate. DHS is going to do their damnedest to prove you're an unfit parent. As of right now, I don't know what their proof is. There shouldn't even be a case for all intents and purposes. Usually a parent has a year to get their act together or lose custody. It's been longer than that for you. That's a red flag I can use right away in our favor."

"What do you mean?" Josh shifts on the sofa.

"About what part?" Bennett asks as he rubs at Harley's back.

I move around the couch, my fingers grazing the butter smooth leather. It's nice, not gonna lie. I take a seat next to Rox. She looks over her shoulder at me and smiles. She mouths 'I saw that' but I ignore her. Just because I like nice things doesn't change anything.

"It's been almost three years since Harley was taken. A parent, in this state, is given one year to get their act together before the child is placed in a permanent foster home. That means the parent is required to attend whatever classes, meetings, etc. What was put forth when the caseworker set the parameters? Lynn must have done something wrong. You can bet I'm going to use that."

"I did everything that was asked of me," Rox tells him, and I one hundred percent believe her. That's just the type of person Rox is. My girl would have done anything it took to get Harley back. Lynn fucked up and I hope Bennett roasts her ass and the whole DHS system.

CHAPTER 9

ROX

I sit in between Josh and Wran as we enter Kingston's city limits, my eyes trained straight ahead. Today went okay. The meeting with Bennett went well. I feel like an idiot though for not knowing the basics of how DHS works. I literally handed over my child to Lynn for this long. Tanner says it shouldn't hurt my chances of winning custody, but I'm not so sure. Why would a judge award me anything when I didn't even know this whole arrangement was supposed to be a yearlong process? I did everything I was supposed to: the drug test, the classes, the meetings. Everything. Why would Lynn do this to me? I have a right to my daughter. I have rights period.

When we pass the first house, I finally turn my head to look in another direction instead of straight ahead. My neck cracks from the movement. Wran is staring at me, but I can't bring myself to make eye contact with him. He probably thinks I'm an idiot too. I got our daughter taken away. He didn't want to let her go after we went on the picnic. It was nice. I couldn't picture Wran being a picnic type of guy when Josh told us what we were doing today, but I was wrong. Wran is most definitely a picnic guy. He rolled around in the grass with Harley and even gave her a piggyback ride. It was the sexiest thing I've ever seen. I didn't even know it was possible for him to be like that. He was never that playful with me when we were younger.

Josh passes the tracks and I suck in a breath. I must go back to Cade's place. I don't want to, and I really don't want to voice that to the guys, but I need what little clothes I do have there. I need to confront him. That video . . . I can't believe he would do that. I saw him smash the phone. I thought that would be the end of it. Guess not.

"I need to go to Cade's house," I blurt out just as Josh goes to turn into his parking spot.

"What the fuck?" Wran asks. "No."

I don't look at him. "Not your choice."

"I don't think that's a good idea," Josh says. "Bennett says DHS will be watching for any slip ups. Do you really think it's wise to go back there after what he did? They will question your morality."

"They're already doing that," I point out. "You think I'm going to get a fair trial? I'm the stupid girl that didn't even know I should have had custody already."

"If that makes you stupid, then so am I," Josh states. "I didn't know neither. Going back to Cade's house will, however, make you seem incompetent. He assaulted you in a diner. With watchers."

I lower my head as disgusts rolls through me. "I know." I lived it.

"Then why the fuck are you thinking about going back?" Wran boasts.

"I need my stuff!" I finally say. It's not the truth though.

The truth is, I want to look in his eyes when Cade sees the pain he's inflicted. I never meant to hurt him, but this was deliberate. I want to see the hurt when I walk away from him. If there's any hurt. He might be at the point where he truly doesn't care about me. I wish that wasn't the case, but I don't see how we can move past this. He released that video.

"Let me go get your stuff," Wran suggests. "There's no need for you to see that fucker."

"No!" There's no telling what Wran will do to Cade. While I might not be extremely sympathetic towards him right now, I don't want to see Cade hurt any further. I've done enough to him. Sending Wran over there will only end in bloodshed. I'm positive.

"Why not?" Josh asks. "It's clear that Cade's not in the right headspace. You shouldn't be around him."

"I said no. I am going. I am confronting him, and neither of you are going to stop me." I turn to Josh. "You can either drop me off or I'll walk. Make up your mind."

"Where are you going to go afterwards?" Josh questions.

"She's coming the fuck home. Where else would she go?" Wran tells his brother.

I shake my head at them both. "I don't know."

It's the truth. I don't know where I'll go. All I know is Wran's is off limits still. It shouldn't be but being around him makes me weak. He makes me reckless and impulsive and crazy. Those are things I can't afford to be right now. Not with Wran. Not when my future with my daughter is on the line. Surely, he can understand putting Harley first.

"What do you mean?" Wran asks. He places his hands on my shoulders and rotates me around. He tilts my chin so I'm looking him squarely in the eyes. "Why aren't you coming home?"

"Because."

"Because why?"

I gulp. "Because I can't be around you. Me leaving Cade doesn't change that Lynn and DHS will. . ."

"Fuck DHS!" he cuts me off, his hands falling from my face and balling into fists in his lap. "You're mine. You're coming home even if I have to drag you there and tie you to your fucking bed."

"Do you hear yourself?" I ask him. "That's exactly why I can't come home. This isn't about you, Wran. This isn't even about us. I would love nothing more than to jump into your arms and sleep next to you, but we don't get that luxury. Not until this mess is over."

"And when it's over?" Wran takes my face in his hand once more so we're looking at each other. His thumb caresses my chin. "What will happen then? I can't stay away from you. You're my whole world. My little lost girl."

"Maybe it's time we both realize that Wendy had to return to the real world too. She couldn't stay lost forever."

Wran's hands fall from my face and those molten brown eyes I love so much turn cold. He yanks the door open and stomps out of the car, all the way up to the house. He doesn't even look back. Sighing, I turn to Josh. He doesn't say another word. Just restarts his car and backs out of the yard. I know going back there is stupid. I know nothing good can come from it, but I still want Cade to explain. I still want my friend back no matter how crazy that might be. Sure, I know that isn't an option anymore. But when have wants ever been rational? Nothing about how I feel for either Cade or Wran is rational. I would do just about anything for the both of them.

"Rox," Josh asks. "Do you know what you're doing?"

I shake my head. "What he did was wrong. It hurts, but surely there must be a way to fix this mess."

"He doesn't want it fixed," Josh tells me and I frown. "Everyone can see that but you. He's brokenhearted and when people feel like their hearts have been attacked, they get reckless and emotional. Do you remember what you were like when Wran left?"

I nod. Of course I remember. It wasn't until I found out about Harley that I simmered down. Nothing before then could stop the ache. My situation is completely different. I didn't walk away from Cade. I stayed.

"He will feel better in time and regret it. I did," I mutter.

Josh shakes his head as he pulls up beside Cade's truck. "This isn't going to get better. It will probably get worse first. He's in love with you. He put everything he's ever wanted on the line for you. And when it came down to it, you couldn't return his feelings. That's not easy to deal with."

I let out a deep breath. Everyone is right. I need to let him go. I want to let him go after that video. It just feels like I'm betraying him even more. Opening the car door, I get out and head up the steps to the house. I wait until Josh is out of sight before I turn around and knock on the door. It opens and Cade's therapist eyes widen when he sees me. He glances over me before abruptly dropping his stare as if he's unable to look at me any longer. He angles his body away from me and the door. I step inside and search the foyer.

"He's in his room." The man still can't bring himself to look at me. He must have seen the video as well.

"How's he doing?" I ask through the dryness in my mouth. My eyes move to the stairs.

"Perfectly. He's still in a ton of pain, but he can stand and walk if he wants. It's mostly mental. The doctors made it sound worse than it was."

I nod. "Will he be able to play football again?"

I know that's his dream. If he can still have that then maybe, just maybe, some of his anger will ebb away and he won't be quite so upset. He wouldn't have given away anything for someone that didn't choose him.

With a wince, the man finally brings himself to look at me full on. He shakes his head. "He'll forever have problems with that knee. He'll be able to coach or do something in the field, but playing professional is off the table."

My shoulders drop and I sigh. I point up the stairs. "I'm going to head up."

"Please remind him that sport drinks aren't water. He had three of them this hour alone."

"I will."

The therapist looks up the stairs before heading out the door. When he's in his car, I close the door and head up the stairs to the spare bedroom I've been staying in. I come to a halt in the doorway when I notice my clothes thrown crazily around the room. I pick up a white shirt laying by the door and sigh. It's one of the ones Cade bought me when I decided to go blond. I pick up the remainder of the things. They're all things he bought me.

Okay then.

I drop the pile of clothes on the bed and look around for my backpack. I know for a fact I dropped it off here before my shift at Aunt May's that night. It should be here. I go over to the closet and pull it open. I inventory everything but it's not inside. I whirl around and come face-to-face with Cade. He's standing on his crutches. His face is flushed, but that is most likely from the physical therapy.

"What are you doing here?" he asks me, taking a step forward. "You haven't been here all week. Thought you weren't coming back."

I shift on my feet. After that night, I didn't think he would actually care if I showed up here. I know he told me to at the diner but still. "Did you really want me to?"

He shrugs. "Didn't bother me either way."

My arms cross over my chest as I glare him down. "If you didn't care, why did you release that video?"

He smirks. "So you saw my masterpiece?"

"No." It's the truth. I couldn't bear to watch it when Lynn's daughter told me what was going on. "I lived through it. I didn't need to watch it."

He laughs. "You and I have over a million views online. Shall I read you some of the comments? I warn you though, some of them are pretty nasty where you're concerned."

I move around him and over to the bed. I begin folding my clothes. "Take it down."

From my peripheral I can see Cade coming over to me. He's having a hard time with the crutches. When he finally makes it to me, he tosses the crutches to the floor. I flinch at the clattering of metal as they land. Cade grabs the dress I'm folding and tosses it back on the floor. I go to retrieve it, but Cade grabs ahold of my forearm.

"Stop folding clothes." His hand tightens around my arm. "What the hell are you doing?"

I look him square in the eyes. "Getting my things so I can leave."

"No, you aren't."

Nodding, I say, "Yes, I am. Being here isn't fixing anything. My presence is only making you angrier."

His nails bite into my flesh and he moves in closer to me, crowding me against the bed. "You don't leave until I say so. You're going to stay here and deal with whatever I feel like throwing at you. It's the least you deserve."

I yank my arm from his grasp and shove him back. "Deserve? I don't deserve this, Cade. I don't deserve your humiliation and torture."

"My life is over because of you!" he shouts, spittle landing against my cheek.

I wipe my face and glare at him. "That's not true. You're only making it true. You can still do other things."

"Like what? My whole life I wanted to be a professional athlete. I chose you though. I chose the dark-haired girl who use to follow me around with her brother. I chose the girl who loved me. And I get nothing in return."

My eyes drop from his, but he grabs my face in his hold and forces me to see him.

"Nothing to say?" he asks. When I don't speak, he tightens his hand around my face. "I'll take the video down on one condition. I'll hire someone and make it disappear altogether."

"What?" I ask through gritted teeth, even though I'm sure I already know what he wants. I've known for a while.

"Choose me for real. Make what I gave up worth it. Be with me. And not as friends. That's what Kiellan would have wanted. For his best friend and sister to be happy. Together."

I shake my head at him. "Don't try to use my brother against me. He wouldn't have wanted me with someone that would do this to me. And do you really expect me to be with you after everything you put me through this week?"

"You've been with Belmont, and I'm positive he's done worse."

"He hasn't," I defend Wran. Sure, he's done things I don't like, but he has never done anything like this.

"Oh, but he has. Freshman year, he told everyone you had herpes."

"He didn't."

"He did. Belmont has said and done so much to keep people away from you. To keep you isolated, but you still defend him. You still love him."

"You don't know what you're talking about."

Cade crowds in closer to me, his hand dropping from my face and down to my waist. I step back and fall against the bed. He presses his front against me so there's nowhere to go. His head lowers to my neck and he place a soft kiss there.

"Choose me, Rox. I'm literally begging you. We could be so good together if you would just give me a chance. I would be an amazing father to Harley and any other kid we have. I could give them whatever they wanted. Belmont can't do that."

"No," I state it as plainly as I possibly can. "I'm not in love with you. I love Wran. Wran is Harley's father, and no matter what he's done in the past, I will forever choose him.

He chose me. He saved me when I needed someone the most. Even when I learned what my father did to his family, he still chose me." I shove Cade off me. "You think I don't know who Wran Belmont is. Then you're wrong. I know him better than anyone."

Struggling, Cade stands and glares at me. "I will make your life hell until we graduate."

I sit up straight on the bed, shaking my head at him. I knew giving him those two weeks when Wran was away would come back and bite me in the butt. I should have never indulged him to begin with. This is all my fault, and I have nothing left to do but accept the outcome. "Fine, Cade. Do what you must, but this is the reason I'm not choosing you. This is not love. This is obsession."

He frowns at me, and his blue eyes darken until they're nearly black. "Don't you dare tell me how I feel." He motions to the door. "You can go, but everything in this room stays. I bought it; it's mine."

I square my shoulders. He must really think I care about all these clothes. I don't. The thing about growing up with nothing, you expect nothing and are grateful for what you do have.

"Fine. I don't care."

That must not have been the response he was hoping for. He sneers at me. "I'm taking back the observatory as well. That was meant for someone you killed."

I shrug. "I never asked for it to begin with. You gave it to me."

A growl leaves his lips, and he shoves me back. He winces but manages to pin me in place. "You belong to me. Belmont is not winning."

I push against his hold but for a guy with a bad knee, he's still quite strong. "Let me go!"

"Choose me!" he yells back. Cade climbs on the bed and he winces from the strain. "I'm not the bad guy. He is. He left you. He abandoned you with a baby. I would never do that."

"Right now, you are being the bad guy. Wran would never do this, now please let me go."

Instead, his head lowers and his lips graze my cheek. He inhales, and I shiver away from him.

"I can make you feel so good." He kisses my neck. "Just like the library." Kiss. "You want that."

"N–no." I turn my head away from him. "I don't want any of this."

He shakes his head back at me. "Your mouth is telling you no. Your brain is telling you no. But your body, your heart, wants me. I've known that since we were six years old. I'll even still let you have Belmont. I can share. He might not, but I'll try. For you."

Cade's kisses continue to rise up my neck and along my ear.

"You'll see," he whispers in my ear as one of his hands go to the button of my skirt. "I'll make you feel so good, babe."

"No!" I shout and shove him back. He takes the hint and moves away from me. I thought I wanted him to explain all this to me, but I'm starting to realize he can't give me an explanation. There is no explanation for why someone who claims to love me would treat me this way.

"I'm sorry okay!" I yell at him. "I'm so freaking sorry that you got hurt. If I could change it, I would. I'm sorry I agreed to give you a chance when Wran went away. It obviously made you think we were more than we are. And I'm sorry I can't be that girl for you. You can hate me. You can torture me, but that's never going to make me yours. I gave my heart away when I was six years old, and I don't want it back."

His face drops but he says nothing. I stomp past him and out of the room. I hear my name being called but I don't turn around. Josh and Claire were both right. Me being here, being around Cade is causing more harm than good. I'm just the stupid girl that couldn't accept that until now. I glance over my shoulder to see Cade standing at the top of the stairs, his eyes slits, hands fisted around the banister.

"Don't walk out that door," he tells me. "You do, this will never be fixed."

I grab the door handle. "If I stay, it will never be fixed."

He let out a frustrated scream and my breath hitches. This is for the best. In time, he will heal and move on. I will heal and move on, but we can't do that together. Not when we want different things. I march out of the house with my head held high. Another yell pierces my ears and the door behind me slams shut. The glass rattles and I squeeze my eyes close. As much as it feels like someone is pounding my heart into dust, I know I can't turn around. I can't comfort him. I drop to the bottom step and take in a deep breath.

I can do this.

I can let him go.

Everything will be okay.

I blink back a few times, to keep the tears at bay. It doesn't work and a few slip past. I wipe my face and pull out my phone. I dial the one person I have left.

CHAPTER 10

ROX

When Raven's phone goes to voice mail, I sigh and start walking back towards Josh's house. I try my friend one more time before I give up and dial Josh. He's the last person I want help from, but there's no other choice. Plus, I need clothes.

"That was fast," he says into the phone.

"Shut up," I chastise and kick at a pebble on the gravel road. "I need your help. Is Wran around?"

"He was gone when I got back. Probably at the apartment."

Just great. "Do you think you can get him away for a minute. I need clothes and I really don't want to discuss Cade with him."

There's rustling on Josh's end of the call followed by a sigh. "And how exactly am I supposed to do that? He's not in the best of moods after you chose to go back to Cade."

I shrug and roll my eyes. "You're his brother. Take him to the gym or to get a beer or something. I just need him out of the apartment for an hour so I can grab some stuff."

"And where are you going to go after that?" he questions. "You could just go home. As a matter of fact, I'm starting to think it was a bad idea ever separating you two."

I move to the side of the road as a white convertible comes racing my way. A plum of dust swooshes up as the car passes and I fan the debris away.

"You are?" I finally say.

"If I had known all of this would happen from sending him away, I would have just let him stay. The outcome would be simpler than all this back and forth mess you two have going on."

"So you regret it?"

Josh doesn't say a word. Truth is, Josh probably doesn't feel guilty for his part in all of this. He was doing what he thought was right, and I can't be upset with him for that. He's been doing it for both Wran and me my whole life. It's who he is. Even though three years ago affected me the most, I wouldn't change it. Josh's actions spared Wran from prison. It's probably the only thing that did.

Then again, if he hadn't sent Wran away, I wouldn't have spiraled to begin with. I wouldn't have lost Harley, and Wran and I would be in a better place. Well, at least I hope that would have been the case. Neither one of us could possibly know what would have happened.

This whole situation is so messed up.

"So," I ask again, "do you think you can get him out of the apartment?"

"Sure. Just don't take too long. You know how he can be."

"Awesome," I tell him as my walk turns into a jog. "I'm headed there now."

I hang up the phone and glance up at the sky. Storm clouds are rolling in, and the sky is an inky gray color. There was only a slight chance of rain in the forecast today, but at least now I know I need to grab rain boots. I jog all the way to the tracks that divide our town and come to a stop. Hunching over, I rest my elbows on my knees and take in a deep breath. Jesus, I need to work out. Lights flash, casting a shadow in front of me, and I rise. I turn around to see Josh coming to a stop in his cruiser.

"You want a ride?" He comes to a stop beside me.

I shake my head. "Don't want to risk him seeing me. Go on ahead."

Josh tilts his head and shoots past me. I watch as he turns down the narrow street that leads to our complex. Slowing my pace, I jog across the tracks and down the narrow street. When I come into view of my apartment, I squat behind a bush and wait. About ten minutes later, the brothers emerge from the top floor. Wran has changed into black sweats and a white shirt. The sweats sit low on his waist and the shirt is sculpted to every part of his torso. I bite down on my lip as I look him over. God, he looks good. Too good for someone in sweats and a t-shirt.

When the brothers finally leave, I dart from behind the bush and rush up the rusty stairs to my home. Opening the door, I come to a complete stop. Everything looks the same. I can still even smell the last bits of burnt coffee in the air from us forgetting to turn off the coffee pot so much. I nudge the door shut and walk inside, my hand gracing the wicker chair facing the TV. I head to the kitchen and open the refrigerator. Bottles of water and energy drinks line the shelves. There's not even a can of beer in sight. Turning around, I open the trash can. To my delight, there's no empty beer cans there either. Just brown paper bags from Aunt May's.

Smiling to myself, I make my way down to my room. I push open the door and go inside. My bed is made and on top the pink comforter sits many of my portfolios. I go over to them and frown. I know that I didn't leave these on my bed. Flipping one of them open, blank spaces greet me. I flip through the whole portfolio to find multiple pieces gone.

Strange.

I know Wran asked about my work when he first made it back to Kingston, but I never thought he would go actively searching for them. Not that they were hidden or anything. Stalking over to my small closet, I retrieve my pink duffle bag and start stuffing as many clothes in them as possible. I make sure to grab a pair of rain boots and a jacket. When I'm satisfied with my selection. I head back out of the room. I go to head for the apartment door but stop. Peeping over my shoulder, I search out Wran's bedroom door. I know it's a bad idea to go in there, but . . .

I turn around and head to his room. The smell of coffee, musk, and cinnamon slams into me. Even though I was just with him earlier today, the smell of him gets me every time. I search the room, not looking for anything in particular. Then my eyes land on the stack of images in the corner. I go over to them and sure enough, they are the missing ones from my portfolio. He took all the ones I did of us. Putting the drawings back, I rise and go over to his bed. The covers are thrown back and pillows look slept on. I set my duffle on the floor and climb onto his bed. I sigh and wrap myself in his scent. Rolling over, I snuggle into his pillow and give it a whiff. God, this man smells so good. My eyes fly open at that thought and I sit up on the bed. I should not be rolling around in Wran's bed.

Not after what just happened with Cade.

I scowl at that.

There's no reason why I should even care how Cade would feel.

He made his choice.

He chose to hurt me. Even though nothing I ever did was meant to hurt him.

I leap off Wran's bed and pace back and forth. This does not make me a bad person. I was perfectly clear with Cade from the beginning about my feelings. Wasn't I?

"Gah!" I scream out. "Then why do I feel this way."

I drop to the floor and take in a deep breath.

This isn't wrong.

I can love Wran.

I should be able to be with Wran without worrying about Cade.

Cade wasn't worried about me when he released that video.

"Ugh! I need to get out of here," I say to myself.

Climbing to my feet, I march to the bedroom door. I stop and glance over my shoulder at the space once more. My eyes stop on his dresser and I still. Maybe . . . just maybe he wouldn't notice . . . I dart across the room to his dresser and pull open the drawer where he keeps all of his t-shirts. They are perfectly folded. Taking the first three off the top, I crush them to my chest and inhale the fresh scent of them. There's still a slight cinnamon aroma, but I can tell he just did laundry. I stuff them inside my bag and rush out of the room. I've already been here too long. Any longer and I won't be able to force myself to leave.

I haul my duffle over my shoulder and head out of the apartment. Pulling my phone from my pocket, I check to see if maybe Raven texted me or something. She hadn't. I glance around my surroundings, taking in the rest of the complex and old houses across the street. My only real option is Raven. I could stay here. There's nothing keeping me from coming home. I'm pretty sure at this point, Lynn doesn't care. Living with Wran isn't going to change our past. And as far as Cade goes, I shouldn't care what he thinks. He knows Wran is my end game, whether we're living together or not. Even I know it. So staying at my own home should not be a problem.

A groan slips past my lips.

Yet, staying here is a problem.

It proves Cade right.

It proves I need the Belmonts.

That I need Wran.

And I don't want to need anyone.

I want to be at our apartment because it's a want. Not a necessity. I want to be able to take care of myself. I want to be able to take care of Harley by myself. Because for three years, I didn't have Wran. And I was a complete and utter mess. I need to prove to myself that with or without him, I can be a good mother. I can be the person I want for myself. That's not going to happen if I come crawling back home.

With my mind made up, I stride down the rusty, cracking stairs towards the high school and to Raven's house. This isn't a long term solution, but it's better than the alternative. Maybe she and her father will let me stay until graduation and I can save up some tips from Aunt May's. I can get my own place and try living by myself for a while. My lips turn down at the mere thought of living alone. I don't really want to be alone anymore. After Harley, all I did was push people away. I became the artistic loner freak that couldn't even paint. I don't want to feel so isolated anymore. If Cade did one thing right, it was reminding me that I do have a right to have friends and a family and a support system. I have rights to be myself.

I come to a stop when I see Raven's Toyota pulled up on the grass. It's parked beside an equally old car that I take to be her father's. Walking up to the porch, I can clearly hear music coming from inside. I set my bag in an old green rocking chair with peeling paint and knock on the door. Voices from inside hoot and holler, and I back away from the door. Maybe this is a bad time. They obviously have guests. I go to grab my stuff when the screen door opens and a tall man in square framed glasses open the door. I look him over and gulp. His hair is sorta longish, and he's lanky like Josh. He has on a pair of fitted jeans and a blue button down that match his eyes perfectly. The first buttons of his shirt is undone, and the sleeves are rolled up. He takes a sip of his beer as he looks me over.

"You must be one of Raven's friends?" he asks me.

I nod. "Is she home?"

He pushes open the screen door for me and I grab my bag and go inside. I hear the door behind me shut as I take in the house. It's small and quaint. The living room and kitchen area is similar to that of my apartment with it being open concept and the kitchen being right across from the living room.

The man walks around me and points down the hall. "She's back this way in the game room."

They have a game room?

I nod and follow him back. As we get farther into the house, the music picks up. I can make out the lyrics to Slim Shady, along with a bundle of laughs. There's a high pitch squeak, and I'm guessing that came from Raven. The man I take to be Raven's father comes to a stop in the door way and the laughter stops. He steps inside, leaving me standing idle in the doorway. Someone cuts the music and all eyes turn my way. I take in the group and table full of chips and cards. Two of the men are shirtless with beers in their hands. Raven is at the head of the table, and she has no chips in front of her.

"Rox?" Raven does a double take as she sees me standing next to her father. She jumps from her seat, seemingly surprised. "What are you doing here?"

She comes over to me and the men in the room eyes drop. I shift on my feet, trying not to pay them any attention. I didn't think she would have company, but I suppose I should have. It is a Saturday after all, and I'm the only one with no social life.

"I, umm . . ."

"What's with the bag?" she questions and points to the duffle I'm clutching for dear life.

My eyes search the room. The man who opened the door is watching our exchange, and for the life of me, I can't bring myself to ask her to stay. Not here. Not in front of all these people.

Raven looks over her shoulder at the room. When she turns back to me, she takes ahold of my bag. "Come with me."

I nod.

"No cheating!" she yells over her shoulders and lead me out of the room.

She leads me back the way I came and up a flight of stairs. Raven shoves open a door on the right and we go inside. I take in the room for a moment. The walls are a deep purple hue. She has a canopy style bed with white covering. The curtains covering the window by a desk are also white but with silver thread running throughout. It's exactly what I would think her room would look like. A little manic.

"So what's up?" Raven asks as she hops on her bed, tossing my duffle to the side.

I shift on my feet and glance back at the closed door. "You look busy."

She swats my remark away. "Nope. Just my dad's usual poker night with his buddies. Are you going to tell me why you're here and what's with the bag?"

My eyes dart around the room, not landing on anything in particular. "Well, I called you. I was kind of hoping you and your dad might let me stay here for a few days?"

"What did lover boy do now?" She grabs her phone from where it sits on a nightstand, and I exhale. At least she wasn't dodging my call on purpose. She hops up from her bed and crosses the space separating us.

"What make you think he did something?"

"You're here," she states. "And you haven't been at school all week. On top of that, he's been in a prissy mood. He literally shoved one of his little cheerleaders off the lunch table yesterday."

I cringe at the thought of seeing Cade that way. "Oh."

"Yeah, oh," she mocks and skips back over to her bed. Patting the space beside her, she says, "Don't just stand at the door, Rox. You can take a seat." She grins. "I don't bite. Much."

I run my hand through my hair and tuck it behind my ear. Giving her a nervous smile, I go over and climb on the bed as well. A strangled laugh escapes me as I finally look Raven in the eye. She's forgiven me, but this is still so hard. Maybe I shouldn't have come here. Maybe Josh was right and it's finally time to go home. I shouldn't be burdening her family home because I'm too chicken to face Wran.

Raven pats me on the shoulder and gives a curt nod.

"This week has been a lot," I finally let out.

"This wouldn't have to do with that video, would it?" Raven asks me and I groan.

"So you have seen it?"

She nods. "Yeah. But it makes him look worse than you. I mean, you're crying in it. And he's getting off on your tears. He looks sick and deprived."

I bite down on my lips and shake my head at the reality of everything. I still can't believe Cade would do that to me. To us. To our friendship.

"Hey," Raven's voice comes out soothing. "He's a jerk. Don't cry over him."

I move my hand up to wipe at the tears. "I thought I could trust him. I thought he was my friend, but friends don't do that. I would have never done that to him."

"It is a bit strange. You two were thick as thieves last month. He was literally following you around with hearts in his eyes. What happened between then and now?"

I search Raven's face for any deception. I trusted Cade and it got me here. I don't want to open up to someone new and end up right back here again. There's nothing but genuine concern on her face though. With a sigh, I tell her everything. I tell her about Wran going away, about Cade asking me to give him a chance, about my mom. I tell her everything. By the time, I've finished my sordid tell, her mouth is hanging open. Raven is speechless.

She is never speechless.

"I really did want to love him in that way," I choke out. "He would have been the right choice if Wran would have stay gone. I thought giving him a chance would draw my attention away from Wran, but it didn't," I tell her.

Raven blinks at my story a few times. She opens and closes her mouth, trying to think of something to say. There's not really anything that can be said with all I just divulged. It's just nice to tell someone.

"Hell, no wonder you ditched us. I would have ditched us." She shakes her head, and her eyes land on my duffle. "Yes."

I tilt my head to the side.

"Yes, you can stay." Her face scrunches up. "Well, I have to ask my dad first, but he's a softy. He'll say yes."

"I'm guessing that's the man that answered the door?" I question.

"Yup. Dear old Dad."

Raven hops off the bed and goes over to her closet. She opens a plastic bin and pulls out a set of pajamas. She brings them back over to me.

"What's this for?" I ask.

"Well, I find that a long bubble bath usually helps me relax after a dramatic day. I have salts and oils and all that good jazz. Then we're going to forget about dick faced boys that are going to peak in high school and beat my dad's friends in poker. You do know how to play poker, right?"

"Yes. It's one of Wran's favorite card games."

"Good," she says and points to her door. "The bathroom is the last door on the left. Try to relax."

I give her a nod and head down the hall to the bathroom. Sure enough, there's a purple bathroom to match her purple room. There's an open closet with folded towels and all the bath products I could ever need. I set the clothes Raven gave me down and start the bath. I don't bother with all the salts and oils. I simply pour in some bubble bath.

Once the water is to a suitable level, I set my phone on the edge of the tub and climb in. I sigh when the warm water hits my stiff muscles. With a quivering lip, I bring my knees up to my chest and wrap my arms tightly around them. Silent tears fall down my face, and this time, I don't wipe them away. Sinking farther into the water, I rub at the tightness blossoming in my chest. I don't know how in one week my life has gone to complete and utter crap. I lost my best friend. I lost visitation to my daughter. I lost my home.

I've lost everything, and I have no one to blame but myself. I knew giving in to Cade would end badly. I knew the moment Lynn found out who fathered Harley, things would turn for the worst.

Maybe all of this is my karma. My dad used to tell me bad girls live bad lives. Maybe he was right and I have been naughty. Maybe falling for Wran was the last straw the universe gave me. A sob breaks free of me, and the tears flow faster at the thought of that. I can't believe I'm being punished. The stars wouldn't have led me to Wran if we were meant to be doomed.

My phone chimes, bringing me back to the now. I wipe at the tears and glance at the name on my screen. Wran. He's calling me.

I press the answer button and listen.

There's heavy breathing on his end of the phone. "You came to the house."

How does he know that?

I don't respond.

"I'm guessing you're the reason Josh tried to get me to go to the gym."

I still don't say anything.

"You know what," his voice is lined with frustration. "Don't fucking talk. Just listen. I don't know what is going on with you. I don't know what fucking spell Cade Jefferson cast that has you thinking you need to make things right with him, but you don't. You don't owe that prick anything."

I suck in a lung full of air and say, "I left."

"I know," Wran confessed.

"How?"

"You think I don't know the way you smell by now? You think I didn't notice my bed had been laid in or that my dresser drawer was open? You think I could go anywhere you are and not feel the presence you leave behind?"

"Wran—"

"Don't talk." He cuts me off. "My shirts, my heart, my pillow are yours. You can have them all, Rox, just please don't shred them."

I blink back more tears at his words. "I would never."

"Good," he says and nothing more.

I pull the plug on my bath and give him a little. "I'm staying at a friend's place. Her name's Raven."

"As long as you're not with that prick, I don't care."

"You don't?" I frown.

"I would prefer you here in my bed, in my arms, but I know demanding that of you wouldn't make you come."

I stand from the tub and grab a lavender towel hanging on the towel rack. I wrap it around me before responding to Wran. "What if I wanted you to demand me home?"

I here Wran suck in a deep breath. "Would you come?"

I shake my head. "No. But that doesn't mean I don't like hearing you tell me to come home."

"Come the fuck home, baby."

"No." I reject him with a smile. "But soon. Maybe."

I hang up the phone before Wran can say anything else. I step out of the tub with a smile on my face and head back to Raven's room. Her face rises from her phone when she notices me and she glances over me.

"You look better," she tells me.

I nod. "Thank you."

"That's what friends are for." She bounces off her bed. "Now let us go roast some old men at poker."

CHAPTER 11

WRAN

My eyes narrow on the tan bag as it swings back my way. In my mind, I can only picture that fucker Cade as I ready my fist for the impact. A grin bursts across my lips as the chains mounting the bag rings out. Jesse lets out an humph as it swings back into him. He catches it and peers at me around the heavy hide. He swings it back my way a few more times and I lay into the thing. If only this bag was actually that prick's face, I would feel so much better. But it's not. And as much as I want to give into my basic need to rip the fucker apart, Rox wouldn't forgive me.

I don't stop punching until my knuckles are split and I can no longer take the pain radiating throughout my palms. Once done, I grab my water bottle from the gym mat and take a swig. With the back of my hand, I swipe at the sweat trickling down my forehead. Jesse grabs ahold of the water bottle from my hold and squirts some water into his mouth and over his already damp head. He tosses the bottle back to me before dropping to the floor and laying back.

"He really has you worked up, huh?" Jesse asks and covers his face with his palms.

I drop down beside him, resting my forearms on my bent up knees. "You have no fucking clue. I want to murder that fucker."

"At least you haven't done that yet," Jesse mutters.

I glance down at him. "Yet. Rox is the only thing keeping me at bay. I called her Saturday night, and she'd been crying. Her voice was all hoarse and shit. I damn near drove to the fucker's house when I got off the phone with her."

"It's a good thing you didn't."

I lay back on the mat. "I don't know how people do this."

Jesse turns his head to look at me. "Do what?"

"Love like this," I tell him. "I feel like I'm going insane. My mind is on Rox all the time. And when it's not on Rox, it's on that fucker Cade. I swear I've made like a million plans to kill that boy in his sleep."

Jesse chuckles. "I'm pretty sure that's normal, man. If you didn't want to hurt him, I would be worried."

"I still can't believe she went back to him after everything he did. After that video."

Jesse shrugs and sit up. "I've known little Roxy for a while, and quite honestly, I think it's just her. She has a habit for drawing in pricks and wanting to fix them."

I sit up and narrow my eyes at him. "What are you saying?"

"I'm saying, she's the same way with you. You were an ass to that girl. Hell, sometimes you still are, but she keeps running back."

"That's not true," I defend Rox. She has a backbone. She knows when something or someone isn't good for her.

"It is true, but you made her that way, so you can't see it."

"What do you mean?" I turn to him and ignore all the grunts around me.

Jess looks down at me. "Do you honestly not see it?"

I shake my head.

He lets out a huff as if readying himself. "The first time she made an actual move on you, Roxy was eleven. Do you remember that? 'Cause I do. We all were watching movies in the basement the day after your sixteenth birthday. You had invited some chick over, and you were palming her fucking tits in front of everyone. When you got up to go get some popcorn, Rox followed. Do you remember what you told her?"

I shake my head.

I don't even remember the damn event. Then again, if it was the day after my birthday, I was probably high. By the time I was sixteen, I had taken a liking to weed on my birthday. It helped me forget my mother's death. And back then, I desperately needed to forget everything. If it wasn't Josh demanding things, it was my pops belittling me. And if it was neither of those two, it was the pain of watching

Rox, knowing she was something I should loath but didn't. My life was a mess then.

"You told her, an eleven year old girl, that good girls do what boys tell them to do. You told Rox to sit there and watch and maybe she'd learn how to please people. And she did just that with a fucking notebook in her hand. And now you wonder why she wants to please everyone. You taught her to."

I shake my head at that. "That's bullshit. I would have never told her that."

"You did."

I shake my head again and sit up. "Even so, she's eighteen now. She should know not to please everybody."

"Habits are hard to break, my friend." Jess claps his hand down on my shoulder. "You better than anyone should know that."

I knock his hand off me.

Did I really teach Rox to be like this?

That was never my intention. I wanted her to be strong. To be able to withstand anything anybody threw at her. I didn't want her desperate to please people. Especially people like Cade-fucking-Jefferson.

Fuck. What if I am the reason she's like this?

What if all my attempts to make her hate me, to push her away, did this?

"You really think I'm that bad?" I ask Jesse.

He shakes his head. "No. I think you were in pain, and you took that pain out on a child. And now that kid doesn't know exactly who she is without following your example."

I bury my face in my palms and let out a groan of frustration. "How do I fix it?"

"Hell if I know." Jess says, "Maybe it's something that can't be fixed. Maybe this is who she is and you'll have to deal with what you created."

"Shut the fuck up," I tell him. This isn't her. "This is just a guilty conscience. It'll pass."

"You can only hope."

I'm just about to tell him to fuck off when my phone rings. I reach around him and take my phone. I frown at the number on the screen. I don't know it. Usually, I just ignore numbers like this, but I don't this time.

I slide the answer key over. "Hello?"

"I'm calling for a Mr. Wran Belmont." The sound of Lynn's voice comes through the speaker, and my fingers tighten around the device. She can only be calling for one reason.

"Speaking. How can I help you Mrs. Adams?" I ask her.

"Oh, Wran, I'm glad I was able to reach you. Your DNA results came back today."

"Okay. I'm sure we both know what the results are. Is that the only reason why you're calling?"

"Yes, I was pretty positive on what the results would be as well, but it's my duty to inform you. You are Harley's father."

"Never doubted that," I grunt into the phone. "So what now?"

Lynn sighs. "This situation is very untraditional. Normally, a guardian would have to file a complaint about what you did, but seeing as you and your brother are informally Roxanna's guardian, I'll be filing the complaint on her behalf."

"Rox is eighteen years old. If she doesn't file it, you can't." My fingers flex around the phone. "Nothing Rox and I did was wrong."

"You raped a fifteen year old girl," Lynn states it like I'm a monster while she damn well knows I did no such thing. "You honestly think that is nothing?"

"I did not rape her," I speak low into the phone. "It was very much consensual."

"A fifteen year old girl cannot consent to being with a grown man. Statutory rape is still considered rape. You put not only Roxanna in this situation but Harley as well. You've ruined two people's lives."

"No, you are," I snarl into the phone. "You are the one ruining people's live. DHS gives foster kids to people who aren't fit, but you're taking one from a family that would do anything for that kid. Don't talk to me about right and wrong when your whole system is fucked up. You are the ones that didn't find a six year old girl roaming the streets after all."

"I understand your frustration, Mr. Belmont, but the law is the law. After the custody hearing, you will have your own court date. Good luck. I'll be talking to you soon."

The line ends and I stare at the phone in my hand for way too fucking long.

That fucking bitch.

How dare she?

How dare anyone at that fucking department tell me what I did and didn't do?

I didn't fucking rape Rox.

I'm not some fucking pervert preying on kids.

I would never do that.

That is not who I am.

"Dude, calm down." Jess steps into my line of vision and pries the phone from my hand. "Just calm down."

"I am fucking calm!" I snap at him.

He steps back and raises his hands in a defensive manner. "Okay. Don't bite my head off."

One.

Two.

Three.

Four.

I count until my temper comes under control. I make it all the way to a hundred before I fall flat on the mat.

"Sorry," I mutter to Jesse. "I hate that fucking woman. I didn't rape Rox."

"Everyone who matters knows that, Wran. Everyone who knows the both of you, know that you couldn't truly hurt that girl."

"Lynn already has my daughter. Now she's going after my fucking life. I don't know what to do."

I get up from the mat and Jesse follow. Grabbing ahold of the punching bag, I ready it for my fist, this time picturing a whole different person. My first hit lands dead center of the bag, a dent where my hand landed. The image of Lynn's broken nose gushing crimson flashes in my head and I send another punch.

And another.

And another.

I don't stop pounding into the bag this time until someone places a hand on my shoulder. A long whistle rings into my ear and I whirl around, my fist ready to hit something other than the brown bag. The guy raises his hand, but the cocky ass smirk on his face tells me he's not afraid in the least. He should be. Everyone should be fearful of me right now.

"You have a mad swing," he states and looks over my shoulder.

I cross my arms, studying the guy before me. "What's it to you?"

Jesse steps beside me and crosses his arms as well.

The dude looks between us before lowering his arms. "I run an underground not too far from here. I'm in search of a new guy. My last one got pussy whipped and bailed. That swing could take you far."

I'm shaking my head before he even finishes. I know all about the Arlington underground. I used to go to some of the fights back in high school. Being a part of that crowd never even crossed my mind.

"Not interested," I tell him. I point over to where some younger guys are battling it out in the ring. "Try them."

The man looks at the ring for only a minute. "Nah. They don't have what you have."

"Look," I state, "I'm flattered. But if your last guy ran off with some girl, then I'm you're worst fucking nightmare. I'm not interested. So run along."

He steps backs. "Okay, okay, okay. I can take a hint."

The guy turns on his heels and strolls across the gym to the ring. I disregard them and turn back to Jesse. He has a shit grin on his face. I shove him as I bend down to retrieve my water bottle again.

"Have you thought about asking your pops to be your lawyer?" Jesse blurts out.

I whirl around to him just as I swallow a gulp of water. It goes down the wrong pipe and my body goes into a coughing fit. What the fuck did he just ask?

"Hear me out," he hurries out. "Your dad was one of the best criminal lawyers. Even you have to admit he was good. Hell, he worked for Roxy's father. If anyone can make this mess go away and make you look like an innocent saint, it's him."

My eyes narrow on Jesse as I manage to get the coughing under control. As much I want to debunk his statement, I can't. My pops was good. Damn good. It's been years now since he's even cracked a case. Over a decade. I doubt he could or even would help me. Not to mention, it would be a miracle if he was ever sober enough to consider it. The last time I saw my pops, his apartment had turned into a junk yard. There were piles of garbage on the floor. Moldy food in the sink. Beer cans littering the countertops. It smelled like the sewer threw up in the house and he didn't smell much better. Not to mention he fired a gun at me.

I shake my head.

Nope.

There's no way.

I'd be better off trying to defend myself.

Jesse leans over and grabs his bag. "He's been doing great, you know."

I pick up my things from the gym mat with a scoff. "And how would you know?"

He shrugs and start walking to the door. "He might have come around 'bout a month or so ago looking for a job."

A month or so?

I would have been held captive at Pleasure House then. I suppose Pops could have made a change in that amount of time. Maybe my little words of encouragement actually made it through the beer fogging his brain.

Running a hand through my hair, I glance at Jess. "You really think that's a good idea? You really think Pops, my pops, could help me get my daughter back and have this ridiculous case dropped before it hits court?"

"I think he's your best shot," Jesse answers as he comes to a stop beside my car. "It's only a suggestion. Take it or leave it. Either way, you need a lawyer."

Without acknowledging the truth in his words, I open the car door and hop inside. Maybe, just maybe, it's time I pay Pops another visit. If anything, I can see if he's truly doing better.

Not that I give a flying fuck about that man.

I come to a stop outside my pop's place. The lawn is trimmed and the smell of rot isn't permeating the air like the last time. That can only be a good sign. I'm not getting my hopes up that my pops is doing as good as Jesse made it sound on the way back to Kingston. The only way to get him to shut it was to agree to come here. I turn to Jesse with a frown. I can't believe I let this fucker talk me into coming here. There's no way this man can help me. He'll probably laugh in my face and tell me I deserve this.

"I can hire a fucking lawyer, man. It doesn't need to be him." I try to change Jesse's mind again about this nonsense.

He leans back against the passenger's door and crosses his arms. "Man up and go talk to your dad."

"Why are you pushing this?"

"When Gramps died, I had no one," he says it like it's nothing. "You are fighting for your life and your kid. This is one of the times when you need your dad. Don't be too proud to ask when you need help, Wran."

I yank my keys from the ignition and shove open my car door. I run my hand across the door's interior and close it on Jess with a much softer hand. I stump my way up the paved pathway and come to a complete halt as the smell of garlic hits my nose. And not garlic that has been sitting out for weeks on end. I blink back my confusion at the homey smell as I wet my lips.

Taking in a deep breath, I knock on the door. A bark comes from inside and I take a step back. When the fuck did my pops get a dog? He never wanted pets around when I was a kid. Always complained about it being another mouth to feed. Another bark comes and then the door opens. Pops stands there dressed in a black apron that says *World #1 Dad* and a wooden spoon in his hand. The garlic aroma is even more potent. Along with it is basil and something else.

I arch a brow at him. "You're cooking?"

A massive dog with shaggy black fur squeezes its way through the space between my pops and the door. It lunges at me and I pat its head.

"I have to eat." My pops eyes me before stepping aside. "Care to join an old man?"

"Um, I can't stay long." I point to Jesse in the car.

"Still come on in." He motions me to step forward.

I move past my father and into the apartment. Glancing around, I take in the wooden floors I can actually make out this time around. There's not a black plastic bag in sight nor a beer can. Maybe my pops has changed. This place certainly has. A hand comes down on my shoulder and I rotate to my pops. Now that I'm past the fact that he actually fucking cooked, my eyes roam over his clean shaven face. He looks at least a decade younger with all that matted mess gone. His hair is even cut close to his head. There's not even a whiff of alcohol coming off him.

Pops crosses his arms in a defensive manner. "You done examining me?"

I gesture to him. "This is just a surprise. After twelve years of you being a fucking drunk—"

"Don't you dare come to my house and disrespect me, boy," Pops cuts me off with something far too familiar.

He straightens, but no matter how he scowls at me and stands like he's actually somebody, the apron and spoon in his hand makes it hard to take him serious. A laugh bubbles out of me and Pops relaxes again.

"I mean no disrespect, Pops," I tell him and it's true. This is the best I've seen my dad in over a decade. I'm not sure this stint will last. None of the others did, but it's better to see him this way than not.

"I'm guessing you didn't come here to smell the spaghetti." He bypasses me and heads into the living room. I follow after him. "So why are you really gracing me with your presence? I've been trying to contact you for a month. Josh's been telling me it ain't the right time to talk."

Josh might have mentioned it a few times that Dad wanted to talk. He thought it might have been good for Dad to come to Pleasure House, but I wasn't about to give this man more ammo to use against me. It's bad enough that I will always be 'boy' and Josh will always be the golden son. Asking him for help on this case, will just solidify how much of a fuck up I really am.

"I need help." The confession comes out cowardly, and I hate it. "The lawyer kind of help."

Pops take a seat in the chair. "What have you gotten yourself into?"

I grind my teeth as I glare at him.

One.

Two.

Three.

I keep counting until my teeth are no longer grinding themselves into powder.

Exhaling, I take a seat across from him on the sofa.

On a new sofa that is not covered in brown stain spots and cigarette burns.

"Roxy got pregnant three years ago." It rolls off my tongue like I've said it a thousand times. "DHS has our daughter and Rox's social worker is filing a sexual assault charge against me."

My pops sits up straight. "I have a grandbaby?"

I nod. "Not one you'll ever get to meet if I'm in prison and she's stuck with some random family."

"Nonsense!" My father stands abruptly from the chair and paces around the coffee table. "That child's a grown woman. No one can file charges but her."

"She is now, but she was only fifteen when she had Harley. Lynn is claiming it as statutory rape."

"Ehh." The noise escapes Pops' lips without him even realizing it. "In that case, I can make a suggestion. I'm not too sure how you will take it."

I look up at him. At this point, I will take any suggestion I can get. "What's the suggestion?"

"Marry her. For a case like this to stick, your girl will have to take the stand. She will have to be questioned, and they will have to question her against you. If you marry her, they can't require it."

I stand from the sofa as Pops come to a stop in front of me. "It's that easy?"

"I wouldn't call proposing to a woman you knocked up three years ago easy."

I shake my head at him. "She'll say yes."

"You sure about that boy? 'Cause if she don't, you have a serious problem on your hand."

Rox will say yes.

Of course she will.

If this is going to save Harley and keep me free, I know she won't deny me.

Besides, she said it herself, no matter what's going on with Cade, her love for me has never wavered.

An annoying beeping sounds around the apartment and a burning smell invades my nostrils. My dad's eyes widen as he races pass me and down the hall. I follow after him only to be swallowed by smoke as we make it to the kitchen.

"Damn, boy, you made me burn my garlic bread," Pops scolds me as he goes over to the oven. Even more smoke rushes out to greet him. Grabbing mittens, he pulls the pan out of the stove to reveal a charred mess. Guess he won't be eating garlic bread tonight.

"Dammit!" Pops shouts. He turns on me and points towards the front. "It's time for you to go. You messed up some expensive bread."

"Garlic bread's not that expensive," I tell him.

"It is when it's not that boxed mess. Now, shoo. I got to salvage this before Cassandra comes."

Cassandra?

"Who is that?" I ask a little curious now. My pops hasn't been interested in any woman since my mother died. That's one thing he was deeply consistent with.

"None of your business. Now go."

"Okay, I'm leaving." I turn and head towards the front of the house. I hear a string of curses as I open the door and step outside in the humid summer night.

Marriage, huh?

I grin to myself. I wasn't planning to ask Rox to marry me this soon. I wanted to woo her. Show her that I can be the man she needs. Make her dreams come true first. But if marriage can fix this mess, there's no need to wait. I know how I feel about her. She's the star in my dark sky. I would have married that girl three years ago if it was legal.

Getting in the car, I turn to Jesse. "Change of plans. We're not gaming tonight."

Jesse's head snap up from his phone. "What? Why? I canceled plans with Layla for tonight."

I cringe at that. "Sorry, but I have a proposal to make."

"Huh?"

"Tell you later."

CHAPTER 12

WRAN

My car comes to a roaring stop outside of Rox's friend's house. I think she said her name was Stacy or Raven or something. I honestly don't care. I'm just happy that Rox has somewhere to stay that's not with Cade. Of course, the best place would be at our apartment but the girl can be stubborn.

I take in the yard. It looks to not have been cut in a few weeks. It's not too badly overgrown. There's a bike laying near the porch and what looks like a bowl by the door. The house itself is quaint with faded blue paint and shutters that need washing. All in all, it's easy to see that the people living in this house are nothing like Cade. Rox's friend isn't one of them.

Pulling down my visor, I check my appearance. I run a hand through my hair and take a deep breath. The door to the house opens and I slam the visor shut. My heartbeat picks up and I run a hand across the back of my neck. Fuck, I should not be this nervous. It's just Rox. It's not like this moment is going to make or break us.

She stands on the porch and smiles, her arms hanging low and crossed in the front. She's in a cutesy little dress with flowers all over and my mind instantly go back to the day I found her. She was in a dress much like this one. Whereas the childhood dress was much puffier, this one is much clingier. It showcases curves Rox normally doesn't show. She tilts her head to the side and cross her legs. She still hasn't moved from her position on the porch.

I get out the car, leaving my door open and up to her. "Something wrong?"

Rox shakes her head. "You said this was a date on the phone."

"Yeah?" I ask, not quite sure what she's getting at. "Why are you just standing here?"

"Well, I haven't been on many dates, but I'm positive you're supposed to get out of the car and come to the house."

I laugh at her statement. "Baby, I'm not that type of guy. You already know this."

"Maybe you can try to be or maybe I can just go back in Raven's house." She points to the door over her shoulder.

Leaning in closer to her, the scent of her hair invades my nostrils. "You know I would do just about anything for you, but don't let your new friend whisper about things you know you aren't going to get. I'm not a hearts and flowers type of man. But I'm down to bend you over my knee and spank you like old times."

A gasp leaves her lips, and pink flows into her cheeks. She licks at her bottom lip before shaking her head. "I–I think I'll pass on that. For now."

I grin at her. "Alright. Let's head out."

Taking her hand, I lead her across the porch, boards squeaking as I do, and to the car. I open the door with a bow. Rox shoves me, but it brings a bright smile to her face. I cross in front of the car and get inside.

"So where are we going?" Rox asks as she buckles up. "You didn't give much info on the phone."

"There's something I need to ask you, but I wanted to go for a swim first. The lake alright?"

She nods. "What do you need to ask me?"

"It's nothing important. It can wait until the end of this."

Rox tilts her head a little like she does when she quizzical about something. I know what my pops told me to do. I know it could fix a ton of our problems. It just doesn't feel like the right time. And it's not even that. I would love nothing more than to just be with Rox, but I don't know how Rox will respond. The old Rox, the Rox before I went away, would jump with joy just from the mention of it. Hell, I wouldn't even be able to get it out before she'd be shouting yes. This Rox is different. I know she cares about me. No matter how much she pulls away, she loves me. But this Rox isn't putting her wants and needs first like she did when she was younger. By no means was she a selfish child. She just knew what she wanted and wasn't afraid to jump at it.

A part of me wishes she was still that way. That made loving her, being with her feel effortless. Now, I'm constantly wondering if everything I suggest is right. It's the worst fucking feeling in the world to not know if you're good enough for the person you love. There must have been some reason other than he's her friend that Rox chose to stay with Cade instead of coming home to me. There must be some reason why she even came to this new girl's house instead of coming home to me.

Thomas would probably tell me I'm thinking too much about her small reactions. To an extent, I agree. I'm obsessing over her. I've been obsessing over her for a long time and it's a habit I need to break. I could always just ask her. Then again, Rox is a woman and they never really say what's on their minds.

"You're being awfully quiet," Rox utters when I turn off the road to the trail that leads to the lake. "You haven't made one sexual remark since we been in this car. You okay?"

"I can make as many sexual innuendos as you want if that's what makes you hot," I tell her and grin.

She rolls her eyes and my grin widens. "Seriously, Wran. You don't ever want to just talk. And now you're all quiet and in your head. Tell me what's wrong."

She got me there. I pull the car up to the lake and cut the engine. I smirk at her as I tug my shirt off and over my head. "Later."

Rox bites down on her lower lip as her eyes roam over me. "Okay." Her voice comes out in a whisper.

God, I love the way she responds to me.

I motion the dress. "You're goin' to need to take that off."

Rox's face heats at the suggestion. She moves her arms to cover her. "You didn't tell me we were coming to the lake. I don't have on a swimsuit."

I raise a brow at her. She's so cute. "Neither do I."

"It's broad daylight." She giggles with embarrassment. "What if someone sees us?"

"Then I will have to kill them. No one gets to see what's mine."

Rox looks down at her dress, still biting that darn lip. I reach over and pry her lip from between her teeth. The red already staining her cheeks turn even deeper. Her eyes land on me, and without looking away, her hands go to the little bow between her breasts. She pulls at the ties and the front of her dress falls open. Fuuuuck. She's not wearing a bra. My eyes drop from her face and I pull my eyes away from her. Why did I suggest this again?

Restraining a groan, I right myself. I didn't come here for this. We are not here for this. I shove the car door open and rush over to the water without taking my slacks off. They need to stay on or I will do something dumb. I can't afford stupid shit right now. I take in a deep breath and jump into the water. It's lukewarm but at least it cools me down. As I resurface, I sling the water from my hair and wipe it off my face. I rotate around to see Rox standing in nothing more than a thong. My eyes take in every feature of her, and I must make some type of noise because she smirks at me. Not the little grin or giggle she usually has but a full on "I know what the fuck I'm doing" smirk. Just like the ones I give her. Suddenly, the lukewarm water is doing nothing to conceal my want. My dick's hard as fucking rock.

And fuck if I don't want to drag her into this lake and fuck her against the shore.

"What are you trying to do to me?" I ask her, clearing my throat as I do so. "When the hell did you start wearing so little?"

She walks, no, struts through the water until it comes up to cover her chest. I gulp as she swims over to me. I need to seriously abort this mission. It's not going at all how I pictured in my head. I want the meek, shy little girl back. The one that wouldn't dare look like this. From the expression lining her face, I know that's not going to happen any time soon.

"What are you playing at, Rox?" I ask her.

She shakes her head, soft curls framing her face like a halo. "I'm not playing at anything. You said date. I'm like this on dates. Well, the one's with you."

She drapes her arms over my shoulders, and I'm so tempted to pull her flush against me. If I do that, she's going to very well know just how much her little act is turning me the fuck on and I don't want her getting any idea right now. The whole purpose of this was to ask her something. Something important. I remove her hands from my shoulders and swim away from her. I submerge myself under the water for a few seconds. I swim in a circle until I'm facing Rox's legs, kicking to stay afloat.

"Wran," Rox calls. "Come back up."

I do as she says and go back over to her. "You look pretty good from down there."

She subconsciously covers her chest. "Shut up."

I frown and send a splash of water her way to show just how I feel about being told to shut up. She shrieks but splashes me back anyway. Swimming over to her, I take her in. She looks so young right now. So free and innocent with the grin on her face. Rox leans back in the water, floating, her hair fanned out around her. Her chest heaves in and out of the water with each breath. Rox is truly stunning. I've always thought that. Even when I was telling myself I hated her for what her father had done.

"Rox?" She turns her head to look at me, her eyes sparkling in the sunlight. When she graces me with her smile, I continue, "I went to see my pops earlier."

She rights herself. "Yeah? Is he alright?"

"Yup." I nod. "He's actually better than alright. He told me he's been sober since the last time I went there."

"Really?" Her brows go up as if stunned at the realization. I don't think Rox has ever seen my pops not completely out of his mind. "You must have done something last time."

"What makes you think that?"

"You're you," she states it like it's the most obvious thing in the world. "You have this way of making people feel crappy for not living up to your expectations."

I frown. "I highly doubt that."

"Maybe. But you must admit you give off this aura. Everyone wants to be liked by you."

"I think Pops just heard what I've been saying for years. Nothing else."

She shrugs and goes back to staring up at the crystal blue sky.

"Anyhow," I continue with my previous thought. "Bennett said he couldn't represent me. Pops is the only other lawyer I know, and he was a fucking good one when I was a kid. Lynn's taking this to trial."

Rox lets out a little huff. "She's being a total bitch."

"Ohh, did Roxanna Raine just say a naughty word?" I tease her. It's very rare that I hear her curse.

"Shut up," she yells and splashes me again.

I catch her wrist in my hold and pull her up right. "Pops gave a suggestion that could absolve me."

She tilts her head back to look up at me. Her eyes narrow at me. I've been beating around the bush since Pops told me to ask her. And I need to get this over with. She can only give me one of two answers.

She arches a brow at me. "Are you going to elaborate?"

I tighten my hold on her waist, silently begging her not to run at the suggestion. Part of me think she won't. The other part thinks she will hightail it away from me as soon as I utter the question. Apparently that's what we Belmonts are good at too. Running when things get complicated and hard.

I lean into her and give her a gentle peck on the forehead. Please say yes.

"Pops think marriage could solve all our problems. You wouldn't have to testify against me. I wouldn't have to testify against you. We would look like a united front and no one could use our age difference against us."

Rox pulls away from me and covers herself with her arms. The look of freedom she had a moment ago is gone. Completely and utterly gone. It's replaced with a sneer that's directed at me and eyes so cold I'm afraid I'll turn to stone. I feel the shock of pain before the sound of the slap resonates with me. My hand goes to my cheek, but it's not so much that it hurts as that I don't understand what the fuck just happened. Rox just did a complete one-eighty for no reason whatsoever. Yeah, I would have expected this a couple months ago when I first arrived back in Kingston, but we've been on good footing for the most part.

Rox turns around in the water and begin swimming back towards the shore. Oh no she don't. I grab her ankle and haul her back over to me, her back against my front. She's not getting off that easily.

"What the fuck was that for?" I snarl in her ear.

She pulls against my hold and the sound of a whimper fills my ears. I turn her around to see tears streaming down her face. I shake my head baffled at what I'm seeing. I just asked her to marry me and she's crying. I clear the tears from her face, but they just keep coming.

"Rox, you have to explain this to me," I coo. "I don't fucking understand what I said or did."

She glares up at me, distain painting her porcelain face. "You asked me to marry you because your daddy told you to."

I search her face for something. I still don't understand why that would send her off. "So?"

"So?" she shrieks repeating my words over. "So? So, fuck you, Wran Belmont!"

Rox pulls against my hold, but I don't release her. We're getting to the bottom of this right now. "You have to say more than that."

"I've said enough, now let me go." Her words come out in a hiss and I do just as she wants. I let her go. She turns and flees. I run my hand over the back of my head as I watch her grab her clothes from my car. She shoves them on and runs up the trail to the road.

I throw my head back and scream, frustration lining my voice. "Ugh! What the fuck did I just do?"

This is the last time I'm listening to my pops.

CHAPTER 13

ROX

I glance above Ms. Flannigan's head at the clock once again. This period is dragging on. I would rather be anywhere than here talking about all the crap going on in my life. Granted, I haven't really said anything which I can tell is agitating the counselor. She keeps raising her brows and sighing in frustration.

"Rox? Are you even paying attention?" Tasha asks me and I pull my eyes away from the clock.

She rotates around in her chair to see the time. There's only five minutes left to sit here and pretend that I care about what she perceives to be causing me anxiety. Or how I can change the outcome of my life.

I so desperately want to tell her to stop listening to everything Josh rambles on about. I know that's where her information about me and Harley and Wran is coming from. He's the only one blabbing to his girlfriend about things that are none of her concern.

"So you're not listening," I finally tune back.

"Nope," I tell her. "But that's not new for you."

"You could at least try to get something out of these meetings. You do the journal entries. Why is it so hard to put in the effort on this part?"

"Because."

"Because why?" she questions even more.

"Because it's none of your business if I'm sleeping with someone. If I wanted to talk boys, I would do it with a friend."

"You and your best friend aren't in a good situation at the moment. If I'm not mistaken, he put pornographic images of you up on the web for everyone to witness. Does that make you feel a certain way?"

I square my shoulders and glare at her. I'm just about to tell her how I feel about this and her when the bell rings. "There goes the bell. Your time is up."

"We have Monday and the rest of the school year."

I roll my eyes at her and grab my tote bag from the floor. Not only did I have to sit in here during my study hall, I now have a test to go make up. A test I didn't have nearly enough time to prepare for because I had to use my study hall to sit in here with her.

Ms. Flannigan and her sessions are wasting my time.

I sprint down the hall and to the class right as the second bell sounds. He made it pretty clear that if I wasn't inside the room when that bell went off, I would be getting an F on this test. An F would bring my GPA down, and I can't have that. Somehow, over the last few months, I've managed to keep my grades in good standing. Most of the teachers here have felt sorry for me, but their sympathy is waning. Of course it is. It seems like I'm ditching classes now just to be ditching. It's not the case, but the end of the school year is too close for anyone to really care what one lone girl is doing with her time.

Taking a seat in the back of the room, I dig out a pencil and calculator.

"Are you ready for this test, Miss Raine?" my teacher asks me.

No. "Yes," I tell him. I'm as good as I can be with no studying.

"Good."

He grabs the prepared exam from his desk and brings it back to me. I flip through the four pages of equations and frown. None of this looks familiar to me. I can't believe that I've missed this much school that a whole module looks like rocket science. I glance up at the teacher. He's watching me and it's unsettling. There's no way he can't tell I'm not ready for this exam.

I scribble my name at the top of the first page. The worst I can get is a zero. And the worst that will bring my grade to is a low B. This is the only class my grade has dropped in; all the others are okay.

Just as I go to solve the first problem, my phone vibrates in my pocket. My head snaps up to the teacher and he shakes his head. I bite down on the inside of my jaw. This could be important. The only people that would call me during class is Bennett or Lynn. I can't ignore either one of them. Pulling my phone from my pants pocket, Bennett's name flashes across my screen.

"Roxanna," my teacher warns. "Put the phone away."

I glance at the number again. "I'm sorry. I have to take this."

Before he has time to say anything I rush out of the classroom and down the hall. I answer the phone just as I enter room 16. It's always vacant the last period of the day.

"Bennett?" I answer the phone.

"Good afternoon. Sorry to be calling in the middle of the school day, but I just got some news that I think you really need to hear," he tells me.

"Good news or bad news?"

"A little bit of both."

"Start with the good news," I tell him. "I could use some good news right about now." Especially since I'm pretty sure I just failed this exam. That was one exam I didn't need to fail. It's just one more thing Lynn and Tasha are going to use against me.

"Well, we found the young man that you claimed drugged you the night of the party. He did confirm what your friend said happened. Although, he claims that the cup was never intended for you seeing as you were, well, pregnant."

"Is he willing to admit that to a judge?" I ask Bennett.

"That's part of the bad news. He doesn't want to admit it. He's worried that it will cost him his scholarship and position on his college lacrosse team."

"Would it?"

"A case like this, yes," he states plainly.

I let out a humph. In no way, shape, or form do I want to drag someone else down. I just want my daughter.

"We could always force the matter, or we could go in a different direction with our statements."

"What other direction is there? That one incident is the whole reason my daughter got taken in the first place. Lynn thinks I was using drugs. Putting him on the stand would solve that."

"It would," Bennett agrees. "But it could cause problems with a very influential family in the long run. We don't want to cause more problems than we can fix."

He's got a point. "So what's the other direction?"

"I can gather testimonial from your peers, from the people that know you best, teachers, employees, and we can persuade the jury and judge to believe it was all a mistake. Josh says your pretty well liked for the most part. It just might be enough for them to grant you custody."

"Okay." It's not like I really have a choice here. I don't want to win custody of Harley only to put a target on her back. "We'll go that route."

"I was hoping you'd agree." Bennett's quiet on the phone for a moment. "Now for the terrible news. I just received notice that Lynn put in for permanent adoption rights of Harley. Her chances of getting Harley are pretty high if we can't convince a judge that you're a decent mother and the drugs were a mistake."

I walk over to an empty desk and take a seat. I shake my head. I know Lynn said she would do whatever is best for Harley, but I never thought she would try to adopt my baby. Yes, she has suggested on many occasions that maybe I should consider letting someone adopt Harley. Never would I have guessed she meant herself. My breathing picks up and I shake my head into the phone. I know he can't see me, but I can't seem to speak. She can't do that. She can't take my baby.

"Rox?"

"No," my voice comes out all choked up. "You have to stop that. S–she can't take—"

"I will do everything in my power, Rox. I promise you. No part of me believes for one second that you would make a terrible mother. I've seen you with that little girl. I've seen Josh with her. I will fight for you all."

I swipe away the wetness leaking from my eyes. "Okay. Thanks."

"I'll call you again if there's an update. Until then, just keep your head down and live your life."

I must be broken. The only thing I can say is okay.

None of this is okay.

None of this is good news.

There was no point in searching for the boy that drugged me if he wasn't going to take the stand and put an end to this. I mean, sure, I knew it would be a long shot. No one wants to admit to something like that, but this was years ago. He was a kid himself. I would at least think he'd want to clear his conscience after so long. I wouldn't have pressed charges or anything. I just needed the judge and Lynn to know I haven't been lying.

I put the phone back in my pocket and head back to the classroom. My stuff is still sitting beside the desk but the test is gone. I turn around to the teacher holding up my exam. Grabbing my things, I go up to his desk and grab the paper. There's a zero written on it in red ink. My gaze drops to the floor. I really wanted to do good on this exam. I knew I probably wouldn't, but still . . . Lynn made my grades a priority when Harley was taken and I know this isn't going to look good.

"Roxanna, this was the last chance to take this test. I don't know what's going on in your life right now, besides what we all see daily, but you need to get your head back in the game and get your priorities straight. You're too close to graduating to let it all slip away."

My eyes meet his. He has no right to talk about my priorities. They've been the same ever since I decided to come back to this school.

And they are damn good ones at that.

I cross my arms and stare down the middle aged man.

"With all due respect, sir, I know where my priorities lie." He gives me a quizzical look. "Do you have a child?"

He shifts on his feet and his expression softens a bit. I can see the unease creeping in. Everyone here knows about Harley. Especially after what the news reported. No one here specifically asked about her except for Ms. Flannigan.

"I do," My teacher finally responds. "I have a daughter in fifth grade."

"And what would your priority be? Her or making sure some student took a test?"

He lowers my exam to his desk. "She would be."

"Exactly. I've been without my daughter for almost three years. And now I'm having to fight for her. If I have to answer a call from my lawyer, then I'm going to. She's more important to me than that test."

He nods and scratches at the back of his neck. His eyes don't meet mine as he slowly shifts back around his desk. "I wasn't aware you were dealing with that. Rules are rules, though, Roxanna. I cannot give you special treatment due to your situation. I would have to allow that for all students."

"I never asked for special. That's sorta why I never mentioned what was going on. All I want you to understand is that my priorities are straight."

My teacher leans back against his desk. "I can see that. I do apologize for insinuating otherwise."

I nod and move my backpack to my other shoulder. I walk out of his class, bypassing the principal's office and out the school. There's no reason for me to go to art class.

It's almost over anyway. I should probably inform Wran of what just happened. He won't be happy, but he still should know that Lynn put in for custody. At least I've gotten to know Harley; he's losing her before even having her.

I don't know which is worse.

CHAPTER 14

WRAN

Josh pulls into the first motel we come across. As soon as Rox informed us of what Bennett told her, I headed out of Kingston. Rox has it in her head that seeing this Travis guy in person will convince him to tell a whole courtroom he drugged a fifteen year old girl. I think Rox is being naive, but I don't mention that. I'm shook that he even admitted to Bennett the role he had in that night. It's something, but it's nothing as well.

I grimace at the motel. The sign is broke and half the lights are blinking, but we all need some sleep. We've been on the road for a while and driving into a ditch isn't going to get us to Georgia sooner. I tap on Rox's shoulder to wake her. She fell asleep about an hour ago, and while I wish I didn't have to wake her, I'm certain a bed would be much more comfortable than the seatbelt she's currently using as a pillow.

Rox groans and snuggles even more into the car door.

"Just carry her," Josh states. "I'll get the rooms."

We scurry out of the car. Josh heads inside while I round the vehicle and open Rox's door. She mumbles something I can't quite make out. Unbuckling her, I lift her into my arm. Her head rolls onto my shoulder, and I nudge the door shut with my foot. I carry her all the way into the dimmed lit lobby and frown. It smells like piss in here and I'm tempted to tell Josh to get back in the fucking car. I will drive through the night if I have to, but I know the girl in my arms needs to rest and a bumpy car ride isn't the place to do it. Her day was already traumatic enough with the news she got from Bennett. I still can't believe she chose to not pursue the one person who could clear her name about the drugs. She would rather come all this way to face him in person.

Neither Josh nor I had the heart to tell her she was wasting our time. Nothing Rox say tomorrow is going to change anything. He's a fucking boy from a rich background. Hell, his family probably told him not to say anything. But if Rox wants to try, I'm not going to stop her. Not that I could. She would have found a way to get here with or without me.

I go over to where Josh stands. He hands the man at the desk some cash before turning to me. He looks over Rox and sighs.

"We have a problem," he says.

I shift Rox in my arms. "What problem?"

"There's only one room available."

I arch a brow at my brother. "How is that a problem? We've all shared a space before."

"It's just different now."

"Yeah, well it's better than sleeping in a car. Let's get her to bed."

Josh leads the way out of the lobby and around the building to our room. I hate these types of motels. They're usually filthy and unsanitary. It's not a place I want Rox to lay her head, but it is what it is at this point. We really should have planned this little excursion out better. Josh unlocks the door and we go inside. Rox stir in my arms and I tighten my hold on her.

I glance around the small room and frown. There's no TV. The wallpaper is peeling off the wall and there are stains on the carpeted floor. I glance at the bed. It has a generic wallpaper print blanket on it. It looks like someone has already spent the night in one of the beds. The pillows are lopsided and thin.

This place is a fucking dump.

"Check the bed before you lay in it," I tell my brother. We really don't need to bring home problems.

"I was told this was a decent place at our last gas stop," Josh says.

"And the person that told you that looked like they lived in a dump as well," I rebut.

"You're being really judgmental for someone that lives in a shitty apartment."

"Fuck you. My apartment is luxurious compared to this." I point at the wallpaper.

"Just get some sleep. We're only here for a few hours."

I drop the subject and go over to the bed that looks at least somewhat put together. Rearranging Rox so I can flip the bedding back, I examine the sheets. They're dark and faded in spots but look decent enough. I lay Rox down and fluff her pillow. She rolls away from me and balls up. I bring the cover up, draping it over her sleeping form. I go to the side I'll be sleeping on and climb onto the bedding. Josh face plants forward. He doesn't even bother turning off the lamp on the one nightstand in between our beds. Or taking his shoes off for that matter. He must have had a long day at the station.

Kicking off my shoes, I try to get comfortable. I turn off the little lamp and lay down. Sleep for me doesn't come. I never did like sleeping away from home, in someone else's bed. Probably why I never went home with any girls. They always came to me. I sit back up and look over at Josh. He's snoring and out cold. I turn to Rox and she's still sleep. With a sigh, I pull my phone from my back pocket and pull up a mindless game.

The game doesn't hold my attention for more than an hour. I glance at the clock to see it's only a little after three. It's going to be a long night if I can't get to sleep. Opening my phone again, I look up the town we're headed to. Blue Ridge. It's less than a six hour drive from Savannah by car and about an hour by plane. My eyes search out the sleeping girl beside me. I could go and be back by the end of the day.

Rox shifts in her sleep and I glance down at her. She rolls over, muttering something. I can't tell if she's having a nightmare or not, but knowing her, it most likely is. I give her a quick shake and she rolls my way. She throws her arms across my legs and melds into me. Once she seems comfortable enough, I go back to looking into the art school here in Georgia that Rox used to dream about. It's not that far from where we are headed later today. I want to check it out for her sake. Rox won't ever do it. She got it in her head that she can't be a good mother and do all the things she wants. It's fucking bullshit, and I'm going to at least attempt to give her what she wants.

I push a strand of hair behind Rox's ear and bend over to kiss her forehead. She stirs, her eyes lazily opening for me.

"Wran?" Her voice is groggy with sleep and her eyes are dull. She's still tired. "What time is it?"

I look over my shoulder at Josh. He's still out. "A little after three in the morning. Go back to sleep."

She shakes her head. "Don't want to."

Setting my phone on the nightstand in between the two beds, I slide down into a resting position alongside Rox. "What were you dreaming about? It seemed intense."

Redness creeps into her cheeks and her eyes fall away from me. It must have been a good dream if her face is growing hot. She doesn't have too many of those. When she finally looks back at me, her eyes are much clearer. Less sleepy. She moves in closer to me, her small frame conforming to mine. Her hand comes from beneath the thin motel blanket and dances along my forearm. Her eyes roam my face and before I know what's happening, her soft lips land against mine.

She pulls back all too soon. "That. I was dreaming about that."

My mind goes blank. I don't know what to say to that.

My body and I know what we want to do about that, but this is Rox. A wet dream doesn't really mean she wants to go there. Then again, she did just kiss me. It's usually the other way around. Rox sucks her bottom lip into her mouth and her hand continues roaming. It doesn't stop until she's playing with my hair. It's grown a ton since I've come home from the military. Not quite as long as it was prior, but I like it this way. Apparently, so does Rox.

"You were dreaming about me fucking you?" I whisper to her.

Her cheeks turn beet red and I grin. "Umm . . ."

I roll her over so that her back's against the thin mattress. My hand moves under the covering and skates across her still clothed legs. Rox doesn't usually sleep in jeans, but with Josh in the room, I didn't think it was appropriate to undress her earlier. I wish I had. Rox lets out a whimper and it goes straight to my dick. I place my spare hand over her mouth and glance back at Josh again. Still sleep.

"You hot for me right now, Rox?" I ask her. She squirms against me. "If I popped the button on your jeans and dived in, would you be wet for me?"

Her eyes widen. This is the first time I've ever been this explicit with her. With other women, sure. Rox was always too young. She's not that young anymore, and if she's having dreams about me, she can take it.

I release the button of her jeans and slide the zipper down. She licks the palm of my hand covering her mouth. My hand dives inside her panties and just as I thought, she's wet. Soaked. All for me. I run my index finger along her center and she whimpers even more.

"Please," she mutters into my hand, back arching to nearer me. I grin down at her. "Not funny."

It's actually very funny to me. Seeing Rox in heat is sexy as hell, but seeing her squirm under my touch, not being able to control herself, is funny. She used to do this same thing to me. Toy with me and think it was hilarious. Now, I get to do the same thing to her.

"Wran, please," she mutters.

Gently as possible, I insert a finger inside. The complete opposite how that fucker Cade dove in without prompting her body. She lurches off the bed, but I shove her back down. Her eyes roll back as she pushes herself into the bed. It's almost like she's trying to run away yet begging for more. I remove my hand from her mouth and cover it with my own. She moans into me as I continue to pump inside her. It's been three years since we've gone this far, and I'm not quite sure what she can take. I'm going to learn her body again though. I'm going to learn every little thing that brings this girl ecstasy and deliver it in folds.

Testing the waters, I add another finger. Rox clenches and tenses around me; I take note of that and remove a finger. She still needs some working over.

She breaks the kiss and pulls back. There's this dazed expression across her face. "More."

I'm just about to do as she requests, when I hear a movement from behind me. Both Rox and I freeze, my finger still buried in her. When I don't hear anything else, I slowly add the second finger back into her. She whimpers aloud, and I slam a hand back down over her mouth.

"You two can't be serious right now," Josh groans.

My fingers come to a complete halt.

Fucking.

Fuck.

Fuck!

Of all the times he could've woken, Josh chose now. He's a fucking cockblock even when he's sleeping.

"We're here on business and you two are fucking around. Go. To. Sleep," he commands with a yawn. "Better yet, Wran, get over here."

Rox gives me a sheepish smile before yawning herself. I pump my fingers into her a few more times before withdrawing them altogether. Rox bites down on the inside of my palm to keep from making any noise. Leaving her like this is fucking painful for both of us, but I can't very well continue now that someone has decided to ruin my fun.

I give Rox another quick peck and whisper, "We'll finish this later."

Her brows jump and her mouth parts. I really don't want to leave this bed. Maybe if we give him a few minutes, he'll go back to sleep. I really need him to go back to sleep. Rox's hand skirts down my chest and dip inside my pants. With a grin, she palms my hard erection. I hold back the strangled sound threatening to come out. Rox grins widen, and I know exactly what game she's back to playing. The little minx thinks she's won.

"Now!" Josh bellows.

I slide out of the bed with Rox and head over to my brother. "We need a second room tomorrow night."

"I couldn't agree more," he tells me.

CHAPTER 15

ROX

My head rests against the cool glass of the car as we drive around curve after curve. There's so much scenery here. We pass a guy on a horse and a creek so blue it seemed unreal. It's quite beautiful. Georgia is beautiful.

I let out a sigh as I feel Wran move my hair to the side. I turn my head from the peaceful view outside and over to him. His lips stretch into a grin and I smile back. Last night comes rushing to the forefront of my mind and my cheeks instantly heat. I still can't believe we did that. And with Josh in the room. It was humiliating. And thrilling. And scary. And so many other things that I can't even comprehend.

"You've been quiet," Wran says and pulls me away from the window.

I rest my head on his shoulder. "Just taking in this view. It's nice."

"You like Georgia?"

"From what I've seen of it."

"It reminds me of Kingston."

I tilt my head and look up at him. "Is that a bad thing?"

Wran shakes his head. "No. I just figured when you finally went out on your own, you would want to go somewhere with a bit more night life."

"I don't need that. I just want to be happy," I tell him.

"Are you happy now?" he asks me. "I know the life I've given you isn't Neverland."

"Yeah, well, I learned that Neverland isn't real. I would much rather have the real deal."

Wran leans down and places a kiss on the top of my head. I snuggle into him. My life may not be picturesque but no one's life is perfect. If it weren't for the two men sitting next to me, I might not even be here today. I don't know if I've ever even thanked them for saving my life that day. They gave me a chance. They gave me a life free of any physical pain, and for that, I will forever be grateful for the life I have. Sure things haven't gone as I've wanted. I never wanted to be a teen mom. I never wanted fall in love and get left behind. I never wanted my one and only friend to turn his back on me, but life is full of obstacles that we must face.

None of those mean I am unhappy.

"We're almost there," Josh voices to neither of us in particular.

I rise and look out the window. We've been driving all morning, and I wasn't too sure what to expect when we decided to come here. Maybe an apartment or a small house or something. It certainly wasn't what is glaring at us through the window. Josh comes to a stop and I take in the rolling green hills encapsulated by a white picket fence. Bundles of hay are scattered across the fields and there are a few horses and cattle grazing. There's a long dirt road with a red mailbox that reads 910. It's the correct address. Over hanging trees encompass the entire road giving some sort of shade. It's magnificent.

Josh backs up and then turns down the road. It goes on for a good mile before opening into a circular driveway with a massive yellow house. It's plantation in style with two floors. Each floor has a wraparound porch with outdoor furniture on it. The house is understated, but I can still tell that whoever lives here has ton of money. They just don't like to flaunt it. Turning off the car, Josh is the first to get out. It's a little more difficult for me to bring myself to get off Wran and open the door. This is the home of the guy that drugged me. This is the home of the guy that changed my life and Harley's life forever. What do I even say to him? How do I even begin to ask him to come clean about something that happened three years ago?

Wran taps me on the shoulder and I glance up at him. "It's going to be okay."

"How can you say that?" I utter to him.

"He's already admitted to what he fucking did," Wran's voice comes out strained and angry. "You only have to convince him to admit it to a courtroom."

"And that's sooo easy." I roll my eyes at him.

"Nothing in life is easy, baby," he counters. "Go."

Taking in a deep breath, I get out of the car and go over to where Josh stands. The door to the house opens as I come to a stop and a guy with auburn hair comes out. A small gasp leaves me when I see him. He's gorgeous. Beyond gorgeous actually. He's lanky and tall with broad shoulders. He has on a pair of deep blue jeans and a long sleeve plaid button up. A giant gold belt buckle sits front and center. I hear a growl leave Wran and I pull my eyes away from the stranger. Taking Wran's hand, I pull him back and over towards to the car.

"Why the fuck were you checking him out?" Wran hisses down at me.

Heat rises up my neck and I shift on my feet. "I wasn't purposefully checking him out. He came out and I just got lost for a second."

"He drugged you, Rox. He is not a good guy."

"I know that," I tell him. "I lived that."

"Then stop fucking checking him out."

My teeth grind together at his jealousy. He should know by now that no matter what, he's who I want. He's who I've always wanted.

"For someone who brought girls back to our house and fucked them so I could see, you get jealous awfully easy."

"That was different," he mutters to me.

Crossing my arms in front of my chest, I give him a pinched expression. "You're gonna have to explain that rea-soning?"

"It just was." Wran stomps away and goes over to Josh. He tells his brother something before Josh drops the keys to the car into Wran's open palm.

My brows scrunch together. Wran walks past me, but I grab his wrist to stop him. "Where are you going?"

"I can't stay for this little meet and greet."

"I need you here." I sound like I'm whining, but I don't care. I want Wran here.

Wran glares down at me. "That boy drugged you. There's only one reason why a man drugs a girl. Do you really want me around this guy? I have control, but not that much fucking control."

I bite down on my lip and let his wrist go. He has a point. As much as I want Wran here with me, I know it's not a good idea. I can't ask him to sit here and listen to this conversation.

"After you went back to sleep, I made arrangements last night for a car to pick you and Josh up in an hour. It'll take you to a bed and breakfast in town. I'll be back by the end of the day."

I look over at Josh and the guy. They are both watching us. I turn back to Wran. "Where are you going?"

"Nowhere you need to be concerned about." He takes ahold of the back of my head and gently pulls me forward. Wran drops a kiss to the top of my forehead and then release me. I watch as he gets in the car, turns around, and drives away.

With a sigh, I plant a smile on my face and turn back around to the guys. It's now or never I guess.

I stride over to where they stand and glance over the guy again. He scratches at his neck and looks me up and down. I can see him gulp as he jerks his eyes away from me. He stuffs his hands in his pockets and rocks on the soles of his feet. I look to Josh for assistance. I don't exactly know how to start this conversation without making things awkward. Then again, it's going to be awkward anyway.

"So . . ." I start.

"How are—" he says at the same time.

I grin at him. "Sorry. Um, Travis, right? Travis Heart?"

He looks over me again. "Yeah. You look the same."

I arch a brow at him. "It wasn't that long ago."

His eyes widen. "I didn't mean anything by that." His eyes shoot to Josh and back to me. I follow his gaze over to Josh who's watching this with curious eyes.

"Do you want to go in the house?"

I shrug. "Sure."

"I would've had breakfast catered or something if I'd known ya'll were coming." His southern accent peeks through as he turns around and briskly walks back up to the house. Josh follows behind but it takes me a moment before I do. Maybe showing up here was a bad idea. Maybe I should have just let this go. It's clear that Travis is nervous. I comb my fingers through my hair. No. He did that to me and now I need him to make this right. This wasn't a freaking mistake.

Walking up the stairs, I head inside the house. It's actually homey. Nothing like the fine lines and white furniture of Bennett's place. I follow the voices until I come to a sitting room with a huge, plushy, tan sofa. There's a flat screen mounted above the fire place, faux trees in terracotta pots, and a gaming system. The guys stop their chatting as I come around and take a seat next to Josh.

Travis shifts at the sight of me.

"Josh here told me why you're here," Travis tells me.

I let out a breath. "Yeah. I'm sorry for showing up like this. My lawyer said you already talked to him."

"I would love to help. I really would, but I can't. There's no way my father would allow the ranch or the Heart name to go through this trial."

I frown at his answer. Even though I knew he would say that, I thought seeing me would at least change his mind.

"Can you at least tell me why you did it?" I ask him.

"I don't think you'll like my answer."

"I don't care. I just want to know. Maybe I'll understand." I would never understand, but he doesn't need to know that.

He scratches at his cheek and sigh. "That was the summer before my freshman year of college. The school year before was my first and last year at Kingston High. My father sent me to stay with my uncle because I had been kicked out of my private prep school. I hated Kingston and I hated my uncle. I tried to do whatever it would take to get out of there. So I started hanging out with this group of guys from Arlington. I didn't know what mess they were into, but I slowly got dragged in. The night of that party, one of them had their eyes on you. Said some things I don't want to repeat. I was high and drunk and in a bad place. When they told me to give you the cup, I did without question."

"So you weren't the one who drugged me?" I ask him.

"Roxanna, I knew about the drugs. I helped prepare them earlier that night. There was four of us in our little group, and we were to each pick a girl and give her a cup. We all had to agree on the girls. I agreed to give you that cup."

"I don't understand what was appealing about me for you all to want that."

Travis let out a laugh. "Even with you being pregnant and wearing clothes three times your size, you were still breathtaking. You had this innocence about you, but at the same time we knew you weren't that innocent. That can be very alluring."

"So I was just one of four girls?" He nods. "What hap–pened to the other girls?"

He looks away from me. "I have a feeling you can guess. Your friend pulled you away at the right time."

"You raped them?" It comes out low, almost a whisper.

"No answer I give you is going to satisfy your curiosity," Travis tells me.

"You did."

Travis eyes flicker to Josh and then back to me. He shakes his head. "I didn't touch them, but I was in the room as they were taken. I watched and I got off on it."

I scowl at his admission and move closer to Josh. How can anyone live with themselves after doing something so heinous?

"I've lived with that ever since," Travis says. "It has been eating me alive, but there is nothing I can do about it now. I can't take it back."

"You can help me though. You can make up for what happened to me," I urge him.

He shakes his head. "No. My father would skin me alive. I'm sorry; I can't."

"I need you to," I practically beg him. "I won't press charges or anything. I just need you to tell them what really happened that night."

"If I tell anyone what happened that night, I'll be carted off in cuffs. I can't do that to my family. Our ranch is underperforming as is. Any bad publicity will wipe my family out. I'm sorry, but my answer is no."

"It's the only way I can get my daughter. There must be some way around jail for you."

Travis eyes search my face. "I wish I could help. I do, Roxanna, but the price is too high. You're asking me to ruin the lives of nine people by coming forward. Nine people who had nothing to do with my mistake. Not to mention their families and their businesses. Coming forward would only ruin them. Too many people depend on my family's ranch for me to help one girl."

My head drops in defeat. I can't believe this. This can't be happening. I get up from the sofa and run out the door.

My name is called but I don't stop. This is actually happening, and there's nothing I can do about it. If coming clean would ruin that many people, how can I even ask that of him? I drop down to the dirt road and bring my hands up to my face. I'm going to lose everything. Absolutely everything.

"Rox." I hear Josh come up behind me, his tone soothing. "We'll figure something out."

I shake my head in my hands. This was supposed to be the solution. This was supposed to help me win my case. Prove that I didn't do drugs willingly. Prove that I never put myself or my baby in any type of danger. Now I have nothing. This whole trip was a waste of time.

"Tanner is an excellent lawyer. I trust him." Josh place a hand on my shoulder. "He will get us our girl back. Harley will come home to her family. You have to believe that."

A sob escapes me at his words. I don't believe that. I don't believe anything anymore. Maybe all this is my fault. I went to the party after all. I might not remember going, but I did. I took the cup. All of this could have been prevented if I wasn't so stuck on Wran. If I wasn't such a mental case when he left. I did this to myself. Losing Harley is my karma.

"Rox." Josh pulls me to my feet and against him. I bury my face in his chest, my tears seeping into his shirt. "Stop crying. Please."

"I'm sorry." I hear from behind Josh. "I'm so so sorry for my part in all of this."

I lift my head and look past Josh. I nod my head in acknowledgment. The devastation is written all over Travis face. "Your apology is accepted."

His brows crinkle and he tilts his head at me. "Why?"

"You could have lied to me. You could have lied to Bennett, but you didn't. You admitted to your part and that takes a lot."

He searches my face for any hint of deception. His shoulders drop and he exhales when he finds none. Instead, he scratches at his cheek and points to the house. "I can get ya'll something to drink if you want."

I peek up at Josh. He nods at Travis. "We could use some water. This Georgia heat is hot."

"Yeah, c'mon back inside until ya'll's car comes."

He turns and Josh and I both follow him. Guess I will have to trust Bennett to win this for me after all. Hopefully, Josh is right about him.

CHAPTER 16

ROX

The door to my room slams open, hitting against the wall with a thump and bouncing back. Raven strides over to where I lay and plops down beside me. She rolls over onto her stomach and rises on her elbows, resting her chin in her palms. There's a frown painted on her pixie-like face.

"You've been moping in this room since you got back." She pouts. "It's senior ditch day and all you're doing is sitting here looking pathetic."

I roll my eyes at her over dramatic statement. I have not been moping.

Not really.

I don't think, anyway.

"I've decided we're going out," she states like it's a fact. "Prom is just around the corner and there's a bonfire tonight. We need dresses, so we're going shopping in Arlington. You, me, and Lex."

I sit up on the bed and move until my back is resting against the headboard. "I'm not going to prom."

Raven's eyes widen and her mouth falls open. "Like hell you aren't. We need our girl with us."

"I don't have a date anymore," I tell her.

Cade had asked before everything happened, but that's a no go now.

"Of course you have a date." She sits up with a bounce and crosses her legs. "Wran, duh!"

I laugh at her. She makes it sound so easy. Go with Wran. Have a good night. "One, I don't think he's even allowed. He's twenty-three. Two, that would just draw unwanted attention. And three, prom is not his scene. I practically had to force him to his own and then he didn't even go because I started my period."

"Maybe he didn't go because the person he wanted to go with was like twelve and having a major life crisis. Someone had to get you chocolate," she says sarcastically.

I shrug. That may be so, but he hasn't even brought up my prom. He must know it's coming up, but he hasn't asked about it since the one time I brought it up. And even then, he got upset because he thought I wanted to go with someone else when I clearly was giving him hints.

Raven stretches over me and grabs my phone from the side table. "Here, call him right now."

"No!" I shove the phone away.

Raven purses her lips and presses the screen on my phone. I smirk at her. There's no way she's getting past my security code. I made it something that even Wran wouldn't be able to crack. My smile drops though when I hear the telltale sound of a phone call and then Wran asking for me.

"Sorry, not Rox," Raven states. "But there is something our dear friend needs from you. Here she is."

I shake my head as Raven thrusts the phone in my direction.

"Rox?" I hear Wran ask again. "You okay?"

Raven shoves the phone against my ear and I have no choice but to talk to him. "Hi."

"Hi yourself. You okay?"

"Yup. Yes. Why do you ask?" I respond.

"You're acting fucking strange," he states.

I let out a sigh. "Raven's just being a pain. That's all."

"No, I wasn't!" Raven shouts. "We're going prom dress shopping!"

"Prom?" The word rolls off Wran's tongue like a curse word. "You ever decide who you're going with? You better not say that prick Cade."

I glance over at Raven. She takes the phone. "Well, she says she doesn't want to go because it's not your thing. So I'm making it your thing. Ask our girl to prom. And give her some money for a dress. She needs a bomb one."

I don't hear Wran's response, but Raven's eyes light up. She hands me the phone, but I don't say anything.

"Prom, huh?" Wran ask.

A flush creeps into my cheeks and I dip my head away from Raven. "I–I mean, it's not like it's important."

My hands begin to tremble around the phone as I wait for him to say something. When there's only silence, I start to pull the phone away. I knew asking him about this was a bad idea. It's not his thing.

"I would love to be your date," he finally says. "All you had to do is tell me you wanted to go."

"You didn't go to yours, so I didn't bring it up."

"That may be, but that doesn't mean I don't want to see you all dolled up in a gown. You still have the credit card. Go get whatever dress you want. Actually, just have fucking fun today. You deserve it. I have to get back to work; talk to you later."

He hangs up the phone and I glare over at Raven. She throws her arms around me, completely ignoring the fact that Wran was coerced into this. I know him better than anyone. If Raven hadn't brought up prom, it would have been a missed event.

"Okay, get dressed. I'll call Lex and let her know to come over. We're making senior ditch day our bitch."

Raven gets off the bed and sashays out of the room. I get up and get dressed for the first time since coming back from Georgia.

I step out of the car and up at the glaring building. The mall has been the last place I've wanted to be since the incident with my father and Harley, yet I'm back here anyway. Raven throws an arm around my shoulder.

"This is going to be so much fun!" she squeals and pulls me through the double sliding doors.

"What type of dress do you want?" Lex asks.

I shrug my shoulders. The only time I've ever worn formal dresses or anything dressy for that matter was when I was a kid. My father used to buy me cutesy little dresses all the time. There was no choice in the matter; I had to wear them. When I ran, my style changed. Dresses like those meant one thing to me. Pain. Torture. Apologies. While I didn't do a one-eighty, my style became a lot more casual.

"I'm not exactly sure. Just not Disney princess fluff."

Raven comes to a halt. "First, we need outfits for tonight. Prom is almost four weeks away. We," Raven gestures between herself and Lex, "need dates. Rox already has her brown-eyed brooding bad boy."

"I'm going stag," Lex tells us as we head inside the first store.

A sweet and spicy smell slams into me as I take in the store. This store is new. I saw them putting it together the last time I was here. The walls are a light pink and fresh flowers, roses to be exact, sit on a coffee table in a sitting area. There's a white velvet love seat that looks too luxurious for a mall store. Magazines sit alongside the flowers.

Lex breaks off and go over to a rack of dark colored clothes. I follow Raven to the other side of the store. She picks up a short mini skirt with cutouts on the sides and holds it out. She examines it before picking up more and more options. Squeezing through the groups of women gathered around the racks, I head to the back of the store. I search for something that looks more me. Running my fingers along the soft material, I come to a stop when I notice a pale blue dress wedged between some white material. I pull the dress out and smile at it. It's cute with a ruched center bodice, girly ruffles, and a skater cut. The dress has little red cherries all over it.

"That's so you," comes from behind me.

I jerk around at the voice and come face to face with Claire. She has a handful of red, pink, and white things. Her signature colors.

"Um, thanks?" It comes out as a question. I glance around the semi-crowded store for Raven and Lex. They've moved to the lingerie section of the store.

"I'm surprised you're shopping at this particular store. They're crazy expensive," she tells me.

My eyes drift down to the tag of the dress in my hold. My eyes bug when they land on the price tag, but I shake it off.

"It's no big deal," I tell Claire. It's a huge deal. "Wran told me to have fun."

"Are you going to the bonfire tonight?"

I shrug. If left up to Raven, then yes, but a bonfire is the last place I want to be. "I haven't decided. Are you and Cade going?"

"I'm going, but I go to everything." She grins at me like we're great friends. "As for Cade, I haven't seen too much of him since the diner thing. It was a bit much for me. He's still part of my group so I do know he's going out of town for the next few days with his dad. So you should come."

"You're actually inviting me?" I ask her.

Claire shoulders drop, and I'm not sure if it's from all the clothes she's holding or me asking her that.

"Look, it's the senior ditch day bonfire, and you are a senior. Besides, I've had time to think about everything with my family, and I'm attempting to be nicer towards you. It wasn't your fault. Will you just accept that?"

I stare at her for a while. She has been trying. That can't be denied, but there's so much history between us that it almost seems unreal that she would even care at this point.

"I found that Travis guy that you told me about." I change the subject. Her brows shoot up. "He seemed nice and regretful, but he can't help me."

"So nice that he drugged you," she scoffs and shifts the clothes in her hold. "Look, I found him on social media after we talked. Apparently, he has this very influential family. I know the type of family, and if he seemed regretful, they will never let him show it."

"Yeah, that's what he said." I glance over at Raven and Lex again. I point to them. "We're here for prom dresses. You want to join us?"

Claire turns around and look at my friends. "They wouldn't mind?"

"Not as long as you don't dump banana shakes on them," I joke.

Claire rolls her eyes. "Get over it."

"So over it," I tell her.

"I would like that. Shopping with you, I mean. It'll be like old times."

"How about we skip you forcing me to buy lingerie like old times and just find dresses?"

She nods. "Let me check out and I'll meet you in the food court by that Chinese restaurant we use to go to."

I give her a soft smile and shove the overpriced dress back on the rack. Heading over to my friends, I notice them already facing my way, whispering to each other. They don't like Claire or any of those people. I know, but hopefully they won't be too upset when I tell them I invited Claire to tag along. She's been really trying lately. And if Claire can own up to her fault in our separation, the least I can do is try as well. Besides, she did tell me what happened the night I had Harley and I never properly thanked her for that or for getting me away from those guys at that party three years ago. After seeing Travis, I know it could have been ten times worse.

Coming to a stop in front of Raven and Lexi, I fold my arms across my chest to brace for their backlash. Raven frowns before I can even get words out and drops the pieces she has in her hold. She storms out of the store. Lex shakes her head at me and follows Raven. My frown deepens and I glance back to see Claire. She isn't even bothered by this. She didn't even see it. Before she does notice any mishap, I step over the clothes and briskly walk out of the store as well. I weave through the throngs of people until I see Raven up ahead. Racing forward, I grab her wrist to keep her from storming any farther.

"Stop!" I shout and glance around. No one is paying me any attention. "Why did you run off like that?"

Raven jerks her hand away from me with a pout placed firmly on her face. Lex stands by her, brows dipped and scowling at me. I literally do not understand what I did to make them so upset all of a sudden. I didn't even get to ask them about Claire.

"I think you're with the wrong group," Lex says.

I turn away from her and to Raven. "What did I do?"

"Ditch us once, shame on us. Ditch us twice, shame on you. It won't be happening a third time," Raven says with disgust dripping from every word. "You can go stay with her."

I shake my head. All of this just for talking to Claire? "No! And who's ditching who? You were the ones that ran away. Not me."

"You were going to!" Raven shouts back at me. "Just like last time. You always choose them. Is their lives so appealing that you will just throw people who genuinely care about you under the rug? What is it about Claire and Cade and all of them that draws you in?"

I search the crowd for somewhere to look but at her. She has it wrong. I wasn't going anywhere. I know who my true friends are. Before was a mistake and I thought my apology was enough for her, but apparently it was not. Apparently, I'm still proving myself to Raven.

"I wasn't ditching you. You ran off before I could even speak. I already apologized for what happened before. What more do you want, Raven?" I ask her. "What more can I do to show you that I made a mistake and it's never going to happen again?"

"If you weren't about to ditch us, what were you doing?" Lex cuts in.

"I was inviting Claire to join us. She's been trying to be better and she gave me the information I needed to track someone down. I figured I could at least be cordial. If she didn't want to join, I wasn't leaving."

Raven's arms drop and the frown on her face softens a little. "Oh."

"Yeah, oh," I mimic her.

"We're sorry," Lex apologizes. "It's just that she used to be your best friend and after everything . . ."

"I know, but you're my friends. If you are constantly going to hold what happened over my head, then this isn't going to work. You guys have to trust me at least a little."

"We do trust you," Raven states. "Just seeing you all friendly with her brought back unwanted feelings. If you want her to join us, she can, but the moment she says one mean thing, I'm throat punching the bitch."

I nod. "So are we good?"

"Yeah, and I'm sorry," Raven says.

Relaxing my shoulders, I let out a sigh. "Good. She asked if we could wait on her at the Chinese takeout place in the food court. But if you want to go back and get your clothes you dropped, Lex and I can go wait."

Raven arches a brow at me. "You live with me. Do you honestly think I can afford a three hundred dollar mini skirt? My dad would skin me alive."

We all walk off in the direction of the food court. The mall is packed today. I wasn't expecting this many people to be here. When we make it to the food court, it's completely full. We spend ten minutes trying to find a seat until we give up and go sit up front by the fountain.

Claire comes prancing our way about fifteen minutes later with an arm full of bags. I stand so she can see us and she comes our way. She glances at all of us before forcing a smile on her face. I know Claire enough to know this is her fake smile. Her nervous smile. I don't know what she has to be nervous about. She's the popular one hanging out the likes of us.

Shrugging a bag loose from her wrist, Claire hands it to Raven. "I maybe saw the little confrontation back there. I bought your stuff."

I glance at the bag Claire is holding out. She bought all of that? I can only imagine the cost of it if that one skirt was three hundred dollars.

"Why?" Raven asks without taking the bag. She's glaring at the thing as if it's made of fire. "Why would you of all people buy me anything?"

"Me of all people? Do you even know me to make a statement like that?" Claire asks and raise the bitchy mask she's perfected over the years.

"I know that you're a mean bit—"

"Hey!" Lex cuts her off and yanks the bag Claire is drawing back.

"One," Claire holds up one of her pointy fingers, "you don't know a damn thing about me. Two, I was trying to be nice. And three," She yanks the bag from Lex. "I'll take the shit back."

Claire goes to turn around, but I grab ahold of her shoulder. "Wait." I turn to Raven. "You were right when you said Claire was once my best friend. I'm not going to take up for the things she's done in the past, but you did give me a second chance. Maybe, just maybe, give her one. I am."

Claire's head turns, but she doesn't say anything towards my statement. Raven's shoulders drop and she lets out a breath. "Fine but be warned. I'm not going to take the shit you dish out. Step out of line and I will relieve you of those overpriced extensions."

Holding the bag back out, Claire states, "I suppose we have a deal."

"Great!" Lex chirps. "Now can we please go shop."

They both nod in unison and turn towards a store across from the food court. It's doesn't have much of anything in it that catches our attention. We move on to the next store and the store after that. By the time we make it to the end of this floor, we finally find a dress shop. It has pretty acrylic mannequins in the window with formal gowns on. We go inside, and I immediately stop. Everything looks too good to be true. From the marble flooring to the crystal chandelier, this store screams luxury.

Raven and Lex break off and head towards the back of the store. I glance around trying to figure out where to start. All I see are pretty princess dresses and none of them are me. I take a step back towards the entrance, ready to bolt. I don't want to be around these types of dresses.

"Are you okay?" Claire asks and I draw my attention away from the dresses and over to her. "You look like you're about to have a panic attack."

I nod my head and take in a deep breath. I'm fine. I'm completely fine. I'm not hiding in a closet behind princess dresses. My father is dead and he can no longer hurt me. I'm fine.

"Yeah. This is just a bit overwhelming," I tell her. "Before this morning, I wasn't even going to prom."

"Figure you wouldn't go to prom," she mutters. She points over to the side away from the puffy monstrosities. "Those look pretty."

We head over to them and I immediately relax when I don't come face to face with layers upon layers of tulle. I finger through the rack, nothing really stands out to me. When I hear a gasp, I turn to face Claire. She jerks a black fitted dress off the stand and holds it up. The entirety of the dress is covered in little black rhinestones with silver and purple one's throughout. It has really thin straps and an excessively low back. I'm not sure how anyone would be able to wear it without the top of their butt showing, nevertheless getting it approved for the prom. Surely that back is against our dress code. It's the bottom of the dress that I love though. It pans out from maybe the mid-thigh or knees and the color fades from black to a pretty light purple. It's a stunning dress, but I can't picture Claire wearing this. It's not red or pink or yellow, which are her typical colors of choice.

"This would look amazing on you. And with the new blond hair," she cuts herself off with a shriek. "It's perfect! Go try it on now."

I take the dress from her without looking at the price tag. I already know I can't afford it. It's too pretty to be something I would normally wear. Even so, I head to the back and try it on.

As I step out, everyone's eyes widen. Even the store clerk stops for a second and looks at me before throwing the dresses in her hand over her shoulder. I drop my gaze from my friends. Them staring at me like this is weird. It's just a dress.

"I was totally right. This is your dress," Claire states.

My eyes stay on the train covering my feet. "It's okay, I guess."

"You guess?" Raven shrieks. "You look fucking sexy as sin. You look like . . . Wow."

Claire comes over to me. She turns me around. "Look at yourself in the mirror. Your pales skin pops against the black dress. And your eyes look even more purple. Don't know how that's possible. You look amazing, Roxy."

I finally force my eyes up to my form in the mirror. A loud gasp leaves me as I take in my body. My boobs are pushed up and they looked to have doubled in size. My waist looks so slim. I turn to look at my body from the side and my own eyes widen. This dress makes me look like I have a butt. Not a big one, but like the perfect little bubble bottom. It is cut as low as I thought, but nothing can be seen. I turn back around to the front and run my hands across all the bead work. This dress really is something.

I smile to myself. Maybe I can see what they see. Grabbing the tag on the dress, I instantly drop it when I see the price. The smile falls and I turn away from myself in the mirror.

"What's wrong?" Raven asks. "How much is it?"

I shake my head. "Doesn't matter. Let's keep looking. Maybe we'll find a better dress somewhere else."

"There is no better dress," Claire states. "This dress was made for you."

She grabs the tag and takes a look. Before I have a chance to say anything, she yanks it off. I gasp and look around for the salesperson. That's not allowed. She can't just do that. Claire walks up to the checkout station and hands the associate the tag. I trail behind her.

"We're taking this."

"What?" I ask her.

"We are taking the dress." I'm not sure if Claire is talking to me or the cashier.

The cashier nods and rings up the dress. She turns to me. "If you go take it off, I can gift wrap it."

I nod and walk back to the dressing room. I can't believe Claire would just buy me a dress. Sure, we used to buy each other clothes all the time when we were actually friends, but those didn't cost over a thousand bucks. Jesus, I can't believe this. A knock on the outside of the dressing room startles me and I jump.

"Do you have the dress off?"

I nod even though the lady can't hear me and hand her the dress. I need to know why Claire is doing this. I need to know this isn't some prank or something Cade put her up to doing. I need to know allowing this isn't going to bite me in the butt come prom time.

Once dressed, I head back to Claire. I pull her to the side. "I need to know why you're being so nice to me all of a sudden."

"Because I have nothing to be angry at you about any—more. After Cade did what he did to you, I finally had the nerve to confront my dad about what you told me he did. Or tried to do. He admitted to it. And he admitted that my mom left because she found out he was having an affair with his secretary. I know, cheesy. It was never your fault."

"You could have just said that instead of paying so much for a dress," I tell her.

"Roxy, I've mistreated you for so long. A simple sorry isn't going to cut it."

"Yes, it would have," I tell her. "Sorry can fix a lot of things."

"Well, I'm sorry. Maybe one day, we can try this friend thing again."

I smile at her. "Maybe."

CHAPTER 17

WRAN

"This place is looking great," Jesse states as he closes the garage door. "Just imagine what it's going to look like when the renovations are complete."

I stare up at the sliding barn door that has been re-painted a blue shade. Not much has been done since we decided to become partners. Mainly because I keep having to run off for Rox, but Jesse understands that. With that being said, the minor tasks that have been done do look amazing. I'm just glad he finally pulled his head out of his ass and relented on making me partner.

"It's going to be something." I scratch the back of my head and tilt my head to the side, taking in the building. "I'll be impressed when the place is back operating and we're actually making a profit. Feels like this place is draining my bank account rather than helping it."

Jesse shoves me in the shoulder. "That's what it means to be in business. Besides, you only paid for the parts for those cars you want to renovate for the Arlington car show."

He got me there. Most of what was spent came from what was already in the budget. However, we couldn't agree on whether the car show would be a good idea. I put my money on the table to prove that the car show at the end of summer is where the profit is at. It'll show everyone what we can do and bring in a new type of customer. The type that likes to restore old cars and don't have a price for their hobby.

"You just wait." I turn away from him and go over to my car. "This time next year you're going to be praising me for this idea."

"Hah! This time next year, you won't even be in Kingston," he retorts.

I glance over my shoulder. "What makes you say that?"

He shrugs and comes over to where I stand. He leans against my car and crosses his arms. "Maybe the fact that you've been looking into houses in Georgia."

I frown at that. I was trying to keep that from him until I knew for sure what Rox would want to do. She hasn't been so keen on talking about the future and college and stuff. Even though she calls me every night, she mostly just babbles on about her day or tell me stories about my time away. Nothing too personal. Nothing really of matter to me.

"I haven't really decided yet," I tell him. "I don't know if it's something Rox will want."

"You know little Roxy would follow you to the end of the Earth."

Shaking my head, I tell him, "Nah, not fucking now. Maybe before. My time away changed her."

"Have you two even actually talked since you been back in Kingston?" He quirks a brow at me. "I mean like real talk. A talk where you're not making out or bantering or making small talk?"

I think back on all the conversations Rox and I have had since I came home from the army. I can't say for sure if we have had one of those talks. Then again, talking like that has never really been our thing. Especially since it took me losing her just to realize I don't hate her. Not even one bit.

"You should go to the bonfire tonight." Jesse points at the sky and I peek up and follow his finger. "The stars are shining and it's the perfect time."

"What bonfire?" I ask him. "And what make you think Rox will be there?"

"The senior ditch day bonfire!" he exclaims like I've lost my mind. "C'mon man, it hasn't been that long since we were at Kingston High. You know the bonfire at the lake."

"Right," I tell him. "Fucking sure that's not Rox's thing. Besides, she's been in a mood since Georgia. I don't know what that guy told her, but apparently it wasn't good."

"You weren't there?" Jesse asks.

I throw my head back with a groan and stare up at the sky. The stars seem brighter tonight for some reason.

Maybe it's a sign that Rox and I do need to finally talk without all the bullshit interrupting us.

Turning to Jess, I shake my head. "Can you really picture me sitting there talking to the guy that drugged Rox and got my daughter taken away?"

"Fuck no."

"Correct. I would be in prison or worse. Then we surely wouldn't get Harley back. Just the thought of him makes me want to kill someone." I straighten up. "Besides, it gave me time to do some things."

I open my car door and get inside. Jesse straightens. "Are we going to the bonfire?"

I put my key in the ignition. "The last time we went to a bonfire, I got piss drunk, got Rox pregnant, and got exiled by my brother for three years. I don't think bonfires and I go too well together."

Jesse grin. "All I'm hearing is that you need a redo." He jogs around my car and hops over the edge of the door. "We're going."

I shake my head at him and pull away from the garage. Turning on the radio, I drive out of town towards the lake. Jesse doesn't say another word as I come to a stop behind an old pickup truck with a taped on bumper. I shake my head in disgust at the monstrosity of the poor truck. That's exactly why we have to get Gramps' back running.

Smoke billows skywards, making it hard to see the stars and an orangish red glow lights up the atmosphere a couple hundred yards away. I get out of my car and walk down towards where I know the fire will be. Jesse follows, and before either of us know it, we're thrust into a throng of bodies. I search the crowd for my girl but don't see her anywhere. I move farther into the mass and come to stop on the edge of the crowd. There are so many people here, it's hard to tell who's who. I do know not all of these people are kids from Kingston High or even from Kingston for that matter. We're a small little town and there's no way we have this many people out partying on a Wednesday night.

"Damn." I hear before I feel Jesse's hand come down on my shoulder. I peek back at him and his eyes are focused straight ahead. I follow his gaze until I find what he's looking at or rather who.

Rox is dancing with three other girls with a solo cup in her hand. She has on a short blue t-shirt dress with thigh high socks and sneakers. Her short blond hair is tied off into two pig tails on the side of her head. Claire throws an arm around Rox shoulder, and they laugh. It looks as if they never had a falling out.

"You let her out of the house like that?" Jesse asks and I notice him rearrange himself. "Man, she looks hot. Maybe it's time to stop calling her little Rox."

I shove his hand off my shoulder. "Maybe it's time you stop staring before I start plucking eyeballs."

"Geez, man. You know I wouldn't dream of going after your girl."

Yeah, I know, but everyone else around here seem to have forgotten that she belongs to me. I watch as a twerp with a guitar goes over to where Rox stands. He says something to her and she nods. I frown, and before I know what I'm doing, I march over behind her and wrap an arm around her narrow waist. She shrieks and glances back. I frown at her. Rox goes to take a sip from the cup, but I take it from her hold and sniff it. It doesn't have a smell, but I'm not taking any chances. I pour the clear liquid out and drop the cup.

"And that's my cue," I hear Claire state as she prances away.

"I was drinking that." Rox points to the cup while she dances to the music. Her ass grinds into me and I tighten my hold on her to keep still.

"Yeah, well, I didn't know what the fuck it was or who gave it to you."

"You could have asked," she says. "It was water and I got it myself."

"Sure it was," I mutter. My hand moves from her waist and slides down her gyrating body. "Water got you dancing like this?"

"No. I got me dancing like this. You told me to have fun, remember?"

There's a loud shout and the song suddenly changes. Rox finally stops moving and turns around in my embrace. She wraps her arms around my neck and pulls herself closer to me. She presses her front to me and for a second, all I can feel is the heat coming off her body.

"What are you doing here?" she finally asks me. She doesn't shout over the roaring music but we're so close she doesn't need to. "Thought you were working today."

I spin us around so that we can see where Jesse stands. He's talking to one of Rox's friends. Lex, I believe. "We just got off. How was prom dress shopping?"

Her smile falls and her eyes search the crowd. I follow her gaze to Claire. I don't know what she has to do with prom dress shopping, but I really don't care.

"You didn't send me a picture," I chastise her. "I would have loved to see you in it."

She turns a back to me with a smirk on her face. "You can see it the night of prom. You're still taking me?"

I nod. "I wouldn't miss it for the world. Besides, it's the after party, I can't wait for."

"I never said there was going to be one," she says and rolls her body against mine.

"Oh, there will be, baby. I can guarantee that."

Her eyes sparkle with amusement as I twirl her around. When she comes back to me, her hands find my chest and fist themselves into my shirt. "You never answered my question. Why are you here?"

I stop rocking against her and draw back. "Come with me?"

Without waiting for her answer, I pull her through the crowd and down the shore of the lake. There's a small cliff with a cave that no one besides us know about. Well, others might have found it, but I always thought of it as our place. The one place Rox and I could go to see the stars.

Rox glances back at the crowd, searching for her friends I take it. "I can only be gone for a moment. I don't want to ditch them."

"Surely Raven would understand." If the girl has nerve enough to ask me to go out with Rox, she can handle being left alone for a while.

"Well, yes, but I still don't want to leave my friends," she says as she kicks at a rock on the ground. "Besides, this is supposed to be senior ditch day. Last I knew, you weren't a senior."

"Like half the fucking people here," I retort and come to a stop at the ledge. I glance down, but all there is pure blackness. I know this cliff so well though. I know that it's about a three feet drop from up here to where we are going. I know that in another five feet is the lake, which I don't want to fall into.

Letting go of Rox's hand, I ease my way down the three feet. When I'm firmly in place, I tap Rox's foot to let her know she can ease down. She does and I guide her the rest of the way, keeping her flush against me. I've dropped her one time and one time only coming down here. She put pink dye in my shampoo bottle and laundry detergent as retribution. I had to walk around in pink clothes until Josh could afford to replace the ones Rox ruined. Needless to say, Josh wasn't happy and I didn't get laid for a whole fucking month.

Now that I think about it, that was probably her plan the whole time. Fucking brat.

I ease into the cave and sit back against the wall. Rox drops down in front of me and rests her back against my chest. I kiss the soft flesh where her neck and shoulder meet and inhale. She always smells so good. Like strawberries mixed with the nectar of the gods. She smells like a goddess that needs to be devoured.

Rox takes my hands in hers and interlocks our hands. "What did you want to talk about?"

"A lot. Everything. Us. We haven't had a real conversation in a long time," I respond. "It's long overdue."

"If I remember correctly, we had one of those a couple weeks ago when you asked me to marry you in that lake." She points down below.

I let out a sigh. "That wasn't my finest moment."

"Do you even know why I rejected you?" she asks.

It took me a while to put it together, but I figured it out. I won't be making the mistake of proposing again because someone tells me it's a good idea. That's one thing I should have known not to do. Even if it would make things simpler with the custody hearing. Rox probably thought I didn't really mean it. I meant every fucking word. But the next time I ask her to be my wife, she's not going to have any doubt that I want her just because I want her. She's not going to second guess my reasoning behind asking. And she most definitely won't be telling me fucking no.

"How about we forget about that and just enjoy today? All I want is to be right here with you under the stars in my arms."

She tilts her head up so she can see me. "You're getting cheesy on me, Wran."

Placing a quick peck on her lips, I shake my head. "No one has ever called me cheesy. This is just for you. Besides, I do have ulterior motives. I need to ask you about something."

"Oh really?" She cross her arms. "And what is that?"

"What happened in Georgia?"

Rox's whole body stiffens in my hold. She shakes her head and starts to ease out of my hold. I pull her back and tighten her to me. She's not getting away that easily. I might not have stayed there with her, but I still need to know what that guy said to her that made her depressed.

"You've been quiet since we got back," I tell her. "Your phone calls haven't been as bubbly. Tell me what the prick fucking said."

Rox pulls away from me and turns all the way around. She sits on her knees, head grazing the top of our little cave and pouts. "And if I don't?"

I grab a fist full of her thin dress and pull her back to me. I need to be touching some part of her tonight. Pulling her down to me so that we're lips apart, I tell her, "I will fucking make you."

She laughs. Full on laughs. "You forget, Wran Belmont. I'm not the people in this town. I know that underneath all that cursing and false bravado is a heart of gold. You don't scare me."

"Is that so, my little lost girl?"

She nods.

I yank at the shirt in my grasp, ripping clean down the front.

Rox jerks back and covers her chest. "What the hell, Wran?"

My lips quirk up at the sight of her braless. While she may not have much, she certainly has more than she did the last time I saw her this way. "You seem to forget, little Roxy. You're not a kid anymore. There's so much more I can do to you."

She gasps, hands still covering her chest. I shrug off my polo and hand it over to her. She scowls and shoves it on.

"You're a jerk," she mutters before taking her place back between my thighs.

I wonder if she can feel just how hard she just made me?

My answer comes when she squirms against me and then positions herself away from my crotch. I take her waist and put her right back where I want her. A low whimper leaves her lips.

"And you're a spoiled brat. Now, tell me what I want to know."

She lets out a huff and crosses her arms. I swat the outside of her bare thigh.

"He just said he can't help. Which I already knew. The trip was a complete waste," she finally says.

"That's all he told you?" I question her. I've known Rox a long time and I know when she's holding something back. This is one of those times. I tap her leg again.

"He said more, but I don't want you to drive back to Georgia and murder someone. I don't think we'll be able to get away with it this time."

"I was in the army," I remind her. "Trust that I know how to get away with plenty by now. So start talking or I'm ripping panties next."

She goes to elbow me, but I grab her arm and lock it in place around her waist, my own restraining it there.

Rox huffs and answers my question. "Travis said that the goal was to fuck me. Him and his friends chose girls that seemed easy, and they were all going to take turns on each of us. He said it wasn't his idea, and I believe him."

My body goes tense at her words. That bastard. "Of course you would believe him. You're too naive for your own good."

"You're right. I was naive. You liked me that way. I've learned a lot since then, so don't call me fucking naive again."

I grin at the back of her head. "Fine. I'll let you have that. Now, what I really want to know is why you haven't applied for any colleges. Particularly the one in Georgia you used to rave about."

It's her turn to stiffen in my hold. "I don't see the point."

"You don't see the point? You're going to college, Rox. Even if I have to apply to them for you and drag you to a campus," I tell her. "You're way too smart and talented to stay here in nowhere Kingston."

She rotates so she is facing me. "And if all I want is to stay here in Kingston to raise our daughter and be with you?"

I shake my head at her, rejecting the idea she wants nothing more than this little life. I know her. She might not believe she can have more, but that doesn't mean she doesn't want it. She's just not letting herself dream of it anymore. I know it's my fault. I've seen firsthand how her hope has been squandered due to my leaving. From having to deal with DHS by herself. I took a lot when I left, but I'll burn this world before I let her give up anything else. She, more than most, deserve to have it.

"You can have me and Harley and college." My hands run up the length of her arms and to one of the pigtails. I wrap my hand around a few strands of her hair. "You can have whatever you want. I will give it to you."

"Harley is all I want. You can't promise me that we will win custody of her. You can't promise me that if we do, I won't turn out like my parents. You can't give me a lot of things."

I didn't even realize turning out like her horrid parents was even a fear she had. It's irrational. Rox could never be like those people. She's the sweetest, kindest, most selfless woman I know. She stayed with that prick Cade just to make him feel better. She stayed with him even though I know her heart belongs to me.

"You're right. I can't promise we'll get Harley, but if we do, I know for a fact that you won't turn out anything like James fucking Raine. You don't hurt people. You would never even imagine killing someone." I press my hand against her chest. "Your heart is too big and powerful for it to hold such evil. I can promise you, I will always be by your side if you do stray. I don't believe you ever will."

Rox eyes flicker across my face as she takes in my words. She nods and her shoulders fall. "Thanks for that."

"Will you please apply to some college other than the community college now?" I ask her.

"Will it make you happy?"

I place a chaste kiss on the back of her neck. "Nothing you could do would ever make me unhappy."

"I'll apply somewhere, but it won't be to art school," she finally agrees.

"Why not art schools?"

"That part of my life is over. If I go to college, it will be for something practical. Something that will provide for Harley."

"You don't think you're good enough?" She's not giving herself nearly enough credit.

"I'm no Picasso that's for sure."

"Personally," I run my fingers underneath the hem of my shirt she's wearing. "I'm glad you're not some stuffy old Frenchman."

Rox giggles. "I'm pretty sure he was Spanish."

"I'm just glad you don't have a dick."

Rox grabs my wondering hand. "With that, it's time I go back to my friends."

I shake my head at her as she crawls away from me. "C'mon, Rox!"

CHAPTER 18

ROX

I shake my head as I rise from the thin, thread worn bed. My eyes shoot from one white wall to another to another and to another. This can't be happening. I run over to the door with the small opening in it. The opening is only wide enough for trays. I grab the door knob and twist. It doesn't budge. I pull on it again and again and again.

Nothing.

This can't be happening.

Different nurses in white short dresses, hair nets, and white sneakers walk past my door. Some have little pill cups while others carry toiletries. I gulp back the fear of what this could mean.

This can't be happening.

I know this isn't happening.

I don't belong here.

One of my fists come down hard on the door as I still continue to pull at the door handle.

"Someone!" I scream. "Help me."

The nurses glance my way but neither one of them stop. It's as if this is normal to them. As if they have seen this all before. I watch them all pass me by, hope slowly draining from me. I shake my head again and step back.

No.

I take another step back.

No.

Another step.

No!

I drop to the floor.

"Please!" I scream out. "Please."

I scoot until my back hits the cool metal frame of the bed. My head falls to my knees and I hold myself. It's not until I hear the twisting of the knob that my head shoots up. The door to my room is pulled inward. A thin nurse comes in with a tray. Her head is down so I can't see her face. She is dressed like all the others. Like they're all carbon copies. Her hair is pulled back and loose. It's long around her waist, and the same jet black that mine used to be.

My eyes flick to the tray in her hand. There's a ton of different pills on it along with a clear cup of water. She takes a step in my direction, head still down. Using the bed as leverage, I rise to my feet once again. I glance down at them just now feeling the cool tile under my feet. My bare feet.

I take in the thin cotton white dress gracing my body and frown.

"I'm going to need you to take your medication," The nurse utters and her voice hits me like a ton of bricks.

I know that voice.

How do I know that voice?

Shaking my head, I tell her, "I don't belong here."

"Of course you do, silly. We all belong here," she chirps, her voice sounding oddly melodious. "Now let's get you these pills."

The lady finally glances up and the force of her purple eyes slam into me. I step back and fall onto the thin mattress. Now I know this isn't real. She can't be here. She isn't meant to be here.

"Mom?" The word comes out a weak question and I struggle to understand what is happening here.

A deviant grin spreads across her lips and she swipes the pills from the tray. It clatters to the floor as she lets it drops. My mom takes a step forward, her grin only getting wider, and holds out her hand.

"Be a good girl and take your meds, Roxanna," she sings.

I shake my head and move back on the mattress. My back meets cool plaster and my retreat comes to an end. "Get away from me."

"Oh, but you have to take your meds. Otherwise, you'll be just like me."

"No." It comes out low, so I scream it again. "No!"

My head jerks up and I come face to face with Raven. There's a fork dangling in her fingers and she is staring at me wide eyed. I glance around and notice that it's not just her. Everyone in hearing distance is looking at me as if I've lost my mind. Sitting up in my chair, I wipe at my mouth to make sure I wasn't drooling. I've been having that same dream for a while now. It's why I haven't been sleeping as much. Raven lowers her fork and gets up from the table. She points towards the cafeteria exit before walking off. I search the room once more. Eyes are still on me.

Briskly, I get up from the spot at the table beside Lex and rush out of the lunchroom. I head down the hall and towards Raven's locker. Sure enough, she's there with a text book in her hands and her Doc Martins untied. I come to a stop beside her and lean against the lockers. It must have been bad if Raven is asking to talk out here away from prying eyes.

"Are you okay?" she asks. "You were screaming."

I run a hand over my hair and exhale. My head falls and my shoulders slump.

No, I'm not okay.

"I'm fine," I tell her.

"You know, I'm really good at figuring out what girls mean. Sorta my specialty. Now what's wrong? I know you think I don't hear you at night, but I do. You're tossing and turning. Having nightmares. Something is going on with you."

I shake my head at Raven. "It's nothing you need to be concerned with. I'm handling it."

"How?" she asks. "From where I'm standing, you're pretending nothing is bothering you when everyone can see there is something. Maybe you need to talk to Miss Flannigan."

I scowl at the idea of truly opening up to Tasha. There's already no clue what Josh has divulged about me. Plus, our mandated sessions are enough. I don't need to talk to anyone. Especially not someone like Tasha. I truly will end up in that place.

"If you can't talk to her, then talk to me. What are friends for if not to help you?"

I stare at Raven for a second. She has a point, and it's not like she's going to report me to the mental hospital.

Giving in, I say, "My mom, my real mom, was committed to a mental facility. She sorta was behind all the stuff that happened a few weeks ago. Getting nearly mauled that time you all couldn't find me. Everything. I've been having night terrors about being locked up with her."

Raven eyes dip, and she places a hand on my shoulder. "Why haven't you mentioned anything?"

I shrug her hand off. "I don't want pity. I have enough of that because of my dad. I don't need people knowing that both my parents are crazy."

"It's not pity when people genuinely care about you, Roxanna." Her eyes grow sad. "We're friends. You're supposed to come to me with things like this. Maybe we can find a solution."

"There is no solution. I've been having nightmares since I was a kid," I tell her the truth.

A locker down the hall shuts, and I turn around to see who's out here. It's no one I talk to and they leave the building.

"Have they been about the same thing?" she questions.

"More or less."

I go around to the other side of the locker, and she turns to face me. "Have you thought about confronting your mom? I would have questions. Maybe you just need yours answered."

Of course I have questions. Do I think I'm going to get them from my mom? No. The woman is bat-shit crazy. Her reasoning behind everything she did is something a mentally unstable person would come up with. And even if she's back where she belongs, who's to say that woman would even want to see me.

"She's crazy," I admit. "She tried to kill me. She shot Cade in the knee."

"But she's still your mom," Raven says. "My mom abandoned me. She ran off with some biker that was passing through town when I was a kid. I guess she just didn't want to be a mom anymore. Or maybe she just stopped loving my father. Either way, that didn't stop me from having questions. That didn't stop me from wondering about all the what ifs. I found out a couple years ago, my mom was killed.

I will never have my answers, but you can still have yours. You should at least go talk to her."

I throw my head back against the locker and groan. What Raven says makes a ton of sense. Of course I have questions, but just like her, some of them will never be answered. My mom can't tell me why the one parent I had hated me so much. She can't answer anything I truly want to know because the one parent I did have is dead. He's gone and he can't explain anything to me at all.

Straightening from the locker, I tell Raven, "You're right. I don't know if that woman can answer anything I need, but she is my mom. I'm having those dreams for a reason. I do need to confront her."

Raven eyes widen. "That was easy."

She mutters that more to herself than me.

"Right now."

"Now, as in right now? Today?" she clarifies.

I nod. "Yes, if I don't do it now, I won't ever do it. I know where she's at. You can take me. Maybe I just need to see her."

"Umm, you do realize we're in school?" she reminds me.

"It wouldn't be the first time I've left."

"Yeah, but—"

"Can you take me?" I cut her off. If I let her get the words out, I know she'll tell me not now. I need it to be now.

Relenting, she nods. "Fine, but we need to be back before last period. I have an exam that I'm not failing."

Biting my bottom lip, I ponder that for a second. The facility is in Arlington. That's an hour drive by itself. So two hours just driving. There's no way we'll be able to make it back by the last period. Raven must see the dejection on my face because her eyes roll. She turns back around and inputs her combo into her locker. She grabs her purse and takes out the keys.

Turning back to me, she holds up the keys. "Can you drive at least?"

I nod. I don't mention that technically, I don't have my license, but I can drive.

"You wreck my car, my ass is grass, and you're finding a new bestie."

I nod again. I understand. "Okay."

I open my palm and the keys drop into it. "I'll be back before my shift at Aunt May's."

She rolls her eyes again and heads back to the cafeteria. I smile to myself. After Claire, I never thought I would have a friend again. I had resigned myself to being the loner freak. I'm happy Raven made a liar out of me. I wouldn't know what to do if she hadn't given me a second chance.

I walk out of the school building and over to student parking. There's no reason to even use the alarm on Raven's car to find it. It's hard not to. While most of the cars that sit here are nicer ones, Raven's is not. It's old with faded black paint. Her car is also the only one using duct tape to keep the passenger mirror from falling off. I should really have Wran do something about it.

Nevertheless, I get in the car and leave Kingston.

Honestly, I can't believe I'm even doing this. Never once did confronting that woman cross my mind. I was perfectly happy letting her rot in that freaking mental hospital. It's where she belongs. She's the reason behind all of this chaos right now. The reason Cade is angry and lashing out. If she would have never made me choose, we all could be blissfully happy. I would still have Cade as a friend. I would be able to love Wran openly without feeling guilty for hurting Cade.

I let out a long sigh as I move in and out of traffic. Who am I lying to? With or without my mother interfering, Cade and I were bound to end up here. I can't give him what he wants and he can't be what I need. He can't be the friend I call about Wran any more than I can turn back time and be the little girl he had a crush on.

Shaking my head, I turn the radio on to drown out my thoughts.

Once I reach Arlington, I follow my GPS to a cream colored brick building that looks more like a fancy schmancy prep school than what I imagine a psychiatric hospital to be. Parking, I head to where the building clearly says entrance. A young man sits up front. I don't say a word until he ends his call.

Hanging up, the man finally looks at me. He takes the clipboard that sitting on the counter and hands it to me. "Please sign in."

I take the board from him and fill in the spots for name and clock in time. He glances over it for a second before setting it aside.

"Who are you here to see today?" he asks. I tell him and he begins typing something into his computer. I watch as his eyes flicker across the screen. "Sorry, but it looks like you aren't on her visitation list."

"I know," I tell him. "But she's my mother. Could you at least ask her if she would see me?"

He searches me as if inspecting me for something before getting up. "Stay here and don't venture past that bench."

I nod and go to sit down. My eyes search the building, but there's not really anything to look at. The walls are bare. Bright white with no artwork adorning them. I suppose I can see why. Anything can trigger these particular types of patients. It's actually quite sad. I know most of the people here probably can't control their mental state. It's something they must live with and be judged and punished for.

With that being said, this place could use something. Anything to make it feel less clinical, even if it is only in the lobby.

The telltale sign of rubber squishing against the linoleum pulls my attention away from the bare walls. I turn in the direction of the attendant and stand. He comes to a stop in front of me and for the first time, I take in his uniform. He's in all white slacks as well. Down to the shoes on his feet are white. I frown at the realization that all personality is wiped clean when you enter these halls. No one, not even the lobby attendant can truly be free. No wonder my mother went crazy in here. I doubt she was like that before my father and her sister tossed her in this place.

"She will see you," he tells me and gestures for me to walk with him.

We venture back the way he just came and go through a pair of double doors much like the ones at the DHS office. The same plain walls greet us on this side. However, if at all possible, the space is even more clinical. Metal tables are placed strategically on one side of the room with white metal chairs. On the opposite side of the room is a lounge area. The sectional in the center of the room is dark gray and pleather. Pleather is probably easier to clean. There's a television mounted on the wall, playing something. There's no sound though.

All of the patients are in the same white scrubs as the man next to me. Some look a bit dingy as if they haven't been washed or changed in a few days. Some look crisp and wrinkle free. It's disturbing.

My sandals flop against the floor as the guy leads me over to a table. I take in a deep breath as we come to a stop and the woman looks up at me. The vibrancy she had when she was trying to kill me is gone. Her skin looks sickly gray. And her eyes like my own are so dark, they look more black than purple. My mother eyes move from me to the attendant, but no words escape her mouth. The woman from before wouldn't shut up.

Taking a gulp of courage, I pull out the metal chair and cringe at the shrill of the metal against tile. I search the open space and a few eyes are watching. For the most part, the patients are acting as if nothing happened. I drop down in the chair and cross my arms out in front of me on the table.

"I'll be back in thirty minutes," the attendant tells me. He glances to my mom. "Behave."

I give him a simple not. Thirty minutes is far longer than I need with this woman. Surely, it won't take that long to get some answers. Some closure. I don't even know if it's possible with her in this state. Whatever medication they have her on has her looking like a ghost.

My mom watches the man leave. When she turns back to me, a grin spreads across her lips, and her eyes light up. My heart stops and unconsciously, I scoot back in the chair, causing a shrill sound to ring out again. The woman's hand comes down on my wrist to keep me in place. I freeze, my eyes trained on where her hand meets my skin. Her hand is so cold.

My eyes travel slowly up to meet her.

"Have you come to play, my little doll?" she asks.

Shivers slide down my back and I yank my hand away from her. I cradle it against my chest and shake my head. My mom gets up from her chair. Picking it up, she places it right beside me without making a noise. She retakes her seat next to me, and I'm already inching to get away. She fingers my hair and pulls the tie keeping one of my pigtails in place.

"You always had such beautiful hair." Her fingers run through my strands before she touch her own frayed ones. "Just like me. It's a shame you don't anymore. You're just like her."

I have no clue who *her* is and I don't care. Shifting in my chair, I clear my throat and try to rein in this conversation. "I'm not here to talk about that."

"Oh deary. Have I gone and made you all weepy? Tsk, tsk, tsk. You're no fun that way."

"Look." I do my best to be assertive. "A friend of mine suggested this."

"Oooh, was it boyfriend number two?"

My hands fist at the mention of Cade. "Don't mention him."

"Oooh, there must be trouble in paradise with boyfriend number two. I'm guessing he didn't approve of your choice."

"Shut up," I tell her.

She wiggles her eyesbrows. "Oh la la, that's exactly it. I guess fun time is over now. Had to end somehow."

"I said shut up," I demand a little louder. "You took my only friend away from me so just shut the fuck up."

"Little girls with naughty tongues get punished," she threatens and runs a finger down my arms.

I turn to face her. "And crazy women who abandon their kids get sent to places like this."

She claps. "Yay! That means we're going to be bed buddies. There's so much I can accomplish with you here with me."

Frowning, I shake my head at her. "That will never happen."

"Well, you said 'crazy women who abandon their kids.' Did you not do the same to poor little Harley? Motherless and alone. Stuffed animals as company."

I shake my head again, denying what she's putting out. That situation is completely different. "I'm nothing like you."

"But you are. You even look like me. So innocent and sweet. So stupid and naive." She touches my cheek and I shove her hand away. "Just admit it to yourself, deary. You're just like me and your father, and that dreadful sister of mine. We're all cut from the same cloth. After all, that's the only reason you would really be here to visit me."

My stomach flips at the truth in her words. I don't want to be like them. I don't want to end up in a place like this because I can't control myself.

"It's only a matter of time. It's in our DNA. We're a bit insane. Just ask boyfriend number two. I'm sure he'd agree."

"Only because you hurt him," I try to defend myself. "He only feels that way because of you."

My mother rises from her chair and perches on top of the metal table. She crosses her legs and shake her head at me. Coming here was a mistake. I don't need anything from her. She can't give anything because she's as crazy as crazy come. I can't talk to a woman that lives in her own head.

I start to get up but she grabs my wrist to keep me in place. She strokes the inside of my wrist before sinking her nails into me. I hiss out and yank my wrist back but to no avail. She doesn't let go.

"You've been having night terrors about our time to-gether?" My body stills at her words. There's no way she can know that. "I know because I used to get them too. Every time your father would touch me. They will stop, eventually. When you stop denying that you are just like the rest of us. All you have to do is admit that to yourself, and like magic, whoosh, they disappear. Then you are free to do whatever you want."

I yank my wrist again, and this time she lets me go. I lean in close to her. "You want to know the difference between you and me, Mommy Dearest?"

She grins and nods.

"I know how to love. You thought you loved my father. You thought he loved you back. But newsflash, he put you here and then spent six years fucking your twin. That's not love."

The grin on my mother's face finally falls and her face ashens even more.

I continue, "I'm different from you because I fight for the people I care about. I don't use them or hurt them or kill in their name to make it okay. Because it's not okay. If you knew how to truly love, there's no way you could have done to me what you did."

My mother's grin doesn't return and her words are silent.

"I hope to never see you again," I tell her.

Her sinister smile returns at that. "Oh you will, deary, and when you do, I'll prove just how much I love you."

I turn away from her threats with a frown. That did not go how I pictured it. Not that I really pictured it going any particular way. Maybe Raven was right. Maybe I did need this after all. Because no matter what my dreams tell me, I know I'm not my mother. I'm not my father. I'm not any of them. Lynn might have implanted in my head that I'm not fit to be a mother, but I know what a parent isn't. I know how a parent shouldn't treat their child. That alone makes me fit. That alone makes me better than every adult figure I've ever known.

Smiling, I head out of the sterile building and back to Kingston. Back to the people who really know how to love me.

CHAPTER 19

WRAN

I log out of my computer and turn to look at Jesse. He has a big grin on his face. I imagine I look quite the same as he. Although office work generally isn't my forte, today has been amazing. We finally heard back from the Arlington Car Show and were accepted. On top of that, we heard back from a contractor. We've had someone working on the exterior, but they bailed. This new guy was highly recommended. He just sent over mockups. The plan is to keep some of the charm that everyone around here knows, but completely gut the interior. All new everything.

"This is going to be great, man. I can picture it already," Jesse states as he rises and retrieves his jacket. Why he needs a jacket in the middle of May in Kingston is baffling, but it is what it is. "You have any plans for tonight? There's this party at the lake if you want to tagalong."

"Aren't we getting too old for parties at the lake?" I ask him.

"Hah! No! We're in our prime, but I guess having a kid does make you older before your time," he teases.

"Shut the fuck up. It's not that." Not really. "The state fair is going on, and I want to surprise Rox."

"Thought you two weren't actually official or anything," he says. "Besides, isn't she at Aunt May's?"

I shrug. Her working has never stopped me before. And it's Aunt May's. That's one woman I know won't care if I whisk Rox away for an evening. "Yeah, but Aunt May won't mind, and Rox can say we aren't together all she likes. We both know we're endgame."

"Truer words have never been spoken. Go get your girl and I'll see ya later."

I finally rise from my chair and stretch. My bones pop from sitting all day, and it feels good to be back on my feet. I head out of the garage and over to my car. I give the garage a look over. In approximately five weeks this place is going to look different. Fresher. Newer. A part of me still can't believe I'm apart of bringing Gramps' Garage back to life. Grinning, I get inside the car and whizz onto the gravel road, kicking up rocks as I go.

The drive to the diner doesn't take long at all. I hop out of the car and race across the road. The door chimes as I pull the door open, and Aunt May looks up from the register. I saunter over to her and throw an arm around the old woman's shoulder.

"Evening, Aunt May." I give her a peck on the cheek. "How's my favorite girl?"

She knocks my arm away and hits me on the chest with her notepad. "Whatcha want, Wran?"

"I got to want something to be here?" I ask her.

"Sure do, and I'm pretty darn sure she's five feet with blond hair." Aunt May crosses her arms and stares me down.

I raise my hands. "Can you blame me? Five feet with blond hair sounds like a dream."

A scoff catches my attention, and I glance down the bar to see Cade sitting. It's the first time I've seen him in person since he sent me that fucking video a couple weeks ago. I narrow my eyes at him.

"Don't start no trouble," Aunt May whispers so only I can hear. "He's done nothing today."

I glance down at the elderly woman. "Maybe you shouldn't let riff raff in here."

"Who are you calling riff raff?" I hear Cade's voice come from down the bar.

Guess I said that a little louder than I meant. I turn to look at Cade. "Wasn't talking to you."

"Yeah, well, you might want to watch what you call people. There could be a whole slew of names thrown at you."

"Like fucking what?" I ask him.

"Boys," Aunt May warns.

Cade ignores her and gets up from his seat. He waltzes over with a grin on his face. My hands clench as he gets closer. He says one wrong thing, and he's going to wish that bullet did more than shatter his knee. I stood back while he hurt Rox. I stood back because I knew she would want me to. I'm not going to stand back if he so much as utters what I think he's going to. He really needs to get it through his head that having money doesn't mean you get whatever the hell you want.

Cade stops in front of me and I snarl at him. A loud smack has me pulling my gaze away from him. I glance at Aunt May and then at the notebook she slammed on the bar in between me and Cade.

"I said none of this in my diner." She glances between the both of us. "I don't care what you two knuckleheads do when you ain't here, but not in my place of business."

Cade sneers at her, and for the life of me I want to bash his head in just for that. Aunt May has been like a mom to all of us since she moved here. This fucker has no right to disrespect her on her turf. Just then the door to the back opens and Rox prances out, a smile on her face and a saucer with chocolate cake in her hand. She looks up and the smile falls. Rox sets the cake to the side and looks around the diner before coming over to where we stand.

"What's going on?" she asks, her voice soft.

Before I have time to answer, Cade does, "I was just informing Aunt May that she should really keep child molesters out of her diner."

My vision turns red, and I storm around the counter.

"Wran!" Both Rox and Aunt May holler.

Someone grabs my arm, and I shake them off. They grip my arm again and pull back. I whirl around to see Rox shaking her head.

"Don't," she mutters. "Please think."

"It's time for you to leave, Mr. Jefferson," Aunt May tells him. "And don'tcha come back 'til your attitude is in order."

"You're kicking me out for stating a fact, but he gets to stay?" he yells at Aunt May.

She places her hands on her hips. "Wran didn't initiate a fight in my diner."

"Of course you would take up for that trash." I turn around to see Cade kick at one of the bar stools. It topples over and Rox's hold on me tightens.

Aunt May doesn't say a word as Cade hobbles out of the diner, a chime announcing his departure.

I let out the breath I was holding and lean against the bar. Rox pulls on my hand and I glance down at her. She motions for me to follow and I do. Rox leads me to the back and towards the breakroom. She closes the door behind me and locks it. I watch her as she paces a little, goes over to the bench to sit, and then gets back up. When she finally looks at me, all I see is disappointment in her eyes. I hate when she looks at me like that. It reminds me too much of how my mother would look at me when I did something wrong. I didn't do a damn thing wrong just now.

"Stop giving me that fucking look," I tell her and go over to her. "If anyone deserves your disappointment, it's that bastard."

She crosses her arms. "I'm sorry. I don't mean to look at you like that. It's just . . ."

"Just what?" I urge her to finish.

Her eyes flip up to mine. "We must be extra careful about how we react to things. Especially while DHS gathers their evidence for this trial. And I know it's hard, but we have to."

"You think I don't know that. Do you have any idea how hard it's been for me not to bash his face in for what he did to you? Do you have any idea how much restraint it takes for me to stand by and watch as people in this town look at you like you're some fucking eye candy because that douche put that fucking video out there? Standing by and doing nothing is not who I am."

She reaches a hand out to me and I take it. "I know that. And I am so, so grateful to you."

"You are?"

She peeks at me from under long, dark eyelashes. Her lips tilt up in a smile. "Yes. I'm sorry if I don't tell you enough."

"You could have told me last night on the phone."

Her cheeks pinken at the mention of last night. It was the first time she called me since I've returned just to talk. Usually, I'm the one calling her just so she keeps to her deal.

One thing led to another and we ended up falling asleep on the phone.

"I was a bit preoccupied," she mutters and takes a step back.

I replace her step and lift her chin up with two fingers. "I only backed down for you. But I'm telling you right now, if he does one more thing to hurt what's mine, I won't hold back again."

"Thought we agreed I'm not yours."

I shake my head. "I never agreed to that shit. You're mine until the day we die. You know it. I know it. Now stop pretending."

I don't give Rox a chance to say it again. Instead I swoop down and capture her lips with mine. She's mine. She will always be fucking mine.

"Say it," I mutter against her lips. "Say you're mine."

She smiles into the kiss, but doesn't say a word. I bite down on her lip and she lets out a whimper.

"Say it, Rox."

She pulls back and tilts her head so she's looking up at me. "I'm yours."

"Again."

"I'm yours."

"And I'm fucking yours. Don't forget it."

I go to capture her mouth again, but a knock on the door has me pulling back. "It's occupied!"

"Wran Belmont, if you don't open this darn door. . ." Aunt May warns and I can practically picture her tapping her itty bitty foot, hands on her hips, and glaring daggers at the door. It's probably best if I don't piss her off any more today.

Rox goes around me and opens the door. Sure enough Aunt May is standing there exactly how I imagined.

"Get ya'll behinds out my breakroom," she tells us. "This ain't no Motel 6."

I let out a laugh. "Yes, ma'am."

Rox and I bypass the old woman and head to the front of the house. I perch on one of the bar stools while Rox grabs the chocolate cake and digs in. She comes over to the register, and I take the cake from her.

"Hey, that's my dinner!" she exclaims.

I lick at the frosting. "Still want it?"

She scoffs. "You are such a pig. What are you really doing here? I doubt it was to fight with Cade."

I take the fork from her hold and she frowns. I eat the rest of the cake in two bites. "Nope. I came to get you. We're going out."

She waves her hand around. "If you haven't notice, I'm at work. I can't just leave."

"Sure you can."

"Yeah, you can." Rox whirls around at the sound of Aunt May pushing through the door. "You might as well, and take that boy with ya."

"Aunt May—" Rox goes to protest but Aunt May cuts her off.

"Didn't that boy teach ya to listen to your elders?"

"I sure did," I mutter.

She narrows her eyes at me and I drop mine. I take ahold of the saucer the cake was on and wipe at the frosting, distracting myself from the woman.

"Wran already told me his reason for coming. You know that boy just like I do and when he gets somethin' in his head, it ain't coming out. You might as well go."

Rox relents and nods. "Okay."

"Have fun, but not too much fun," she says.

Rox nods again and heads to the back. I watch her go and then turn to Aunt May. "You going to be okay here tonight?"

She swats at me. "I been runnin' things on my own for a long time. Besides, it ain't busy. Where you takin' our girl anyway?"

"The state fair. I think she needs to remember what's it's like to have fun. She's been too focused on this trial and putting up appearances lately."

"Oh, I've noticed. You make sure she do have some fun. Win her a bear."

"I will. For you." I laugh.

Rox comes back out and I take her hand, kissing her knuckles. "M'lady."

Rox pulls her hand from me. "Show off." She turns to Aunt May. "See you later."

Aunt May shoos us and we head out of the diner.

"So where are we going?" Rox asks as we make it to my car.

"To have some fun."

CHAPTER 20

WRAN

I watch Rox's face morph as we pull in line, her eyes widening and grin spreading. We haven't been to the fair since she was a kid. The last time didn't end so well. I sorta maybe hooked up with some random girl after Rox tried kissing me on the Ferris wheel. I'm hoping this time goes a lot better for the both of us.

"The state fair? You could have told me. I could have went home and put on more comfortable clothes!" she exclaims.

I drive forward. "I wanted it to be a surprise. Our last date didn't go quite as planned."

"Yeah, well, you shouldn't go around asking people to marry you if you don't mean it."

I slam my foot on the brakes. The car behind us honks their horn at us, but I pay them no mind. "I meant every word I said to you that day. I might have asked you for the wrong reason, but that doesn't mean I don't want it."

Rox bites down on her lip as she stares at me for a second. Her eyes flicker across my face before her gaze moves to the window. "You said we were here for fun. Let's just have some fun, okay?"

"Fine, but we're talking about this later."

The corner of her lips tilt up. "Yeah, now park. I want to ride the bumper cars."

I shake my head at her. The car behind us honks again and I lower my window to flip them off. Rox smacks my arm, but the amusement doesn't fade from her face. I can already tell this is going to be a great night.

We're guided onto a gravel lot and we park. The keys aren't even out of the ignition before Rox has her door open. She bounces over to me and pulls my door open, urging me to hurry up. I grin at her enthusiasm. She takes my hand and leads me through the rowdy crowd. We don't stop again until we're standing at the ticket booth. We get two armbands and head straight for the bumper cars. I don't even remember the last time I was in a bumper car, but if this makes her happy, I'm happy.

The attendant straps us in separate cars and Rox eyes narrow on me. "I'm going to ram you," she shouts of the fair noise. "Get prepared."

"I'm pretty sure I'm the one that supposed to do the ramming, baby!" I shout back.

As soon as the buzzer sounds, I accelerate. I slam into Rox and I can see her lurch forward a bit.

"Not fair!" she shouts. "You distracted me."

I smirk at her and reverse my car. "By all means, try to catch me."

She does exactly that and for the next five minutes we go at it. I let her get in a few hits, but for the most part, I keep dodging her attempts. Her little pouts are too cute for me not to.

When the buzzer sounds ending this ride, Rox hops off and grabs my arm. She smiles up at me and points over to another ride. For the next half hour, we spend time going from ride to ride to ride. It's not until her stomach growls that we decide to take a break. I lead Rox through the crowd and to the one vendor we used to go to all the time. She squeezes my arm when we come to a stop at Fried Cheese and Things.

"You remembered," she says, but I think it's more so for herself.

"How could I forget? You use to spend all my money here on loaded blooming onions. I've never seen an eleven year old eat as many onions as you." She shoves me and mutters something I don't quite get. I put in an order for her blooming onion, but she adds on fried pickles and fried tomatoes. I look her up and down. There's no way she's going to eat all of that.

Another thirty minutes later and I'm proved wrong. Rox eats all that plus most of the fries I got myself. I honestly don't know where she puts it. I gather all the empty containers and then take them to the trash. When I come back, Rox is already up and ready to go. She grabs ahold of my hand and entwines our fingers. It's the first time in a long time that I'm starting to see the girl I use to know peeking through. The girl that wasn't afraid to grab my hand or try to kiss me when she knew it wasn't going to happen. I squeeze her hand in mine. Coming here was definitely a good idea.

"What now?" Rox asks.

I look around the fairgrounds. "How about we play a game and I win you a bear?"

"Do I really need another stuffed animal?" she asks me.

Honestly, no. She has way too many of them from when we used to come here. But back then, I was winning them because I knew they made her happy and all the other kids were walking around here with them. Now, I want to win her one because she's my woman, and she deserves the fucking best prize this fair can offer.

"No, you don't need it, but I want to win it for you anyway."

She pulls me to a stop in the middle of the crowd. They part and go around us. Rox stands on her tiptoes and plants a gentle peck against my cheek. My hand instantly goes to my cheek. We've kissed many times since my homecoming. But for some reason, that one feels different. Special. More powerful. Maybe now is finally our time. She goes to walk away, but I pull her back to me. Her chest slams against mine, and I kiss her in the middle of the crowd for all to see. For the longest time, I couldn't do that. We've had people telling us this was wrong so much, but there is absolutely nothing wrong with us. There's nothing wrong with a boy liking a girl and a girl being in love with a guy. We make fucking sense. We always have.

"How about we skip the games and go somewhere else?" she suggests.

"I would love—" My response is cut off when I hear crying. I search my surroundings and see a small boy standing alone with a rubber dolphin.

"What is it?" Rox asks.

I point to the kid. "That little boy."

I take Rox's hand in mine and pull her over to the little boy. When we reach him, I bend down to him. He wipes his face and holds the rubber toy.

"Hey you." I smile at him. "You okay?"

He doesn't say a word. Just keep looking at us and then out at the crowd.

"Are you are lost?" Rox bends down next to me. The little boy's head snaps to Rox and his eyes widen. He nods.

"You sound pretty," he says, not relinquishing his hold on the dolphin.

"Who are you here with?" I ask him.

The boy looks around again before he says, "Momma."

With a gentle smile, I stand and hold out a hand to him. "How about we help you find your momma."

The kid nods and takes ahold of my hand. I haul him up on my shoulders. Hopefully, that will allow him to see better. We make our way through the rowdy throng of people, stopping every couple to feet to ask people if the boy belongs to them. Most people ignore us, but the ones that do answer tell us no. It takes an hour or more of searching until we do come across a woman with guards searching the crowd.

"Momma!" the little boy yells from my shoulder and the woman's head snaps in our direction. She yanks on one of the security guard's shoulders and then come running at us. I lower the boy to the ground and the woman drops to her knees in front of us, pulling the child to her chest. She's sobbing and muttering something, but it's hard to make any sense of what she's saying over the loud buzzing and zapping of the fair rides.

She gets up with the little boy in her hold. "Thank you, thank you, thank you."

I shake my head at her. "No problem."

"What do I owe ya'll?" she asks.

I shake my head again. "Nothing, ma'am. I only did what any decent person would do."

She places her hand on my arm. "Thank you again."

The woman walks off, peppering the little boy in kisses. I turn to Rox to see her staring up at me. She's biting her bottom lip, eyes hooded, and she looks flushed.

"You okay?" I ask her.

She nods and steps closer to me. Her hands go to my chest and she clutches my shirt in them. She rises on her toes. "I never imagined seeing you being so fatherly would be so freaking hot."

My eyebrows shoot up. Okay then. She likes when I'm fatherly. I'll remember that.

"Let's get out of here," she tells me breathily.

My body comes alive at her suggestion. Fuck. Definitely remembering she likes this. I take ahold of her hand and maneuver us through the crowd, the laughter and sounds becoming nothing more than background noise. A man is standing in front of the gate leading to the gravel parking lot chatting away with a group of people. I don't have time to wait for him to move, so I shove him instead. Rox giggles and I see nothing funny at all. She just gave me the go ahead. She just asked to get out of here and there's no fucking way I'm letting her change her mind. I can already picture her sweet little body next to mind. A groan leaves my lips. It's been way too long.

As we make it to the car, I open the door and practically haul Rox inside. I'm on my side and in the car before she even has time to right herself. Rox scoots over to me and places her hand strategically against the front of my jeans. My dick hardens instantly. I grab ahold of her hand and move it aside. If I didn't have to drive us home, it would be on. There's no way in hell I can get us back to Kingston if she's touching me like that.

I look down at her and she's smirking at me. She flutters her lashes as she moves in even closer to me, my arm pressed against her breast. She moves her hand back over to me. I can't help the noise that leaves my mouth.

"Fuckin' hell, Rox," I groan.

"What?" she asks all innocently. There is nothing innocent about her in this moment.

"At least let us get home."

Her smirk turns into a grin. "I'm not stopping you from driving, but you might want to hurry."

My eyes widen at the suggestive way she's talking. I haven't heard her talk like this since before I left, and now she's . . . Fuuuck. Maybe I should have taken her on a proper date sooner. Swerving out of the lot, I don't wait for the people guiding the line. I hit the accelerator and speed past them. Rox giggles and it goes straight to my cock. I got to get this girl home and fast.

Her hand on my leg moves up and I glance over at her, taking my eyes off the road for a second. She fingers the button of my jeans and it comes undone. I grab her hand to stop her. If she goes there, we're not making it home.

"What are you doing?" I question her.

"I want to taste you," she tells me.

"You can't say shit like that to a man driving."

Rox doesn't say anything back. Instead, I feel her pull the zipper of my jeans down. Her hand goes inside my pants before I can stop her roaming. My feet slam on the brakes at the touch of her soft hand and I moan aloud, the sound echoing off the car walls. Rox slides forward on the seat.

I throw my arm out to keep her from slamming into the dashboard. She giggles and starts pumping me.

"Jesus-fucking-Christ girl. Where did you learn to do that?"

"You," she states. "Now drive. We don't want to get pulled over."

I close my eyes for a brief second, taking in a deep breath, and then begin driving once more. "I didn't teach you this."

"I learned everything from you. Now it's time to see if you were a good teacher."

Her head lowers and before my mind comprehends what she's about to do, I feel her soft mouth around me. My hips buck and the car sputters with my movement. This girl is going to kill us on a back country road. I glance down at her. She turns her head to see me and smiles. I knew this girl was the devil. You can never trust sweet ones.

Her mouth moves back to my cock, and instead of simply testing out the waters, she dives right in. She encompasses as much of me as she can. I squeeze my eyes shut, trying to stay in control of this. When her slurping hits my ears though, I know this is a losing battle. I search the street, but I'm the only car on it. That won't last for long, especially when people start leaving the fair. There should be enough time to finish this.

I jerk the car over and off the road. Rox stops what she's doing and lifts up. She looks around, but there's nothing for miles. Just open corn fields and blackened streets.

I remove my seatbelt and urge her back. Her eyes widen.

"What are you doing? I wasn't done," she says.

"Yeah, you are."

I slam my mouth down on hers and a burst of saltiness floods my mouth. I ease her back on the seat without breaking the kiss. My hands roam up her side and under the shirt she's wearing to cup her perky breast. Rox whimpers, and I smirk into the kiss. Not so fun now that she's on the receiving end. I break the kiss to stare down at her. Her eyes flutter open and I can see the lust written all over her face.

"I'm going to taste you now," I tell her. That's one thing I've never done. To anyone. I so desperately want to know what my lost girl tastes like though. I bet she's sweet.

Rox shakes her head. "I don't . . . What if—"

Her words cut off when I squeeze one of her tits. Her eyes roll back in her head, a sigh of pleasure leaving her pink lips. I make my way down her legs peppering kisses along any exposed flesh. I don't take my sweet time popping the button on her denim shorts. Instead, I just drag them down and off her legs. Rox parts for me like it's the most natural thing in the world and I love it.

I search her sweet sex, salivating at the wetness I see there. I ease a finger inside her and she yelps, rising a little from the seat. I pull it out of her only to press her back down. I can feel the rise and fall of her sternum as her breathing picks up. She looks down at me and I lower my mouth to her center. A moan escapes me as the taste of her gushes across my tongue. Fuck, she does taste sweet. Like strawberries and something else. Rox squirms. I tighten my hold on her and really go in on her. Whimpers get louder, and the sound of her make me slurp her up even faster. I insert my finger back inside her and Rox lets out a loud cry.

"More," she begs, and I insert a second finger.

She tenses beneath me and I know she's right on the edge. I lift my eyes to watch her. I want to watch every emotion flicker across her delicate face. Rox's eyes are closed. Her left hand palms her breast, and fuck me, if it's not the sexiest fucking thing I've ever seen. She grabs ahold of my hair and urges me on. I don't even think she realizes what she's doing, but I'm not going to complain. I slurp up everything she has to give me. It's too good to leave behind.

I apply pressure to her center and she bucks. "Yes. That's it baby."

"Wran..." she moans breathily. "God, Wran."

Rox doesn't stop writhing beneath me and her little noises intensify. She's clamping down on my fingers and any moment now, I know she's going to erupt.

Bright light catches my attention though followed by a blaring horn. I yank my fingers from Rox and she jerks up, hitting her head on the ceiling of the car.

"What was that?" she shrieks.

The car bypasses us and I glare at it in displeasure. Stupid bastards. She was almost there.

I turn my gaze back to Rox and her face reddens. She brings her legs up to her chest and searches the car. The moment's over and I didn't even get her off. I grab her shorts from the floor and hand them over. Frantically, she takes them and shoves them on. I tuck myself back in my jeans, my cock still hard as all fucks.

"That was—" I start.

"Amazing," Rox finishes for me.

A grin spreads across my face at her admittance. I thought she was going to say a mistake. She tends to say the things we do are just that.

"Really? Even though we got interrupted?"

She nods and bites down on her lip. "I've never done that before."

Her eyes squeeze closed and I move over to her. I lean in and place a gentle kiss upon her lips. "I would have never guessed that."

"So," she gestures to my crotch, "that was okay?"

I laugh at her innocent question. "That was more than fucking okay, Rox. Matter of fact, I'm thinking we should head home and finish this up."

Her face falls, and I know that's not going to happen. This was just a moment between us. A fun, spontaneous moment, but Rox isn't going to go any further. Not tonight.

"Umm," she bites her lip, "I think it would be best if I go back to Raven's house."

I shake my head, not wanting this night to end. Tonight's been what we've both needed. Time to just be us. I don't want to let her go that easily.

"How about you spend the night with me? We don't have to continue this, but I would like to hold you tonight," I tell her.

"No sex?" she asks.

"Not if you don't want to."

She thinks about my offer for a moment before nodding. I start my car back up and pull off the side of the road, headed back home. With my girl in tow.

CHAPTER 21

ROX

Some works of art speak for themselves. They move you in a way that only art can and have you reflecting on life. After the conversation, if it can be called that, with my mother the other day, I came back to school and started painting again. I haven't painted anything in a long time. That little session made me feel lighter somehow. I left knowing I wasn't going to be a bad mom to Harley. I left knowing that wanting things doesn't mean I'm going to turn out like them. It's not ingrained in peoples DNA to automatically be bad. I don't know why, but I had it stuck in my head that if they birthed me, I could only ever be like them. Even if I was only ever with them for a short while.

I wipe my hand down my blouse and then scowl at myself when I realize what I just did. I stare at the black paint on my pink shirt with distaste. There is no way that is coming out. Mrs. Zannah comes over to where I stand and takes in the piece with me. She smiles at the woman holding the universe in her hands, caressing the earth like a child with stars gleaming in her eyes. It's a very literal painting, but most of my work is. It kind of started out as a way for me to get my feelings across to Wran without having to use words. And he is not the most abstract person.

"It's stunning," Ms. Zannah tells me. "The way you captured her surrealness is absolutely breathtaking."

I smile to myself. "Thanks."

I wasn't sure if her making her skin midnight with stars scattered across it would portray what I was going for but if she likes it, then it must be good. Ms. Zannah is a sweet woman, but when it comes to art, she's as serious as it gets. She lives for the craft in any form, whether it's sculpting, painting, or pen and ink sketching.

"This just may be one of the best pieces I've seen come from you." She turns to me. "What prompted this change? You haven't been interested in the arts in recent years."

I set the paint brush down on the easel and cross my arms. Smiling at her, I give the most honest answer. "I finally realized that wanting something doesn't mean I'm a bad person."

"You thought that?" she asks me.

I nod. "After Harley, things got complicated."

My teacher nods along. "I heard about that. You've been all over the news as of late, young lady."

"My family," I try to think of an appropriate word to describe my fucked up family, "is toxic. My dad was a murderer. My mom wasn't my mom. And my real mom tried to kill me. I thought . . . How could I be a good person, good for Harley, if I come from that? Bad people don't deserve good things. So I stopped painting. I stop wanting. But I'm not a bad person."

"Oh, Roxanna." She sighs. "We all could have dug a little deeper where you were concerned. We didn't do our jobs and we let you down. You never should have thought that. You are an amazing girl with a very bright future."

"Thanks," I mutter. I don't know if I quite believe it yet, but I promised myself I would try. I would give myself a chance to live.

My art teacher turns back to the painting. "I wasn't fibbing when I said this was one of your best pieces. I would like to enter it into a competition. It's for a scholarship that I believe you would win hands down. The prize is twenty thousand dollars to any school but you have to major in a fine arts program."

Twenty. Thousand. Dollars.

For a painting?

I take in my piece and frown. Is it even that good? Hardly any time was spent on it, and I know for a fact that the shading looks rough. It's not perfect. It's not good enough for that type of money. Not to mention, I still have no idea if I'm going to college. I put one application to the community college in Arlington. The thought of applying other places never crossed my mind. I never thought I would go. Not with Harley here.

"Umm, maybe you should offer that opportunity to another student."

Ms. Zannah is already shaking her head. "As much as I love all my kiddos, none of them have your talent. None of them are as good as you. I know for a fact you could win this. Let me enter this piece."

I bite down on my bottom lip. Twenty thousand dollars is a ton of money. More money than I will probably be offered for my academic work. I could use that.

"Maybe I have another piece that's even better," I suggest. I really don't think this one is as good as she believes it is.

"No," Mrs. Zannah states with all confident. "This is the piece. Yes, it's not perfect, but it's completely raw and unfiltered which is what you need for such an emotional piece."

"Okay then. You can enter it."

She beams. "I will send it in today."

Today? Yikes.

I'm just about to ask for another day to work on it, when my phone rings. I pull it from my pocket and cringe at the name on the caller ID. Lynn never calls during school hours. Something must be wrong with Harley.

Turning to my teacher, I point at the phone. "I have to take it."

"Go." She shoos me and I walk out of the art room.

I head towards my locker as I answer the phone. Lynn doesn't speak right away.

"Hello?" I ask.

"Good afternoon, Roxanna. You're on your lunch break, correct?" she asks me.

I nod even though she can't see my movements. "Yes."

Normally, I would be with my friends in the cafeteria, but I really wanted to get this piece completed this period. It's the first real piece I've completed in a long time.

"Is Harley alright?" I ask my social worker. "Do I need to come to Arlington?"

"No. She is quite fine actually. My daughter is giving her lunch as we speak. This is more of a courtesy call."

Courtesy call?

"What do you mean?" I come to stop in front of my locker and open it. I pull out my tote bag and grab the notebook Ms. Flannigan gave me for writing things down. I have yet to do her log and I need to have that done before our session next period.

"I put in my application for custody of Harley."

"What?" I shriek and cringe back at how loud that was. I knew this was coming. Bennett already told, but it sorta escaped me. Calming myself, I ask her, "why?"

"I told you back in February that my priority is that little girl. Not you. And I don't believe you are the best option for her right now. She needs a family to actually be there for her, and I'm sorry, but that is not you. Not to mention, I don't believe the Belmonts are a great bunch to be around."

"You can't do this. I am her mother. She is my child. You cannot have her. I won't allow it!" I shout into the phone, my calm demeanor vanishing altogether.

"It's not your decision, Roxanna. Your trial is in a few weeks. I can't picture a judge granting you custody. Your lawyer will have to be pretty amazing."

"Pretty amazing or just know the law. You're not even supposed to have Harley now. I was supposed to get custody back after a year, wasn't I? You had no grounds to keep her from me."

There's a long pause on the line. "The law is complicated on the length of time. It all comes down to whether we believe the parents are capable or not."

"That's bullshit," I tell her. "You can't just keep my kid for no reason. I've done everything you've asked of me. What reason did you ever have for keeping Harley?"

"I don't believe you are fit to be a mother. You might have done everything that was asked of you, but can you truly tell me you are ready for the responsibility of having a toddler? I told you I would have someone watching your every move. In the span of three weeks, I've caught you making out in a lake, being featured in a sexual video, ditching school, and so much more. You are not ready for this, Roxanna Raine. It is my job to make sure I do what is best for that little girl. You are not it."

"I love her. I would be the best mother to her."

"I'm sorry," Lynn apologizes, but her words are weak. They mean nothing. "Like I told you before, you still have a chance. If you are granted custody in a few weeks, Harley is yours. I can't stop that. In the meantime, I will be doing my diligence to try to give her what I believe is best. And you can let your lawyer know he can stop with the accusations. Everything I have done has been within law."

I don't get a chance to say anything else because she hangs up on me. I stare at the phone in my hand for what seems like forever. Just glaring at it. Willing her to call back so I can give her a real piece of my mind. This whole time, I thought she was doing what was in the best interest of the family. Isn't that what DHS does? Protect the family as a unit? I am Harley's unit.

And I am more than capable of protecting my family. Her belief and opinion shouldn't even play a part in how this should have gone. I don't care if she believes I am too young or too naive or too whatever. Harley is my child. Mine! Not hers, and Lynn is not taking her from me. I will rot in hell before I go down without a freaking fight. She might tell me that everything she's been doing is above the table, but I trust Tanner over her any day at this point. If he believes we have a chance, I'm running with it. Lynn isn't getting Harley. She just can't.

I would die.

With a groan, I bang my head against the locker, once, twice, and then a third time. I can't believe Lynn is doing this to me. Everything she has ever asked of me has been completed without any rebuttals. Now she wants to take my daughter. And not only take my daughter but adopt her.

Make Harley her own. And no matter how hard I try to beat her at her own game, she's probably going to win. Harley has been with Lynn her whole life. Lynn is who she knows. Harley might know I'm her mom, but I'm not the one feeding her. I'm not the one who changed her diapers or held her when she cried. Lynn did it all and now she wants my baby. Now she wants to take the only thing I have ever wanted.

I soft sniffle leaves me.

There is nothing I can say that will make Lynn change her mind. She made that pretty clear during that call. I was so stupid to believe she ever had my best interest in mind. I should have seen all the red flags. Every time she changed her argument about why I wasn't ready to take Harley home should have been a sign. All the tasks she required of me . . . Everything. I don't know when it started or how it started, but Lynn was never going to give me my baby.

"Must suck watching your world go up in flames." I jerk my head over to see Cade.

I roll my eyes at him. I seriously don't have time for Cade's self-pity and games. "Go away."

He walks over to me, and I notice he's without the crutches again. He didn't have them at the diner a few days ago either. Cade leans against the locker beside me, leaving just enough room between us so we're not touching.

"How do you always find me?" I ask him as I take a step away from him.

"I have my ways," he mutters and steps forward.

So he wants to play this game. "You're stalking me then?"

"I like to think of it as keeping an eye on what's mine. And make no mistake, you are still mine. I don't care if you're with Belmont right now. He's hurt you before and you came running to me. He'll hurt you again, and I'll be right here."

I shake my head at his delusion. I don't know why I didn't notice this before, but Cade needs help. Everyone in my life seems to be crazy.

"That. Is. Never. Going. To. Happen," I say it as clearly as I can, shaking my head as I turn to go.

Cade grabs ahold of my arm and pulls me back. I slam against his chest with a thump, knocking the air out of me for a mere second. He seems to be a lot better. He didn't even flinch or wince or anything.

"Guess your knee is feeling better," I say sarcastically.

"When you have money," his fingers skim up the outsides of my arms, "you're able to get just about anything you want. You can't imagine all the different things scientists have come up with that makes this knee painless."

"So you're doing drugs now?" I ask him.

"If that's how you choose to see it."

"What does your physical therapist think about that?"

"Had to let him go. He wasn't helping."

"Cade—"

"We're done talking about me," He cuts me off. "You want Harley back, right? I have the money to make that happen. All I have to do is call dear old Dad. You know, he doesn't even know I found you again. He would be ecstatic to see you."

My breath catches at his offer. I know money can get you a ton of things. Money equals power. My father had a ton of it and it corrupted him. There's no way I want that amount of money or power. No matter how tempting his offer may be. It corrupted him too.

"I don't want your money," I whisper to him and it feels like I just gave up the one real chance I might have at getting my daughter back. I know if I were wealthy, I would have a better chance at persuading people. But I want to do this the right way. I want people to see that I'm a good mother. I'm not like my own.

"How about you and your fake offer get the fuck away from me?" I suggest.

"It's not fake. It's just not free, but then again nothing in this world is free. I'm shocked you don't remember our parents saying that all the time when we were kids."

My nails pry into his arms keeping me pressed against him. "I try not to follow the preaching of psychopaths. You would do well to follow my lead. We don't want to turn out like them."

"You always have to have the last word," he mumbles.

I relax in his hold. "Cade, let me go. And stop following me."

"Never."

"Why not? There are plenty of other girls. And you weren't like this before Wran came back."

"That's the problem!" he yells.

I flinch at his tone. I search the hallway, but it's clear. I should have stayed in the art room. It's not like people don't know about Harley at this point. They do. Staying in there would have been much better than this confrontation.

"I am so sick of Belmont," he hisses in my ear. "First, I couldn't talk to you because he threatened every guy in this school. Then he leaves, and I have to give you space to grieve. And now he's back. It was meant to be the perfect time for us. I've waited for you my whole life."

"You shouldn't have."

"But I did." His hold lessens as he inhales a large gulp and then lets it out. His body is still tense against my own. "I will help you get Harley back. The price is an easy one to pay. You've never been intimate with anyone other than Belmont, so you don't know what it's like with someone else. Give it a chance. You might find that I'm better."

My body goes rigid in his hold. "This is all about sex to you?"

"No. It wasn't. You made it that. All I wanted was to make you happy. If sex works to get you were I need you, then I will use it. I will twist it to work in my favor."

I finally manage to jerk away from him. I rotate so I'm finally facing him. "I will never have sex with the likes of you. You sealed our fate the moment you decided to treat me like a piece of property. Besides, we've been intimate.

Remember the library event you like to keep reminding me about? Yeah, well, Wran went down on me. And he's gotten me off with much better skills."

I don't have time to react. One moment, I'm standing there, and the next a loud bang sounds out and I'm on the floor. My vision darkens around the edges. I blink back a few times and glance around, searching for the loud ringing. I attempt to get up, but a sharp pain on the side of my head keeps me from getting too far. I bring a hand up to my head. Something sticky drips onto my fingers and I pull my hand back. I gasp at the red lining my hand. I look up at Cade attempting to make sense of what he just did. His eyes are wide as he stands there like a statue, mouth agape. Managing to get to my feet, he starts shaking all over.

"I didn't . . . It was an accident," he says. "I didn't mean to. . ."

"Don't." I tell him as the pain finally registers. "You hit me."

Tears spill over at the realization that the boy I liked is truly gone. No matter how much I wish it, Cade is lost.

He reaches out a hand to me. "Rox."

"Don't touch me!" I scream at him and step back. "Don't ever touch me again."

His eyes search my face and his face falls. The bell ending our lunch period rings and I whirl away from Cade and race down the hall before anyone can see me. I don't stop until I'm at the counselor's door. Josh eats with Ms. Flannigan most days. I've seen him around the halls. Shoving the door open, I halt when there's no sign of Josh. The counselor stands with a questionable look on her face, but I shake my head and run out of her office. She calls after me, but there's no way I'm stopping for her. I head out of the school building. I glance to my right. That's where Raven's house at, and that's where I'm staying. Raven's here at school though, and I don't want to be a burden on anyone that may be at her house.

I go left down main street and walk until I get to Aunt May's diner. The bell chimes as I go inside and heads pop up. One of them being Wran's. He's sitting in a booth with Jesse. At least I think it's Jesse. I haven't seen him since Wran was in high school and even then, I was barely around him. Wran leaps to his feet and rushes over to the door.

His hands go to my face, and I wince. "What the fuck happened?"

I shake my head. I didn't think he would be here. Aunt May is usually here at the diner for the lunch shift. She would have been able to help me clean this. Wran searches the rest of me for any injuries, but I'm pretty sure it's just my head.

"Who fucking did this?" his voice is low and deadly. The hand holding the side of my face falls. "Was it Cade?"

My face must betray me. Wran's expression grow even steelier. He steps around me and out the door. I reach back and seize his arm. "Don't."

He yanks his arm away from me. "That fucker dies."

"Stop, Wran, just stop!" I shout at him and everything in front of me swims. I feel a presence behind me, and I glance over my shoulder to see Jesse. He gives me a small wave.

Wran points to me. "Get her cleaned up. I'll be back."

"Please don't go," I beg him.

Wran looks over his shoulder at me. "I let him get away with blowing a whistle at you. I let him get away with posting that video. He's not getting away with this."

I grasp at Wran, but Jesse draws me back. "You can't let him do this."

"You know Wran just as well as I do. When his mind's made up, there's no changing it. Besides. I agree with him. No guy should put his hands on a woman unless it's to please her."

I bite down on my lip and the taste of copper floods my mouth. My hand goes my mouth and I wince. My lip must have gotten cut.

Jesse turns me away from the diner door. "Let's get you cleaned up. No need to stand here and wait. He'll be back."

My shoulders drop and I let Jesse lead me away. I really hope this doesn't set Wran back. His anger has been in check since his stint at Pleasure House. I don't want him to go overboard because of Cade. Because of me. I give one last glance out the diner door and sigh. Wran can handle this. I know he can.

CHAPTER 22

I yank the door to the school open, barging in like a raging storm. That fucker is going to wish he never laid a hand on my girl. He thinks his career is over now; there won't be anything left to salvage when I'm done with him. How dare that fucker even think he has ever had the right to touch her. Any part of her.

I slam one classroom door open, and everyone heads snap in my direction. I search the students. When he's not in that room, I move on my way. Door after door gets yanked and slammed. Each group giving me the same curious and shocked expression. I pay them no mind. It's not until I'm halfway through all the rooms that I finally find the fucker.

All eyes land on me.

Cade's face goes pale and his eyes bulge out of his head at the sight of me. He jerks from his desk and backs away. I chuckle. There's nowhere for the prick to go. And it's funny he thinks I would even give him the chance. Cade bumps into the desk behind him as he vigorously shakes his head at me. I give one sharp nod just as Mr. White takes a step forward to intervene. On a subconscious level, I can admit to feeling a tiny bit bad about barging into this teacher's particular class. I always liked Mr. White in school. This is personal though.

Everyone scatters from their seats as I make my way over to Cade, stepping on backpacks and kicking anything in my path. Cade grabs the first thing his hand lands on and throws it at me. I dodge his pathetic attempt at defense.

"Mr. Belmont!" Mr. White yells after me. When I don't acknowledge his authority, he demands the students, "Someone, go get the principal!"

I yank Cade up by the collar of his blue polo and slam him down on the desk. There's a collective sharp intake of breath behind me, but I ignore it. This fucker has wanted to be the center of attention since he walked into Rox's life again. Now he has my attention.

The first punch to his pretty boy face has his head slamming against the desk surface. The second, I hear a deafening crunch. I guess it's a good thing his daddy has fucking money, 'cause he's going to need it when I'm done with him.

"I–it was an a–accident!" he sputters out, blood dribbling from his cut lip. "I love her. I wouldn't hurt her like that on purpose."

"Love? Hah!" I scream in his face. "You don't know a fuckin' thing about love!"

I punch him again and again and again.

"Wran!" someone behind me screams. "Stop!"

My hand stops midair as I glance over my shoulder to see who has the audacity to stop this. Claire stands in front of the growing crowd, her hands perched on her hips, face stern, and blond hair pulled up into a ponytail. Cade takes the opportunity to scurry away from me like the coward he is. Fucker can't even finish a fight he started.

"Get the fuck out of here," I respond to her, but my words are for all the people here.

"No." She stands strong. "Look around you. You're being a fucking idiot. This is a public school!"

I march over to Claire and glare her down. Her defiance is really reminding me why I hated her as a kid.

"He touched her. He hurt her," I spit out. "You didn't see the fucking blood on the side of her face."

She gulps, knowing whatever she says isn't going to simmer the rage I feel right now. She still tries. "Roxy and I may not be as close as we once were, but I know her. And I know she wouldn't want you here fighting. Whatever Cade did, Rox wouldn't want you to lose yourself in the anger."

I search the girl's face but this is the sincerest I've ever seen Claire. And she's right. Rox wouldn't want me here. She begged me to stay with her at the diner and I left. I fucking left her with Jesse so I could come beat up some punkass fucker. I glance behind Claire at Mr. White and the students. They all look at me as if I'm some ticking time bomb. With fear and disgust.

My eyes search for Cade and I find him in the back of the crowd. The principal and nurse are helping hold him up. His face looks like someone took a meat grinder to it. It's swollen and bloody. Rox's scratches look like nothing compared to his. My face drops and I take in the blood on my hands and the cracked skin at my knuckles.

Fuck.

Fuck.

Fuck!

"You should go," Claire's voice is low as she says this. "Pretty sure the principal called the police."

I laugh at that. "Josh isn't going to arrest me."

"He may not have a choice. Go, Wran."

For once, I do as she suggests. I push through the crowd and come to a stop in front of the principal and the nurse. I look Cade over once more before turning my back to him. I snarl at the sight of him. He's lucky Claire was here. I would have done so much worse if she hadn't stopped me.

"T-tell her I'm sorry," Cades voice cracks.

I stop but don't turn back to the fucker. "No. And don't ever fucking come around her again."

I barge out of the school building and rush to my car. Getting in, I sit there for a moment, my hands gripping and releasing the steering wheel. I take in a few deep breaths and begin counting. When the red doesn't clear from my vision,

I know what I have to do. I turn on the car and drive. Right out of Kingston.

My car doesn't come to a stop until I'm glaring up at the massive red brick building that was my home for an entire month. The grass seems greener, and this place doesn't seem nearly as creepy as it did the first time I stepped foot here. I still think this place should rename their facility. Seriously, Pleasure House? It's cringe.

I turn off my car and head inside. Crosses still cover the walls and nuns in dark red robes are still walking around with their heads down.

I go over to the help desk. "I need to see Dr. Thomas Harding right now."

The girl looks from her book, the bible I bet, and acknowledges me. She wasn't here during my stay. "Dr. Harding is in a group session at this time. You may come back on his break in a couple hours."

I shake my head at her. "No can do. I'll just join the session."

"That's not really how . . ."

Her words trail off as I walk away and down the hall. I know my way to the courtyard. It doesn't take me long to get there. There's a woman talking as I approach, so I take a seat behind the group on the fresh grass. Thomas' eyes move to me, but I make no move to answer the obvious question in his gaze. The girl takes her seat and the next person recaptures the doc's attention.

I sit in the back the entire session. I get a few question-ing looks, but no one really says anything. When the session ends, I wait until everyone besides Thomas leaves before getting up and raking the grass from my pants.

He comes over to me. "It must be dire if you're coming back here."

My fingers rake through my hair and I let out a groan. "Something happened."

"Let's head to my office." He walks away first and I follow.

Once inside the room, I plop down on the sofa he has stationed by the window. He sits at his desk and crosses his arms.

"So what happened?" he asked when I don't elaborate. "Must have been something bad if you decided to venture into hell once more."

I sit up and place my elbows on my knees. I let out a long exhale. "Cade hit Rox."

His brows jump. "That's interesting. That seems unlike the Caden you've told me about."

I shake my head. "There was a situation that occurred when I was here. It resulted in him getting hurt. I'm not sure what happened between him and Rox, but he's been out of control since. I overlooked the video, because Rox asked me to. I couldn't overlook him hitting her."

I sit back and rest my hands over my face.

"When you say you couldn't overlook it, what exactly do you mean Wran? Is he okay? He's not. . ."

I remove my hands from my face and glare at Thomas. "Of course he's not dead."

Thomas raises his hands in a defensive move. "I wouldn't be doing my job if I didn't ask, especially after Roxanna's father."

Annoyed, I nod. "Rox's dad was a one-time thing. I don't make it a habit of murdering people."

"I'm aware," he tells me and removes his glasses. "So what exactly did you do?"

I tell Thomas everything that happened. How I saw Rox's face and barged into the school. He takes it all in as if he were listening to a child tell him about a coloring project. When I'm done rambling about it all, he sits back in his chair, running his thumb over his chin.

"Do you want to just vent or do you want me to give you my opinion about this?"

"Well, I came to you," I state. "Kinda need you to fuckin' doctor me."

He sighs. "Wran, there's nothing wrong with you. This was quite tame compared to some of the things you've mentioned to me before. I think what made you go off is the fact that your and Cade roles in Rox's life seemed to have gotten reversed somehow. He's now you, and you see the parts of yourself you loath in his actions."

"I'm nothing like that fucker," I disagree.

"You ended up here the first time because you hit Rox. You hurt her. Am I right?"

I don't respond. He knows very well why I was here.

He continues, "I might not know exactly what's going on with Caden, but I do know what I've been told. I believe, and this might be putting it lightly, that both of you are envious of the other."

I go to rebuke his accusation —there's no way I'm jealous of that fucker—but he lifts a hand to stop me.

"Hear me out," he tells me. "You and Caden are similar in so many ways. When you first came home, he and Rox were close. Your sudden presence changed that. So yes, he's probably bitter and upset. Just like you were when you found out about Rox and him."

I bite down on the inside of my cheek, hating the comparisons he's drawing. I don't want to be anything like that prick. I know I'm nothing like that prick, but at the same time I can't deny any of what he's saying.

"You let your anger get the best of you today, because it was a reminder of all the times you hurt Rox. You couldn't defend her from yourself, but you could defend her from Cade."

My eyes meet Thomas' from across the desk, but I can't bring myself to say a word to him. When I saw Rox's face, it was like I was back in our apartment the day I hit her. Her face stunned by what had happened. Rox never expected me to hit her, and I bet on my life she never expected the guy that protected her from me to do the same. Cade and I are toxic to her, yet neither one us seem to be able to let her go.

I glare at Thomas for making me admit that to myself. I don't want to be like that prick.

"I suppose I can see your point," I relent.

"If you want honesty from me, I believe you're being too hard on yourself. Especially about today. There's not many men that would let someone hit their woman. I wouldn't recommend the barging into high schools though. That's getting into tricky territory."

"Got it." I rise from the sofa. "I should head out. Thanks for seeing me."

Thomas stands from his chair. "You can come here anytime to vent. That's what I'm for."

I nod and exit the office.

The drive back to Kingston is a lot less hectic and frantic. I stop in Arlington to get Rox's favorite takeout. Hopefully, that will ease her anger of walking out on her when she was hurt. It's a little before seven when I pull up at Raven's house. She's sitting on the porch with their other friend whose name escape me, but there's no Rox in sight. Opening my door and grabbing the takeout, I go up the two girls.

"Hey," I greet them. "Is Rox inside? I brought takeout."

I hold up the bag. Raven gets up from the wicker chair and grabs the bag. She looks inside it, and I frown. That was meant for Rox and I.

"Rox isn't here. We haven't seen her since before lunch when she went to the art room. I figured she was with you since you stormed the school like a crazy person earlier." Raven pulls the container of noodles from the bag. "What was that about anyway?"

"Um, nothing." I point to the takeout. "Keep it. I gotta go find Rox."

She nods and hands the bag over to the other girl. I go back to my car, contemplating where Rox could have gone. I know she didn't stay at the diner. Most of the students hang out there in the afternoon. And I don't think she would have gone to Josh. While they are on better terms, he wouldn't be Rox's first choice. Maybe she went to the apartment. Maybe I'm being wishful.

Without putting too much thought into it, I head to my apartment. There's only a handful of places she would go and well, this is technically her home too. I hesitate in my car before finally going up the rusting stairs. Inhaling, I open the door and step inside. At no sign of her, I exhale and drop my keys on the table next to the door. I head into the kitchen and grab a bottle of water. This is one of the times she doesn't want to be found. If so, she would have been here or at Raven's.

I take a gulp of the water and walk down the hall to my room. I shove the door open and come to a stop in the doorway. Water goes down the wrong pipe as I gasp at the girl laying on my bed in one of my old Star Wars t-shirts. Using the back of my hand, I wipe my mouth clean and go to her. Rox sits up and looks me over. Her examination stops on my hands. I completely forgot they were cracked and covered in that fucker's blood. Thomas didn't mention it.

Rox rises from the bed and comes over to me. She grabs my hand and leads me out of the room and down the hall to our little bathroom. She lets the toilet seat down and points at it. I do as she says and take the seat. Opening the medicine cabinet, Rox pulls out a bottle of ointment and peroxide. She grabs a clean towel and wets it. My little lost girl comes back over to me and drops to her knees. She takes my hand in hers and dabs at the blood. When my hands are clean enough to her liking, she pours peroxide on the cuts and seals them with the cream. The entire time she's silent, and I so desperately want her words. I want to know what she's thinking and feeling. I want her to yell at me for leaving her. I want something.

After returning the items to the medicine cabinet, she comes back over to me, taking the spot on the floor she was a moment ago. She lays her head in my lap, and I can't resist touching her.

I run a hand through her hair before moving it around to lift her head. She meets my eyes and I notice the tears in hers.

"You okay?" I question.

She nods. "Yes." Her eyes drop to my hands again. "What happened?"

"He got what he deserved."

Rox wets her lips and peeks up at me. With a strained voice, she asks, "Is he okay?"

I want to take offense to that, but I can't. I know Rox is only asking because that's just the type of person she is. And if I tell her no, she's just going to assume it's her fault.

"Cade's fine. A little beat up, but he's alive."

"I should be used to your anger. And I am when it's directed at me. But don't ever do that again. I lost you once because of Josh. I don't want to lose you again due to your stupid anger and getting arrested. Some people said the principal called the police."

I slide off the toilet seat to sit down with her. Drawing her into my arms, I place a peck on her head. "Don't ever cry about that. Today was a mistake. I acted rash, but I promise you nothing like that will ever take me from you. Being away from you is my deepest fear, and I won't allow that to happen."

She tilts her head back and looks up at me. Her purple eyes are shiny. Using my thumbs, I wipe the wetness from her eyes.

"You promise?" she asks.

I nod. "I do."

I stand from the bathroom floor and reach for her hand. She places her small one in mine and allows me to pull her up. I swipe her off her feet, cradling her against my chest and exit the bathroom. I take us back to my room. Gently, I set her down on my bed. She lays back and glances up at me. She makes room for me and I crawl in beside her. Tonight I only want to hold her. That's it. Turning on my side, I draw Rox into me and drape an arm around her waist. She takes ahold of my arm and cradles it against her as tightly as possible. Her body's warm against mine, and if I had to do this for the rest of eternity, I would be happy. She's here. In our apartment. With me. And that's all I need.

CHAPTER 23

ROX

Smiling to myself, I push open the door to Raven's house. Last night actually turned out pretty perfect considering how my day started. I fell asleep in Wran's arms for the first time in a long while. It was nice. Okay, more than nice. It was the best night I'd had in forever. There were no expectations on neither Wran's or my part. When we woke up late last night, we watched a marathon of Star Wars and didn't go back to sleep until early this morning which is why I am currently walking into Raven's house at almost five o'clock in the evening. I didn't even go to school today.

"What's that smile for?" My head snaps up at the sound of my friend's voice. "I know that look!"

I can't wipe the grin from my face, not even to hide my embarrassment from being caught. This time of day, Raven tends to be with Charlie. Her and Lex watch him rehearse. He's been having gigs in some club in Arlington every Saturday for the past month. I haven't been able to attend because well . . . Saturday.

Raven looks towards the couch and I follow her gaze. Her dad sits there flipping through the channels. She gets up from her spot at the old wooden table and grabs my wrist. She hauls me up the stairs to her room and slams the door. I whirl around to face her, but she's already in my face.

"You had sex with Wran." She bounces and shrieks.

While I wouldn't have turned Wran down, it didn't happen. I don't know why it didn't; I made myself very available to him after the whole bathroom sob fest. I mean, I was in his shirt for crying out loud. I ground my butt up against him the whole night. He didn't bite. Still, it was a pretty amazing night.

"No I didn't." I go over to her bed and sit down. I grab the pillow at the foot of her bed and hold it to my chest. "We just watched movies like old times."

Raven shakes her head. "No. I don't believe that. You're still in his clothes!"

She jumps on the bed beside me and I take in the shirt I'm still wearing. I completely forgot to do my laundry and change.

I shrug my shoulders at her statement. "I thought putting the shirt on would ease whatever tension there would be after he got back."

Raven's still shaking her head as if my story is so hard to believe. "C'mon, you got to give me something." She points over to the kraft paper bag on the desk. "He brought take-out!"

I laugh out loud at that. "So that's what happened to my dinner?"

My friend rolls her eyes. "I was hungry and you weren't here. Care to tell me what yesterday was about and how you got that?"

She points to the bandage on the side of my head. My hand goes to the cut and I frown. "I don't really want to talk about that."

"Did Cade do that to you?" she questions.

I fall back on the bed and groan. "How bad was it?"

She lays back beside me. "Bad. Wran barged into my class. But he left after searching the room. A lot of people said he did the same to theirs. I personally didn't see the fight, but from what Lex says, it was pretty brutal. Cade's face is shit."

"He told me it wasn't that bad." I groan into the pillow.

"So did Cade really do that to you? I mean, I knew he was a douchebag, but he seemed really taken with you."

I turn over on my side to face my friend. "It's complicated. Actually, it's not that complicated. He wants me to be in love with him."

Raven moves so we're face to face and brings her arm up so that her head is resting on it. "But you're in love with Wran."

"In another life, Cade and I would have worked. I see it so clearly. If my father never did what he did and if Wran never took me in, I would be with Cade. And I would probably be happy with him."

"But your life didn't go that way," she says what I neglect to add. "And now he feels cheated out of what could have been?"

I nod. "I know he didn't mean to hit me. I saw that on his face the second it happened. And I probably shouldn't have said what I said to him. I wasn't thinking about how he felt. Everything is setting him off, and until he calms down, there's no way for us to be friends anymore."

"How do you feel about all of that? It sounds rough," she states.

I bite down on my lip and shake my head. "It feels like losing a piece of myself. I feel like he brought me back to life. But if I have to choose between having him as a friend and having Wran, then Wran always win. He's the one I can't live without, and I don't want to."

"Jesus girl. I do not envy you."

I shove her shoulder. "Thanks."

She laughs. "I guess it's a good thing I invited the girls over for a sleepover. You need something to take your mind off boys."

"Girls? As in more than just Lex?" I ask her. I don't know any other girls that Raven would actually invite to a sleep over.

"Uh, yeah. I sorta, maybe was being friendly." She rolls over and buries her face in her pillow. "I invited Claire."

"What?" I shriek.

Raven sits up and grabs another pillow. "I was being nice. She helped Wran. And I sorta maybe had a good time with her when we went dress shopping."

"Oh my god, you like her."

"It's not like that!" Raven shrieks and covers her mouth. "I mean, maybe it's like that. I don't know."

I grimace at my friend. "I hate to tell you this, but Claire is straight."

"You sure?" Raven asks me. "Because I was getting different vibes at the mall."

"Yeah, I'm a thousand percent sure. Claire likes guys. Like a lot."

"Oh my god, and I invited her here!" Raven falls back on the bed and screams into the pillow.

I cover my ears and laugh. "If it helps, I'll try to help with the awkwardness."

"Thank you," she mutters through her pillow.

I actually find it cute and who knows, maybe I'm wrong. It has been some time since Claire and I were really close. She could have changed during the time we spend apart. I don't think that's the case considering she did warn me against Cade, but like I said, who knows with her.

Raven exhales and shakes her head. She gets up and throws the pillow aside. "Enough with relationship drama. We have a sleepover to get ready for. Help me make snacks?"

I smile at her. "Sure."

The next hour and a half, Raven and I spend time in the kitchen baking cookies, brownies, and making three different types of dips. We even make a run to our little grocery store to pick up drinks. I don't know who she plans on eating and drinking everything. From my experience with sleepovers which isn't much, they're usually awkward. I went to one with Claire when we were like twelve, and it ended in disaster. And considering that Lex doesn't like Claire and Raven is currently crushing on Claire, I can only imagine the night is going to be just the same.

Lex gets here at exactly eight o'clock and like always, she bombards me with questions about yesterday. About why I wasn't at school after lunch. I give her the bare minimum. Unlike Raven, I haven't really gotten that close to Lex. Probably because every time we're together, all she wants to do is ask me questions. I understand her curiosity. I would be just as curious if it was someone else's life. It's mine though, and sometimes things get awkward. I do like her though. When she's not prying, she's quite fun to be around.

Lex walks over to the kitchen table where all the snacks are laid out and takes a brownie. She takes a bite of it before coming over to us in the kitchen and leaning against the sink. Her gaze moves over to Raven's dad who's playing a game on the PS5. She sighs and take another bite of the brownie. Raven shoves Lex.

"What?" Lex protests.

"Stop looking at my dad like that!" Raven exclaims low enough that her dad doesn't pick up on what's being spoken about.

"Don't blame me because he's a total dilf," Lex whisper back. "Look at him."

My eyes move over to where Raven's father sits on the couch. I take him in for the first time since I've been here. I suppose to someone else he is attractive. I can see the appeal, but he wouldn't be my type. He looks too polished and clean with his perfectly styled hair, dress shirt, and slacks. Although, playing the game does make him look a little more appetizing.

"Lex's got a point," I take up for her. "He's okay."

"Eww, eww, ewww!" Raven cringes.

"What are we whispering about?" We all look at the door as Claire walks inside. She has on satin pink pajamas and an overnight bag in her hands. Her hair is braided on both sides of her head, and she's makeup free. This is the first time in a long time I have seen Claire not all dolled up. It's surprising.

I hear Raven take in a gulp. To help her out I step forward. "Nothing really." I lower my voice. "Just about how hot Raven's dad is."

Claire takes a peek over her shoulder and takes in the man. "He is hot. In a nerdy, corporate, I-wanna-fuck-your-dad kinda way."

Raven's face reddens, and she turns away from us. "Dad? Aren't you supposed to be heading out with Uncle Cam for poker night?"

Her dad pauses his game and comes over to us. "Hey girls." He faces his daughter. "You trying to get rid of me, sweet pea?"

Raven nods. "Yes. You said I could have the house tonight."

"Alright, alright. I'm headed out. You girls better behave."

"Yes, sir," Lex says way too flirty for what's appropriate. Raven's father shakes his head at Lex, dismissing her and walks out the door. Raven runs around to the exit and locks it.

"Okay, rules," Raven says and looks pointedly at Lex. "No more fantasizing about my dad."

"But he's so easy to fantasize about. You know how many dreams he's starred in?"

"Lex." Raven's all too serious about this.

"Fine, fine."

Claire opens her bag. "I raided my dad's liquor cabinet." She pulls out a bottle of Jack.

I shake my head. "I can't have any."

"C'mon, Rox. You used to live off this stuff at our parties."

"That was before Harley."

Claire's playful tone drops. "Right. Sorry."

I dismiss her apology. It's fine. I know the person I was pre-baby.

"Sooo . . ." Lex walks back over to the snack table. "What are we going to do tonight? Men are obviously off the table."

Claire giggles at Lex.

"I have some games," Raven says. "Come help me, Lex."

They head up the stairs and leave Claire and I alone. She leans against the counter and takes in the small house. It's nothing like her place on the other side of town. This house is small and homely. A standard middle class house. This isn't the type of event I would ever expect Claire to show up at. I wouldn't even expect her father to allow her on this side of town.

"So, you showed up? Raven told me she invited you." I try to make conversation with her. It should be easy after the mall, but it's not.

"Well, it is different," she says as she takes in her sur-roundings. "But that doesn't mean bad. Your apartment was always smaller than my house."

"True."

Claire sets her bag down on the counter. "Besides, big house doesn't mean big, happy family."

"Things are still bad with your dad I take it."

She snorts and it's so unladylike. So unlike the picture she puts out for the world to see. "That's an understatement, but you know what my dad is like. Smile in everyone's face, creep into everyone's bed, and pretend it never happened. He got it in his mind that he wants to be mayor. That's the only reason he allowed me here tonight. It looks good to socialize with the less fortunate. His words."

"At least you're going off to college in the fall." I try to look on the bright side. Claire doesn't have to put up with him for much longer.

Claire rolls her eyes. "Yeah, to a school where he still has full control over me."

"Surely—"

She interrupts what I'm about to say. "You know my dad. You know what he's like. Do you really think he'd let me out of his sight to do whatever I want?

I grimace at the fact that she's probably right. It'll take a lot for her to pull away from him and for him to relinquish control. Her father is not the type of man to let even one person around him slip through his cracks.

"Anyway," she points to the bandage, "how are you? Yesterday was insane. I've never seen Wran like that."

I drop my head to the counter. Here we go again. "I'm fine. Wran's fine."

"I'm guessing you don't want to talk about it?" she asks.

"It's not that," I tell her. "Okay, so maybe it's a little that. It's tiring always answering questions about us."

"You remember when we were kids and all you wanted was for him to fight for you?" I nod. "That's what he did. It was insane to witness but romantic. I'm glad I got him out of there before the police showed up."

I life my head to her and smile. "Thank you. He mentioned you helped."

"So," her eyes drop from me and she leans back, using the countertop as an anchor. "Does this mean you and Cade are officially over?"

"Pretty sure you knew we were over back when you told me I was being a clingy friend. Besides, there was never really a Cade and me. I should have never given in to him."

"I mean, well, yeah. But you were still around, and I don't know, I wasn't completely sure it was over, and—"

"Claire, get to the point," I interrupt her rambling.

She rests her arms on the countertop, her fingers weaving together over and over. It's her nervous tell. "You wouldn't mind if I maybe asked him out?"

"You want to go out with Cade?" I question.

Her eyes close as if this pains her. "Look, I know what he did to you, and while I didn't agree with it, I know he did it because he was hurt. Cade's not a bad guy and he's going to need someone to help him move past you. I want to be that someone. I've wanted to be that someone for a while, but you always had his attention."

"I only just started talking to him this year," I tell her. She could've been with him.

"That may be, but he's been obsessed with you since freshman year. But then you sort of vanished from school. Now feels like my time."

"I'm guessing that's why I got a banana shake tossed on me at the beginning of the year?"

"You called dibs on Wran, I called dibs on Cade. Even if you didn't know."

"Well I think you should go for it. He needs someone that cares about him as much as possible."

Claire face lights up. "Really? You wouldn't care?"

I shake my head.

"Thanks."

Raven's admission comes to my mind, and I frown. While I knew Claire was as straight as they come, my friend did invite her here tonight thinking the opposite. I should probably tell Claire so that she doesn't make Raven feel bad. I'm just about to bring it up when Lex and Raven come bouncing back in the kitchen.

"Alright. I got the games set up in my room. Let's head up." Raven eyes flick to Claire for a second before they drop. I glance over at Claire to see her reaction, but she looks as if it didn't bother her. Claire probably hasn't picked up on Raven's crush.

We all crowd into Raven's room and I take the chair at her desk. Lex hops on the bed and Claire makes herself comfy on the floor.

"I figured we could play truth or dare first," Raven suggests and I quirk a brow at her.

"Actually," Lex says before anyone else can but in. "I want to ask you something."

She points to me. "Me?"

She nods. "Don't get mad at Raven, but she mentioned your court hearing. And you know me. I love the gossip, so . . . She said you were worried about the possibility of Wran going to jail."

I stare at Raven, not sure how I feel about her telling Lex that. The girl asks enough questions as it is. Raven slaps a hand over her face and groans. Claire turns to look at me with questioning eyes.

"Wran's going to jail?" Claire asks.

"No!" I tell her. "I don't know. Maybe. It's a possibility. Lynn keeps calling what Wran and I did something that it's not, and they're not listening to me. They just keep treating me like a child."

"What if I told you I had an idea that may help?"

I narrow my eyes at Lex. "What type of idea?"

"Well you see, my aunt is a news anchor for the local news. How do you feel about telling your side of things? Getting ahead before the court can twist the story into something perverted and wrong."

"Rox, that's a good idea," Claire states. "It might actually win Wran favor in the eyes of the public, which you both would need to beat this."

"And your aunt would air this?"

Lex nods. "She's all about helping those that can't be helped. I think she would jump at this story, especially with a social worker trying to fight for custody of a child she shouldn't even have."

"Alright. I'll try anything," I tell her.

Lex bounces on the bed like a kid at Christmas. "I'll go get my camera."

I glance from Raven to Claire and back again. What did I just agree to?

CHAPTER 24

WRAN

Josh comes to a stop in front of some fancy ass restaurant with a valet. I frown at the pretense of it all. Of course Tanner would have us meet him somewhere we can't even afford to get in. Hell, we'd be lucky to breathe the same air as these people. Rox wiggles in my lap and my eyes move away from the penguin suit wearing fucker and to my girl. I probably shouldn't have planted her ass in my lap when we got in the car earlier, but I missed the feel of her against me.

Clasping ahold of her thigh, I stop her from moving any more. There's not a chance in hell I'm going in there with a raging hard on to sit across from Tanner for God knows how long. Nope, not happening today.

Rox glances over her shoulder and smirks at me. "Un–comfortable?"

I smirk right back at her. "Nope."

Josh grunts something about immaturity, but I pay him no mind. Rox has been letting loose a lot lately, and it's hot as fuck. I'm not sure what's gotten into her, but whatever it is she needs to keep doing it. Rox's been reminding me of the girl I fell for and not the one Lynn turned her into.

The valet finally makes his way over to us and I frown again at the suit. Josh mentioned before we left that I should dress nicer. He also said we were just having lunch. I should have known something was up when Rox came out of Raven's house in a mini floral dress and heels. Don't get me wrong, Rox can dress just fine, but she's normally in something a little more casual.

Rox reaches for the door and I swat at her hand. I shake my head at her. "I can get the door."

"Then why haven't you already?"

My cock instantly hardens at her sassy tone. Rox's eyes widen just as she realizes how much I like it when she give me sass. She wiggles on my lap for only a mere moment before wrenching open the passenger door and hopping off me like I burned her. My lips tip up as my gaze follow her around the car and into the restaurant. Josh catches my eyes, and he shakes his at me.

"Must you two do that when I'm around?" He grimaces and gets out of the car.

I follow my brother's lead and go around to him. "The only time I really get to see her is when you're here. Excuse me for seizing the moment."

"Yeah, well, try seizing when I'm not sitting right next to you. Voyeurism isn't really my cup of tea."

I clasp my brother on the back as we make our way inside the restaurant. "You think she would be into that?"

"Wran, seriously?" Josh scolds.

"I lost three years of learning what she may like. I'm making up for that now."

Josh shoves my hand off his shoulder. "Then discuss it with her. I don't want to hear about my brother fucking a girl we raised."

A laugh escapes me at the shiver that runs up my brother. He really hates picturing me with her. I honestly can't see anything wrong with us. Yes, she's young. Yes, we technically raised her. But we were kids ourselves. This feels like the most natural thing in the world to me. Being with her. Making her smile even on days like today. At least I was able to get her mind off the news Tanner has to deliver and the fact that it's a Saturday and she isn't getting to see Harley.

We come to a stop in front of a stand with a woman wearing a similar penguin suit to the man out front.

"Welcome to Verona. Do you have a reservation?" the hostess asks us.

I nod. "Yeah, we're meeting Bennett Tanner."

The hostess beams. "I can show you to your party."

She steps aside the stand and heads towards the back of the restaurant. We follow her all the way to a dark corner in the back. She gestures to Tanner and Rox already seated.

I dive for the chair next to Rox and grab at the breadsticks on the table. There's also glasses of water already stationed for us.

"When you are ready to order, just signal. Someone will be right with you," she tells us and heads back to her post.

I take in the restaurant. It's nothing like Aunt May's, and I'm not sure I like it. It's dark and gloomy and all the tables are spaced too far apart. I suppose for the type of conversation we are having, space and privacy is a good thing, but if Tanner really wanted privacy, we could have met him at his house or office. Rox grabs one of the menus in front of us, and I take it from her. I open it and frown. It's all in some foreign language. French or Italian. I hand the menu back to her and take another breadstick.

"Why'd you choose this place?" I ask Tanner.

"I'm meeting another client in a bit, and it was convenient," he says as he picks up the water and takes a sip. "This meeting shouldn't take too long."

"You said you wanted to tell me something?" Rox speaks up.

Tanner nods. "Your custody hearing has been pushed up."

"That's a good thing, right?" Josh asks.

Bennett shakes his head. "It could be. In our case, it's not."

"What do you mean?" I ask just as a waitress in black slacks and a white button down comes up to us. She takes the glass sitting in front of Tanner with a smile and walks off again. No one says anything until she returns with the water glass.

"Are you ready to order?" she asks.

Bennett rambles off some items in French and the waitress writes it all down. I have no clue with he just ordered for us, but at least I'm not making a fool of myself trying to pronounce shit I obviously can't pronounce.

When she leaves again, Tanner finally answers my question. "As of right now, Rox's only witnesses are May and her teachers. I tried contacting your friends, Claire and Cade, but there's been some difficulty in that area."

I'm the only one at the table that notices Rox's wince at Cade's name. Honestly, I don't even know why Tanner is trying to recruit that fucker at this point. He would hurt our case more so than help.

"Surely, she doesn't need them," Josh says. "Is there no one else?"

Tanner lets out a long sigh. "Her teachers think her focus has been waning in past months. May would have to testify about Rox's attendance at work. While May and her teachers have amazing things to say about Rox, Lynn is going to make it look like they are being elusive with information. Claire and Cade can attest to what Rox was like prior to having Harley and what she is like now. We need that."

I twirl the uneaten breadstick in my fingers and glance at Rox. She's biting down on her bottom lip and her hands are strangling the fork in her hold. Her eyes remain down. I pull my gaze away from her and back to Tanner.

"What can we do?" I ask him. "There must be something."

Tanner's gaze flicker to Rox. "You could try talking to Claire and Cade. Maybe you can make better leeway than I can. If that doesn't work, I can always subpoena them. That's my last result as it tends to upset the witnesses. However, once they're on the stand, they can't lie."

"Excuse me for a moment," Rox announces as she swiftly rises from her seat and darts away from the table.

I watch until she disappears, my leg switching underneath the table as I itch to follow her. Rox probably wasn't expecting to hear any of this today. We knew Tanner would be contacting people, but it seems like no matter who he calls to witness, Lynn is going to use them against us. At this point, I don't even see any options for us.

Slumping back in my chair, I cross my arms and glare at Tanner. "You have any good news?"

He meets my glare head on, picks up the glass of water and takes a sip. "I'm Roxanna's lawyer. I'm only talking about this case when she's present."

Josh sits up and pull my eyes away from Tanner. "How about Wran?"

My brow scrunch together at my brother's question. "What about me?"

"Can you give us some insight on the charges he will face if he loses his case?" Josh clarifies.

The mention of what that woman is doing has me seeing red. I grip the edge of the table and slowly begin counting in my head. I'm not going to let that woman occupy any time in my head. Tanner scratches at his chin and his mouth turns down. That look alone answers the question. My chances aren't good. I'm going to prison. A chill runs up my spine at the thought of that. Fuck, there's no way in I could survive prison. Someone would piss me off, and I'd end up shanked in the middle of the night. Granted, I'd give any one of those pricks a run for their money. Prison and anger problems still don't make the best match. I'd never see my girl again.

"Wran's case is going to depend solely on the jury," Tanner finally acknowledges. "They could see him as a young man in love with a girl who had the same feelings. Or they could see him as someone who groomed Roxanna. There is a very thin line there and there's no telling what way the wind will blow. I can say for certain, if he is found guilty, he will face up to a year in prison."

A year?

I suppose it could be worse.

But can I really spend a year without Rox. That first year I was away was pure fucking torture. I almost drove myself crazy just listening to her voicemails on repeat. Now, I wouldn't even have those to keep me company. And who's to say my girl would even wait around for me a second time. I'm just now getting her back. Truly back.

A plate is placed on the table and I look up to see our waitress with a plethora of dishes. She sets them all in the center of the table and then leaves. I examine each dish with a frown. It's all fancy finger food.

"You really don't know your guest," I say to Tanner as I pick up a long white and purple looking tentacle.

"Calamari." Tanner points to the tentacle in my hand. "It's octopus."

I drop the octopus so fast and scoot my chair. "Yeah, no thanks. Order me cheese sticks. I'm going to go check on Rox."

I jet away from the table just as fast as I dropped the squid. I head down a narrow hall, the way I saw Rox turn, until I see a sign with a lady on it. Restroom. I knock on the door, and I can here rustling coming from within.

"Just a moment," Rox calls.

The door swings open and Rox comes to a stop before me. Her eyes are swollen and her face is red. She's been here crying. Shoving past her, I shut the door and lock it, trapping us both inside. I take her hand and pull her over to the little black podium sink. I pick her up and place her on the edge of it. A tear leaks from her pretty purple eyes and I swipe it away.

"What's wrong?" I ask her. "Why are you crying?'

Rox doesn't say anything but the tears start to flow even more. I pull her to me, resting her head against my shoulder. Gently, I run a hand over her back to soothe her.

"Whatever it is, it's okay," I tell her. "We've survived so much. Nothing is going to keep us down, baby."

Rox shakes her head on my shoulder. "I'm going to lose her."

Harley. This is about our daughter. "No, we're not. I'll do whatever it takes so that won't happen to us."

"I called Claire. She won't testify. Her dad won't let her. And Cade," she chokes on a sob at the mention of him, "Cade doesn't care. How can he not care?"

"Because he's a fucking prick that only cares about himself." I draw back from Rox and lift her face, swiping even more tears as I do so. "Don't cry over them. They aren't worth it. Tanner said he can subpoena them. Let him. It's time for you to think about you. Not them. So what if they get mad? They will get over it. If we lose Harley, we're not getting her back."

Rox shakes her head again. "I can't lose her. You have no clue what it did to me when Lynn took her the first time. I can't lose her again."

"Shh," I soothe and pull her closer and kiss at her tears. "We won't."

Rox eyes searches my face for a second before her soft lips slam against mine. Her whole body leans into the kiss, her arms wrapping around my neck and her fingers diving to the hair at my nape. I cup her cheek as I attempt to slow her down. Not that I'm opposed to this, but she is. She's not thinking clearly, and I'm not about to fuck up the progress we've made.

"Rox," I warn her as her mouth trails down to the side of my neck. "We're not doing this here. Josh and Tanner are waiting."

"I don't care," she mumbles against my skin. "I want you. I need you now. Please."

Gulping I tilt my head back and stare at the black ceiling. She just had to throw in the please, didn't she? She slides off the sink and down my front. I shake my head at her as she descends to her knees. This girl is going to be the death of me.

"You seemed to like this in the car." She unbuckles my belt and I let out a pathetic groan.

Fuck.

I want this.

Way too much.

But . . .

The release of my zipper snaps me out of it and I pull away from Rox. "No."

Rox stands with a pout, her arms crossed like a petulant child. "Then I will find someone else that will help me."

My vision instantly goes red at the thought of someone else touching what is mine. I step closer to her and crowd her in against the sink. Her throat bobs as she looks me over, a little whimper leaving her. I grab ahold of her waist and yank her flush against me. Her hands come up to rest against my chest, pink tinting her cheeks.

"What did you say?" It comes out as a growl.

"I–I . . ." she starts.

"Don't you dare repeat that." My free hand moves to the bottom of her dress and underneath it. She gasps as I get a handful of her feminine part. "This belongs to me. Don't you ever talk about giving it to someone else. Do I make myself clear?"

She nods. "Yes."

Her voice comes out all wispy and wanton. I grin at her and tear her panties off, ripping them in the process. Rox gasps and looks around the small restroom as in someone is watching. When her eyes come back to mine, her pupils are blown and there's not a hint of a tear in them. Her breathing picks up and she clutches my shirt in her hand.

I shove her panties in my back pocket and smile. "My little lost girl like that?"

Rox shakes her head, then nods. "I don't know."

My finger inches to her opening and I run my knuckle over her warm center. With a gasp, she leaps in my hold. I tighten my arm around her waist to keep her in place.

"You're soaking," I whisper in her ear.

"Wran," she whimpers. "Please."

I release her then and step back. She frowns at my departure and shakes her head. I smirk. "I think you need to stay like this for a while."

"What?" she shrieks. "No."

"Maybe next time you'll think twice about trying to make me jealous."

I watch as her emotions play out on her delicate face. She goes from confused to irate in a matter of seconds. "You bastard."

She shoves me and I grab her wrist as she does. "Be a good girl."

Her eyes narrow on me, and I can see the moment she decides to play. It's like watching a switch flip on and I'm suddenly transported back to when we used to do this. Rox steps away from me and lifts herself up on the sink. It creeks from her weight, but she has my full attention. Resting her back against the mirror, she spreads her legs wide, allowing me the perfect picture of just how turned on she is for me.

"If you don't finish me off, I will," she threatens.

I step into her open legs and grip the back of her knees, drawing them up around my waist. Her hand glides down the front of her chest and down to the pushed up hem of her dress. She dips her fingers inside herself and lets out a quiet whimper. The sight of her pleasuring herself makes me even harder and the rigid material of my denim jeans is making the discomfort even worse.

Fuuuuck.

I want to give in.

I want to give in to this girl so bad.

But as much as I want this, want her writhing and panting for me, I'm not going to take advantage of her. She was literally in here fucking crying about our daughter. Now is not the time for this.

Grabbing her wrist, I pull her fingers from her center. "Stop, Rox."

Her eyes pop open and she gasps at the emptiness. She frowns and yanks her wrist from my hold. I feel the sting across my face before I even notices she has gotten down from the sink. Rox shoves me, but I stand firm. She goes to shove me again and I capture her wrists. I pull her into me and spin her around so that her back's pressing against my front. Her shoulders heave a few times before a splash of water lands on my arm restraining her. I glance up at the ceiling, but there's nothing dribbling down. Turning Rox around in my arms, I notice the tears have returned.

I shake my head at her. "Don't cry. Not over this."

She sniffles. "I've lost everything else. You could at least let me have you."

"You have me. You more than have me. I'm so wrecked for you, there's no chance of resurfacing," I tell her. It's one of the most truthful things I've ever told her. "Spend the rest of the weekend with me and we can do whatever you want."

She smiles up at me. "Whatever I want?"

I nod. "Within reason."

"Okay," she agrees and swipes at the tears.

Tilting her chin up, I place a gentle peck against her pink lips. "You're going to get our daughter back. No matter what I have to do, Rox."

She nods, but all the feistiness has left her system. Taking her hand, I open the door and lead her back out to our table. Rox lowers into her seat, head down, and doesn't say a word. I grab a couple pieces of the squid tentacles and place them on her plate. She still doesn't move. Glancing up, I catch both Josh and Tanner eyeing us in question. I shake my head to warn them from asking any questions.

We nibble on the food in silence until the waitress comes over with the receipt. The octopus actually wasn't as bad as it looked earlier. A little chewier than I would have liked, but not a bad taste. Tanner pays for the ticket and rises. Rox gets up and I look at her plate. She's eaten nothing. I take ahold of her hand and pull her over to me. She peeks up at me through wet lashes and manages a smile at me. She turns to look at Tanner.

"Do it," she tells him. "Subpoena them. Whatever it takes."

I let go of Rox's hand and guide her in Josh's direction. He starts to question me but thinks twice. He takes Rox's hand and head towards the front of the restaurant. I clamp a hand down on Bennet's shoulder to keep him from leaving. He arches a brow at me, and I take in a deep breath.

"There's something we haven't considered where Rox and Harley are concerned, and I need to know a potential outcome," I tell him.

"I assure you, Wran, I've considered everything," he tells me.

I shake my head in disagreement. "What if I confess that I raped her? Would that give her Harley?"

Tanner searches the restaurant before giving me his full attention again. "Why would you confess to something you didn't do?"

I run a hand through my hair. "There's not much in this world I give a fuck about. That girl is the main one that I do, and I've hurt her so much already. I left, and that's why we're in this situation. If I can give her our daughter, then I'll do whatever."

"Do you even understand the gravity to admitting to something like that. You'd never be able to see Harley or her. You would be labeled a sex offender. I think you really need to think about what you want, because that's not it."

I disregard his words. "But would it work?"

He doesn't answer me right away, letting out a deep sigh and searching the place once more. "Possibly, but she didn't lose custody because you're the father. She lost custody due to the drugs in her system. You admitting to sexual assault could be seen for what it is, fooling the jury. That would only lead you somewhere you don't need to be."

"I want to make her happy. I want to give her a future with our child, even if I can't be a part of it," I confess. "I would do anything for her."

"Then try working on Cade. That little shit has been a pain to talk to. Get him on her side, and you both could walk away from this."

My teeth grind together at the mention of him.

That fucker.

I should have known we'd need that prick.

Tanner leaves me standing in the dark corner fuming.
Fucking fuck.

CHAPTER 25

ROX

The shrill of the bell sounds and I set my pencil down. No one makes a move until Mr. White nods for us to leave. Stuffing my book into my backpack, I pick up my assignment and place it in the tray on the way out of the room. I come to a stop when I notice Charlie and Lex leaning against the wall next to the door. Someone squeezes past me and I make out the purple hair of Raven before she comes to a stop beside me, her book pressed against her chest.

"Jesus! What took so long?" Charlie exclaims.

"You know what Mr. White is like," Raven answers.

I roll my eyes at that. "He is literally the only teacher who's acting like we're not graduating in three weeks."

"He's still giving ya'll work?" Charlie asks.

Raven and I both nod.

"And that's why you should be in regular classes. Not this AP crap," Lex says. "My teachers stopped giving us work right after senior ditch day."

Senior ditch day was two weeks ago. If anything, all of my teachers have been trying to cram as much down my neck as possible. I still have an end of course paper to turn in about the principle of electricity and magnetism for a physics class. Granted, I did complete it already, but there's still the work cited page and editing and all of that.

"So why are you two creeping outside of our class?" Raven asks our friends.

Lex pats Charlie on the shoulder. "He said he needed to talk to us all in the library."

Raven shifts on her feet. "It's lunch time. Why do we—"

Charlie holds up an envelope to cut Raven off. "It's from Julliard. I've been freaking all morning and wanted to open it with you all."

I give him a sheepish smile and step back. This is probably meant for only Raven and Lex. It seems like something that only his close friends would be a part of and seeing as I haven't really been a part of the group for long, I don't want to overstep and intrude. I go to turn around but am stopped with a hand on my wrist.

I look down to see rather large hands holding me. Glancing over my shoulder, I take in Charlie.

"Where are you going?" he asks. "Didn't you just hear me?"

"I, um, thought you meant them." I gesture to the girls.

He shakes his head at me in disapproval. "Raven has adopted you into our group. That means you are a part of this."

Butterflies swarm in my stomach as I take in the meaning of those words. I haven't had a group of real friends since Claire back in middle school. This seems so surreal, but I'm not going to question it. If he wants to share this moment with me, then I will happily be a part of it. Although, I don't know why he's so nervous. The envelope is rather large for a rejection.

Raven takes ahold of my hand and pulls me down the hall. Everyone heads to the library and to an empty table. My body instantly tenses as I notice Cade farther down at a spare table. He's by himself and reading. He doesn't notice me so I take a deep breath and relax. I thought he wasn't going to be back for a while, but I guessed wrong. I haven't seen him since Wran came here after he hit me. I don't know what I expected to happen after that whole situation, but I didn't expect for Cade to just vanish. I take in the boot on his leg and the sling holding his arm. As if he can feel my gaze on him, he lifts his head and glances around. I jerk my eyes away from him and turn back to my friends. Raven brows dip and she runs a soothing hand up my arm. I give her a weak smile and give Charlie my full attention.

"So, it's a rather large envelope," I tell him. "You totally got accepted."

Lex nods. "Totally."

"We know you got this," Raven cheers him on.

Charlie nods and pries open the envelope. He pulls out a packet full of papers. His eyes move back and forth but the corners of his lips fall. I tilt my head in confusion. There's no way he didn't get in. I know Julliard is a very prestigious school, but I've seen Charlie perform. I've heard him on the piano. He's amazing.

"What's wrong?" Raven questions, noticing the way his expression falters as well.

"I got in," he says and Lex throws herself at him.

"See!" she exclaims. "We've been telling you for weeks not to worry."

"It doesn't matter." Charlie tosses the letter on the table and takes a seat in a chair. "All the rehearsing and practicing was for nothing."

"I don't understand," I say and take a seat. "You got in. That's great."

Charlie crosses his arms and pouts. My fingers twitch around the strap of my backpack as I watch his reaction to getting into one of the most coveted and prestigious schools in the country. At least he gets to go off to college. At least he gets to follow his dreams. What more could he want? If you ask me, he's being really selfish right now. Someone else who didn't get in would be crying with joy right now. This is an honor and he's acting like it's the most horrible thing in the world. He gets to go to freaking New York after high school. I'm going to be stuck here in Kingston waiting tables. Sure, it's my choice, but when you have a kid, not much of anything is about you.

"That's not it," Charlie finally says with a huff. "I'm glad I got in. Only five percent of applicants get in, but it doesn't matter because they didn't offer me a full scholarship. Without that scholarship, my folks can't possibly send me there."

Oh. Money. I should have known that would be the issue. He's been talking about that scholarship for a while. I try to think of something to say to make him feel better about this situation. I mean, there's not much I can really tell him. It's not like I spent my time this year focused on things like this, but there still have to be options for him.

"Can't you apply for like grants and stuff?" Lex asks. "Or loans?"

Charlie shakes his head. "I don't qualify for student aid. Dad makes too much. And I'm really trying not to die in debt."

"That sucks," I mutter. "Maybe some other school will offer you a full scholarship."

"I wanted Julliard. Acceptance there only comes around once in a lifetime."

I nod but keep quiet. I still believe he's lucky. Even if he can't go to that particular school, he at least gets to get out of Kingston. That's more than half of the people at our school is going to get. It's more than I am ever going to get. I shake off the self-pity and sit up in my chair. I'm just about to tell him that he should still be happy when the door to the library is yanked open and Claire stumbles inside. She stops and glares around the room as if searching for someone when her eyes lock on me.

I gulp at the fury painting her features.

Uh oh.

Claire marches over to the table. Her clickety clacking shoes sounding throughout the library. She slams her palms down on the table and glares at me. Both Raven and Lex retreat a step at her anger.

"What the fucking hell, Roxy?" she shouts.

Yep, she's definitely upset if she's back to calling me Roxy. "What's wrong?"

She tears a piece of paper from her back pocket and tosses it in my face. "We need to talk. Now!"

I pick up the paper, but don't have a chance to read it before her nails are digging into my forearms and dragging me up from the chair. I yank my arms away from her as she point to one of the private rooms. I search the library to find Cade eyes on me. His face is blank, like he's looking straight through me. I pull my gaze away from him and head to the private room. Claire follows behind and locks the door. She whirls on me.

"Why?" she shouts, and I cringe away. "Are you trying to ruin both of our lives? You really had me subpoenaed. If you have to force people to testify for you then maybe you really don't need custody of Harley!"

I stare at her with wide eyes, unable to say a word to her. Of course, I knew Claire would be pissed about this. Especially after she and her father had already rejected

Tanner. If I had any other choice, I wouldn't have done it. She must understand though that I need her. I don't like that I need her, but Claire truly is the best person to testify for me. She knew what I was like prior to that night and she witnessed the deeds of it too. If anyone can clear me, it's Claire.

"I'm not sorry," I tell her. "Bennett said he asked and your father turned him down. I need you."

"If I said no, Rox, it was for a damn good reason. Do you really think my father, the man running for mayor, is going to let me tell the truth about anything? Especially that night? It would look bad on him. And I'm pretty fucking sure you know that. A fourteen-year-old at a party with college kids drinking? He will kill us both before he allows me to utter that."

I slump in defeat. Yeah, I'm very much aware of what Claire's father is like. I was on the receiving end of his ire more times than I would like.

"I know," I tell her. "And if I thought I could get my daughter without you, I would. But you are all I got. Cade's being a dick. And Travis is too afraid to come clean about the drugging. This is my daughter, Claire. I haven't asked you for anything in four years. I'm asking this of you though. I want my daughter."

She shakes her head. "I want to help. I do. We used to talk nonstop about kids and family and who we would marry, but I'm telling you, if your lawyer makes me take the stand, I will lie. I'm sorry. But it's you or me. And I've had to deal with my father far too long."

All of my hope vanishes at her confession. I know her father is terrible, but would he really make her lie under oath? It's against the law and a man running for mayor should at least have some values. I scoff to myself. Of course he would. This is the same man that came on to a fourteen-year-old girl.

"Okay. I'll see if Tanner can rescind the subpoena."

Claire's shoulders drop as she stares at me. Her eyes soften. "I really am sorry, Rox. If there's anything else I can do, anything besides that, I will help."

I look up at her and take in a deep breath. "Can you . . . maybe speak to Cade? I know Bennett sent him a letter as well."

"Do you think that's a good idea?" she questions.

I shrug. I don't really have much choice left. "I don't really have many options here."

"I'll talk to him, but I don't think it's wise to put Cade on the stand after everything that's happened," she tells me. "He could ruin you and Wran."

"He can't possibly hate me that much."

"You underestimate what a broken heart can make people do." She slouches against the opposite wall. "I'll still see where his head is at."

I nod. That's really all I can ask of her.

"Rox?" I glance at her. "For what it's worth, I think you would be an amazing mother. If anyone knows how to treat a kid, it's the girl that got so mistreated."

A tear slides from the corner of my eyes and I bat it away. "I'm going to lose her."

"You got to have faith," she tells me. "The video we made is going to air soon and that will be a win in Wran's favor. It will help."

I nod at her words. That video is the only thing I'm holding on to right now. While I don't see how it will help with the custody trial, I can definitely see it helping Wran. Even if I don't get Harley, at least I will have him, I suppose. Wran will help me through this.

"I'll let you know what Cade says," Claire tells me. "Just please get your lawyer to rescind that."

I nod at her. I'll ask Tanner, but I'm pretty sure he's not going to do it. I'm also pretty sure Josh and Wran aren't going to allow me to ask.

Besides, Claire said it herself.

It's her or me.

And I'm pretty confident that Tanner can talk her into a corner.

CHAPTER 26

WRAN

I pull out of Bennett's yard and head back towards Kingston. I should have known what he would tell me. It's nothing I haven't heard a million times from Josh. Part of me never really thought I would actually see real fucking jail time for loving Rox. But I can't keep pretending that it's not a possibility anymore. It doesn't matter if Rox truly means the world to me. I did something I shouldn't have. I messed up, and if Lynn gets her way, I'm going to pay the price for that.

I fucking hate that woman.

It's not enough that she wants my child, now she wants to take Rox from me too. I don't understand what she gets out of all this. There has to be something more to this than just her doing her job. This is heartless. I don't care how she dresses it up, Lynn is tearing a family apart. She's taking a child from a family that actually gives a fuck. If Rox and I were some fucked up individuals, I could understand. We're not though. Rox has been more than cooperative.

My car doesn't come to a stop until I'm at my pops' apartment. He needs to know what I found out today. I don't even think he'll be able to get me out of this mess at the rate Lynn is going. Hopping out of the car I go up to the door and knock. It opens a second later. Pops stand there freshly shaved, eyes clear, and in actual clothes. Slacks, a nice blue dress shirt, and a tie. His hair is even combed. I haven't been back here since the time he told me to ask Rox to marry me and that blew up in my face. Even though he said he was clean, he was still not as put together as this.

"Going somewhere, old man?" I ask him.

"Nothing that can't wait. What brings you by, son?"

I run a hand over my hair and then scratch the back of my neck. It's been a long time since he's called me son. "Um, you want to go get something to eat at Aunt May's?"

Pops glances at the watch he's wearing, like a legitimate watch with numbers. "You know what, I could certainly use some food."

I examine his get up. "You sure about that? Looks like you had something planned."

"It is not as important."

I don't know how to feel about that statement. For so long, I'd been the least important thing in my pops' life. This is going to take some getting used to. I wave to the car and Pops locks up the place.

We make it to Aunt May's in no time. I frown as I walk inside. It's pretty busy and some of the people turn to see us. More people than not wrinkle their nose at my pops, and I turn to stone in the entryway. Kingston doesn't shy away from shunning people they don't seem fit to exist in this small town. That's exactly what happened when Pops went off his rocker and we lost almost everything. It's fine when it's just me by myself, but I really don't want to hear the whispers.

Pops places a hand on my back and walks past me to one of the booths. I glance at the pedestrians and then make my way over to the booth. Pops look up from the menu and eyes me.

"You seem nervous," he states.

"Nope," I tell him and take the second menu. I don't need to look at the menu to know what I want. I've been eating the same thing since I was eleven years old. Pops doesn't need to know that Aunt May fed Josh, Rox, and I when he was too hammered to cook or when Josh was too tired to. Nope. Pops doesn't need to know any of that.

"So, son, what is the real meaning of your visit? It can't have to do with the trial; you'd call for that."

"How about we just eat first, Pops?" I ask him. I don't want to discuss the trial anywhere someone can overhear.

"Doable." He lowers the menu. "What's good here? Your brother used to mention this place regularly." I snort at that. If only he could remember just how much this place became our home . . .

"Rox and I always get the chicken pot pie. It's pretty good. Taste like Mom's," I tell him.

"That's high praise. No one made better pot pie than your momma."

I leap up from the booth. "I'll put the order in."

I rush away from him and that conversation. Now is not the time to reminisce over Mom. Not that I want to anyway. I ring the bell at the counter and Rox walks out from the back. I forgot she was working today. She's been working on Saturdays since Lynn restricted her visitations. I think this is a way for her to keep her mind off of not being with Harley.

"What are you doing here?" Rox asks she comes to a stop in front of the register. "Shouldn't you be at the garage overseeing construction or something?"

"I told Jesse I wouldn't be in today. Had to deal with some things." I point to the notepad in her hand. "Can I get two of our usuals?"

"Two?" I point down to the booth my pops is in. "Oh."

"Yeah."

"You need a buffer?" she asks. As much as I want to tell her fuck yeah, I don't. I need to talk to Pops about what Bennett told me and I don't want Rox anywhere near that conversation. Not after I promised her she wouldn't lose me again. I might not have a choice.

"Nah, I'm good."

"Alright. I'll get this out to you."

"You do that."

She rolls her eyes and walks away, back into the kitchen. I return to the booth and notice the woman in the booth behind us glaring at Pops. I sit down and ignore her.

"So, that was the little girl you and your brother took in, I take it?" My head snaps up at that. Pops' eyes are on the door Rox went through.

"Why do you say that?" I question him. He shouldn't know what she looks like. Yeah, he's heard of her, but Josh and I took care to keep Rox away from the house when he was around.

"You just loosened up the moment she came out," he says, returning his attention to me.

"What do you mean?"

"When you're a lawyer, son, you have to be able to read people. You walk around like the world is on your shoulders. Just now, your shoulders dropped. You relaxed against the bar. And there was a smile on your face. I'm guessing the only person you're like that with is Miss Roxanna Raine."

"She doesn't like to be called that," I correct him. "But yeah, that was her."

"She's a beautiful young lady. I'm glad you have her."

"Yeah, me too," I tell him.

Rox comes out of the kitchen with our bowls and places them in front of us. She smiles at me and then turns to my pops. "It's good to see you better, sir."

My face drops. When the fuck was Rox around my pops?

My father gives Rox a grin. "You too, Roxy. And good to see you not hiding out in my cellar."

"I loved that cellar. It was my home."

"You have a real home now," Pops tell her.

Rox walks off, back to the kitchen, and I glare at my father. "When did you meet her?"

"Considering you and your brother left a child in my house, I met her on many occasions. Most times I didn't say a word to her. We acknowledged each other and went on our way."

"You never said anything," I comment.

"It's hard to say something when my boys are being better men than me."

"Pops—" I begin, but he cuts me off.

"Wran, I know I was a shitty father. When your mother died, a part of me died with her. And I lost my job, and then it felt like I couldn't even take care of my kids. I went from one of the top lawyers at a top firm to no one wanting to hire me because I worked for that girl's father. My ego took a hit, and I couldn't handle it. I couldn't handle the pressure. I never meant to put that on you boys."

"I understand that pressure," I tell him. "Maybe we should get this to go. I have something I need to talk to you about."

"Sure thing, son."

I have Rox box up our lunch and we head out.

Once back at my dad's apartment, we head inside. The place smells good, like he's been burning some type of candle.

Never did I expect yelling at him to make such a difference in him. I'm not sure if this will last, but I'm proud of him. I'm glad he's trying to get back to where he was before everything happened with Rox's dad.

Pops take a seat on the couch and turns on the TV. I glance at the photos he now has on the wall. I didn't even think he had pictures of us from our childhood. Well, what little childhood we had. There's a photo of all of us together, him, Mom, Josh and me. We're in matching pajama sets. I remember the day we took this photo. It was right before Mom got really sick with cancer. It was the last Christmas we had with her.

I turn away from the photo to find Pops looking at me. He sighs. "Your mother would be happy of the man you became."

A snort mixed with a laugh comes out. "I doubt that. She would probably be pissed that I knocked up a fifteen-year-old girl."

"You seem to keep going back to the fact that this happened when Rox was fifteen."

I shrug. "Everyone's making a big deal out of it."

"It would be a big deal, if I hadn't watch you two grow up together. Everyone in this town knew it was going to happen. You loved her too much and vice versa. It's not a bad thing. It's only a bad thing that they found out."

"You telling me this as a lawyer or a father? Because if this is coming from my lawyer, then you're fired."

"No, I'm talking to you as my son." Pops flips through the channels and decides to land on the news.

There's a man discussing the crazy heat we're having right now. A rain shower is supposed to come in later this week, but I doubt it. We haven't seen hardly any rain this month. It's been humid and hot and sticky. The man's segment flashes over to a woman with dark hair. A photo of Rox pops up on the screen. I go around the couch and grab the remote from Pops. I turn the volume up as high as it can go and take a seat.

"Many of you might have heard of the infamous James Raine of Raine and Sons Law Firm. Earlier this year he was released from prison. Shortly after that, he passed away in a horrific accident. Today, I have an interview with his one surviving heir, Roxanna Raine."

"What the fuck?" I whisper to myself.

"What's this?" my father asks.

I shake my head, keeping my eyes on the television. "I don't know."

"Miss Raine here has been battling for custody of her two-year-old daughter. We're here today to hear her side of the terrible misunderstanding that has caused a young girl a chance to get to know her child."

I stare at Rox as she goes into the story of us. How we met. How Josh and I took her in. She paints me as this savior when in reality I was anything but that. Then she gets to the night things happened.

"Wran and I have always been close. He was my best friend so of course we were. The night we," Rox stops and looks at the camera, "well, you know. He was out with some friends. He came home drunk. That was the first time he'd ever been drunk in my presence. It was baffling. Then he was angry. He kept repeating he wasn't good enough. That he would never be able to give me things I deserved. I didn't know what it was all about, and all I wanted was for him to feel better. So I kissed him. It was just a kiss. It was never met to go any further. But then it did. I didn't stop it. It's every girls' dream to have the guy she likes show her that much attention, so I took it. The next morning we woke up, and he didn't know what had happened. We were on the couch and he was confused. I didn't know what was going on. I didn't think he was so out of it the night before that he wouldn't remember. When I told him, he was upset. We spent the next week apart and on his twentieth birthday, he left."

"That must have been rough on you," someone off camera asks her.

Rox nods her head. "It was the hardest thing at the time I had to get through. The boy that had been my savior, my best friend, was all of a sudden gone. And I was left wondering what I had done wrong."

I turn the TV off, having heard enough. I sit back on the couch. "What the fuck?"

"Son?"

"What the fuck?" I scream out. "When the hell did she film this?"

"Son!" my father shouts and shoves me in the arm. "She just saved you."

I shake my head at him. "No. She just ruined this trial."

"Did you hear what I heard?" Pops' asks me.

"Yeah, she just told the entire state that we fucked."

"No. She told the entire state that you didn't know what was happening. She told them that it was her. That it was all her. She just told them how guilty you felt about the whole situation."

"I didn't feel guilty. That was all fucking lies," I tell my pops. "I remember everything."

"That's not the point, Wran. When people see you now, they're not going to see a potential child molester. They're going to see a man that was put in an unthinkable situation and did the only thing he could do. Leave."

"And that's a good thing, Pops?"

"It's better than the alternatives and it might just save you from jail time."

I throw my head back against the cushion. I can't believe Rox did this. I can't believe she would put all the blame on herself.

"What are the consequences for her? For her admitting this?" I ask my pops.

That depends on the judge at the court hearing. "Many judges would see this for what it is, a child admitting to doing something that got taken completely out of control.

She was fifteen. It was her first time. And like she said, she didn't know any better. You may be asked if you would like to press charges, but if you say no, there's nothing to be done about the situation."

"I need to go see Rox," I tell my father and get up from the couch.

I don't wait for a response from him. Racing out of the house, I jump into my car and race back to the diner. I race inside and see Rox setting a plate down at a table. I jog over to her and grab her hand.

"Hey!" she yells at me as I haul her from the diner. "What are you doing? I'm working."

Leading her to the side of the building, I slam my mouth down against hers she struggles for only a second before letting me take control. I shove her up against the wall and kiss her like I'm giving my very essence to her. When I finally break the kiss, I lean my forehead against hers.

"What's wrong?" she asks me.

"Nothing. I just saw your interview."

"Oh. That." She shifts on her feet. "Are you mad?"

"No. Rox the night we made love was the best night of my life. I had wanted you for so long. I hope you don't believe anything you said."

She shakes her head. "No, Lex sorta walked me through what to say and not say to make you sound innocent."

"Well, my pops seem to think it worked. I think you're fucking crazy."

"Then I guess I'm crazy. I would do anything to keep you Wran. Besides it wasn't all a lie." She props her hands on her waist and perches her lips. "You did ghost me for a week after that and you did leave."

"I ghosted you because Josh found out. He said it was clear on my face. I left the following week on my birthday because if was getting hard to pretend I didn't want you and I knew if I let myself have you like that again, I couldn't blame it on being drunk."

"You can have me now. All of me."

My mouth descends on hers once again. "You have no clue how much you mean to me."

Rox wraps her arms around my neck and press her firm body into me. "Show me."

I take ahold of her hand and together we run across the road to my car. I press her up against the passenger car door and steal another kiss before opening it and letting her in. She giggles as I slam the door and dart over to my side. The keys fumble in my hold as I attempt to start the car. Rox slides across the seat and picks up the keys. She puts them in the ignition and I'm off down the road before another giggle has time to leave her pillowy lips.

Rox doesn't give my car time to come to a complete stop when we pull into the driving lot of our complex. She's out of the car and rushing up the stairs within seconds. I follow after her, not even setting the alarm on the car. By the time I make it into the apartment, her shirt is already off. The door shuts behind me with a thump, and I grab Rox. I rotate us around and pin her against the same door.

She rises on her toes and presses a firm kiss against my mouth. "I want you now."

"Be patient."

"No." She shakes her head. "I've been patiently waiting my whole life for you to see me as your equal. I've been waiting three years to have you again. I'm done waiting, Wran Belmont. So take me now."

I stare at the beautiful girl before me, taking in every aspect of her. If only she knew exactly how she makes me feel, she would already know she's my equal. She's everything I've ever wanted and more. She's it for me.

"Rox, from the moment I met you, you have been my equal. Even when I blamed you for the way my life turned out, you were my equal. Because the day I saw you in the snow, I thought my mother had sent me an angel. A beautiful, frozen angel of my own."

"Show me," she tells me again.

My mouth crashes against hers again, and I do just that.

CHAPTER 27

WRAN

A subtle warmth against my side has me cracking my eyes open. Platinum blond hair fans out over my chest and I grin at the sleeping girl. Last night flashes to the forefront of my mind and my grin widens. I've thought about being with Rox so many times over the last three years. I know admitting me thinking about her in that way sounds creepy as fuck, and I would murder any other man that thought it, but I'm done shaming myself for wanting her. For wanting things with her. She's been my destiny since the day I found her and there is absolutely nothing wrong with us.

Nothing at all.

I ease the hair covering her face away. Rox looks so relaxed right now. Like nothing can harm her. It's different. I'm used to her dreams terrifying her into my bed. Seeing her sleeping like this is a bit nerve-racking. I like it. At least now she's here because she wants to be and she's not running from her terrors.

I ease away from under her, doing my best not to wake her. She turns the second I'm free and curls up into a ball. It's cute. She's cute. I watch her for a few moments before I have to force myself out of the room and down the hall. It would be all too easy for me to crawl back into bed with her and recreate the magic of last night. To consume her. But I know she has to be hurting after what we did.

Once wasn't enough for either of us. Hell, we didn't even make it to the couch the first time. I had her against the door. It was fast and rough and depraved. I'm not sure either of us really cared; we were too far gone to stop. Fuck, I really need to stop thinking about last night.

Adjusting myself in my boxers, I head into the kitchen. The time on the microwave catches my attention and I scowl at it. I had nothing to do today, but I don't normally sleep past noon. I wash my hands in the sink before heading to the fridge to see what I can make Rox. I know she has to be starving. We didn't eat yesterday, and it's been well over sixteen hours since I dragged her from Aunt May's.

I frown at the slim pickings. Since Rox has been staying with other people, there hasn't been much food in this house. I either eat at the diner or grab something at Josh's place. That's a decision I'm really starting to regret. I grab the bread, eggs, and milk that I hope isn't expired and begin working on some French toast.

A creak from down the hall lets me know that Rox is awake. The pitter patter of her feet coming my way distracts me from the bread sitting in the milk mixture. My eyes roam over her dressed in my shirt from yesterday and the very obvious bed hair. She comes over to the bar and looks at the ingredients before giving me her attention.

"Are you hungry?" I ask her.

She nods and comes around the island to me. She wraps her arms around me from behind as I place the bread in the sizzling pan.

"I'll have breakfast done in a bit." Even though it's nowhere near breakfast time.

"I'm not hungry for that," she whispers against my bare back as her small hands make their way into my boxers. Her soft caress instantly wakes me up and I turn the stove off.

"Rox." I turn to her. "There's no fucking way you're ready for me. You have to be in pain."

She shakes her head and drops to her knees. Her big purple eyes look up at me through thick lashes. "I have a lifetime of pent up want. And I'm not waiting anymore."

She tugs my boxers down. The moment she takes me in her delicate hands, I know nothing else is getting done today. I've created a little fiend, and I fucking love it. Rox strokes for a second before her hot mouth descends on me. Gripping the back of her neck, I pull her in closer, forcing myself farther down her throat. She coughs around me and attempts to pull back, but I don't allow it. She started this, but it's going to go my way. And right now, I don't want her soft kisses and barely touches. I want to see her slobbering on me and panting in heat. I want to see that blond hair plastered to her sweaty skin.

Rox grips my thighs as she does exactly what I want. I watch her pretty little head bob as I lean back against the stove. A guttural groan escapes me as she takes me fully and licks at my base. My eyes drift close as my body tenses. I shake my head; this is not freaking ending. Not right now. Twining a hand through the hair at the base of her head, I pull her precious mouth away from my cock.

"As much as I like this side of you, I'm not coming down your fucking throat right now," I tell her.

She stares at me from where she's still perched on her knees, brows dip. "And if I want to taste you?"

I shake my head at her. "You'll have to wait until after I make you fall apart first."

Her cheeks redden as I lift her from the floor. Her legs go around me and I stop when I feel her warm core against me. Her wet, bare, warm core. Fucking hell! This girl is going to be the death of me.

"Rox," I say as calm as possible. "Where are your fuck-ing panties?"

"They would have been in the way. Besides, I'm pretty sure you ripped them yesterday." She turns her face so that I can't see the pink moving up her neck and to her face. I don't have to see it to know it's there. I know her. I know her body. I know her soul.

I know it all.

Because she's mine.

Mine.

Mine.

Mine.

I set her on the edge of the island counter. Her eyes still don't fully meet mine like they did a moment ago when she was sucking me off. Instead of waiting on her attention, I plunge a finger inside her wanting body. She's already ready for me. I pump my finger a few times as I drop to my knees before her and take her all in. I always knew her lips were the only part of her body that held any color. It's true about these lips as well.

Rox grinds against my finger, chasing more pleasure. Whimpers leave her as my speed picks up. I lick my lips as her essence seeps out onto the counter. I rise enough to lick it up. No part of her is going to waste.

"Wran." My name crosses her lips like she's in pain, yet her writhing clearly tells me it's the opposite. "More. I want more."

I want more too.

More of everything.

More of her like this.

More of her taking my cum.

I want the whole fucking shebang. The white picket fence. The dog running circles around our feet. Her pregnant with my kids. My body immediately goes still at that thought. Fuck. I didn't even think to ask Rox how she feels about any of this. We went bare all yesterday, and I was just about to do it again. She might not even want more kids. Fuck, I hope she does.

"Wran?" Rox asks me when she notices how still I am. "What's wrong?"

"Rox, we've been fucking since yesterday." I rise completely from the floor and stare down at her. My eyes linger on her covered torso a little longer than necessary. While I'm not opposed to any of this, she might have some reservations about it all. I don't want her thinking with her libido and not her head. This could go to shit fast if none of this is truly what she desires.

"I'm aware," she mutters as she closes her legs and pulls down the hem of my shirt.

"Are you on birth control?" I straighten up ask her.

Her whole body turns a bright shade of pink as she shakes her head. No. Okay. I simply have to figure out where her head is at about having another kid. I mean, she did get pregnant the first time we did anything. The probability is pretty high. I tone down my excitement at the potential opportunity. I don't want to freak her out, but fuck, I want that. I missed everything the first time around; I want to fully experience a pregnant Rox.

"I never really thought about getting on it. Josh took me to the doctor after Harley was born, but I just didn't make it a habit of taking the pills. There was no point since I wasn't, well, active when you were away."

I nod at her explanation and hate what I'm about to ask. But I need to know. "So you and Cade really never—"

"No!" she cuts me off and tugs on the shirt to cover her more. "It never got that far. We made out and he touched me and stuff, but we never took it farther."

I'm not going to admit to being surprised by that. The way the boy has been acting, one would think they'd been doing more than making out. I'm glad as fuck that they hadn't, but that still doesn't change anything here.

"Okay . . ." I grab her fidgeting hands. "So how do you feel about having more kids? With me?"

She gulps and says nothing.

"I just need to know if I need to go to Arlington and get you a plan B or something," I tell her. I don't want to do that at all, but I don't want to scare her either. If she doesn't want more kids after what she's gone through with Harley, then that's okay. I'll deal. I just want her happy.

"You don't have to," she tells me, and a weight is lifted off my shoulders. "Not unless you don't want more kids. In the future."

"I want a whole fucking football team," I admit to her.

Rox chokes on a laugh. "I don't know about that."

"So you would be fine if you were to get. . ." I point to her stomach.

She smiles at me. "Things aren't ideal. I would like you to put on a condom now, but I wouldn't be upset. I like being a mom. I just don't like the situation with Harley."

I grin at her and pull her to the edge of the island. Gripping her legs, I wrap them around me. "So what you're really saying is if there's a little Jr. in there, we get to keep him?"

Rox wraps her arms around my neck and kisses me softly. "You, Wran Belmont, would actually want to be a father? Like a real father to kids we actually get to keep?"

"With you," I say between kisses, "more than anything."

Her legs tighten around me and I can see the moment she's back to wanting me. A soft whimper leaves her lips as she begins to grind against my stomach. I grip the edge of the shirt she's wearing and pull it over her head. I want to see all of her. I want to see her body take me. She stops though, just as I'm about to take one of her pretty pink nipples in my mouth.

"I want all of that," she tells me. "But in the future. In like five years. Not right now, Wran. Put on a freaking condom."

I groan in protest. I don't want to wait that fucking long. I don't get a chance to tell her that as my phone goes off in the other room.

"Ignore it," she tells me.

I stare at her for a long time. I should fucking ignore it. I should stay here with my girl and be in this moment and fantasize about our ten kids, but I can't. That could be Jesse about the garage or Pops or Josh. I need to answer calls from all of them. Especially Jesse. I can't fuck up the opportunity he's given me.

"It's a Sunday," Rox protests. "It can wait until tomorrow."

"Baby, it will only be a minute."

She pouts not liking my answer to that.

"You know, that pout makes you look like a fucking kid."

The pout morphs into a scowl.

"I'll be back." I lean down and kiss her. "You just be ready when I do."

I walk away from her before I change my mind and down the hall to my room. The ringing stops only to start right back up. Pops' name flashes across the screen as I take it from the nightstand. I instantly answer.

"What's up, Pops?" I ask and sit on the edge of the bed.

"Lynn's lawyer contacted me," he says right away and my entire being tightens. If that woman is contacting Pops on a weekend, it can't be good. Hell, it's never good when Lynn-fucking-Adams demands attention.

"And?" I ask, waiting for him to tell me my life is officially over.

"You're free. She saw the interview too."

My mind doesn't register what he's saying right away.

"Son, do you hear me?" Pops asks when I say nothing.

Free?

"No jail?" I finally answer.

"She dropped the case."

"I get to stay with Rox?" I ask him.

This seems fucking unreal. Tanner assured me there was no way I wasn't going to face some time. I've been preparing this entire time for Rox and Harley to be taken care of. I had Jesse set aside a fund just for them in case I was sent away.

"Wran? Son, are you okay?" my dad asks me. "You get to keep your family."

I choke on my words. "Thank you, Pops."

"I did nothing," he tells me. "Just don't go around getting anymore minors pregnant."

"Not a chance in hell. I have my Rox."

"You should formally introduce us now. And I want to see my grandbaby."

I nod even though he can't see me. "We have to get custody of her first, but you have my word that you will see her as soon as I have her back. I'm gonna tell Rox the good news now."

"Right, right. Talk to you later, son."

He hangs up without another word. A grin breaks across my face. I'm free. I'm going to be able to be here with Rox. I'm not going to lose my girl over some dumb ass lawsuit. I lay back on the bed and stare up at the glowing stars on my ceiling. Maybe we'll get our Neverland now. Maybe now I can be the man I know I can be and give Rox all her dreams. Even the ones she doesn't know she still wants.

I get up from the bed and head back into the kitchen. The smell of cinnamon permeates the space as I watch Rox at the stove. She's back in my shirt and flipping French toast. She glances up from the pan and smiles at me. I guess my two minutes was longer than the one I promised her. I go over to her and pick up my boxers in front of the stove. I slide them on with ease before wrapping my arms around Rox and pecking the top of her hair.

"What was that for?" she asks and sets two slices on a plate.

"When we first met, you wanted me to be your Peter Pan and fly you to Neverland. I was so full of rage that I couldn't see how perfect you were for me. I couldn't see that I needed you just as much as you needed me."

Rox looks over her shoulder at me, her brows dipping in confusion. "Are you okay? Who called?"

I turn her around and take her face between my palms. My mouth descends on hers and she stiffens, not sure how to take this. But when I don't stop the kiss, she kisses me back.

Pulling back after a moment, I place my forehead against hers. "I'm okay. I'm better than fucking okay. I have you and I will never take you for granted again. I will do my best never to hurt you again. You, Roxanna Raine, are it for me."

Her eyes flicker across my face. "You're freaking me out. Who called?"

"My dad," I tell her. "He got a call from Lynn's lawyer. She's dropping my case. I'm not going to jail. I'm not going to be labeled as a fucking perv. I get to keep you. I get to keep the love of my life."

Rox throws herself into me and I feel her tears against my chest immediately. "I can't believe this. I was so terrified for you. I thought I was going to lose you again."

Tilting her chin up, I shake my head at her. "I'm never leaving without you again. I can't. You are my heart and living without it the first time was hell. I'm not putting either of us through it again. You hear me?"

Nodding, she wipes the tears away and turns in my hold back to the French toast. She removes the remaining two from the pan and sets them on a separate plate.

"I made you breakfast," she says. "You know, since you couldn't get that done without distraction."

"You are the best fucking distraction in the world," I mutter into her hair.

She hands me a plate but I take both of them.

Heading over to the couch, I blurt out, "Move back in. It's not going to matter if you're living with me or not anymore. I want you back here."

Rox drops down beside me and takes her plate. She draws her knees up as I turn on the TV and find something to watch.

She cuts a corner of her food but doesn't eat it. "Okay."

Did I hear her right?

"Okay? I question.

She pops the food into her mouth and nods. "Yes. I'll move back in, but there are conditions."

"Conditions?" I set the plate on the coffee table and give Rox my full attention. "What kind of conditions?"

"First, no alcohol in the house. I never want to see you that way again."

"Done," I tell her. "I haven't had a drink since I started at Jesse's."

"Second," she holds up two fingers, "you have to stop nagging me about working at Aunt May's. That diner feels like home too."

I hold back a rebuttal on that point. It's not like she's going to be there much longer. "Fine."

"And third, you have to give me all the orgasms you refused me over the years."

Fucking hell.

I grab her ankle from where it's tucked underneath her and pull her to me. I remove the plate from her hands as she straddles me. "Done, done, and fucking done. Anything else?"

Rox shakes her head. "Not as of right now."

"Good." I pry her lip from between her teeth. "I think now is the perfect time to start on those orgasms."

She giggles, but I show her just how serious I am.

I spend the rest of the day consuming her.

CHAPTER 28

ROX

I let out a deep breath as I look over my last exam. Today has been long. All of my teachers agreed to let me take my finals early due to the custody hearing this week. So for the last six hours, I've been sitting in this room listening to the tic tic tic of the clock while I do my best not to break under the pressure of three sets of eyes on me. Honestly, I don't know why the principal had to sit in on this. Surely, he had actual work to do beyond watching me overthink math equations and scramble to remember theories.

The buzzing of the timer goes off, and I frown at the test. I set my pencil down with reluctance. There're still five questions I didn't get to and I'm not even sure I did that well on the rest of this exam. My plan was to study over the weekend, refresh my mind, but then Wran showed up at the diner and my plan went down the toilet. Hopefully, I did well enough that my standing is still fine.

Mr. White comes over to the table and retrieves my test. I finally look up to everyone only to see them all smiling at me. Even my principal and I didn't think he liked me much.

"We are so very proud to have been your teachers," Mrs. Zannah speaks.

My brows dip at her comment. She's my AP Art teacher. I didn't do anything in her class besides hand out supplies. The only reason she's here is because none of my academic teachers had time in their schedules to watch me take these. She volunteered.

"Thank you?" It comes out more like a question than a genuine thanks. I actually am thankful to these people. If I lived anywhere else, if anyone other than the Belmonts would've found me, I probably would have been in a foster home or state custody. None of the teachers here turned me in. None of them turned their backs on me, even when things got hard and I started flaking.

"I probably won't see you again until graduation, so I wanted to give you something," Mrs. Zannah says and comes forth.

I tilt my head at her. While she's been my favorite teacher, I wasn't expecting much for doing exactly what everyone else is doing. The door to the class closes and I glance over at the door.

"The competition ended," she continues, and I give her my full attention. "Your piece came in fourth, which I honestly think is utterly ridiculous. That was some of your best work."

I cringe at that. That piece was not my best work. It was rushed and streaky, and my shading was absolute trash. I only entered it because it felt good to actually be painting again. Mrs. Zannah pulls a chair over and takes a seat in front of me. She pulls out an envelope and hands it over.

"While you didn't win, there was a ton of interest in the piece." I open the envelope. "Someone bought it. I hope you don't mind that I sold it for you."

My mouth falls open at the check in my hands. "Someone paid $5000 for that painting?"

She nods.

"Who?" I ask. It's hard to believe anyone would pay that much for that piece. It was horrible.

"He asked me not to tell you, but I've seen the turmoil in you both. And I think it's time you two make up. Cade bought the painting."

My curiosity falls away and I push the check back over to Mrs. Zannah. "No. Give it back."

"Roxanna."

"Mrs. Zannah, no. Too much has happened. I don't want anything from him."

She blinks at me a few times. "I can see that, but can I give you some advice?"

I nod. There's not anything she can say that's going to make me change my mind about accepting anything from him. I trusted Cade. I would have done anything for him. He broke us and then threw everything he did for me in my face. I'm never going to give him the chance to do that again.

I might not know what game he's playing with buying my piece, but I'm not falling for it.

"I saw the video." That's the worst thing she could have admitted. "And Cade has talked to me about everything. He opened up when he bought your painting. Roxanna, people make mistakes. But it's about how they grow from those mistakes."

"I haven't seen any growth from Cade. I haven't seen an apology or anything," I tell her. "Whatever you think you see in Caden Jefferson is a lie. He is a spoiled rich boy and I'm done letting him live rent free in my head."

Mrs. Zannah sighs as the bell rings. "You won't even consider forgiving him? You two were close."

I shake my head. "I'm so tired of caring about everyone else but myself. Forgiving him isn't an option at this point. He'll never accept that I don't care about him the way he wants. And it would be unfair of me to force him to live through such pain. This is best for us both."

My teacher crosses her arms and nods. "I suppose I can understand your point. You should still talk to him though. Clear the air."

Giving her a small grin, I stand from my desk. "I'll think about it, but I should really be going. I need to see Tasha before I head out."

She doesn't say anything else as I make my way out of the class and into the empty hallway. There are a few stragglers hanging around but for the most part, it's just me and the boisterous ticking of the massive clock hanging above the glass entrance of the school. I head down the hall to my locker and open it. My eyes dip at the emptiness of it. Only the small crossbody bag and the journal Tasha gave me earlier this year sits inside. The faint sound of giggling catches my attention as I take my belongings. I glance to the sound of the giggles and frown. A girl with red hair is leaning against the wall, twirling her hair, and beaming up at a guy like he hung the moon and stars. She's looking at him the exact same way I used to look at Wran. Like he's her whole world crammed into one human being.

A part of me wants to tell her to run. I know she can't be any older then fifteen or sixteen. And she has her whole life to live. However, another part of me doesn't want to begrudge her the opportunity of finding her person. And who knows, he just may be her person. Just because mine was snatched away and my life turned into a Lifetime movie, doesn't mean hers will.

Deciding to mind my own business, I bypass the couple and head to the counselor's office. Tasha's door is open but her head's down. I tap on her door to get her attention. She looks up and beckons me inside. I leave the door ajar since this won't be long and I'm only here to drop off the notebook one last time. Taking a seat before her, I hand over the journal. She takes it and sets it aside without even reading it, which has been her go to since giving me the thing. She would much rather I tell her what I wrote, confide in her, rather than snooping through the book.

"You did really well on your first couple of exams today," she finally speaks. "I'm sure you did just as superb on your last."

My nose scrunches up at her words. I tanked the last one. I'm almost positive about that. "I think I did so–so. Am I still in the running for valedictorian?"

She nods. "You will be this year's valedictorian. Your only real competition was Claire, but I can't see her surpassing you. Yes, there is a possibility if she aces her exams this week, but as of right now, your standing is still intact."

I should have known Claire would be right behind me. The way her father pushes her to be the best at everything just so he can tear her down in private, I'm honestly surprised that she isn't ahead of me. I know I had the motivation to work my butt off the last three years but still. I don't think I worked that hard. Not harder than Claire.

"That's good," I say and rise from the chair.

"Wait," Tasha stops me. "I actually wanted to talk to you about a few things. You might want to close the door."

I look from her and then to the door. That sounds serious. I take the few steps to the entrance and pull the door shut. I go back to her and sit down, bringing my bag around and clutching it for dear life.

"You can relax," Tasha tells me. "I just want to see where your head is at with this trial."

I shrug again. "There's really only two ways this can go. Either I get custody or I don't."

"What happens if you don't?" She straightens in her chair and tilts her head at me, eyes searching my face for truthful answers.

My eyes drop from hers and I fiddle with the buckle on my bag. "I haven't really thought about it, but I can't lose her."

"You have an entire community backing you and Wran," she tells me. "But if for some reason this trial doesn't go as we all think it should, I want you to make a promise to yourself."

Biting on my bottom lip, I hesitate to answer. A promise like that could be anything. I don't know if I'm at a place right now where I can promise anything. Especially not to myself.

Before I have a chance to voice my thoughts, Tasha raises her hand to stop me. "I know what's going on in your mind right now. But if you take anything from the sessions we've had together, please let it be that you know you are worthy. You are worthy of so much more than what you are allowing yourself to have. I want you to promise to live your life to the fullest, whether that's with Harley or without. I can imagine the thought of moving on from your child is painful, but if things don't happen the way you want, you need to know that you can move on. Harley will grow and ask questions, and eventually she will come looking. You need to give her something worthwhile to find if that so happens to be the case."

I shift in my seat. That will never happen. I will never stop fighting for Harley. Even if things don't go as planned,

I'll just search for another way. Lynn can't win this. She can't just decide she wants my baby and take her. Besides, what type of life would it be knowing I didn't give it my all for the one person that means more to me than anything? I can already feel the guilt eating away at me for Tasha even suggesting that I move on from Harley. Things will go my way this week. I will get my child. I must. They have to see that I don't deserve what Lynn has put me through. And I certainly don't deserve to lose custody of my child because of something that happened to me. I should have been more responsible, yes, but I was a child and I've grown so much since then.

"Rox?" Tasha pulls me out of my head.

"I can't promise you that. She's the only thing that truly matters to me," I tell her. "Besides, it's not like I have a place outside of this town and Aunt May's. Not one college has gotten back to me. I'm a big, huge, red flag to them."

A grin spreads across my counselor's face as she sits back in her chair and crosses her arms. "I wouldn't say such a thing. I would bet a lot on Roxanna Raine and Roxanna Belmont. You've lived an interesting life."

I mimic her position and sit back. "If that's the case, how come not even the community college has accepted me. All of my friends have gotten letters. I've gotten nothing. I appreciate you helping, but no one wants me."

With a sigh, Tasha sits forward and opens her desk drawer. She pulls out a handful of envelopes and fans them out in front of me. "You've gotten a letter back from every school we applied to. And even the ones I applied to on your behalf. Just because things have happened in your past doesn't mean you aren't worthy, Roxanna. I believe in you. Wran believes in you. Kingston believes in you. You need to start believing you are more than this little town."

My eyes flicker across the letters laid out in front of me. There's eleven of them. That's six more than I applied for. Scooting forward in my chair, I pull one letter forward. It's not the big flashy envelope like Charlie got from Julliard, but a regular sized one like most bills arrive in. It's thick though. I glance at all the letters. Right away, I can tell some are acceptance letters. They're in the flashy envelopes. Others are in plain white ones. Some look jam packed with papers and others don't.

"What are you waiting for?" Tasha asks me. "Open them."

I do as she says and open the first one. I don't read past "You've been accepted." I pull the next letter and the next and the next until all of them are opened. I get into all but three, but I knew it was a long shot with the Ivy schools. They look for more than exceptional grades. They want well rounded students, and I have not been lucky enough to have the opportunities of my peers.

Tasha hands me a tissue and I look up from the letters. "See? I told you there was a future after all of this."

I nod. She might have been right, but none of these letters change the fact that Harley comes first. I have to get her back, and if it doesn't happen this week, I can't just up and leave the state as if nothing happened. Maybe the community college, but that's all I'm hoping for until after the hearing is over. If I win, then maybe I'll let myself think about the other offers.

"You don't look like you're happy," Tasha says. "This is a joyous moment!"

"I am happy," I manage to tell her. "Truly, I am, but none of it matters until after the trial. I can't make a decision until then."

"That's understandable. I simply wanted you to know that you do have choices. And people do want you. All of you."

I give her my acknowledgement and rise. "Thank you, Ms. Flannigan. These sessions have been helpful."

"Even though you were forced into them?"

A laugh escapes me. "Yes. Writing helped. More than I thought it would to be honest."

"I'm glad." Tasha stands and glances behind me. I look over my shoulder, but the door is still closed. "Um, this is going to be weird, but I have to ask."

I turn back around at the sound of Tasha's unsure tone. "What?"

"Um, has Josh said anything about me recently?"

I shake my head. "No, not really. Why?"

"Nothing you need to worry about."

Crossing my arms, I arch a brow at her. She knows all my dirty little secrets. Now it's time for her to spill. "What has he done?"

Tasha scratches the top of her head. "I just haven't heard from him in like two weeks."

"Well," I try to come up with a reasonable explanation for Josh's behavior. "He has been pretty busy with Tanner and the trial. I'm sure it's nothing. I mean, c'mon, it's Josh."

"Yeah, you're right. Go enjoy the rest of your day. To-morrow's going to be big for you."

I nod and turn for the door. Stopping just short of it, I glance over my shoulder to see Tasha staring at her phone on the desk.

"Josh is like a brother to me," I say, pulling Tasha's attention away from the phone. "I might not know him the way you know him, but I do know him. And I know that when Josh loves, he loves hard. He loves with all his heart and he'll do anything to protect those he cares about. He made you one of those people. If he's not calling, there's a reason why. Just be patient with him. As much as he gets on my nerves, I do love him. And he deserves happiness too."

Tasha's frown slowly but surely turns upright. "Okay, I'll give him some time."

"Good," I state and head out of the office. Unzipping my purse, I pull out my phone and pull up Josh's number. He answers on the first ring, and I don't give him time to say a word. "We need to talk."

CHAPTER 29

ROX

I twist my hands in my lap as I sit in the backseat of Tanner's fancy car with Wran right beside me. Today is the day and for the life of me, I can't remember how to breathe. Ever since opening my eyes this morning, it's felt like someone has been holding me down and covering my mouth. I've been hot then cold and then hot again. It's the nerves, I know, but it isn't helping, and neither is the white dress I'm wearing. Long sleeves with a lacy delicate bodice and flowing, loose fitted skirt. Tanner said that it's meant to make me look virginal, lovelorn, but I feel anything but innocent today. I'm going there to fight for my child. No judge is going to be fooled by this look.

Wran takes ahold of my hand and pulls it over to him. He places a peck in the center of my palm before placing our joined hands on his thigh. Tanner didn't want Wran here today. I had to fight to get him to agree to let Wran come. Wran promised to be on his best behavior and to sit in the back away from prying eyes. Tanner's hope is that my interview will draw a crowd. I'm not sure how that will help me, but Tanner seems to think it will.

"Are you okay?" Wran whispers to me.

I turn to him and shake my head. "How can I be okay with this? It's not fair."

Wran unbuckles my seatbelt and slides me across the black leather. He lets go of my hand only to drape his arm around my shoulders and pull me closer. He leans down and kisses the top of my head.

"Nothing in life is fair, Rox. But you are my little fighter, my Wendy, my lost girl. If anyone can handle this, it's you. Just remember that you did nothing wrong. It's not wrong for us to love each other."

"But it was." I drop my head against his chest. "I was a kid. And you kept telling me we couldn't happen-"

"Rox," Wran cuts me off, and lowers his voice. "We were going to happen no matter what. I was in love with you. I am still in love with you. None of this is your fault. I was the adult. Not you. Let all that bullshit go. I don't care what Tanner prepped you to say, I want you to tell your truth. All the ugly bits of us. All the amazing bits of us. Your truth is what's going to get us our child, because no one can hear our story and think it's anything other than what it is. A girl and a boy falling in love."

I glance up at him and nod. The car finally comes to a stop outside a massive, red brick building with white stone pillars. The US flag hangs from the very top of a clock tower and I frown at it. That flag is supposed to represent justice and freedom. Yet there's nothing just about today.

I glance from the flag to the press standing on the steps waiting. My trial isn't the only one happening today, but I know they are here for me. Looks like Bennett's getting what he wants. I bite down on my lip, wondering what they are going to think about Wran and Josh both showing up here with me. Since the interview, I've heard whispers at school. There's been speculation about Josh and me, but I kept quiet as Tanner suggested. I hope the press doesn't think that. I hope that Lynn doesn't think that. When everything first happened, Josh was Lynn's target. We were close after Harley was taken.

Wran squeezes my leg. "You got this."

I look up front to where Josh and Tanner are. Tanner gives one sharp nod before he opens his door. Wran opens his door and steps out. I take in one last deep breath, trying to get as much oxygen as possible, and get out as well. The sound of the press is deafening. Cameras point at us, and questions are cried out. Wran pulls me in close to him as I do my best to ignore the questions. Tanner takes the lead and we all follow up the matte white steps, the brothers flanking me on both sides.

"Roxanna Raine!" I hear someone yell. "What would your father think about this if he was alive?"

My body tenses and my feet stop moving.

"Ignore it," Wran whispers into my ear.

"Do you think he would approve of you and the Belmont brothers?" another reporter asks.

I turn around, even though I'm well aware I shouldn't.

"Don't," Josh hisses so only our little group can hear.

I ignore him and glare down the reporters. "My father's opinions haven't weighed on me since I was six. He's exactly where he belongs."

I turn away from the onslaught of questions to find Tanner and the Belmonts all glaring at me. I push past them and into the building. A pristine white atrium greets me, but I don't get a chance to take in much as someone gestures for me to proceed into another set of doors. I come to a complete halt when I see the sheer number of people present in the room. Every pew is filled and there's even some people standing along the wall.

A slight shiver runs up my spine and I gulp. This courtroom is the most intimidating place I've ever stepped foot. But maybe that has more to do with the fact that my life is about to change today more so than the people filling the benches.

"This way, Miss," the guard says as people start turning around in their seats. I can make out Aunt May and Wran's father. Ms. Zannah is here and so is Tasha. My friends are here, but everyone else is strangers.

My gaze quickly moves from them and to the cherry wood wall barricading the judge's bench. It's empty. I don't linger too much on that nor the empty witness stand as I head down the aisle. They won't be empty for long. Instead, my eyes drift to where Lynn stands dressed in her usual black sheath dress and court shoes. Harley stands before her in a pretty pink dress that reminds me of the ones my father used to dress me in. My daughter's dress is not too different than the one Tanner put me in except her bodice is laced with flower embroidery and the skirt is full on tulle.

My feet stop and the crowd starts whispering.

Lynn turns back to see what the commotion is about when she spots me. She squares her shoulders and smiles. I don't return her phony gesture. As I draw closer, Harley finally turns as if she could sense me. Her eyes widen and a grin breaks out on the toddler's face.

"Mommy!" she shrieks and takes a step in my direction. Lynn bends down and tells her something before Harley can get too far. My daughter pouts and I'm tempted to go to her. Someone squeezes my hand to keep me in place. I look over my shoulder to see Wran. His eyes are glued on Harley as well.

"We will win this case," he says so only I can hear. "She will be coming home today. Just stay calm. You can do this."

I give him a slight nod. Whether I could do this part has never been the question. I know I can do this. What I don't know is if I can handle what happens if I lose.

I yank my head away from the toddler and rush the rest of the way to my seat. I plop down, my eyes focused straight ahead. I hear Harley whimpering, but I know if I look for one second at her, I'm going to rush Lynn and take my baby. I can't allow that to happen.

Bennett takes the seat next to me and starts unloading his black briefcase. He has so many different papers that I honestly don't know where to look. As if feeling my eyes on him and what he's doing, Tanner looks up from his paperwork. He gives me a sharp nod and I turn back to the front of the room.

An officer in the corner of the room clears his throat and turns to face us all. "Please stand."

I stand with the rest of the room as a man adorned in a black robe emerges from somewhere behind his seat. He searches the room taking in me and then Lynn. I turn to look at her and my daughter too, but Harley isn't up front like she was a moment ago. My eyes instantly go to the back of the room to search out Wran. Sure enough, he and Josh both are standing against the back wall. Both brothers look as if they are mere spectators. Like this hearing doesn't bother them at all. I wish I could be as calm as them. Right now, it feels like everyone can see me falling apart.

The judge takes his seat and picks up the cherry wood gavel. He bangs it down once and I flinch. My heart instantly begins racing.

"Court is now in session," he announces.

Everyone but Lynn's lawyer drops to their seat and the courtroom gets quiet.

"We're here today to discuss the custody of Harley Raine. I've had the chance to go over the initial trial that took place two and a half years go along with the new evidence delivered on behalf of Roxanna Raine. Will the defendant please proceed?"

A man in a navy two-piece suit step forward. "Good morning. I'm here today to defend the state on their decision to withhold custody of Harley Raine from Roxanna Raine. Our plaintiff is going to try to paint a picture of an innocent girl who was never in the wrong and deserves every right to a toddler she bore at the tender age of fifteen. I am here to prove that same girl is a child herself and has not yet fully grasped the responsibility it takes to care, provide for, and maintain the health of a toddler who is truly innocent in this case."

Shame washes over me at Lynn's lawyer's statement, and I slump a little in my chair. Is that really what Lynn thinks of me? That I'm an immature child? I tried to do everything she asked of me. From the AA meetings to the random drug tests. I did everything. There's nothing more I could have done besides roll over and hand her Harley.

"All evidence may be presented now," the judge announces. "Mr. Cavanagh, will the defendant please present their case?"

Lynn's lawyer, Mr. Cavanagh turns to face the room. He runs both hands over his already slicked back hair, eyes flickering in my direction for only a mere second.

"Ladies and gentlemen, if you would please turn your attention to the screen," Mr. Cavanagh gestures to the left of my table as a blank projector screen lowers, his voice coming out strong and resilient. An image of me sitting in Cade's lap flashes across the screen and my heart plummets. I shake my head at the screen. This can't be happening. They can't possibly show this to a room full of people.

I turn around in my seat to see Wran glaring at the screen, his hands fisted. My gaze quickly moves to Aunt May. She wasn't in the diner the night this happened, and I never told her. She never brought up the situation, so I figured she didn't know. I turn back to meet Mr. Cavanagh's eyes.

"As I mentioned earlier, Roxanna Raine's maturity has yet to reach a point where she is capable of protecting herself, let alone a toddler. The footage I'm presenting shows clear evidence of that."

The lights in the courtroom go out and the video starts playing. I hold back my tears as I hear my own whimper play out. How can playing this video be allowed? I had no choice in this situation. Cade literally forced my hand.

"Cade please," comes from the video and I cringe. I sound like I'm begging and not in a positive way. Not in a way that makes me look like the victim in that circumstance. I bite down on my lip and force myself to stay collected throughout the rest of the footage. When the lights come back on, I don't raise my head to look at Lynn's lawyer. My eyes stay trained on the wooden table before me. This is humiliating.

Do not cry.

Do not cry.

Do not cry.

I tell myself over and over until I'm able to look up at the lawyer and judge again. They're both watching my reaction, the judge to see if I can handle this. And Lynn's jerk of a lawyer to see how I will break. This video hurts. I'm not going to lie. People shouldn't have the right to witness me in a vulnerable state, but Cade didn't break me. Neither is this footage playing for this audience. I did nothing wrong in this situation. And I'm not going to feel like some kind of sleazy, immature child because of something that happened to me.

The lawyer's eyes moves away from me and to the room. "As you can clearly see, Ms. Raine made no attempt to protect herself. She sat there and let a boy physically pleasure her in an open space with people present."

"Objection," Tanner calls.

Lynn's attorney turns to Tanner. "On what terms?"

"You cannot assume my client is feeling any type of pleasure from the acts performed in this video," Tanner counters. "The sounds she made could mean anything."

"Sustained," the judge bellows and Mr. Cavanagh turns away from the table. "Move along."

"As I was saying, Roxanna Raine made no attempt to release herself from the hold of Mr. Jefferson. As you can clearly see, she sat there and let him do that. Tell me, are those the actions of a person suitable for parenthood? Will she be able to protect Harley if such thing were to happen or would she merely watch like a spectator?"

My eyes fall back to the table as I sit through the rest of his defamation of my character. He pulls up photos from the bonfire. Photos of me leaving school in the middle of the day. He even has images of me before Harley was even born partying with Claire. Lynn's lawyer throws everything he can at the judge to make me seem like a red flag. By the time he takes his seat, I'm even starting to feel like I'm not worthy of having Harley. It's not logical to think that way, but Mr. Cavanagh is good at this job. Too good.

Tanner stands and heads to front. "I would like to call Caden Jefferson to the stand."

My head snaps up.

What?

I was under the impression that Cade wouldn't be here. Tanner told me he never responded to the letter, and Claire never told me what he said to her. I figured Cade would have bought his way out of being subpoenaed.

CHAPTER 30

ROX

I turn around in my seat and lock eyes with Cade slowly walking down the aisle on crutches. His gaze meets mine as he passes me, but he turns away. His eyes are less bloodshot than the last time I saw him and I hope that's a good sign. He climbs into the witness seat and turns to Tanner.

"Mr. Jefferson, to you promise to tell the truth, the whole truth, and nothing but the truth?" the judge asks.

"I swear," Cade says, his eyes coming back over to me. "I promise."

That last bit feels like it's aimed at me, so I nod. I know I probably shouldn't, but this is Cade. As much as I have wanted to completely lose faith in him, as much as I have told people that he means nothing to me now, that I cannot forgive him, he is still the guy that was my best friend. He's still Cade.

"Mr. Jefferson, how do you know Roxanna Raine?" Tanner questions.

"My father was part of her dad's law firm when we were kids. We used to hang out all the time," he tells my lawyer.

"Rox ran away from home at a young age after witnessing her father murder her nanny. When did you reconnect with her after that point?"

Cade looks at me before answering. "For me, the first time we reconnected was at the end of middle school. She and her friend Claire were shopping at the mall in Arlington, and she accidentally ran into me. Her bags fell. At first, I didn't recognize her. I was too engrossed in something else, but when I bent down to pick up her bags, we met eyes for a second and I knew. She didn't seem to know me though. I let her walk away. I searched all summer until I figured out where she was. I talked my dad into enrolling me in Kingston High for high school. We wouldn't officially talk again until the beginning of this year."

My brows dip at Cade's answer. I remember the day he's talking about clearly. It was the day Claire talked me into trying more with Wran. We were at the mall to by lingerie. I bumped into him, but my mind was on whether or not Wran would like the blue piece Claire picked out for me. The guy handed me my stuff and Claire spent the whole ride back to Kingston swooning over the guy in the mall. He never crossed my mind after that.

"Since you've admitted to searching for Roxanna, I'm assuming you kept watch over her until the beginning of this year?" Tanner continues.

"Yes." Cade shifts in his seat. "We had run-ins but nothing substantial."

"I'm also assuming you knew about Harley before now?"

"Yes."

"Can you please tell the courtroom what Miss Raine was like during the time after Harley's birth?" Tanner asks.

Cade nods. "She was quiet. She kept to herself. She worked. She seemed very forlorn. Anyone could tell that she was sad. However, she always came to school. She always went to work. She didn't party like the rest of us. If I'm being completely honest, she was stagnant. She was doing everything she was supposed to, but she wasn't really living. That didn't really change until this year. She was happier, and while I would like to claim to be the reason for that, I know I am not the cause."

"The video that you made of the both—" Tanner begins again.

"I didn't make it," Cade cuts him off. He turns to me. "For clarity's sake, know that I didn't make that video. At the time, I truly thought I had destroyed it. I only realize he had it in the cloud a day later."

I know all of that. He doesn't have to reassure me. I did live the whole night.

"Okay, then. Did you release the footage?"

Cade nods and his head drops. "Yes. I was angry." He raises his head, and as if magnets, our eyes drift to each other. Cade's eyes are red and glassy. "I was stupid. I was jealous. I wanted her to hurt as badly as I hurt. Releasing that footage was the worst mistake I could have made. It cost me my best friend. I will forever regret that choice. I am so sorry."

I bite the inside of my jaw and nod, letting him know I hear him loud and clear. I accept his apology. It doesn't change anything. We could never go back to what we once were, but at least the hostility on his part can come to an end.

"One last question, Mr. Jefferson," Tanner tells him. "Would you consider this normal behavior for Miss Raine?"

Cade tilts his head to the side and his brows lower. "I'm afraid I don't understand the question."

"Does Roxanna Raine normally let men such as yourself, abuse and mistreat her? Does she have a pattern of reckless behavior?"

Tanner crosses his arms and eyes Cade down. Cade's mouth quirks up in the corner, but only slightly. I'm probably the only one that even noticed the change. Cade mimics Tanner's posture and turns to me. He looks me over. I gulp. If he tells the truth here, I'm ruined. This one question could end this entire hearing and leave me with nothing. Cade's eyes shift again, but I don't follow his gaze to the back of the room. I don't want to draw attention to Wran. I don't even want for a split second for them to think Wran is abusive to me.

Cade lets out a deep breath and shakes his head, lying. "No. That was a one-time thing. She doesn't normally associate with cruel, abusive jerks with anger problems."

I cringe at the insult to Wran. He isn't that bad. . . Okay, so maybe he used to be that bad. But his anger issues have been somewhat under control since he came back from the Pleasure House. Sure, his outburst on Cade was a bit much, but if the roles were reversed, Cade would have done the same thing. Any decent man would have defended his woman.

Tanner nods his head at Cade before turning to the judge. "I have no more questions, Your Honor."

Cade is just about to get up when Lynn's lawyer rises from his seat. "I actually do have questions for Mr. Jefferson."

"Proceed," the judge tells him.

I turn to Lynn's lawyer. What could he possibly wish to ask Cade? He's already answered everything.

"You say that Roxanna Raine doesn't normally hang around abusive men, right?" Mr. Cavanagh asks.

Cade nods.

The lawyer continues, "But your school has a recording of Wran Belmont physically assaulting you."

Cade's eyes snap to the back of the room and everyone turns in their seats to see what he's looking at. I don't make a move to turn; I already know who's back there. Cade then looks in my direction and I gulp. I know where this is going to go. Cade might be willing to lie for me, but he's not going to do it for Wran.

"Y–yes," Cade mutters low. "He did."

"Care to tell us all why that was?" Mr. Lawyer pries.

"Objection," Tanner calls for the second time. "The reason behind Mr. Belmont's behavior has no weight on Miss Raine or this hearing."

"It's does," Lynn's lawyer says. "And I'm getting to my point."

"Then get to it. We do not have all day," the judge urges.

"As you well know, Mr. Jefferson, Wran Belmont and Roxanna Raine were living together. Our reports show that she moved into your house about two months ago. Care to tell us why that may be?"

I stare at Cade. Sweat beads down his face as he glares at the lawyer and then back to me. Biting the inside of my jaw, I nod at him, letting him know it's okay to tell the truth. I don't want the courtroom to know the real reason, but I don't want Cade in trouble either. I've ruined his life enough.

"I don't know," Cade tells the lawyer.

"Is that so, Mr. Jefferson?" Cade nods, but even I can tell it's jerky at best. "Because footage I have claims something different."

The lights go off and my eyes drift back to the screen on the wall. The front of Josh's house comes into frame. Cade's truck pulls up outside. He darts out and over to where Wran is sitting on the steps, a flask in his hands. Seeing as whatever device recorded this had to be across the street from the house, it picked up amazing sound. Wran hops up from the step and drops the drink. He goes to reach for the handle of the house, but Cade grabs him by the back of the shirt and slam him into the stone exterior of the house.

"You no good waste of space!" comes through the courtroom speakers loud and clear. "You ever hurt her again and I will kill you."

Wran laughs in Cade's face but doesn't respond. The video zooms in and the footage gets even more grainy, but it's clear enough. Cade draws his fist back and slams it into Wran's face. He stops laughing. I can't make out the expression on Wran's face. It can't be good though. Wran takes a step forward. Cade doesn't move.

"You know what's funny?" Wran asks.

"That I got the girl?" Cade taunts.

Wran shakes his head. "No. It's funny that you think you got the girl. Cade fucking Jefferson comes in on his white high horse and takes her away from the big bad wolf. Rox will never be yours. You can give her all the fucking gifts and support in the world, but that girl is mine. Nothing you do can change that. We belong together. I gave her the one thing you never can."

"Shut up," Cade snarls. "She's with me. I win."

"She's with you because I allow it. She's with you because I knew if I didn't let her go, I would cause her more pain."

The video cuts off and I turn to Cade in the witness stand. His face is ghost white as he looks at me. I woke up that night and he wasn't there with me. He stayed long enough for me to cry myself to sleep. The next morning when I woke, he was downstairs making me breakfast. I didn't attempt to ask him where he went. I knew. I knew he would go back to Wran the moment I asked him to let that situation be. As much as neither guy likes to admit it, they are very much alike. Cade might not have as bad of a temper as Wran, but they both like to protect what they think is theirs. They both have heads as hard as stone. And they both think their word is law.

Cade doesn't meet my eyes. When I turn around in my chair to see Wran's response to the video, he just shrugs. Like this is nothing. I suppose to him, it is.

"I ask you again, Mr. Jefferson, why is it that Roxanna Raine went to live with you?" the lawyer asks. "Why did you go there that night?"

"Because," Cade's eyes shift around the room. "Because he hit her. And I wanted to show him he couldn't get away with that."

"Who hit who?" the lawyer pushes.

"Wran Belmont assaulted Roxanna Raine," Cade confesses.

The courtroom gasps, and the lawyer stands down. "No more questions."

I turn to Tanner. His usual light heart demeanor is rock hard. "Did we just lose?"

"No," Tanner whispers back. "We still have a chance, but he just made Cade's testimonial useless."

I sigh and slump back in my chair. The gossip around us picks up, and I do my best to keep a straight face. The judge slams his gavel down again to gain everyone's attention.

"We'll have a short thirty-minute recess before we come back and finish the testimonials and a final decision is made. We are dismissed for now."

Cade hobbles down from the witness stand, and before I have a chance to ask him any questions, he disappears through a side door. I stand and make my way through the crowd to the back where Wran is still standing against the wall. He reaches for me just as the crowd shoves out the door.

"Let's get lunch," he says to keep me quiet. "We'll talk when it's more private."

I nod and allow him to lead me out the small court-room.

CHAPTER 31

WRAN

I pull Rox into the women's restroom and lock the door. We don't need anyone coming in here. Rox leans against the row of sinks, her face finally falling. I go over to her and pull her into a hug. Having that fucker Cade up there had to be hard on her. And he had the fucking nerve to try to apologize after what he did? I hope Rox didn't fall for his antics. She was nodding at the prick, and I really don't know how to take them two silently communicating. That use to be a Rox and me thing. Now it's a Rox and fucking Cade thing. I don't like it, but today isn't about what I like. It's about getting through this hearing and getting my daughter. Not sure how well that is going after that little conversation between Cade and I have finally came to light.

"Are you okay?" I finally ask Rox when she stops shaking.

She tilts her head back and looks up at me. "You didn't tell me Cade came back."

"You were mad and rightfully so. That didn't seem too important. How the fuck did they even get footage of that?"

Rox shrugs, before adding, "Lynn said she was watching me. I guess she wasn't bluffing."

A low buzzing goes off, and Rox draws back. I frown. She pulls her phone from her purse and stares at it for a second. I move to her side so I can see the number. It's unknown. Rox answers the phone with a shaky hello before her back goes ram rod straight.

"You're here?" she asks. "Like at the courthouse?"

She goes silent and listens to whatever is being said on the other end. Her eyes widen and I'm tempted to take the phone and see who the hell is calling her.

"Don't hang up," she tells them and walks towards the door. "Let me find Tanner. Stay on the phone."

Rox races out of the restroom and I follow her. She searches the many faces in the lobby, before pushing out the double doors. The press turns around and the lights instantly start flashing again. I take ahold of her hand and pull her through the onslaught of vultures. We head to Tanner's car. He's sitting inside with the doors locked. His windows are so tinted, that we can't really make out his features. Rox taps on his window, and we hear the doors unlock.

I yank open the door and urge Rox inside. Slamming the door in a reporter's face, I slide across the seat to where Rox is.

"Drive," I tell Tanner.

"What's wrong?" he asks, his eyes flickering from me to Rox. "Did something happen, Roxanna?"

She shakes her head. "No, but someone wants to talk to you."

"Someone?" I ask her. "Who's on the phone?"

She ignores my question as Tanner peels away from the group of photographers snapping pictures. He drives around the corner, away from the courthouse, but close enough that we'll make it back before the recess is over. When he comes to a stop, Rox hands him the phone. I turn to her and still. She has a grin plastered across her face. It's the first time today she has truly looked hopeful.

"Who called?" I ask her again.

"We're going to win this." She throws her arms around my neck. "I'm getting my baby back."

"Rox, what the fuck is going on?" I question her.

I need fucking answers.

She shakes her head at me. "Something good. Just know that if this goes well, we could be taking Harley home. I knew Claire was good for something."

I still at Rox's words. I've wanted my daughter by my side since the moment I found out Rox had her. And while I knew getting her back was the goal today, I haven't had much time to sit and prepare myself for a life as a father. Yes, I can support both of my girls, but there's more to being a father than that. I should know. The moment mine lost a way to provide he went haywire.

"Wran, why do you look like that? This is a good thing," Rox tells me.

I nod and run my hand over my head. Of course it's a good thing. It's the best fucking thing. I want this more than anything. I want my girls with me. I want the white picket fence and summer nights looking at the stars and all the fairs in the world. I want every single moment I can squeeze from them. At the same time, I have no actual experience with being a father. I don't want to fuck Harley up like my pops did to me, even if it's unintentional.

"You don't look like you want that. Have you changed your mind?" she asks me. "If you don't want to be a dad, I can do it myself."

"What?" I shake my head at her. "No. Of course I want my family. I want you. I have always wanted you. I just got lost in my thoughts for a second."

"What were you thinking about?" She shifts in the seat and grabs ahold of the seatbelt, using it as a distraction from what my answer could be.

"I was thinking I have no experience caring for a kid," I tell her honestly. "I don't want to fuck her up."

She pulls my face to look at her and she smiles. "That's not true. You raised me. You have twelve years of experience, not counting the three you left me."

"It's different."

Tanner turns around in his seat and hands the phone back to Rox. He now has a grin on his face. After Lynn's lawyer questioned Cade, Tanner looked grimmer than the reaper. I was sure we had lost this case. Now, I'm not so sure. He and Rox both have the 'we already won' thing going on.

"Who was on the phone?" I try again, but neither one of them answer me.

"Let's get back to the courthouse," Tanner says. "There's a vending machine if you're hungry, and I need to prep the judge for what's about to happen."

Rox nods and Tanner does a U turn to get us back to the court as fast as possible. Tanner doesn't stick around to talk to us. Instead, we head back into the courtroom where everyone else is waiting. Josh is still leaning against the wall on his phone and the pews are still filled to the brim. I pull Rox over to where my brother stands and it draws his attention away from his phone. He looks over my girl before drawing her into a hug.

"You okay?" Josh asks her.

She nods and pulls my arm around to her front. She settles into me and I don't reject.

The rest of the break is spent talking to a bunch of different people. Aunt May comes over and hugs Rox , apologizing for not being there the night Cade took advantage of her. Rox assures her that it wasn't her fault and that it would have happened regardless. She even tries to make up an excuse for that fucker, which I'm having a hard time wrapping my head around. She needs to stop doing that shit. She needs to let us take the fall for our own misdoings.

By the time the judge finally calls court to order again, I'm on fucking edge. The atmosphere has changed. Everyone is eerily quiet, and I can't figure out why that is. It's like this is the end all moment. I lean against the wall and let out a breath as Tanner gets up from his chair. He heads to the front of the room and turns to the judge. I grab ahold of Josh's hand and squeeze. I need my brother. I need to know that everything is going to be okay. Rox and Tanner both might think this case is won, but I'm not holding my breath. Lynn's lawyer is good. Too damn good, but I expected nothing less when I saw him in that damn two piece double breasted suit and slicked back hair. He screams arrogant, and I saw that look on lawyers a lot as a kid. Rox's dad had it, and my pops had it. Only the good lawyers walk into a room already thinking they won. Josh squeezes my hand back just as Tanner begins.

"Your honor, Roxanna Raine lost custody of her child due to drugs found in her system the night she went into labor, correct?" Bennett asks.

"You are well aware what transpired. Please continue, Mr. Tanner," the judge tells him.

"Miss Raine has let her caseworker know on many occasions that it was involuntary. That she was drugged. Recently, we've found proof that absolves Roxanna Raine from any ill will towards herself and her child. And I would like to call a new witness to the stand."

The doors to my left open, and I step forward to see who's walking through. The moment I peep red hair, a grin breaks out over my face. Dressed in a gray button down shirt and black navy trousers, Travis Heart walks into the courtroom. He heads down the aisle and to the witness stand. He looks already defeated, like admitting to what he was a part of is killing him. Rox told me what he confessed when we went to Georgia. It only made me want to kill the fucker even more. Rox likes him though. I don't know why and I don't understand it, but at least he showed his cowardly ass here today to make things right.

"Travis Heart, please tell the courtroom why you are here today."

The fucker twiddles his fingers as he looks out over the audience. "I drugged Roxanna Raine the night she gave birth to Harley Raine."

His head drops and he starts shaking. The crowd instantly gets rowdy, and I hear exclamations thrown all over the courtroom.

"Silence!" the judge bellows. "Order in this courtroom."

The crowd calms somewhat, but there are still a few murmurs going around. The judge tells Tanner to continue and he questions the guy more. Travis goes through all the events of that night and how his friends were acquiring the drugs to supply to the girls. He doesn't name anyone outright, but he does admit that he's sorry.

By the time Tanner is done questioning him, I know we have this case in the bag. There's nothing Lynn can say that will convince the judge not to side with Rox. She was the victim. She lost three years with her child because Lynn didn't believe her. Because the system is flawed and wrong. Travis exits the stand, and Lynn's lawyer rush up to the podium, whispering something to the judge. The judge shakes his head, and the man returns to his seat.

Turning to face the crowd, the judge speaks, "I have made my decision, and based on the evidence presented here today, I'm granting Roxanna Raine full custody of Harley Raine. This case is dismissed."

The courtroom burst into applause. I dart from the back of the room and up front. Rox hasn't moved from her seat next to Tanner. Her face is planted firmly down on the table. I tap her shoulder and she looks up. Tears line her delicate doll like face. She stares at me for a long tense moment as I block out all the noise around us. I only see her right now. I only see the mother of my daughter. My future staring at me. Rox scoots back in the chair and stands. She tosses herself into me and I wrap my arms firmly around her. I knew today would go our way. We've had to deal with too much crap in this life for us not to have the one thing we created.

"I really get to keep her," Rox weeps into my shoulder.

I run my hand over the back of her hair. "Yeah, we do."

Rox pulls back and wipes at the tears. A little laugh shakily leaves her before she throws herself into my arms again. Her mouth slams down on mine and I sink into it. My arms wrap around her more, too afraid of letting a little bit of space between us. We get our child. I get my daughter. We finally get to make our Neverland.

A throat clears from behind us. Rox and I break apart to see Lynn standing before us. Rox tenses, and I frown at the woman. I step in front of Rox, ready to handle this lady if I have to. We have both put up with too much from her, and I'm not about to let her say anything that might upset my girl right now. Lynn wants my lost girl, she has to deal with me. Rox wraps her arms around me from behind, her face buried in my back.

"What do you want?" I ask Lynn, ignoring the people around us watching. They can watch all they like.

"I would like to speak to Roxanna, if you don't mind, Mr. Belmont."

"I do mind. You've done enough to us."

Lynn takes a step forward. "Please keep in mind, Mr. Belmont," her voice drops to a whisper, "that none of this would have happened to Roxanna if you hadn't left a fifteen-year–old pregnant and depressed."

I glare at the woman. She has some nerve. "You're right. I did leave her. I thought that was the best thing for her. Don't get it wrong, I will never leave her again. Stay the fuck away from my girls. And just so you know in advance, I have filed charges against you for negligence on behalf of Rox. Kiss your position goodbye; you will never have the chance to do this to someone else."

Lynn's eyes narrow and she stomps off. Rox comes around to face me. "You did?"

I nod.

Her amethyst eyes flicker across my face. "But you didn't know if we would win."

"I had complete and utter faith in you, babe," I tell her and take her hand. "Now, let's go find our daughter."

I lead Rox through the crowd of people and to the lobby of the courthouse. We come to a stop when we see Cade leaning against the round table that is placed in the center of the room. When he sees us, he rises on his crutches and stands as straight as possible. I glare at the prick. He might have told his truth today, but my truth is still very different. Cade Jefferson is nothing more than an entitled little rich boy who threw a fit when he didn't get the girl. For all I care, he can rot in hell alongside Lynn.

Rox pulls away from me and goes over to him. The tip of their shoes meet as if dancing around each other. I go over and stand behind her, backing her. If he tries anything, I will lay his butt out in this courthouse.

Neither one of them speak for a long while. They just stare at one another. When Cade glances at me above Rox head, I shake mine no. I'm not leaving. He scratches the back of his neck, letting one of his crutches fall against the table.

"I'm sorry," Cade whispers. "I am so fucking sorry, Rox."

She nods. "Thanks."

"I never thought I was that person. I never wanted to be that person, and I'm not going to make any excuses. I fucked up."

Yeah, he did, but at least his fuck up was my win.

"Can you forgive me?" He grabs his crutch and shifts. "Do you think we can ever be friends again?"

Rox lets out a sigh and shakes her head. "I forgive you, but we can never go back to what we were. You hurt me. And while I know I did the same to you, mine wasn't intentional. I would have done anything for you."

"I understand," he sounds defeated. For a split moment, I feel sorry for him. I know how it feels to have Rox, to have her undying love, and then have to give her up. I know all too well what that does to a guy. And the fact that someone else has to go through that . . . geez, I couldn't survive losing Rox again. I'm just glad it's not me.

"Wait!" Rox calls as Cade goes to leave. Rox turns to me. "Give me a minute."

"You serious?" I glare over her head at the rich prick. "He's done enough. Don't give him a chance to do worse."

Her eyes plead with me, and I relent. I give her space. She may be giving him a few minutes of her time, but I'm the one who'll get to love her for a lifetime. A few minutes away won't hurt. Besides, I really want to see my daughter.

CHAPTER 32

WRAN

Harley jumps on my bed, the creaking of the mattress springs making me even more nervous. I run my hands over my hair one more time and take in a deep breath. Going over to Harley, I scoop her up in my arms. She grins up at me, before reaching for my hair. It's different than what she's used to seeing. But for tonight, and tonight fucking only, I decided to gel it back and look more presentable. Rox is going to look amazing, so I want to look like I belong with her.

"C'mon," I tell Harley. "Let's go wait for Mommy up-front with Uncle Poshy."

"Poshy, Poshy, Poshy," she chants over and over as she bounces in my arms.

Josh has been staying at my apartment in Rox's room every night since we won the trial. At first, it was because he was the only one that could get Harley to stop crying and asking for Lynn. Neither Rox nor I thought about what it would be like taking her away from the only real home she's known since birth. It's been hard. Josh being here makes things so much easier. Harley doesn't cry nearly as much when he's around, which really fucking sucks. Josh isn't going to be around all the time. We really need Harley to get used to us.

As soon as I step foot in the living room, Harley wiggles her way down my side and runs over to Josh. My brother catches her in his arms and starts tickling her. Harley's laughter rings out, and it's the best thing in the world. I never knew I was missing this before. Sure, I wanted her. I wanted my daughter like the oxygen I breathe. I just never thought I would need her just as much as she needs us.

"How's my big girl?" Josh stops tickling her and settles her on his knee.

"Poshy, look." Harley points to me and I glance down at myself, trying to see what she sees.

"Yeah," Josh coos. "Daddy cleans up nice. At least I taught him something."

"Hey!" I argue. "You never taught me to tie a tie. Rox did."

"Sure." A door opening shuts Josh up.

Harley eyes that match my own widen and she gasps. "Princess! Mommy a princess!"

I run my hands down my trousers and gulp. The nerves hit again as I turn around. My eyes widen and I gape at her. She dyed her hair back to black. The color it is naturally. The best color. It's curled. My gaze moves down to the bright red lipstick she's wearing. I gulp. Fucking hell. Rox looks amazing without all that, but those lips tonight. Fuck, I bite down on my lip. I want her around me so fucking bad right now. Rox takes a step forward, and my eyes dip to the deep V of her dress that exposes way too much of her chest. When the fuck did she fill out like that? I take a step in her direction but stop when deep curls zip past me.

"Mommy, mommy, mommy!" Harley pulls at the tulle of Rox's dress. She raises her arms up to Rox, and Rox bends down to retrieve her.

Harley immediately goes for the small little crown thing Rox has in her hair and pulls it out.

"Ouch!" Rox exclaims. "You have to be gentle, sweetie."

Rox untangles her hair from the combs and hands the hair accessory to Harley. Wiggling down, Harley sits at Rox's feet and plays with it. When Rox is sure Harley is occupied, she steps around our daughter and comes to me. She flattens a few strands of hair, and then run her hands down the fitted dress. The little beads on it look like stars.

"What do you think?" she asks me, her fingers playing with the jewels on the bodice.

I pull her hands away from her dress and wrap an arm around her waist. I hoist her closer to me, her chest to my chest. "I think we should send Harley and Josh back to his place and we skip the prom to work on giving Harley a sister."

Heat creeps into Rox's cheek, and she fidgets against me. She shakes her head and pulls away. "I told Raven we would meet them there, and Claire wants pictures of me in this dress."

I groan at the idea of sharing her with everyone else. We haven't had time together at all this week, and right now, I really want to show her just how much I like her in this dress. I adjust myself in my pants and turn to my brother.

"You sure you're good?" I ask him.

He gives me a pointed look. "Are you forgetting I'm the one that took care of both of you. I got this. Go have some fun." He glances to Harley. "Try not to get pregnant again."

I turn to see Rox's face turn beet red. She grabs my hand and pulls me out of the apartment. I lead her down the stairs and to my car. Rox starts for the passenger door, but I pull her to a stop. She glances over her shoulder at me. I close the small distance between us. Cupping her cheeks, I lean down and kiss her. I feel the shiver run through her as she rises on her toes. Even in heels, she still as short as a fairy.

Breaking the kiss, I lean my forehead against hers. "I got you something."

Rox attempts to control it, but a smile breaks out over her face anyway. "You did?"

"I figured we're going to prom. Every girl needs a corsage." I reach into my suit pocket and pull out a small white wristlet. "I would take credit for this, but then Aunt May would stop feeding us. She told me what to get."

"Well, I like it." She rises up and places a swift peck against my lips. An owl hoots and I smile down at her.

"I'm glad you like it. I had no clue what color to get."

"When in doubt, go neutral."

Rox turns to go again, but I catch her forearm. "Please remind me to thank Claire for picking out this dress. She's my new favorite person."

Rox full on laughs. "I thought you hated her?"

"I changed my fucking mind."

Rolling her eyes, she heads to the car. I don't stop her again. Instead, I get in the car and speed off towards Kingston city limits.

My senior prom was in the high school's gym. By no means were they trying to rent out a ballroom in a swanky hotel in Arlington for us. I guess this class was better deserving than mine. I pull in behind a black SUV. A kid in a black suit gets out and hand his keys to a valet. In no way, shape, or form was Kingston High ever this posh before. I glance over to Rox. Her attention is on the hotel lit up like it's Christmas in June.

The vehicle in front of me pulls off and I take its place. Rox's hand moves for the door, but I grasp her arm to keep her in place. This is her night. She wanted to go to prom, she wanted this date, then I'm going to give her the best night of her life. That doesn't include her opening her own door. Rox turns around with an arched brow.

"Stay," I tell her. "I got you."

The door to my car opens and I hand my keys to the valet. He's a punk-looking kid that barely seems old enough to drive. I frown at him.

"If there's even a scratch on my baby, I will kill you." The boy's eyes widen at my threat and shakes his head. I step aside and go to Rox. Opening her door, she leans forward. I have a straight view of her chest and I groan. Tonight is going to be fucking torture. No way is anyone going to look as good as Rox. I had to threaten kids when she was fourteen to keep them from looking. This dress is going to have every eye in the place on her. Fucking Claire. I guess I do still hate her.

Rox takes ahold of my outstretched hand and pulls herself out of the car. She falls into me. We fit together so perfectly; it's hard to believe I ever thought I could truly loathe this girl. She's my world. My Neverland. And I can't wait to get her away from this place.

"I love you," I announce.

"Yeah, he does!" someone from behind cheers.

Rox giggles, her head falling against my chest. "I love you too, Wran Belmont."

"Let's get this over with," I tell her and pull her away from my car and inside the hotel lobby. Music blares and strobe lights tint this place in pink. There's a huge white sign that reads "Kingston's Senior Prom" hanging in front of a set of open double doors with a black and silver balloon arch around it. There's a woman sitting at a table collecting tickets. As we get closer, I can clearly make out Mrs. Zannah, Rox's art teacher.

I pull out the tickets Raven got me.

The teacher beams up at Rox. "You look so beautiful tonight. How are you?"

Rox gives one of her shy smiles. "Honestly?" Mrs. Zannah nods. "All of this seems fake. Like I'm dreaming. But I don't want to wake up."

"You're not dreaming, Roxanna," the woman tells her. "You deserve your happiness as much as the next person. Enjoy your night."

We leave the table and venture inside the lit up ballroom. Rox leads me to where everyone is taking pictures against a white background. The photographer directs us on how to stand and we do. On the last photo, I bend down and place a peck on Rox's cheek. I want that one for myself.

It takes no time at all for us to find her friends. They're all sitting at a table on their phones. I glance around the space to see many of the kids doing the same thing. The dance floor is practically empty. I'm not a dancing man, but even I know prom is meant to be spent with having fun. Not on your freaking phone. Raven's eyes pull up from her device as we approach.

"Oh my god!" she screeches and leaps from her seat beside the other one who's name I keep forgetting.

I search the small group until my eyes land on Claire. This isn't normally her brand of bandits, but I suppose anyone can change. I release Rox's hand and go over to where Claire sits. I drop down in the chair beside her.

"Thanks," I force out. No part of me enjoys thanking her. Not for the dress or for her getting Cade to show up at the trial. "She looks amazing in that dress."

Claire turns to me with a wicked grin on her face. "Does this mean you're done being Kingston's community peen? She deserves better than that."

"If I recall, you tried to hop on this peen the moment you found out I was back in town," I remind her.

She rolls her eyes. "I was still pissed at Rox. Not so much anymore."

"You think you two will ever be as close as you once were?" I ask her. I can't see Rox ever getting that close, but anything is a possibility. Especially if Claire wants it.

Claire shakes her head. "She's replaced me."

I glance over to where Rox and Raven are enthralled in conversations. As much as I don't like Claire, I wouldn't write her off so fast. Yes, Rox has a new friend. But Raven doesn't have the history that Claire has with Rox. If Rox can forgive me for all the bullshit, she can forgive Claire for it as well.

"Have you mentioned that you miss her?" I ask.

She scoffs. "Seriously, Belmont. Do I look like the missing someone type?"

I nod. "You're hanging out in the background. The Claire I knew was never in the background. Talk to Rox. If she can forgive me for everything I've put her through, there's hope for you two. Besides, you know our history better than anyone. I doubt Rox is going to willingly open up to Raven about it. You are going to have to make the first move though. This is Rox. She's stubborn."

"How about you fuck off, Belmont? I can handle my own relationships," she says and gets up from her chair.

Rox glance over Raven's shoulder to Claire and then over to me. She tells Raven something before coming to my side. She grabs my hand and pulls me up. I let her. She drags me across the vacant dance floor and stops. I shake my head at her.

"Dance with me," she mutters and drapes her arms round my neck. "We used to dance all the time."

I chuckle at her reasoning. "Yeah, when you were a kid, and it was more goofing around than anything. You know I don't dance."

"And you're also not the hearts and flowers type of guy, but that doesn't mean you haven't been for me."

We sway back and forth. I notice a few other people joining, but Rox has my full attention. This night has my full attention. I run my palms down my pants again, feeling the small little box inside my left pocket. Tonight is definitely the night. She's happy. I'm content. I have my family and things have been great. I've wanted to re-ask Rox to marry me so many times since I fucked up the last proposal, but there was always something more important. There's nothing standing in my way now. And what better way to ask than at the prom?

Crossing my arms, I grin down at her. "What do I get if I give in to your demands?"

Rox stares me down, the grin falling from her pouty red lips. "It's not a demand. It's a request. And what does the infamous Wran Belmont want for a dance?"

I glance around the room, and sure enough we have eyes on us. The only person that knows I've got the ring is Raven. Mainly because she's been secretly helping me out with stuff. Rox was talking to her, and I needed to know what Rox was talking about. It helped that Raven was team Belmont and despised Cade as much, if not more, than me.

I pull the ring from my pocket and drop down to one knee. All playfulness leaves me as I stare up at the girl who's had my heart since I was eleven years old. Gasps go off around us, and the music cuts. I glance around the room, noticing that people have stopped what they're doing. I gulp and turn back to Rox.

"I want your future," I say loud enough for our audience. "I want all your smiles. I want all your tears. I want all your stress. I want you. I haven't always been kind to you, but I have always loved you. I'm pretty sure I'm going to fuck up every day, but I promise not to end those days without fixing it. Roxanna Raine, take this fucking ring and marry me."

Rox is nodding, even before I finish. She takes the ring from the box and slides it on her finger. She throws her arms around me and nods into my chest.

"Of course, I'll marry you, Peter." She grins up at me.

I cup her face and lean down, giving her a quick peck on the forehead. My thumbs stroke the apple of her cheeks. "And I promise to always protect you, my little lost girl."

EPILOGUE

WRAN

Harley sits on my shoulders as we watch Rox walk across the stage and receive her diploma. I scream out for her, and she searches the crowd for me. A sheepish smile spreads across her lips when she sees Harley and me. The trial ended two weeks ago, and things have been amazing. Rox moved back into our little apartment, and even though I'm sure it's not what Harley is used to, it hasn't been too difficult getting her comfortable.

Rox walks off the stage, and I retake my seat, bringing Harley down. She points at Rox walking back to her seat.

"Mommy graduated," she says.

"Mommy sure did. I'm proud of her," I say more to myself. This is all I ever really wanted for Rox. When Josh and I first put her in public school, things were difficult. She didn't really want to be there. I don't know all of what happened during the time I was away, but I do know school wasn't the easiest place for her to be. I'm so proud she stuck it out.

"Me too," Harley says.

When the rest of the ceremony ends, we wait for Rox. She stops a few times to talk to teachers and friends, but it takes her no time at all to get to us. She comes to a stop in front of me, the ring on her finger glinting in the sunlight. Rox takes ahold of Harley's hand before leaning up and pressing a sweet kiss against my cheek. She looks around and I already know who she's searching for. Cade. He's not here though. Ever since their final goodbye on the court steps, I haven't seen him. Rox says she is fine with everything, but I know my lost girl. She misses him. I'm just glad she has more friends to keep her from thinking too much about him.

Speaking of friends, Raven runs over and throws her hands around Rox.

"We did it, girlfriend!" she shouts way too loud. A few people glance our way, but I pay them no mind. At least they aren't looking because Rox and I are finally together. Out in the public. Or because Rox has a child. For the first week after the trial, we would get stares. Rox had to keep me from saying a few choice words on more than one occasion. We are in Kingston after all, and things like this in Kingston are usually looked down upon. Aunt May being Aunt May, however, didn't listen when Rox told her to ignore customers. Pretty sure old man Townsend is still covering his ears.

"Doesn't it feel amazing?" Raven asks her. "We're adults. We can do whatever we want, and we have the whole summer to not listen to boring teachers."

I shake my head at Raven's last statement. I haven't had the time to tell Rox the good news. Well, its good news to me at least. I don't know how she will take it.

Rox hugs Raven back. "I just wish you weren't going so far away. What am I going to do without you? I need you."

Raven shakes her head. "You and Harley are going to get sick of seeing me. I'm going to be around all the time. You can't get rid of me that easily."

"We'll see," Rox mutters. The smile she had a moment ago falls though, and her eyes aren't as vibrant. I know Rox has been concerned about all her friends going away. She hasn't said as much. Actually, she's been really fucking quiet about all of this. She didn't want to even walk across the stage. We had an argument about that. Rox put in the work. There was no way I was going to sit back and let her receive her fucking diploma in the mail.

"I'm going to go find everyone else. See you later?" Raven asks.

Rox nods. Now is the perfect time to finally tell her the good news.

"Rox—" I start but Harley cuts me off.

"Mommy." Harley reaches up for Rox.

She bends down to pick up our daughter. Harley immediately goes for the tassel on Rox's cap.

"Yes, sweetie?" Rox answers her.

"I wanna go home."

Rox glances over at me. "You heard her."

I give a curt nod. The news will have to wait a bit. Rox sets Harley back down and takes her hand. She walks off in the direction I parked the car. I follow close behind. Once Harley is buckled in her car seat, we weave our way through the crowd and down Main Street. Rox is silent the entire way home and I hate it. It makes me want to just blurt the news out now. I take a peek at her and then at Harley in the backseat. My daughter's playing with the brown bunny Rox had when I first found her in the snow.

"So . . . how do you feel?" I ask her.

She looks over at me. "About what?"

"Graduating? This chapter of your life ending?"

Rox shrugs.

Fuck it.

Now is as good of time as any, and she needs something to make her excited about the future.

"You remember I made a slight detour when we went to Georgia?"

"Yeah."

"Well, I sorta, maybe went and viewed the art school there," I tell her. I pull up outside our apartment and cut the car's engine. I turn to gauge her expression, but she just looks confused.

"Why?" she finally asks.

"Because you're a fantastic artist that need to do something with your work. I put in an application for you, and

Raven helped me submit a portfolio. I got the letter a week ago. You've been accepted."

"What?" she shrieks and shakes her head. "Why would you do that?"

"Because you're going to college."

"No," she states. "I–I can't. Harley. And that's in a completely different state. Are you crazy? I'm not leaving my daughter."

"Rox." I place a hand on her arm to calm her down. "No one said anything about you leaving Harley. I also, maybe, sorta bought us a condo close to the school. I don't want to separate my family any more than you do."

"You," Rox eyes flicker, searching, "you what?"

I look her straight in the eyes when I tell her this. "I bought a condo for us. All of us. Even fucking Josh if he wants to come. You agreed to marry me, and I want to give you the world. That means college, where you can be with your friends. A home that isn't this little cramped apartment. A life. A real life where you can live and grow. Where we can grow."

Rox bites down on her lip and her eyes get glassy. She looks in the backseat at our daughter and I follower her gaze. For the past three years, Rox's life has been centered around that little girl. I haven't been here for the most of it. I got to live and have fun and do stupid stuff. I want that for her too. And if that means moving to Savannah, leaving Kingston and the garage, I'm going to do it.

"But . . . you just made partner," she states. "You're going to give it up? You love that place."

"I do, but I love you and that little girl more. I told you once before and I'm telling you again. You are my whole world. You have been since I found you in snow when I was eleven. There's nothing I wouldn't do to make you happy. Besides, Jesse and I have already come to an agreement on the garage. I'll be more of a silent partner. I've already hired a mechanic from Arlington to take over that aspect of the job."

Tears stream down Rox's face. She swipes them away again. "I love you."

"I know. I'm kinda hard not to fuck—" Rox throws a hand over my mouth, cutting off my words.

She tilts her head to the backseat. "Kid back there."

I shake my head at her. "But that's my favorite word. It fits everything so perfectly."

"You're going to have to find a new one."

I glance back at Harley and smile. "I can do that."

Leaning across the seat, I capture Rox's mouth with mine. She kisses me back just as gently.

"Eww, Daddy!" Harley exclaims.

I pull back and laugh. My daughter would be the one blocking this.

"So what do you say?" I finally ask Rox. "Are we going to Savannah?"

She nods. "Yes, yes, a thousand and one yeses. I'd follow you anywhere, Wran Belmont. To Neverland and back."

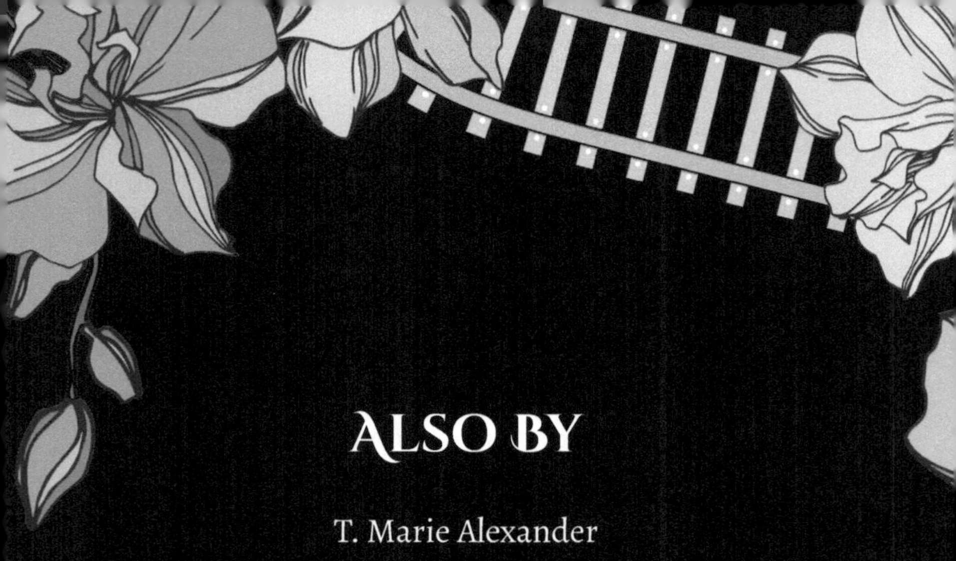

ALSO BY

T. Marie Alexander

Completed (Kingston City Limits Series)

The Lost and the Scarred (Book 1)
The Saved and the Sorry (Book 2)
The Worthy and the Willful (Book 3)

(Standalones)

Revelation

Follow T. Marie at:
Facebook: @authortmariealexander
Tiktok: @authormariealexander
Instagram: @authortmariealexander

You can even check out my website:
www.tmariealexander.com

www.ingramcontent.com/pod-product-compliance
Lightning Source LLC
Chambersburg PA
CBHW050958210726
48287CB00004B/1284